A FEW DYING WORDS

CASE CLOSED:
THE CRITICS APPLAUD
PAULA GOSLING
AND HER BLACKWATER BAY NOVELS

◇

"The author has an especially fine touch."
—*New York Times Book Review*

◇

"Good writing, an inventive plot, and a nice balance of humor and horror make this an appealing mystery."

—*Booklist*

◇

"Not many writers get better with each book, but Gosling never fails to fascinate."

—*Sacramento Bee*

◇

"Her characters leap from the pages, alive with full-fleshed delineation."

—*Arizona Daily Star*

◇

"Her novels are not only cleverly plotted, but brim with power and emotion. . . . Sure to whet an American's appetite for classic British crime fiction."

—*Rave Reviews*

more . . .

A FEW DYING WORDS

Paula Gosling

THE MYSTERIOUS PRESS

Published by Warner Books

A Time Warner Company

For my American cousins

Finnegan—
Begin Again—

He was running, weeping, strangling on his own breath. Overhead, beyond the high twisted web of naked branches, the night sky seemed almost light, its pale moon mantled by gauzy, racing clouds. Suddenly he fell, hard, stunning himself. Sprawled facedown, he could feel the ground vibrating as the pursuing steps came closer, closer. He had to get away! He struggled to his feet, but it was too late. Someone was already there, a menacing shape with clawed, upraised hands—

He screamed, but no sound came....

Tom Finnegan sat up, sweating, and stared into a different darkness, his breath coming as fast now as it had then. New pain in his chest, though. New pain everywhere, worse each day.

Gradually his breathing slowed. The sweat chilled on his skin and he shivered once, twice, then lay back, eyes wide and unblinking. It was not terror than kept him staring into the darkness now, but guilt. A guilt that had been eating at him for far longer than his illness. The race was no longer between quarry and hunter—now it was between his nightmare and his death.

Finnegan—
Begin again.
Before it's too late.

He had survived the worst summer of his life with his

1

For most people the sight of a Great Lakes summer resort when the season is over is a bleak prospect. What was a summertime mecca of fun and freedom has become just another small town, a blip on the highway from here to there.

The temperature slides from the high nineties to the low forties. Suddenly Main Street goes quiet. No net bags full of garish beachballs hang by ever-open doors. There are no tempting displays of snorkels and fishing rods, no inviting pyramids of plastic shovels, painted pails, kites, Frisbees, paper plates, fat romantic novels, or any of the other paraphernalia traditionally required for a brief holiday from life's cares and woes. There's no longer live music every night. No big-name movies showing. No summer stock with old plays performed by even older ex–film stars. No midnight swims. No barbecues. No dancing. No *magic*.

The little shops that blossomed after Easter to serve the vacationers just as suddenly shed their bright petals on the first brisk morning after Labor Day, leaving the local inhabitants with only the ordinary year-round shops and the throbbing headache of a morning after.

And yet, as he walked down Main Street digesting his breakfast, Sheriff Matt Gabriel did not feel bleak. Indeed, he was a happy man.

He had survived the worst summer of his life with his

kingdom more or less intact,* and he had the entire winter to recuperate. He smiled at everyone he passed, and most people returned his smile. Some said "Hi," and a few paused to share an item of news or a worry. As a result, his progress toward his office was syncopated but generally steady.

Not even the cold wind dismayed him. He took a deep, slow breath. There was a smell of leaf smoke and the sharp sting of an approaching freeze. Unlike many others, he welcomed it. Life was settling down to walking speed again. Maybe he'd have time to pull out that biography of Wittgenstein he'd been trying to get around to reading all summer.

That morning there had been a brief fall of pellet snow. Little skeins of it were still dancing and scurrying across the pavements and drifting for a few moments against trees and fences before melting away. Next week or the week after, when the final red and yellow leaves fell, fat white flakes would replace them. After that things would get really serious: heavy snowfalls, wind, and below zero temperatures would arrive. Ice would form on the Bay, eventually becoming two or three feet thick and cluttered with the ramshackle huts of the ice fishermen.

This winter coat of ice and snow would enrobe the county right through until February or even March, buttoning the inhabitants up tight. Sweltering all summer in temperatures of over a hundred, only to be plunged into winter lows of twenty below zero is hard on the psyche. Screens and suntan oil one minute, storm windows and frostbite the next—some kind of sneaky attack each time you step out the door. Every year the local inhabitants hope for deliverance from the extremities of this unique Great Lakes weather pattern. Every year they are cruelly disappointed.

Overhead, a thin double trail of white marked the passing of a couple of jet fighters from the Greenleaf Air Force Base across the lake. The sound hit the ground just as a car with out-of-state plates went past, a lone man at the wheel. As Matt's eye followed the unfamiliar car down the street, he noticed a Halloween jack-o'-lantern leering at him from the window of the children's section in the library. Pumpkins

* *The Body in Blackwater Bay*

were heaped on the sidewalk in front of the grocery store, and each shop he passed seemed stuffed with orange and black crêpe paper, masks, broomsticks, corn stacks, and a thousand other macabre decorations.

He frowned. Damn.

It wasn't time to rest easy after all.

There was still the Howl to get through.

Sheriff Gabriel sighed, his happy mood suddenly fraying around the edges.

Known officially as the Blackwater Bay Halloween Carnival, the Howl was a local event, strictly for the year-rounders. In a way it was a protest against the coming winter, a last fling of silliness and insanity, a defiant cry against the dying of the light. Everyone dressed up and let loose around the bonfires and barbecues. Games were played, and crazy competitions were set up that created new enmities between old challengers—you beat the man who beat you last time, but seven new guys got mad at you for seven different reasons. This meant lively conversation in the bars when the snow got deep.

What was even *more* interesting and gossip-worthy was the collapse of morality among certain sectors of the population. Less than loyally affiliated husbands and wives suspended their marriage vows for twenty-four hours or even changed partners permanently. Newly matured teens discovered sexual attraction where there had been only friendship before. Affairs were begun behind the masks and costumes that would warm the participants during the coming months. But the worst aspect of the Howl, as far as Matt was concerned, were the Howlers—practical jokes played between tacitly consenting victims competing to outdo one another.

High spirits induced by freely imbibed spirits led to imaginative vandalism that left rocking chairs sitting in treetops and many a door and window removed, some never to be found again. Cars were detired and left on blocks in the middle of shallow ponds, dogs and cats were dyed bright blue, and houses were covered in aluminum foil from roof-tree to basement. The small communities of Blackwater County vied with one another to mount the most outrageous prank of the night—the winner achieving the front page of the *Black-*

water Bay Chronicle, which always ran one of its color features in the week following October 31.

Matt Gabriel shook his head and crossed the street to his office. Better check out the boys and the equipment and make sure everything was ready. It looked like poor old Wittgenstein was going to have to be shoved aside for just a little longer. Peace had not quite *yet* come to Blackwater Bay.

On the wide inner windowsill of the Blackwater Bay Sheriff's Office, a big, battle-scarred ginger tomcat was stretched out full length, gazing balefully at a catnip mouse that lay just out of his reach.

From beyond the back wall of the office came muffled sounds of hammering and sawing, where supposedly men were working to convert the heretofore perfectly comfortable sheriff's office into what someone in the state capital had recently ordained to be vitally necessary—a modern, up-to-date, computerized, and fully sanitized law-keeping facility. The work had been going on for the past six weeks and at the present rate of progress would probably be going on for the next six decades. The laughter and talk of the workforce employed on this worthy endeavor played a light obbligato over the clatter and hum of their various tools and machines. The resulting susurrus of sound plus the gentle warmth of the sun was having a pacifying effect on the cat's lust for herbal mayhem. His glare at the catnip toy was gradually diminishing into a heavy-lidded doze.

"Dammit!" shouted George Putnam, banging his fist down hard on his desk blotter.

Startled, the cat leaped up. Ears back, spine arched, he prepared himself for attack. When nothing further occurred, he blinked, sat down, and gave the catnip mouse a vengeful swipe that sent it skittering into the corner.

"Now you've upset Max," Tilly Moss observed.

"Sorry, Max," George said, automatically.

The cat glanced at him and looked away disdainfully. The chief deputy of Blackwater Bay was not only extremely noisy—he also had big feet. Big feet could land anywhere, without warning, and all too frequently did just that. Such gross habits did not encourage even a tough and experienced cat's affectionate regard.

"I can't decide how old I want to be," George was complaining as the door opened and Matt entered.

Tilly looked at George across her computer keyboard. "About seven and a half, I'd say. Maybe eight on a good day."

George did not dignify this with an answer. "I can't even decide what *country* I want to be," he continued. "Hey, Matt," he called out as Gabriel hung up his coat and hat. "What are you going as?"

Obviously George's thoughts had been running in the same direction as Matt's own—the Halloween Howl. Matt bent down to stroke Max, who was checking out the smells accumulated on his shoes during the walk to work. Having thus paid tribute to the Scourge of the Alleyways, Matt sank into his chair, which creaked its usual refrain. He considered several tart replies to George's question and settled for none of them. "I'm going as myself," he said. "That ought to scare everybody."

Tilly grinned but said nothing. When Matt growled like that he reminded her of Ted, his late father, who had been sheriff before him. She had worked for both and was as devoted to the son as she had been to the old man. Matt liked to pretend that he was lean and mean, when actually he was a kind and thoughtful man, slow to anger, patient, fair.

Unless crossed, of course.

The policing of Blackwater Bay County was not generally an onerous occupation. Situated north of the huge city of Grantham, it was composed primarily of resort villages and properties that edged one of the larger bays off one of the Great Lakes. The relatively small county extended back through farming areas, forests, dunes, and parklands for less than fifty miles. Almost crescent-shaped, it had been created during Prohibition, largely because of the enthusiasm of the locals for "importing" illegal alcoholic beverages from Canada, which lay only a swift motorboat ride away. It was thought at the time that a concentration of specialized lawmen would overcome the unique problems of the Bay area, and to some extent the ploy was successful, even allowing for the fact that a few of the specialized lawmen "special-ized" in the occasional profitable motorboatride themselves.

After Repeal, nobody had seen the necessity of going through all the fuss of dissolving the county and its attendant rather idiosyncratic bylaws. After all, it was only really alive during the summer months and for the balance of the year slumbered peacefully beside the waters, its local population no more than several thousand at best.

Or, in the case of the Howl, at worst.

"Aw, Matt—come on," George said, disappointed. "Everybody *else* gets into the mood, makes an effort." He paused. "After all, you're up for reelection next year," he added slyly.

Matt sent him a disgusted look. "If you think putting on some stupid costume and prancing around like a jackass is going to win me any extra votes, you're more naive than I thought, George."

"I keep telling him," came Tilly's voice, fading away as she struggled with deciphering Charley Hart's handwriting.

"People like to see that someone is taking care of busi-ness," Matt went on. "When all hell breaks loose on Hal-loween night—"

George chuckled to himself. "And it will."

"—then they'll look around for someone to straighten things out," Matt continued. "How would it be if I was stand-ing there in a hula skirt or a clown outfit? Do you suppose the kids who've driven over from Brewster already half-soused are going to stop their usual tricks if a knock-kneed man in a toga tells them to?"

"All right, all right, I hear where you're coming from," George said. "Does that mean I can't wear a costume, ei-ther?"

"I'd be happier if you didn't," Matt said.

"But you're not saying I can't."

"I—"

"Because I've had this *terrific* idea," George went on. "How about if we dress *up* as policemen? Maybe English bobbies, or French gendarmes, or something like that? We'd still be police officers . . . but sort of more in the swing of things. How about that?"

Tilly had stopped typing. "Good heavens, George. That's not a half-bad idea."

"There you go," said George, tilting his chair back onto its rear legs and doing his McCloud imitation.

Matt gazed at him in annoyance. He was annoyed because Tilly was right—it *was* a good idea. Or, at least, a reasonable compromise. But it still meant "dressing up," and something in him rebelled at the idea. Partly it was because of personal shyness (not the greatest asset for a sheriff to have), but mostly it was because of his size. It is not easy to find a costume rental store that carries a really great assortment of disguises for someone who is six foot four, is as wide in the shoulders as a kitchen door, and has arms that look as if they'd been pulled out of their sockets when he was a kid and never quite snapped back.

"That still gives you quite a varied choice," Tilly said encouragingly. She herself was going as a Victorian lady-in-waiting. "Why not English bobbies—Victorian ones?"

"They had those hats," grumbled Matt. One of those high British police helmets would suit him about as much as a thimble suited a gravestone.

"Not the *top* officers," George said, "I've got a book right here." He slammed his chair legs back down onto the floor and rummaged in the bottom drawer of his desk. After pulling it out, he thumbed quickly through the pages, then held the book up facing Matt. "See? You could go as Sir Robert Peel himself. And I could go as what they called a Peeler." He turned the book back and gazed with some satisfaction on the picture, rather liking the idea of himself in that particular guise. But then George was easily pleased when it came to his own reflection. As far as he was concerned, as long as his face was above it, any costume would be a winner.

Matt gazed at him patiently. George Putnam was not a bad young man, but he was vain, as awkward as an adolescent goat, and about as smart. On the other hand, he was loyal, reliable, physically strong, and enthusiastic. My God, Matt thought for the thousandth time, George is enthusiastic. He was sitting there now, like some puppy with a new rubber bone, waiting for it to be thrown in the air so he could leap twenty feet straight up and catch it.

"Well . . ."

George took his hesitation for acquiescence and grabbed the Yellow Pages. "I'll see what we can find," he said, and began riffling the thin sheets excitedly. Matt and Tilly exchanged a mutual glance of weary and wary amusement.

The telephone on Tilly's desk rang. She answered it, then looked over at Matt. "Tom Finnegan for you," she said, and replaced her receiver when he punched the lighted button on his own instrument and picked it up.

"Hey, Tom—how's it going?" Matt said with a grin. The grin faded as he heard the older man speak. Tom Finnegan's voice was rough-edged and urgent.

"I have to see you, Matt. Got something I have to talk to you about."

"Sure, Tom. The trouble is, I'm leaving for Hatchville in about ten minutes—I have to give evidence in a case. Can George help? Or should I send one of the patrol—"

"No, no—it has to be *you*, Matt. It's not—I mean, there's nothing wrong, exactly. Nobody's broken in here or stolen my car or anything. It's not like that." There was a pause, then Tom spoke again in a more reflective voice. "Well, actually, it *is* like that, in a way, but not now. Not today. Or last night. I mean"—He gave a heavy sigh, exasperated at his own inability to communicate. "The thing is, I just need to talk about something, that's all. To get it straight in my own mind. It *is* the kind of thing you should know about."

"I see," said Matt, who didn't see at all. Tom Finnegan was an old friend. Until his retirement two years ago he'd been the town pharmacist, running the big corner drugstore that had now been taken over by a chain. Aside from his family and his professional duties, his only real passion had been to build the best banana split in Blackwater County. Hardly the responsibility of a trained pharmacist, but when Tom Finnegan ran it, the drugstore had been the old-fashioned kind, with a long marble counter, stools that spun until the rider was dizzy, and a few straw wrappers always dangling from the ceiling because Tom only stocked the wrapped kind in his dispensers. He bought them deliberately so that customers could lick the wrappers, shoot them off, and bet on whose would stick the longest. The counter was gone now, and a display case of hairdryers stood in its place.

Nobody in town considered it an improvement.

"Are you all right, Tom? I mean, you don't need the doctor or—"

"No, no, I'm fine. It's nothing to do with *that*," Finnegan said impatiently. The "that" he referred to with such irritation was cancer. Tom had been fighting it for months, and his gradually diminishing size and energy testified to the fact that it was a losing battle. He was normally a cheerful man, and as far as Matt had observed he had been dealing with his illness courageously. But now he sounded far from brave or strong.

"Well, listen, Tom—maybe I *could* swing around there on my way to court—" Matt began.

"No, no—don't bother. I need more than just a few *minutes* of your time. It's . . . complicated."

"Okay. Well, how about tonight, then? Say, right after dinner? I'll drive out—"

"No, I'll drive in," Tom interrupted hurriedly. "Dorothy is having her damn sewing circle here tonight. Biggest bunch of gossips in town."

That startled Matt, too. Tom Finnegan had never been given to speaking ill of anyone, yet his voice was tinged with definite dislike when he spoke of the local group. As far as Matt knew the Blackwater Bay Magpies—for such was the name of the quilters group to which Mrs. Finnegan belonged—were not particularly gossipy. At least, no more so than any group of women. Or men, if it came to that.

"Okay—if you feel up to it," Matt said.

"I can still drive myself," Tom snapped.

Something was wrong, really wrong, to have shortened Tom Finnegan's fuse, Matt thought. "I'll be in the office about seven-thirty, then. That all right for you?"

"It will have to be, won't it?" Tom replied. There was another pause, and this time when he spoke again his voice was almost a whisper. "Sorry, Matt, didn't mean to bite your head off," he said. "It's just—when you make up your mind to do something, the least thing that stops you—you know—when there isn't a lot of time . . ." His voice trailed off.

"I know," Matt said. "Listen, if the court case finishes early, I'll give you a call, maybe drop by on my way back, how's that?"

"Great. That would be great, Matt. Thanks."

"Sure. But if you don't hear from me, then it's seven-thirty here at the office, okay?"

"Okay. Thanks." Finnegan rang off.

Matt frowned at the phone after replacing the receiver. Tilly spoke from her desk.

"Dorothy Finnegan says Tom's been going downhill fast," she informed Matt. "She thinks the drugs Dr. Rogers gives him for chemotherapy have been affecting his mind. She told me he hardly sleeps, and when he does he has these awful nightmares—"

"Are you telling me to take whatever he has to tell me with a grain of salt?" Matt asked, turning his chair to face her.

Tilly Moss was large of girth and heart, a woman who knew a great deal about what went on in Blackwater Bay. People talked to Tilly freely and frequently, knowing their troubles would receive a sympathetic hearing and knowing also that the talk stopped there. Tilly Moss was not given to telling tales—except to Matt, and then only if it was pertinent. She seemed to think her information concerning Tom Finnegan's state of mind qualified for transmission.

"I'm telling you what the man's wife told me," Tilly said, firmly. "You'll have to use your own judgment."

"I always do," Matt said.

Tilly sniffed. "We *all* always do," she said. "Doesn't mean we're all always right. I'm not saying Tom Finnegan is going to tell you lies, I'm just saying . . . listen carefully."

Matt smiled. "Okay. Thanks."

Tilly smiled back and returned her attention to her work, her big, dark eyes flicking back and forth from scrawl to screen as she translated and inserted Charley Hart's left-handed chicken tracks into the computer files.

"Gendarmes! They've got gendarmes' uniforms in all the right sizes!" George shouted suddenly, pounding the desk in

glee and waking Max yet again. The cat sat up, gave George a look of vast disgust, stretched, stepped lightly around the hat stand to his personal entrance flap, and departed.

Matt stood up, too. It was time he left for court. "*Très bon,* George," he said resignedly. "Now all you have to do is grow a mustache you can twirl."

George fingered his upper lip and glanced at the calendar. "There's not much time," he said doubtfully.

Matt sighed heavily. "Say good-bye, Gracie."

"Good-bye," George said before he could stop himself.

As he drove to Hatchville, Matt couldn't decide who worried him more, George or Tom Finnegan.

2

Sycamore Avenue was one of the oldest streets in Blackwater. Lined on either side with huge Victorian frame houses converted to guest accommodation, the street had an air of museum hush about it, broken only by the sound of Dominic Pritchard's weary footsteps and the clacking of the bare branches overhead. He'd had a long day and was looking forward to a good meal and a quiet evening.

The street itself seemed already half-asleep. Lawns that had been lushly green all summer were now browning, their straw-covered flower beds bristling with topless stems. The curbsides were empty, no longer lined bumper to bumper with the cars of vacationers. In the rear gardens of the guest houses that accepted children, swings hung motionless and the polished slopes of the slides were hazed with condensation. Lawn furniture was folded away, with only bald scuff marks to show where sandaled feet had rested under the summer sun.

It was a proud street, still, although some of the houses badly needed repainting and one was closed and completely boarded up. Two of the "smaller" places had been converted back into private residences—even Blackwater Bay had its yuppies—and they were bright with fresh paint and clean windows. As a result the houses on either side of them looked a little worse than they might have in more sympathetic company.

Dominic came to the path that led up to Mrs. Peach's Guest House and turned in. As he let himself in the front door he was immediately engulfed in the fragrances attendant on this evening's meal. He inhaled, smiled, sighed. Confronted with Mrs. Peach's cooking, even a strong-willed man found himself sliding inexorably toward gluttony. He was attempting to compensate by walking to and from the office—but it was an effort he felt would soon be inadequate. If he weighed himself tomorrow and found he had gained any *more* weight, he would have to start spending his lunch hour in Mayor Atwater's gym. Better the torment of bench presses and the rowing machine than denying himself second helpings from Mrs. Peach's table.

He went to his room, stripped off his dark blue suit, hung it up carefully, washed, and put on a comfortable pair of slacks and a pullover. Clean and neat was all Mrs. Peach required of her winter guests. If he was still here in summer, it would be shirt and tie every night, but he knew he could never afford Mrs. Peach's summer prices. His boss, Carl Putnam, had gotten him in here until he found a more permanent place of his own. He was very grateful. It was hard enough trying to adjust to a new town and a new way of life without having to worry about whether your next meal was coming from McDonald's, Pizza Hut, the Golden Perch, or the supermarket. He hated making wrong decisions.

Down in the front sitting room, the other winter guests were gathering. Having winter lodgers of any kind was a new innovation apparently, brought about by Mrs. Peach's daughter, Nonie, and the urgent need for repairs to the old house. Nonie was a plump, pretty woman in her late thirties. Her work as a certified public accountant required intelligence and precision, but her efforts to be dignified were all too frequently undermined by a robust sense of humor and an awareness that what life offered to most intelligent women was, in general, a series of banana peels. Stepping carefully had its drawbacks, however. In the end it came down to choices—and her latest one had been pretty final.

She had been doing rather well down in Grantham. But after a long talk with Dr. Willis she had decided that her mother's continued good health was far more important than

either her career or anybody's tax returns, so she resigned
her partnership and stopped commuting to stay home for
good. She did a little accountancy work for local clients but
now devoted most of her time to running the guest house.
She had not only been blessed with a cool head for figures,
but had also inherited her mother's cool hands for light pastry. Thus the Peach tradition seemed assured of continuance
for at least one more generation.

Nonie had confided all this to Dominic while polishing the
brass one Saturday afternoon. He had listened with interest
and agreed that her choice had been the right one. Nonie had
been grateful for his support, for she was still running on city
revs, and had not yet geared down successfully to the slower
pace of Blackwater. Somehow telling him had made it all
feel a little better. Dominic had not yet met Tilly Moss, but if
he had, he would have recognized a soulmate. People tended
to confide in him, too.

There were six people presently boarding at Peach's Guest
House: Mr. and Mrs. Stevens, whose house was being reno-
vated after a fire; Sheriff Matt Gabriel, also temporarily displaced by the noise and mess of construction work; Miss
Biddy Tillotson, a kindergarten teacher substituting for
Grace Mayhew, who was in Europe on a year's sabbatical;
Mr. Clarence Toogood, a writer who was trying to finish a
novel about a storm-door salesman gone wrong; and Dominic himself—recently admitted to the state bar and even
more recently taken on by the local law practice of Crabtree
and Putnam.

Dominic was a well-built young man whose natural good
looks were not at all spoiled by a broken nose received at the
knee of a sneaky left tackle from Cornell. He was bright, ob-
servant, and eager to find his place in this very idiosyncratic
town.

Blackwater had not been a casual choice. He had spent the
summer lifeguarding at nearby Butter Beach, simply to get
the feel of the place before finally accepting the position with
Crabtree and Putnam. This caution was typical of him. He
liked to look and look again before he leapt—because when
he *did* leap it was with a yell of enthusiasm and full commit-
ment. As far as he had been able to ascertain, practicing law

in the county of Blackwater Bay was going to be extremely interesting, if a little unsettling. It was merely a matter of being on one's guard at all times.

He was pouring the predinner drinks that were a custom of the house when he saw Matt Gabriel coming down the stairs. Dominic grinned and reached for the malt whiskey. Matt looked as if he could use a strong one.

Mr. and Mrs. Stevens, perched side by side on the chaise longue, were sipping sherry. They blinked at him simultaneously over the rim of their respective glasses. They were an awkward pair, both bony and pale, all too ready to dominate any conversation with their own problems and equally ready to solve everyone else's at great length. Even that would have been bearable—they were neither unintelligent nor unkind—if it had not been for their voices. Mrs. Stevens had a corncrake screak that rasped on everyone's nerve ends, and Mr. Stevens's drone was like a bagpipe endlessly readying for a melody that never began.

Mr. Clarence Toogood, a small round man of indeterminate age and hairline, bounded over to shake hands with Matt. He always shook hands with everyone, morning, noon, or evening. Dominic had told Matt he was in serious danger of developing calluses on his right hand thanks to Mr. Toogood's eager grip. It wouldn't have been *quite* so bad if Mr. Toogood hadn't also felt it necessary to augment his hand clasp with further evidence of bonhomie. Women he merely patted in an avuncular way, but men invariably received a hearty buffet on the arm, knocking them off balance if they were unprepared. It was almost as if he considered general disablement a necessary adjunct to saying hello.

"Hello, hello, hello," said Mr. Toogood, grasping and thumping Matt enthusiastically.

"Evening, Clarence—everybody," said Matt, who had automatically braced himself for the Toogood onslaught. "Nice to see a fire tonight."

"Yes, yes, it *is* getting brisk, isn't it?" Clarence agreed. "A winter of discontent will soon be upon us, I fear." He did not appear to view the prospect with dismay—quite the contrary. But then, Clarence Toogood viewed everything brightly. This evening he wore a red sweater under a brown tweed jacket and reminded Matt of a plump inquisitive robin determined to find worms *somewhere.* Unlike the Stevenses, his constant nosiness was cheerful. He said it was an author's curse to be interested in everyone and everything. He spent his days walking around the town "picking up atmosphere" and his evenings dozing in front of the television. When he actually worked on the novel he claimed to be writing, nobody could quite discover, but when asked he always assured them that it was "going really well."

Dominic came across with Matt's drink. "Bad day in Blackwater?" he asked. His voice was low and quiet, but it had a carrying quality that was most effective in a courtroom. Carl Putnam said it was like the purr of a cat before it pounced. Putnam was quite taken with his new assistant, according to George, who was more than a little jealous of this new competitor for his father's attention and affection.

"Have you come up against 'Rancid' Randall yet?" Matt asked, referring to the defense lawyer he'd been facing that day.

"No—but I've heard about him." Dominic grinned. "Maybe I should have poured you a double."

"No, this is fine. It's just that he stretched a half-hour case into a whole day's worth—and there was someone I was hoping to see before dinner," Matt said. "I didn't get called to give my two minutes of evidence until almost five o'clock."

"Mr. Putnam says it's because Randall never forgets that he charges by the hour." Dominic smiled. Matt Gabriel and he had had several late-night conversations since he'd joined the guest list here, and he had been surprised to discover that the big, angular man was actually a doctor of philosophy. When he'd ventured that it was an odd qualification for a lawman, Matt had agreed but said that in moments of stress it was comforting to reflect on how many angels could dance on the head of a pin. Despite the ten years' difference in their ages, they were well on the way to becoming friends. Now he watched Matt sit down beside Miss Tillotson and thought he looked worried.

"I can't say a fire has the same cheery message for us that it *used* to have," Mr. Stevens observed gloomily. He took a sip of sherry with pursed lips. "Every time I see an open flame—"

"The children are getting very excited about Halloween," said Miss Tillotson, in a bid to change the subject before the Stevenses began talking about their house fire again. She was sitting closest to the blazing grate, and her cheeks were quite pink. She was a woman of "mature years"—but dressed as if she were barely old enough to vote. She had a good figure, so from the back the illusion was successful. It was when she turned and smiled her wide, toothy smile that the shock set in. As she taught very young children, this effort to deny the years was perhaps understandable. There was always about her the air of someone who had just built a sand castle and was looking forward to the finger paints.

With a wary glance at Mr. Stevens, who was glowering at the grate and seemed poised to continue his diatribe against anything that burned, she continued to wax enthusiastic. "I'm pretty excited myself, to tell you the truth. I have my costume all planned, and I intend to really let myself *go*, because I understand everyone *does*. Are the amazing things I hear about Halloween in Blackwater Bay true, Matt?" She blinked at him coyly, but with an air of considerable innocence. The flirtatiousness was a semiautomatic weapon, resulting from a postwar upbringing surrounded by women's magazines and a mother who *always* wore an apron. Miss Tillotson wouldn't really have been happy with a policeman, or a farmer, or a lawyer, or an accountant, and Matt had a feeling that deep down within herself, she knew it. What she really needed—and would probably never find—was a toyboy. In *every* sense.

"Depends on what you've heard," he said cautiously. "I'll have to admit, there are a few high jinks."

"Mmmph," sniffed Mrs. Stevens. "Low jinks is more like it."

"Seems like the Howl is getting wilder every year," observed Mr. Stevens. "You'll be glad of those extra men they've given you, Sheriff. Something tells me they'll be needed. I've heard some nasty rumors about kids with grudges from last year's state football championship being won by Lemonville. A lot of beer has been sold already. And what if that firebug strikes again?"

"Oh, no—not *another* fire!" Mrs. Stevens moaned.

"Now, there's nothing to worry about," Matt said quickly. "Last year was an exception—Blackwater High hasn't a hope in hell of winning the cup this year, besides which all the boys involved in last year's fights have gone on to different colleges. We found out that barn fire was set by the farmer himself for the insurance. And as for school—we're keeping a close eye on liquor sales throughout the county."

"They'll find it somewhere," Stevens grumbled.

"Well, they won't get it inside the grounds," Matt assured him. "This year the Howl will be the same as it used to be—just for fun. The only fire will be in the fireworks—and the only fight might be among the candidates for queen of the Howl. Those teenage girls can get pretty feisty when it comes to who's going to wear that tin crown."

The Stevenses didn't look convinced, but Biddy and Clarence began to look quite excited.

There was a brief silence.

Dominic cleared his throat and had opened his mouth to speak when Mrs. and Miss Peach appeared, pushing aside the sliding doors leading to the dining room as if drawing the curtains on a Broadway production. Then they turned and faced their guests.

"Dinner is served," they said together, and beamed at them, each as round and glowing as a Rubens portrait in modern dress.

Behind them the long table was covered with a snowy cloth and set with old silver that gleamed like satin. The first course of the evening's meal lay waiting—a steaming bright red tureen of soup next to a delft platter artfully displaying thick slices of freshly baked bread and small, crisply crusted rolls. Around this centerpiece sat ten dishes containing various items designed to "sting the appetite a mite"—crisp, thin cucumber slices in sour cream, cannelini beans vinaigrette, green tomato relish, watermelon pickle, hard-boiled eggs in mayonnaise, shrimps in creole sauce, green and black olives, artichoke hearts, smoked haddock mousse, and a sweet-pepper pâté the recipe for which was still Mrs. Peach's secret, even from her daughter. Deep blue bowls of creamery butter spangled with icy dew completed the picture.

"Ah," said Mr. Stevens, standing up. "Food."

Clarence Toogood stared at him, glanced at the lavish repast that awaited them, and shook his head. "I bet he also called Toscanini a band leader," he murmured to Dominic.

The young lawyer smiled, and they all went in together.

They were just leaning back in their chairs, enjoying a very necessary pause between the chicken fricassee and the pineapple upside-down cake, when Nonie came in, looking concerned. "Phone for you, Matt. It sounds bad."

He excused himself and went into the hall. "Yes?"

It was George. "Duff Bradley just called in, Matt. There's been an accident out on the old post road. It's Tom Finnegan. He's still alive, but not for long. And he's asking for you."

3

As he came around the bend, Matt immediately knew that if Finnegan wasn't dead already, it was some kind of miracle. As he pulled up behind Charley's patrol car at the edge of the road, he could see Fred Boyle, the local high school chemistry teacher, standing beside a dark green sedan, looking shocked and distraught. There were no marks on his car, at least none Matt could see from where he was.

Matt got out of the car and began to run. The scene was strangely peaceful—a few birds were still singing their evening songs, and crows argued in a nearby field. A light breeze tugged at Matt's hurriedly donned jacket, and the rough weedy grass swished and crackled under his feet.

He might have considered it a lovely evening, except for the fact that Tom Finnegan's vintage red Corvette was plastered against the wounded bole of a massive beech that towered over the road. The tip of the tree's golden aureole of leaves was gloriously alight in the final rays of the setting autumn sun, but beneath it shadows had already gathered. In the distance he could hear the rise and fall of an ambulance siren.

Taking in the curving black tracks across the road and the deep gouges through the mud of the shoulder, Matt jumped over the smashed remains of Riley Newcombe's split-rail fence and ran across to where Charley Hart was kneeling on the yellow carpet of fallen beech leaves. Tom Finnegan lay outstretched under a rough gray blanket, apparently unmarked save for a small trickle of blood coming from a cut over one eyebrow. However, a closer look revealed the concave outline of a crushed chest and darkness spreading on the blanket from the broken body beneath it.

Charley moved aside to let Matt get close. Tom opened his eyes and stared into Matt's face for a moment or two, as if trying to place him. Then he spoke, and the sound was not much louder than the rustling of the leaves overhead.

"Wanted to tell you . . . not an accident."

Matt looked at Charley and then back at the curving tire marks between the highway and the tree. He looked down at Tom. Was he saying it was suicide? It would not be surprising. Everybody knew Tom was dying of cancer. His features were knife-edged under the loose skin of his face, and his hand, as it groped for Matt's, was skeletal. Perhaps the pain had become too much. Perhaps as he drove along in the autumn dusk he had been suddenly seized with despair at the prospect of the dark winter coming and his pain increasing, while his wife could only wait and watch. Nobody really would have blamed him for wanting a quick end to it all. Matt took the hand and held it, trying to reassure him. "I understand," he said. "It's all right."

"No . . . you *don't* understand. Nobody did—not even your father," Tom whispered, sounding oddly irritated.

Matt frowned. "My father?"

Tom closed his eyes, and there was a long silence. Matt thought he had gone—but then the almost transparent eyelids fluttered open again, and Tom Finnegan was staring at him, his lips moving soundlessly, struggling to explain something that was obviously very important to him. Considering the severity of his injuries, Matt was amazed he'd held on as long as he had.

". . . and it was the same with Jacky Morgan," Tom said, his voice suddenly taking on substance.

Matt looked at Charley, who shrugged. He was paying more attention to watching for the ambulance than to the faltering words of a dying man. If the ambulance came in time, maybe he wouldn't die. Charley was an optimist. Matt

looked down again at the old man, whose breathing was faint
now and who seemed as fragile as a broken bird fallen out of
the tree that rose above them. The bony hand stirred in his
and suddenly gripped with unexpected strength. "I promised
never to tell, but I don't want to die with it on my conscience
. . . I *told* him that." The grip relaxed, Tom shivered suddenly, and his voice faded away even though his lips kept
moving.

"Get another blanket over here," Charley called out just as
Tom's voice became barely audible once more, and Matt
missed the words.

"What? Tell me again, Tom." He bent closer.

"He forced me." Tom's voice was suddenly clear, propelled by anger and frustration, and Matt jerked back, startled. "He *forced* me, dammit!" As Tom shouted in outrage,
there was an abrupt inner convulsion and his final words
were drowned in blood.

The sound of the siren was loud, and then it, too, was
choked off abruptly. A screech of brakes, doors slamming,
running feet approaching—but they were too late.

Tom Finnegan was dead.

"And you didn't see anyone?" Matt asked Fred Boyle.

Boyle was clearly still upset. Charley had told Matt that
Boyle had come upon the accident as he was driving back to
town, and it was he who had pulled Finnegan clear of the
wreck, fearing an explosion or fire. Then he had summoned
help on his car phone.

"No, Matt, I can't remember passing or seeing a single car
going away," Boyle said in a shaky voice. "You know, I got
the car phone for when my wife was sick—I was going to
give it up, but I guess—"

"They can be useful," Matt agreed, talking as gently as he
could. It was clear that Boyle was rattled. If he had seen a car
before coming upon the wreck, it was unlikely he'd remember it now. Maybe later, when he'd calmed down. Certainly
there were no marks on his own car to indicate he had any
involvement in the crash. Of course, Tom Finnegan had said,
"He forced me"—and he could have been referring to Boyle,
but Matt doubted it. Neither man was known as a careless or

reckless driver, although this long bend on the old highway was notorious for luring even sensible people into taking chances. That Boyle had done it deliberately seemed even less likely. As far as he knew, the two men had no kind of relationship at all, neither friends nor enemies, although they were certainly acquainted. Boyle must have taught Finnegan's kids at the high school—he'd taught there for the past twenty-five years, at least.

Even at the best of times, Boyle was a sad figure. His suit needed a good dry clean, his hair needed cutting. He'd been going steadily downhill ever since his wife had died. "I wish I could have done something for Mr. Finnegan, but I could see he was in a pretty bad way."

"Yes," Matt said. "I'm surprised he survived for as long as he did."

"Terrible thing," Boyle said, and looked away. "So *many* people seem to be dying lately," he added in a vague, faint voice. "It's like when you stand on the beach and the waves pull the sand out from under your feet. You start to sink and you step back, but the waves keep coming, and coming—"

Matt patted him on the arm and went over to one of the paramedics. "I think you'd better have a look at Mr. Boyle over there. He's pretty shocked."

"He cause the accident?" the paramedic asked.

"No, but he pulled the victim out of the wreck," Matt said. "And he's . . . a little sensitive."

"I'll give him something," the paramedic said.

Matt looked back at the smashed Corvette. It was too late to give Tom Finnegan anything. They put the dead man on a stretcher, covering him completely with a blanket.

Matt grimaced. Now it was time for all the *if only*s to begin, starting with his own—if only he hadn't had to be in court. If only he could have dropped by Finnegan's place on the way home. If only he could have gotten here quicker. If only people didn't have to die.

"If only he could have made it to Christmas," Mrs. Finnegan said, impatiently wiping away the tears that trickled down her face. She had taken the news of her husband's death quietly, neither crying out nor giving way. But her tears were

not under control—they continued to come unbidden,
welling from her eyes and spreading over her pale cheeks.
They seemed, somehow, to annoy her. Mrs. Toby, sitting beside her, patted her hand encouragingly.

The Blackwater Bay Magpies had been holding one of
their monthly meetings at the Finnegan house that evening.
When Matt had arrived it was to a living room full of chat-
tering, stitching women, their heads bent over their quilts as
their needles went in and out of the material and in and out
of the reputations of various Blackwater Bay citizens. Their
gossip was more delicious than malicious, for they were a
generally good-natured group, but there is nothing more
pleasant to discuss over a quilting project than somebody
else's love affair, or the bargains to be had at some shop, or
the difficulties of raising one's own recalcitrant teenagers.
Tea, sympathy, and beeswaxed thread were the mainstays of
the Magpies. Once Matt had broken the news to Tom
Finnegan's wife, there was no keeping it private, and the
ladies—having hugged Dorothy sympathetically and gathered up their quilts—had departed discreetly, leaving only
their senior member, Mrs. Toby, to give further comfort to
the new widow.

Dorothy Finnegan was a very neat woman, dressed simply
in a matching skirt and sweater, with graying blond hair cut
short. She wore no makeup or jewelry except for her wedding ring and a small gold wristwatch. Matt couldn't ever remember her looking anything but tidy and organized, even
when she was younger and surrounded by four lively children and a pair of leaping dogs. "Competent" was the word
that came to mind when he thought of Dorothy Finnegan.
She smiled easily, laughed often, but never giggled. Even
now, faced with this terrible shock, she still retained that familiar air of efficient intelligence.

Except for those steadily flowing tears.

"What happened, Matt? Did something go wrong with that
damned car of his? I always told him it was too much for a
man his age. And he'd gotten so weak. . . ."

"I don't know, Dorothy. The state police garage will be
taking a look at it, but—" He paused, thinking about the skid
marks, the two small streaks of white paint on the side and

front fender of the Corvette and the half-moon gouge in the mud at the very edge of the paving, parallel to those Tom Finnegan's tires had made but returning to the highway.

Another car had been there.

And it had not been the car belonging to Fred Boyle, the frightened man who had come upon the wreckage and called for help on his mobile phone. His car was dark green.

"Tom braked, hard, before he went off the road. He didn't *want* to crash," Matt told her.

Her eyes met his, and she nodded, understanding only that he was releasing Tom from any accusation of suicide. "That tells us that the brakes were working, anyway," he continued. "It could have been a steering failure, or a blowout—two of the tires were torn apart. They'll have to reconstruct everything. It will take a little time before we know for sure." And, he added to himself, the white streaks could have gotten there days ago in a parking lot somewhere.

She nodded and was quiet for a moment. After a while she said, "Tom was coming to see you."

"Yes—he called me this morning. He seemed rather upset about it. Do you know why?" Matt asked.

Dorothy shook her head. "No."

"Oh." He was disappointed, hoping that she might throw some light on Tom's last words.

"But I know somebody didn't *want* him to see you." A little anger stirred in her voice.

"Oh?"

"I heard him on the phone this afternoon—he thought I'd gone out shopping, but I came back to get my list—I'd left it on the kitchen table, you see." She paused and, to his amazement, began to blush slightly. "I heard him talking and I thought . . . well . . . I went and stood outside his study . . ."

He realized suddenly that she was not embarrassed to have been eavesdropping, but because she'd suspected her husband of talking to another woman. "I don't know who it was, but he was arguing that he didn't want something on his conscience anymore . . . that he'd lived with a lie long enough."

Classic phrases—no wonder she'd been suspicious, Matt thought. He thought back to Tom Finnegan as he had been in the past few months—bald from the chemotherapy, pale, shaky, ravaged by his cancer—and hoped that the man had realized how much his wife adored him. She had remained blind to the cruel changes in him and had been afraid another woman, not cancer, was taking him from her.

She'd faltered momentarily. Now she cleared her throat and continued. "He said he couldn't go on with it, no matter whose reputation it would ruin. He said, 'You should have thought of that when it happened. If you'd told the truth then, it would have been better for everybody.' That's when I realized . . ." She stopped again, the blush more apparent.

"When you suddenly realized he *wasn't* talking to another woman," Mrs. Toby said with some asperity. "Would have suspected the same thing myself, Dorothy, hearing those first words. Any wife would. Perfectly natural."

There was gratitude in her glance. "Yes. And then I thought that if he had waited until I was out of the house to talk to this person, then it was something very private indeed, and I should respect that. So—I crept away and went shopping." She smiled ruefully. "I even let the car roll down the drive so he wouldn't realize . . . silly, I suppose."

"And you have no idea who he was talking to?"

"None."

"Or what it was all about?"

"No, I'm sorry. I wish I had asked, now." She looked at him speculatively. After a moment she added, "It had something to do with Halloween, I'm pretty sure of that. Or maybe more with the Howl."

"How do you mean?"

She sighed and looked around the room, seeming to take comfort from the well-worn familiarity of it. "It's difficult to explain," she said. "I don't want to create trouble for anyone."

"Now, you go right ahead and create," Mrs. Toby encouraged her. "It might be important, and you can trust Matt to be careful, you know that. Say what you have to say." Her wise old eyes turned to meet Matt's and there was sudden speculation there. "It was an *accident,* wasn't it . . . Tom's crash?"

He waited a moment, then answered honestly, "I don't know."

"Ah." Mrs. Toby nodded. "I see."

Dorothy Finnegan hardly seemed to hear this exchange. She looked at her hands, then lifted her eyes and looked around the room. Her gaze paused momentarily on a photograph in a silver frame at the end of the mantelpiece—a wedding photo—herself, younger and darker, her husband, full-faced and beaming. She turned back to Matt as if the sight burned her eyes, then leaned back and took a long breath. She held it for a minute, then let it out as if it carried with it all her reason for living. "Every year around this time, Tom would get very moody, very quiet. And when it came time to take the kids to the Howl, it would have to be *me* that took them, not Tom. I'd ask him about it—well, of course I would, it made me so darn mad—but he'd just laugh it off and say he was afraid of ghosts. It seemed there was just something about Halloween he couldn't tolerate. He'd be quiet for a few days afterward, too, but gradually things would get back to normal and we'd forget all about it. Until the next year, and then it would be the same thing all over again."

"Tsk." Mrs. Toby shook her head and patted Dorothy's hand again. "Men get these notions, you know. Like children, some of them. My Haskell was just the same over Thanksgiving, went into a proper droop every year, said it should be renamed National Indigestion Day. Didn't stop him eating turkey, though. I used to get so exasperated!"

Thanksgiving was one thing—the late Haskell Toby had made some kind of sense there—but Halloween was quite another. Here was a side of Tom Finnegan he'd never noticed, never heard about, a man he'd known practically all his life and known—he thought—rather well. So Tom Finnegan had been "funny" about ghosts and goblins. Well, everybody was a little strange about something, his father used to say. Certainly some people were "funny" about Christmas, real Scrooges, but Tom Finnegan—a grown man—spooked by *Halloween?*

Or something more?

"I know, I know," Dorothy said, understanding his puzzlement. "But that's the way he was. It got so we just accepted it, hardly noticed it, really. Just Tom's way, so to speak, not worth making a fuss about. I thought perhaps he'd had some traumatic experience as a child and didn't like to admit it. All I know about his childhood is what he told me from time to time, the way you do. But he didn't talk about it very much, so I assumed it hadn't been a happy time and didn't press him about it. I wasn't born here, remember—I only came to Blackwater when I married Tom. People assume you know, you see, so they never explain. And it's not the kind of thing you can ask other people about." She gestured, vaguely, encompassing a lifetime of moments missed, stories, recollections, and histories known to others but hidden from her. "Well, after a while it got easier. We haven't had anything to do with the Howl since the kids grew up. Oh, on the actual day he'd be quieter than usual, go into his study or out for a walk in the evening. Something like that. Not big gestures in themselves, but he'd manage to shut me out, one way or another."

"Or shut himself in?" Mrs. Toby suggested.

Dorothy Finnegan nodded. "Exactly. Because it was like it was something he had to *face*, every year." Her voice seemed to skid sideways in her throat, and she paused to swallow. "You know about the cancer?"

"Yes."

"Well, whether it was that or something else—*this* year the moodiness was worse than ever. He started brooding about two weeks ago, and he got to be more and more of a misery each day that passed. He kept having nightmares, and lay awake at night as if he were afraid to go to sleep. It wasn't the pain—he had pills for that, and it hadn't gotten really . . ." She paused again.

"I think I'll just go out and make a nice pot of tea," Mrs. Toby said suddenly. "You could do with it, Dorothy. You need to boost your blood sugar." And she marched out purposefully.

Matt was grateful for her discretion. He leaned forward and put his hand over Dorothy's, seeing the tears gathering in her eyes. "It's all right. If you want to leave this for another—"

"No, I want to tell you," she insisted a little more loudly than necessary. "I do. Because when he got into his car tonight, he was different. He seemed to have come to some kind of a decision." She hesitated. "I think he was going to confess something to you. Did he?"

Matt was perplexed, but not surprised. Something very important had made Tom Finnegan fight to keep himself alive until he could talk to Matt. What could it have been? Tom had been the only pharmacist in Blackwater for many, many years. What could he have known about? A wrong prescription that had killed someone? A secret addiction? An illness that carried some stigma? But he wouldn't have been alone in such knowledge. And why was it worse for him at Halloween? For a moment his mind veered wildly—was there a werewolf in Blackwater Bay? Settle down, Gabriel, he told himself, you've been watching too much late night TV.

"Does the name Jacky Morgan mean anything to you?" Matt asked.

She frowned. "No, it doesn't."

"Then I'm afraid I don't know either. Tom was still alive when I reached him, but . . ."

"But he never got to say what it was," she said in a flat voice, like a machine.

"Well, he *started* to . . . he got out the name Jacky Morgan, and something about promising not to tell . . . but then . . . he just slipped away. I'm sorry."

She looked at him for a long time, then seemed to come to a decision herself. "I wasn't going to tell you this, but if it *wasn't* an accident . . ." She paused again, waiting for him to answer the question she didn't want to ask.

"Please tell me anything you think might help my investigation," he said carefully.

Her eyes widened momentarily. He *had* answered the question. She took another deep breath. "It was the last thing I heard Tom say . . . before I went away and left him on the phone."

"Yes?"

"He said—'There's no statute of limitations on murder, my friend.' " She spoke with a kind of dawning agony and repeated the last words. "My *friend.* "

And then she broke down.

4

It was after eleven when the sheriff got back to Mrs. Peach's. The house was quiet. Mr. and Mrs. Stevens had gone to bed. Biddy Tillotson and Nonie were busy in the back parlor, making papier-mâché Halloween masks for the children in her class. Dominic Pritchard and Clarence Toogood were slumped on two armchairs in the front sitting room, bathed in a weird flickering light from the television set, where a character in a horror film was muttering imprecations at someone. The dialogue was accompanied by occasional snorts and snufflings—Clarence was asleep. Matt tried to move quietly down the hall, but Dominic spotted him through the archway and rose to join him.

"Are you making coffee, by any chance?" Dominic inquired.

"Definitely," Matt said, and they went into the kitchen together. Matt clicked on the light by the door and gazed with pleasure on the clean surfaces of the old-fashioned room. There was something very calming about a neat kitchen, he decided, and he felt his taut muscles begin to relax. Especially one with bright blue-and-white-checked curtains and a fatly cushioned rocking chair by the range. On the scarred and scrubbed pine table in the center of the quarry-tiled floor lay a tray of brown eggs, set out ready for the morning. When he went to get the coffee from the pantry, he saw two huge bowls of dough draped in muslin and set on the marble slab of the cold shelf. Already a slight mound was visible in the center of each stretched white circle of cloth—tomorrow's fresh breakfast rolls were gently on the rise.

Mrs. Peach did not allow guests into her kitchen when she was cooking, but she had told Matt he could help himself to coffee anytime, because he kept such irregular hours. During the day there was always a pot kept hot, but after dinner he was on his own. Dominic looked around a little nervously— he had not been extended the same privilege and seemed to half expect Mrs. Peach herself, or Nonie, to leap out and cry "Interloper!"

He sank onto a chair beside the big table, plucked an egg from the tray, and idly spun it with one finger as Matt moved about the kitchen, preparing the percolator. When it was grumbling to itself satisfactorily, Matt removed his portion of pineapple upside-down cake from the pantry and carried it to the table, collecting another plate and two forks on the way. As usual, the portion Nonie had left him was enough for two. Dominic's polite refusal was less than convincing, and soon they were both tucking into the succulent dessert. By the time they had finished, the coffee was ready.

Dominic, whose timing was excellent, finally spoke. "Was it a bad one?" His tone was sympathetic rather than curious—he was asking Matt about Matt, not for any prurient details of the accident.

"An old friend killed out on the highway," Matt said. "Crashed his car into that big golden beech tree."

"I'm sorry," Dominic said. He could see Matt was upset and wondered how he managed to distance himself from the suffering his job must cause him to witness from time to time. Or even, as in this case, his own pain. It was something that worried Dominic, because he didn't know if *he* would be as successful at it as Matt apparently was. Unlike a lot of "modern" young men, he was proud of being sensitive and empathetic, yet the thought of looking after clients in a malpractice case or a custody situation terrified him. Could he maintain his cool? Could he control things in court and out? Lawyers had to be hard these days. There were too many sad stories.

And there were too many lawyers.

"I suppose some would say it wasn't a tragedy," Matt said slowly. "Tom was dying of inoperable cancer, had only a few months more to live. He had a lot of pain to face up to—and he's been spared that. On the other hand, he and his wife were counting on spending those last days together. A lot of things were left unsaid. Unfinished." He stirred cream into his coffee. "Including why he was coming to see me in the first place."

"You mean he was on his way here?"

"To my office," Matt said. "He called me this afternoon, said he needed to talk to me about something. He was obviously worried—but I had to appear in court today. So we arranged to meet tonight, at my office."

"Ah." Dominic carefully replaced the egg he'd been toying with. His tone was reflective.

Matt glanced at him and smiled. "You're right—he didn't want his wife to hear what he had to say. When I asked her, she said she had *no* idea what it was all about."

"Oh?" Dominic asked dubiously.

Matt grinned. "Right again. She had an idea all right—but not a very clear one. She said she thought he wanted to confess something."

"Deathbed conscience?"

"I think so." He told Dominic about the scene of the accident, about Finnegan's struggle to stay alive until he came, and then his broken series of statements. He also told him about the marks on the road and car and, last of all, the conversation Mrs. Finnegan had overheard.

"She thinks someone forced him off the road to prevent his talking," Dominic said when he'd finished.

"Maybe."

"You have only her word for this conversation."

"True."

"Do *you* think he was forced off the road?"

Matt hesitated. "He more or less said he was."

"He said he was 'forced'—it could have been off the road, it could have been referring to the secret he kept," Dominic pointed out. "And he *was* rambling, you said so yourself."

"You want me to believe that they were both rambling—

he *and* his wife?" Matt snapped. "He knew damn well he was dying."

"Yes—but you don't know what 'forced' refers to," Dominic persisted. "Did she suggest the possibility of murder or did you?"

"I never actually—"

"But you left the question open—left her to wonder and put things together, the moods, the overheard conversation . . . ?"

Matt sighed. "I guess maybe I did. I was so suspicious myself—maybe I communicated it to her."

"And *then* she remembered this conversation."

"Yes." He spoke ruefully. "Leading the witness?"

"It could be," Dominic said. "On the other hand, you might both be right, he might have been forced off the road." He paused briefly, then spoke quickly. "What color car does his wife drive?"

Matt looked at the young lawyer, startled. Then he smiled. "Bright blue. And her guests were still there, quilting away, when I arrived. They'd been there since before Tom left."

"Ummm," Dominic said neutrally.

"But I did make a call when I got back to the office," Matt acknowledged. "As far as their regular agent knows, Tom's life insurance is adequate, no more."

"She needn't have gone through their regular agent. He could have had an old paid-up policy. He could have bank accounts somewhere. There are lots of ways to hide money," Dominic pointed out.

Matt looked at Dominic with a slightly refreshed attitude— there was a good lawyer's mind there. Naturally suspicious, exploring all the angles, wanting every question answered. "So what are you telling me?"

It was Dominic's turn to look startled. He had been considering it purely as an abstract problem, forgetting that the dead man had been a friend of Matt's, had been a beloved husband. He flushed slightly. "I'm not telling you anything. It's just that suspicion can grow in shallow ground with very little fertilizer. You don't want to go off half-cocked without facts."

"The state police were not convinced," Matt said slowly.

"They arrived *after* he died, of course. They didn't hear what he said—or what she said. The SP forensic guy did take a moulage of the tire tracks by the road. We saw right away they weren't from Fred's car—he's the guy who came along later and called for help. *His* car is green, so it couldn't have left the white streak on the Corvette. They could get the make of the car that left that from the chemical formula of the paint itself—but I didn't get the impression they were too eager to bother. They didn't think the white scrape was fresh."

"So what are you going to do?" Dominic asked.

"The only thing I can do," Matt said. "Nothing—for the moment."

"People often forget that doing nothing is a perfectly viable alternative," Dominic said solemnly.

Matt laughed. "How long have you been in Blackwater?" he asked. "Two months?"

"No, more like five. I started working for Mr. Putnam just over a month ago—before that I was lifeguarding at Butter Beach. I wanted to look around the town before I made up my mind to settle."

"Summer isn't the same as winter here."

"I know that. I wasn't interested in the tourists—just the locals. I like to take time over my decisions—especially the important ones."

"Very sensible. But I don't remember seeing you around town."

"Well, I was here—whenever I wasn't pulling kids out of the water, that is. I don't like to draw attention to myself. I just sort of—wandered around."

Dominic thought back to the hordes of cruising young men who had infested Main Street, looking for girls on summer evenings. It had been easy to blend in with them, wearing the ubiquitous uniform of saggy shorts and sweats, or perhaps jeans and T-shirt, allowing him to become invisible and to stare freely at everyone and everything.

"How did we measure up?" Matt asked with genuine interest.

Dominic grinned—and it was a sudden, wolfish grin. Matt saw him anew and was abruptly wary. For all his seeming modesty, there was an animal inside young Dominic Pritchard, and a carnivorous one at that. The broken nose suddenly made more sense. This was a person who went for the kill when you least expected it, who watched and waited patiently for his chance and then took it without warning. His sheep's clothing of polite conversation and calm intelligence served him well. Matt wondered if Carl Putnam knew just what he had hired.

Dominic spoke briskly. "As far as I could see, Blackwater is growing but not grown, solid but not set, has plenty of variety—emotional *and* geographic—and, legally speaking, is unique. Your local bylaws are absolutely amazing."

"Blackwater County was carved out of Michimac County during Prohibition," Matt said.

"So I understand. Judging by the framework they set up then, they must have been drunk themselves, at the time," Dominic said. "I had a professor who would love to get his hands on some of those statutes for a book he's writing. Why didn't they reamalgamate after Repeal?"

"Nobody much gave a damn," Matt said. "I think it was more or less on the basis of 'If it works, don't fiddle with it.' They let it all ride. I recall your boss telling me once that when he tries a local case he just applies what's useful and the hell with the rest. Isn't that general practice?" he added slyly.

Dominic laughed. "Maybe. Anyway, once I had a look at it all, I couldn't resist it. I can't say it will fit me to work anywhere else, but it will be an experience."

"Not planning to stay long?" Matt asked, surprised.

"Not planning anything," Dominic said. "Just going along."

"Be careful—that's what got *me* stuck up to my armpits," Matt said.

Dominic looked surprised. "Aren't you happy here?"

"Oh, sure. Maybe too happy," Matt said. "It's the old frog/pond dichotomy. Sometimes I get the feeling I should rejoin the real world and contribute something to the betterment of humanity. But, if I sit still long enough . . . it passes."

They relaxed in peace for a while. Then Dominic stirred.

"That name Tom Finnegan said sounds vaguely familiar," Dominic murmured with a frown.

"Jacky Morgan?" Matt asked. "I looked in what files of my father's I could reach—but I couldn't find a damn thing. There's no telling how far I'd have to go back—and even then there's no *guarantee* it would help. Anyway, Morgan's not an unusual name. I can place about ten Morgans in the county offhand."

"But no 'Jacky'?"

"Nope. Don't even know if it's a man or a woman."

"Funny—I can't remember where I heard it or saw it . . . but I *have* come across it—sometime in the past few weeks."

"Well, what have you been *doing* in the past few weeks?" Matt asked.

"Going over old cases, cleaning out files, generally tidying up and reading up, so as to get well settled in before Mr. Putnam starts taking the time off he says he wants. He handles a lot of family business, you know. I have to know the background of each one. Of course, he'll be on the end of the phone—"

"When he isn't on the end of a fishing line, golf club, or tennis racket," Matt put in.

"Right—but I can't stick a client in the waiting room while I phone him and get the lowdown on some obscure relationship. It's not that big an office, frankly—they'd overhear me asking who the hell they are. A man could lose respect that way." He chuckled, then grew serious again. "I wish I could remember. . . ." He shrugged. "Sorry. I can ask Mr. Putnam tomorrow, of course—unless you'd rather I didn't."

"Not just yet," Matt said. He felt disinclined to draw any more people into what could easily be a wild goose chase at best. "It's not as if it were directly relevant. Of course, if the state police decide it was murder—"

"Haven't you already decided that?" Dominic asked quietly.

Matt looked at him. "Not officially," he said carefully.

"That's what I thought," Dominic nodded, and was quiet once more.

Matt was disappointed. For a minute there he thought "Jacky Morgan" might have dropped into his lap, that he could have picked up a thread and followed it to some conclusion or other that would settle things. Too easy, of course. Too much to expect. He could be so wrong. He looked around the room, gently kicked the leg of the table. But, then again, he could be right.

"Well, hold on a minute," he said. "You've been doing *other* things for the past few weeks, too. Watching TV, for instance, going to the movies, reading the newspapers, reading books—"

"Say—*that's* a possibility," Dominic interrupted.

"Which one?"

"Newspapers. What about the *Chronic?* Don't they keep files there, back issues, that kind of thing?"

Matt smiled. Dominic had obviously learned a few local abbreviations, such as the *Chronic*—their weekly newspaper, so nicknamed because of all its typographical errors and its tendency to look on the dire side of ordinary events. (Just the way *he* was doing at the moment.) "They're bound to keep back issues. Mr. Gibbons is an editor of the old school, as they say."

"Well, then—why not look there?"

Matt shook his head. "It would take too long, and I—"

"I'll do it," Dominic heard himself saying. "You said Tom Finnegan got depressed and upset around Halloween, so whatever was bothering him must have happened then. It's just a matter of going back from one October to the last. One thing might remind me of another—I might pick up the connection with whatever it is *I'm* trying to remember. I could do it on my lunch hour."

"Why the hell should you?" Matt asked.

Dominic shrugged elaborately, pretending innocence. "Well, I haven't got all that much to do in my spare time at the moment. And I'd like to help."

"Oh, yeah?" Matt asked doubtfully.

"Yeah," Dominic said negligently. "Why not?"

Matt regarded him. The young man's mouth curved up in a slow smile—a smile reminiscent of the expression on the face of a wolf running behind the troika when the horses were tiring. Matt stared at him for a long time—and then he remembered.

Emily Gibbons worked on her father's newspaper.

And Dominic Pritchard had been in town all summer.

Looking around.

5

"*I*'m sorry about last night," Matt said.

"So am I." Daria Grey was by the window looking out over the bay.

They were standing in her new studio—converted from what had been an open redwood deck that had spanned the front of the big house on the tip of Paradise Island. Sleety rain obscured the horizon and slid in wavering streamers down the glass roof and walls that now enclosed three quarters of the space—only the leading edge of the deck had been left open to the weather. There the uncaulked boards were darkened and glistening with icy wetness. The planters along the railings had puddles in their empty earth, and from one a small trickle of muddy water was dripping down.

Below, untended lawn stretched to a narrow strip of sandy beach. Even though the morning was overcast, there was a pearly light in the studio, a light without shadow that Matt knew was perfect for Daria's painting. It was obvious she'd come here to work, for a prepared canvas stood on her easel, but her paints were still capped, and her palette lay clean and empty beside the bottles of linseed oil and turpentine.

The ribs that supported this new structure were wired for lighting that would enable her to continue work when night fell. Next summer, people out late on the water would see her at her easel, seeming to float in a rectangular bubble of light above the rest of the house and the grounds.

He was interrupting her work and he knew it, but he
needed to talk to her. It was a need that was growing daily.

She turned, now, and smiled at him. The smile was loving
and a little sad. "But I'm glad you were there when Tom
Finnegan died. He was a lovely man—he used to make me
double chocolate tin roof sundaes with extra peanuts." Her
smile stretched to a wry grin. "He would say there were
always plenty of nuts in Blackwater Bay, one way and
another."

"Amen." Matt nodded. He gestured to the glass that surrounded them. "They did a good job on this."

"Yes, it's wonderful. But I think I'll be glad of the air-
conditioning in the summer—I'd suffocate without it."

He didn't want to talk about the changes in the house any
more than she did. Here their conversations always became
stilted. In this house, which had held so many terrible secrets, he still felt awkward and uncomfortable. So did she,
but he knew she was fighting to overcome it. Perhaps that
was why she had come here today to face her easel. It was
certainly why it was being transformed from top to bottom.

Daria had recently purchased the newly christened Hope
House from its previous owners. She was a brilliant and
gifted artist and had just begun to establish an international
reputation when her wealthy and insanely jealous husband
had commenced a campaign to destroy her, body and soul.
Now he was dead and she was free. The returning desire to
commit herself to canvas had proved to her that she was at
last triumphing over the agonies of the past few years, when
she had been unable to work or even think of working.

Therefore, her most urgent and wonderfully welcome need
had been for a studio where she could begin to paint again—
hence the precipitate purchase of the big house.

Once the studio was completed, the builders had been
turned loose on the three-storied interior of the big house to
create comfortable living and working accommodation for
about eight people plus staff. Next spring, when the conversion work on the house was complete, she planned to grant
one-year scholarships to promising art graduates in order that
they might have a breathing space to sort out their priorities,
to begin to build a body of work, and—hopefully—to create

reputations and careers of their own. She had used the balance of her late husband's money to establish a trust fund for that very purpose—an action she viewed with wry pride.

Despite all the horror he had caused, her late husband *had* provided the financial support that had permitted her to begin her career without the worry of when and where her next meal was coming from. Now that she could live comfortably from the proceeds of her own work, the money she had inherited from him was superfluous. Therefore, knowing the decision would have enraged him (as it had certainly enraged his family), she had determined to use it to provide that same golden freedom to others. After the destructive experiences of the previous months, Daria Shanks Grey wanted to put a little creativity back into the world.

Her first intention had been to move into the house herself, but after long discussions, she and her peppery aunt Clary had decided to continue living in their own little cottage farther back down Paradise Island. It was where the orphaned Daria had grown up and where she felt at home. There she and Matt could relax and enjoy the affection that was growing between them. In her new Main Street gallery or here at Hope House, she was the famous artist. In the old cottage she was just Daria, as she had always been. Unfortunately, also there in the cottage was Aunt Clary, as *she* had always been.

Aunt Clary Shanks was an old-fashioned and respectable woman. She approved of Matt and of his courtship of her niece, but that approval did *not* extend to accommodating what she called "hanky-panky." At first this did not interfere with their physical discovery of one another—by the end of the summer Daria had become a regular visitor to Matt's small flat over the garage. But now that Matt was rooming at Mrs. Peach's, the sexual aspect of their relationship had taken on farcical dimensions.

If it all hadn't been so new and tentative, it would have made them laugh. As it was, it only made lovemaking seem either deliberate and therefore cold or a matter of missed connections—as with last night—and therefore alienating. Theirs was not a grand passion, where sexual gratification took precedence over everything else, driving them to any extreme for consummation. Rather, it was a growing acceptance that their individual lives, however incompatible, were also incomplete without one another. She had been badly hurt in her first marriage, as had he in his. Perhaps they were being overcautious. Certainly it would have helped matters considerably if they had been able to worry less about it and just go ahead and risk making things permanent. But that wasn't in either of their natures.

Blackwater was worried about them.

Even Aunt Clary was coming to the conclusion that she should visit her distant cousin in Miami for the winter—hanky-panky unseen is hanky-panky unheard—in the hopes that she could return to a spring wedding.

"There's too damn much about 'being sure' in you, girl," she told Daria. "That's what happened to me, you know. I was so busy being 'sure' I had the right one that he got fed up and went off with the wrong one—the one that was willing. I don't hold with living together, you know that—but great God almighty, marry him before I die, will you?"

Looking at Matt Gabriel now, with his hair wet on his forehead and his new uniform fitting him like a glove, she felt almost overwhelmed by desire. For a moment the suggestion that they make love right there in sight of the rain and the seagulls burned the tip of her tongue—and then she heard the shout of the builders within the house and pressed her lips together.

Matt, too, wanted to take her in his arms—not from overwhelming physical desire, although that was always with him, but from a need to affirm life, to feel her warmth and her reality in the face of his confusion concerning Tom Finnegan.

"I wish to Christ it wasn't raining!" he suddenly burst out, startling her.

"Why?"

"Because I could use a walk. I find it easier to think when I'm walking, and I need—I want—to know what you think I should do, if anything, about Tom."

"What about him? His funeral, you mean?" She was puzzled by his vehemence. "Won't his wife be arranging that?"

"No. Yes. Yes, of course." He took three quick steps toward her and, grabbing her arm, started toward the stairs.

"Hey—I was planning to paint—" she began.

"This won't take long."

"I don't *want* to walk in the rain, Matt," she protested.

"Then we'll drive. I just want to get away from here," he said. He snatched her coat off the hook by the door, draped it over her shoulders with the rough affection of a parent readying a child for school, and rushed her out and into the car. Five minutes later they were on the highway, heading toward Hatchville.

"This was necessary, was it?" she asked in a level voice. She hadn't decided yet whether to be irritated or not. On the one hand it was satisfying to be close to him in the smaller space of the car, but on the other hand he hadn't even asked her whether or not it was where she wanted to be. A girl liked to be asked. She was on the verge of opting for irritation when he spoke.

"I think I'm scared, Derry."

All thoughts of irritation, mock or real, fled. "Of what?"

"Either I'm nuts—which is a distinct possibility—or somebody *forced* Tom Finnegan off the road and into that tree. Someone who knew he was coming to tell me something they didn't want told."

"Good heavens—are you serious?"

"Yes." And he explained.

She was silent for quite a while, and when she spoke it was gently, as if she were humoring an overimaginative child. "Are you sure you haven't got murder on the brain?" The windshield wipers tsk-tsked disapproval.

"Because of last summer?" he asked.

"Mmmm."

He shook his head. "No—I wondered about that, too—wondered about it most of the night, in fact. I know what you're getting at—the excitement of the chase and all that. Is that it?"

"Well, sort of. I only meant that you might have become supersensitive about murder. Do you want to become another Jack Stryker?"

"I could do worse."

"Jumping Jack" Stryker was a lieutenant of homicide in Grantham, the large city well to the south of Blackwater. Locals here referred disparagingly to Grantham as "The Big Dirty," and it was indeed a city filled with death and pollution, an urban sprawl of contrasts, housing a state university, huge factories, world-class museums, and a reputation for violence and decay.

Blackwater, on the other hand, was a small and beautiful lakeside area that had largely escaped the inroads of "progress" until the previous summer, when murder and hatred had rocked the small county and in particular the small and elegant island called Paradise. Jack Stryker's fiancée, Kate Trevorne, had grown up on Paradise Island, and they had been vacationing here when Matt had been faced with the first real homicide investigation of his career. Stryker had given up his holiday to help Matt close the case. Working with an experienced, educated, and brilliantly intuitive detective had been an enlightening experience for Matt—and a serious loss of innocence.

"You could do better, too," Daria said. She liked Jack Stryker well enough, and Kate was one of her best friends, but she didn't relish Matt becoming as cynical or as reckless as the city detective.

"I hear what you're saying," he conceded. "But I don't think I'm just looking for trouble. You weren't there, Derry. You didn't *hear* Tom, didn't see how he'd hung on so *hard* just in order to tell me what it was he wanted me to know. And then he couldn't get it out. Whoever had wanted to silence him got his way."

"What do the state police think?"

He shrugged. "Oh, I pointed out things to them—but I got the impression they weren't convinced. I'm positive they're going to label it an accident and shove it to the back of the drawer. But it wasn't. I'm *sure* it wasn't."

They were no longer racing down the road raising a tail of spray between the fields and woods that flashed past. His first burst of energy and exasperation had faded, eased by telling her of his confusion. He glanced across at her, taking his eyes briefly from the gleaming half-river of the road. She still had her raincoat wrapped around her like a cloak, and the collar was awry behind her head. Her short curls twinkled with icy raindrops. A few more spangled her cheeks, and one clung to the end of her nose. It was her nose he loved best of all—long, angular, chiseled at the end, a sweeping counterpoint to the fluid line of her jaw and the prominence of her cheekbones. She wasn't laughing at him—she wouldn't—and she wasn't trying to deny the possibility he was suggesting.

She was thinking about it.

He knew, then and absolutely, that she loved him.

"What are you going to do about it?" she finally assked.

"For the moment, nothing." They drove on. "Does the name Jacky Morgan mean anything to you?" he finally asked.

She frowned. "It sounds familiar, somehow."

"Yes, to me, too. Our records and files are in a hell of a mess with the conversion work going on. I had a fast look last night, but I couldn't spot anything. Dominic Pritchard is going to look at the *Chronicle* back issues for me."

"Why don't you do it yourself?"

"Too official. For the moment it seems better to accept the 'accident.' When I find out more, I may have a clearer picture of things."

"Why Dominic?"

"He was handy." Matt finally managed a smile. "And he volunteered. I think he's getting bored with Blackwater Bay already."

Daria looked over at him, noting the lines of tension and the hard set of his mouth. He was not a natural lawman. He belonged on a college campus somewhere, debating Descartes under a tree. Forcing himself into his father's persona had been difficult for him—but he'd seemed to feel some obligation to take on the responsibility. Now the lines between what he was and what he felt he should be were beginning to blur.

She knew what was bothering him the most—not murder itself, although that was bad enough, but the disruption to the town and the way of life he'd been brought up with and hoped to preserve. Blackwater Bay was being dragged into the twentieth century, dragged screaming and begging to be let alone. For so long a gentle existence had seemed safely possible here. Now the dream was dissolving around them.

Maybe it had always been an illusion, but if so, the sheriff—father or son—would have been in a perfect position to know. And he hadn't known anything of the kind—until last summer.

She knew, watching him, that he now felt increasingly helpless to stop whatever was going wrong in the town. Right for the job or not, he felt personally responsible somehow for not being able to hang on to what it had been, to hoard and protect its elusive sweetness.

She wished she could extend her world to enclose him, but he would neither appreciate nor accept it. In the years ahead he would have to learn, as she had, that some things you just can't hang on to, and that maybe it was wrong to try. He wasn't a fool; he would absorb the lesson. She wished she didn't have to witness this painful education, but loving him meant she had no choice. All she could do was hide his eyes occasionally.

"So you're not going to do anything about Tom Finnegan right now?"

"No—like I said—"

"Then take the next left," Daria said.

"What?" He glanced at her again.

"The next left. That little lane—there."

He did as he was told, and they bumped down the graveled lane into a stand of trees. "Stop here," she commanded.

"What the hell for?" he wanted to know.

"And turn off the engine."

He complied, then turned to her. "Well?"

"I understand the seats in this fancy new car of yours actually fold right down flat," she said. "I read it in an advertisement. Is that true?"

Matt stared at her and began to smile. "Oh, yes," he said.

She turned to face him. "Show me," she said softly.

Dominic had fully intended to go over to the *Chronicle* the first thing next morning, but man is not always master of his fate—particularly a new man in a junior position. Two new contracts came into the offices of Crabtree and Putnam, with at least two hundred clauses, conflicts, and contradictions in each to consider. It was, therefore, well past noon before he cautiously entered the offices of the *Blackwater Bay Weekly Chronicle.* Indeed, it was so quiet within that he wasn't certain the place was open for business during the lunch hour—even though the street door had been unlocked.

No alarms rang out, so he closed the door behind him and looked around with interest. It was, he supposed, what a small-town newspaper office should *really* look like—a neat and modern layout of desks and files—totally without the customary Hollywood addition of a crusty old man in arm garters and a green visor, sitting with his feet up on a rolltop desk, smoking a pipe and reading a book by H. L. Mencken.

In fact, there was only a girl there. She wore jeans and a light blue sweater, no arm garters. She was eating a croissant and absently brushing the crumbs off her admirable front. The book propped up in front of her was by Peter Drucker, and on her lap was a half-finished quilted cushion cover. A truly modern girl, then—torn between business management and the more womanly arts.

She looked up as he closed the door. Her eyes were like melted chocolate, so dark they seemed almost without pupils, startling in a face where the skin was delicately pale despite the sun of the just finished summer. Her hair was brown, too, and her figure, though curvy, was definitely on the elfin side. She gazed at him for a moment and then asked, "What do you think of string?"

He considered. "I think there are many instances when absolutely nothing else will do."

The dark eyes came into sudden and sharp focus. "Okay," she said with a grin. "You pass."

"Good for me. Who fails?"

"Your call, not mine," she said. "It's an individual test with individual criteria. Personally I reject anybody who says 'Huh?' or 'Did you say string?' or 'I dunno.' Who would *you* fail?"

"Is this the second part of the test?" he asked warily.

She was momentarily disconcerted. "I suppose it could be, at that. Anyway, come on, move on, don't spoil your record," she said, standing up. The quilting project started to slide to the floor, but she caught it on the toe of her boot and kicked it up onto the desk.

"Back issues," he said. "I need to look something up."

"Okay. How far back?" She leaned over the long high counter that separated the reception area from the working office and propped her chin on her hands. He decided the sewing bit was a temporary aberration and would never be finished. He had asked around about her—very discreetly. He knew she was twenty-three, unattached, and full of hell. Close up, you could see the snap and sparkle in those dark, dangerous eyes.

"Twenty years back. Maybe more."

"Mmmm. Attic stuff. You'll get that Armani jacket filthy," she said, giving him a comprehensive once-over. "Sure you wouldn't like to come back tomorrow in overalls?"

"I am a loyal supporter of the dry cleaners of America," he said. "They live for my challenge."

She went to the end of the counter and lifted a portion of it to give him access. "Passing through or settling down?" she asked over her shoulder as he followed her between the empty desks.

"Undecided," he said.

She grabbed a pad and pencil from the last desk. "Name?"

"Dominic Pritchard."

She hesitated a fraction and then went on. "New junior associate of Mr. Carl Putnam, local legal eagle?"

"Almost exactly."

"I see. And you just out of law school. You must be good."

"You must have asked."

She glanced up at that, her cheeks growing pink. She dropped the pad and pencil back on to her desk. "I'm a reporter. I'm *supposed* to ask."

"I'm a lawyer. I'm supposed to ask, too. I asked about you."

"Oh, really?"

"Yes."

"You must be hard up for entertainment. Learn anything interesting?"

"This and that. Nothing *very* bad."

"Then you must have been talking to the wrong people,"

she said briskly. She went to a door at one side of the room and opened it. "This way to our beautiful library—and watch out for the spiders."

"Do they bite?"

"No, but they can be *really* sarcastic."

He was delighted with her. Enjoying the view as she preceded him, Dominic climbed the steep, narrow staircase with a hopeful heart. At the top he found himself in an overstuffed but orderly "attic." Long lines of shelving seemed to fade into the distance, for the room extended the length of the building, over what he assumed must be a printing plant at the rear of the ground floor.

Emily turned and waved a graceful arm. "Our presses started rolling just after the Civil War. Daily then, weekly now. Some say very weakly. Personally I think people just read slower these days. Bound copies go up to 1988, raw copies stacked by month up to last week. All the really *good* stuff happened during Prohibition—after that it was all weddings and funerals. We get journalism majors working summers sometimes. We set them to work up here, sorting and binding. If they last more than a month, we figure they might be serious."

He regarded her with amusement—she'd only finished college herself a couple of years back. "How long did *you* last?"

"Actually, I was born to it—my father owns the paper," she said, flushing a little.

"Never turn down a lucky break," he said with a grin.

"Maybe. Mind you, some are harder to take than others," she admitted. "If you're good, they say you take after your old man, but if you're *bad* nobody says a word. It's hard to learn that way."

He looked around for a reason to prolong the conversation. "I thought newspaper offices were supposed to be noisy, full of people shouting 'Hold the presses!' and demanding rewrite men, whatever *they* are," Dominic said. "Where *is* everybody?"

Emily Gibbons spoke to the raftered ceiling. "Another disappointed customer, led astray by Hollywood." The dark eyes fixed him to the spot once again. "Would you like me to shout something for you? I can do 'Copy boy!' in four languages."

"*Wow!* No *wonder* they left you to run things alone." He put more sarcasm into his tone than he'd intended. "I mean—"

She looked at him as if undecided between irritation and disdain and eventually settled on pity. "We publish once a week, on Thursday. Today is Friday. It's breather time before we start putting together our traditional Halloween issue. Dad's at home making himself a suit of armor out of cardboard for the Howl, Mother is probably doing her yoga exercises, our three thousand highly experienced reporters are *both* out to lunch—most of the time—and our incredibly talented photographer has turned artistic on us. He's hanging himself in the new art gallery across the street." Her tone was only slightly weary.

"Well, what if some big story breaks?"

She raised an eyebrow. "What kind of big story do you think we get around here? A cut-price sale on piece goods? Our erstwhile body-building mayor dropping a dumbbell on his toe? I think I could handle it." She raised both eyebrows, and he involuntarily stepped back a pace. It struck him belatedly that she was not one to play by anyone else's rules.

"*Say,*" she said in a speciously eager voice. "You wouldn't be an ax murderer on the quiet, would you? I mean, it would be really *great* if you'd let me write up your life story before you cut me into pieces. I might even get a byline."

"Sorry—I hardly ever chop up girls before dinner."

"Oh. Pity." She gazed at him for some time with an intensity he found somewhat disconcerting. *He* had come to do the gazing, after all. "Why were you asking about me?" she demanded abruptly.

He could hardly tell her the truth—that he'd seen her in the Golden Perch three weeks ago and been so stricken with unexpected lust that he'd spilled his drink in his lap, and that by the time he'd dried off she'd left with some bastard who wasn't good enough for her. "Aren't you flattered?" he asked edgily.

She looked him over. "No."

A low blow, but he rallied. "Hey, I'm just a poor boy from the Middle West seeking encouragement and friendship in a hostile environment," he said with his most winsome smile.

"And I'm just a poor girl from Blackwater Bay seeking a bucket to puke in," she said wryly. From below there came the sound of two telephones ringing in a syncopated rhythm. "Sounds like that big story is breaking after all," she said. "Lucky me."

"*Un*lucky *me*," he heard himself say in an oily voice, and was filled with a kind of horror.

She looked at him and sighed again. "I would have been disappointed if you hadn't said that," she said.

Dominic realized, too late, that his pursuit of Emily Gibbons was doomed from the start. She was lovely, she was sharp, and she was the kind of girl to whom he would *always* say the wrong thing in the wrong way. Tasting premature defeat and finding it bitter, he considered throwing himself out of the nearest window and wondered if it would make the front page. Probably not.

She pointed toward the shelves as she turned away. "There's a table in the middle of all that, paper and pencils provided. If you need anything else—snake oil, tooth polish, a whetstone for your ax—just lift the tin can on the string and whistle."

"If I do, will you answer?"

"No chance." She started down the stairs, then turned, her head just visible above floor level. It was like being addressed by Anne Boleyn after the ax had fallen.

"You know, I'm not surprised somebody broke your nose," she said.

She left him alone with the feeling he'd gone three rounds with a Cuisinart. He shook his head and turned to the shelves filled with the news of years past, silent and waiting to be news again as he turned the pages. Six high, narrow windows on either side of the long room admitted angular shafts of light. In the nearest two, dust motes still spun lazily in the breeze of Emily Gibbons's departure.

"Pritchard, you're an ass," he muttered aloud. "Four years

of college, three years of law school, and you *still* haven't learned how to handle a simple conversation. Torts, yes, precedents, yes, contracts, yes. Women, *never*." With a huge sigh, he turned toward the maze of shelves and the task at hand.

Listening at the bottom of the stairs, Emily grinned to herself. She'd almost given up hope that Dominic Pritchard would find an excuse to talk to her. After all, he'd been around town for *months*, first over at Butter Beach and then in Putnam's office. She'd spotted him, watched him, managed to put herself in front of him at every opportunity, and waited.

And waited.

And waited.

Now he'd appeared and actually spoken, but if the past ten minutes were any indication, it would be Christmas before he asked her out. She went to answer the nearest telephone, shaking her head in exasperation. Some men were so *slow!*

"Get down from there before you break your fool neck!" Nell Norton said. "I swear, Margaret, you haven't the brains you were born with, climbing on rickety chairs at your age. Pretty rickety yourself, if you ask me." She took hold of her friend's hand and helped her down from her admittedly precarious perch.

Margaret Toby was oblivious to the criticism, caught up as she was in the splendor of her latest quilt as its rich blues and purples glowed against the white wall of the gallery.

"Doesn't that look grand?" she enthused, clasping her hands before her chest in a tiny arc of triumph. She turned to Daria Grey, who stood at the far end of the room. "It could be a painting!"

Daria turned and smiled. "It *is* a work of art," she said. "You work in textiles instead of oils or watercolors, but the creative process is just the same."

She put down the framed watercolor she'd been contemplating and came slowly up the room, her heels clicking on the broad, highly polished floorboards. The floor had been one of the pleasant discoveries made when they had been exploring the old premises and had influenced her strongly when it came time to decide which of three old Main Street stores she would purchase to become her local gallery. "It never ceases to amaze me how incredibly strong your grasp of color and composition is, you know." She neglected to add that it was even more amazing that the plump little widow with the white hair and the fluttering manner could produce such wildly innovative abstract results within the boundaries of an old and traditional form. Truly, Margaret Toby was one who transcended the gap between craft and fine art.

"But to be in a proper gallery . . ." Mrs. Toby breathed.

Daria looked at her and raised an eyebrow. "None of that giggling modesty, Margaret, you know damn well you're good."

"Just what I tell her," Nell Norton said.

"Well, that doesn't mean I don't appreciate an opportunity to strut my stuff," Mrs. Toby said briskly. "I just wish I'd had time to finish the yellow one last night. They're meant to be a pair, you see—winter and summer."

Nell Norton scowled. "Would have, too, if Tom Finnegan hadn't killed himself in that sports car of his."

"Well, for goodness' sake, Nell, he hardly did it on purpose!" Margaret said. "It was terrible, Dorothy finding out like that with all of us sitting there. Anyway, he didn't kill himself. Somebody else did it, or so the sheriff thinks."

"Now there you go, manufacturing mysteries again," Nell challenged her. "He never said any such thing, and you know it, Margaret."

"He didn't have to *say* it," her friend rejoined. "But he made it clear."

Daria looked from one to the other. "I know Matt is worried about the accident," she said quietly. "But there's no real evidence that it was anything *but* an accident, you know." She could see the entire thing growing and expanding until the whole town was taking sides, and that wouldn't help Matt at all.

"Dorothy was real upset," Margaret went on. "I felt so sorry for her. I know how I felt when Haskell died."

"Relieved, probably," Nell said dryly.

"Nell Norton, you take that back!" Margaret snapped.

Nell looked at her calmly. "Do you deny it?" They stared at one another.

Margaret surrendered first. "Well, no . . . but—"

"Tell it like it is, kiddo," said Nell.

"Oh, sure, when it's *my* husband," Margaret said. "But when it's Dorothy Finnegan's husband—"

"How long do you think it will take you to finish the yellow quilt, Margaret?" interrupted Daria. "We can leave space for it if it's going to be ready soon."

"I'll have it done by Friday, *if* I'm not interrupted," Margaret Toby said, glaring at her friend in mock anger. Their flare-ups were invariably for their own amusement.

Nell stuck out her tongue, and leaving them to discuss artistic matters, she walked over to where Harry Foskett was sorting out a selection of photographs for his display. Harry was a freelance photographer who worked for the *Chronicle* as well as doing all the usual bridal, baby, and pet shots required by the editor. Lately he'd begun working seriously on his own, however, and had accumulated a number of striking images that Daria had considered well worth displaying. He was tapping in a nail to support a shadowy study of an old man.

"Heard anything about Tom Finnegan's accident?" Nell asked Harry in a low voice.

"I was out there this morning to get a picture of the car," Harry said. "Hell of a mess."

"Look like an accident to you?"

Harry glanced at her. "Shouldn't it have?"

Nell shrugged. "There's been talk," she said.

"Well, it looked like a straight skid to me," Harry said. "Not saying I'm an expert or anything. Mind you, the rain's been coming down since five this morning. Might have looked different last night."

"Mmmm," Nell murmured. She and Margaret Toby were widows who shared a cottage on Paradise Island. Margaret had come home full of details about what Matt had said and what Dorothy had said and what Margaret herself had said, going on and on until Nell had been forced surreptitiously to spike her friend's cocoa with an extra sleeping pill just to get a good night's sleep herself. Both she and Margaret were inveterate gossip collectors, but there was something about Margaret's proximity to this particular drama that made it too real for her liking. Shocks taken second- or third-hand are one thing, but to be right there when the tears flow is something else. It wasn't good for Margaret. She'd have to keep her off the subject—unless something new developed.

"Doing anything special for the Howl?" Harry asked over-casually. In his experience, people weren't always ready to share their intentions. Nell, however, had no such inhibitions.

"I have plans," Nell said. "Last year Harriet Crabbe doused me down with garlic juice. Took me a week to get the stink out of my hair. I reckon to return the favor with a new vegetable dye Fred Boyle showed me. She'll be purple for days."

"Fred's a good man to know around Howl time." Harry nodded approvingly. "He's been so depressed since his wife died, thinking up nasty little tricks for nasty little people like us to do over the Howl is the perfect distraction for him. He's made up this special paint for me to spray all over Archy Ventnor's precious Edsel—bright pink. It'll look *awful.* After Archy's screamed and hollered for a while, I'll tell him how it washes off with soda water." He hung the picture of the old man alongside one of a young girl. The contrast was somehow flattering to them both. "It would be good if Fred could get married again."

"Isn't that Emily Gibbons?" Nell asked, looking at the girl.

"Yeah—took it last year. She's a pretty thing, isn't she?"

"Pretty is as pretty does," Nell said in a disapproving voice. "She's a wilful little piece, her mother tells me."

"Always was," Harry agreed. "Works with us over at the paper now. Has plans to be a big-city reporter—if she lives that long. Got a tongue on her like you wouldn't believe. Real amusing when she's in a good mood, but when she isn't—watch out."

Nell looked at him. "Don't you like her?"

"Sure I like her—as long as I'm safe behind a nice, long

lens," he said as he patted the picture. "She can't talk back when she's hanging on a wall."

Seeing that Margaret and Daria were still absorbed in their discussion—they were scribbling on a piece of paper bag now—Nell took a circuit of the big open room, looking at the various paintings that were already "hung."

Primarily for selling professional work, Daria Grey's new gallery would also feature promising local amateur talent. Hence Margaret Toby's quilts and Harry Foskett's photographic prints being added to the collection for the grand opening at the weekend.

For a moment Nell thought she was hearing an echo of Harry's efforts—hammer taps seemed to be outside as well as in. She turned to look through the glass door and saw that across the street, Mr. Naseem was nailing some of the windblown posters for the Blackwater Bay Halloween Carnival back onto the telephone poles. Somewhere on those posters, in the small print, would be a notice of her own cookie and baked goods stall. Back at the cottage the freezer was stacked with the dozens of items she'd be offering for sale on Halloween night, and she'd be baking right up until the carnival opened.

Nell sighed. She had mixed feelings about the Howl. The older locals kept to the largely innocent displays of imagination that were traditional—like Harry's paint and her temporary dye—but the young seemed to be developing different ideas. Last year somebody had set a barn on fire, there had been a fight between the senior boys from Blackwater High and a contingent from Lemonville, a girl had been deliberately pushed from one of the carnival rides, and just after midnight a drunken plumber from Brewster had crashed a pickup through the front of Tyrone Molt's Supercar Showroom, causing a lot of damage. Despite all the mayhem, nobody had been seriously hurt, but the opportunities were always there.

Matt Gabriel had a bigger force now and probably would keep things under control, but Nell had an uneasy feeling about it. Margaret sometimes accused her of being psychic. Normally Nell would have nothing to do with such nonsense, but she couldn't deny the fact that she was getting what some folks called "bad vibes" at the moment. The Howl was in real danger of getting out of hand.

Somebody might even get killed.

Maybe Tom Finnegan was only the first.

6

Tilly Moss was furious.

"Dammit, George, have you been at my files again?" she demanded, glaring at the jumble within the drawers. The chief deputy, in the act of raising his third cup of coffee to his lips, could have posed for any Victorian artist portraying "Innocence." He blinked, smiled, sipped, and sighed with contentment.

"Not guilty," he said. It wasn't a phrase he could use often, and he savored the moment.

"It was me, Tilly," Matt admitted wearily as he hung up his jacket. After dropping Daria off at the gallery, he'd spotted a bunch of teenage kids surrounding a fight and had gone over to break it up. He'd spent a while trying to sort the problem out, but he knew it was a useless exercise. Hormones and the approaching Howl, as usual. "Sorry."

"Well, for goodness' sake, you only have to *ask* for what you want," Tilly huffed. She began plucking, tucking, and generally tidying the top drawer of the first tall cabinet. "I'm usually right here, you know."

"You weren't here last night," Matt said. "For crying out loud, Tilly, we *allow* you two hours of sleep out of every twenty-four, the least you could do is take it at a convenient time."

Tilly grinned as she pushed back the top drawer and began on the next. "Well, what were you looking for, anyway?"

"Some of Dad's personal records."

"Louis Armstrong or Bix Beiderbecke?" George asked, still reveling in the novelty of not being to blame, for once.

"It's to do with Tom Finnegan's accident."

"But that was last night," George said in some surprise. "How could it be in your father's stuff?"

"Something Tom said keeps nagging at me, something about my father being wrong about something." He explained about Finnegan's last words. "I don't know if Jacky Morgan is a man or a woman, what happened, why—"

"Oh, *that* would be in one of those boxes in the back row," Tilly said with some exasperation. "I keep *telling* you I can't do anything about having those old daily reports microfilmed until we get the new storage rooms organized."

"They have to get finished first," George put in, referring to the snaillike pace of the builders, who for all their noise didn't seem to be accomplishing much.

During the murder investigation that had taken place the previous summer, media attention had been drawn to the fact that the Blackwater County Sheriff's Department was sadly understaffed and underequipped.

The fact that until then it had also been largely underoccupied, the local population being both small and law-abiding, was ignored. More help had been poured in from the state capital than anybody had needed or wanted. As a result the office had been quickly redecorated, and now the extension was being built that would house a private office for Matt, another for Tilly (now officially referred to as their "office manager"), two storerooms (one general and one secure), a comfortable lounge with refreshment dispensers for off-duty deputies, and four electronically locked and monitored cells, each with built-in television sets and toilet facilities. On the second floor would be an apartment for Matt, replacing the rather ratty couple of rooms he'd been occupying above the old garage. They'd suited him all right, as his physical needs were few. He and Max had been content with warmth, a couple of comfortable armchairs, two rings to cook on, a table to eat from (or under, in Max's case), and a bed to sleep in. Unfortunately, before the new extension could be built, the garage had to be demolished.

As a result, the cat was camping in the office full-time, and Matt had taken up residence at Mrs. Peach's Guest House. The displaced cat's only compensation was that all the old records from the past sixty-odd years had been boxed up and stacked along one wall of the office. This meant that he had a vast choice of places to settle for a nap. He had already reduced reports from 1929, 1934, and 1981 to crumpled masses dotted with paw marks.

The sheriff's department had also been supplied with a complex computerized records system that could be connected with the interstate network. In addition to that, four new patrol cars had appeared (courtesy of Molt's Supercar Showroom), and a generous uniform allowance had transformed the men's generally ramshackle appearance to that of neat, smart models of efficiency. (It had taken almost three weeks to break in the new uniforms sufficiently for them to be able to sit down comfortably, and there was still an overpowering smell of oiled leather jackets if all the deputies came into the office at one time for a briefing.)

That was another problem as far as Matt was concerned. Until the previous summer he'd made do with George as his deputy in the daytime and Charley Hart as his night man. He'd had a list of ten or fifteen local men he would swear in as temporary deputies during the summer or in case of emergency, but that was about it. Now he not only had George and Charley (as chief deputies, officially titled, and didn't *that* knock George's socks off), but also four additional permanent day patrolmen for whom he had to think up schedules and duties, plus two permanent night patrolmen, ditto.

Between the state, whose public relations experts had been horrified, and the town council, whose members had at first been stunned and then made vainglorious by the attention drawn to the town due to an extremely sensational case of murder on their very own doorstep, Matt's heretofore simple existence had been made extremely complicated.

Matt was staring at Tilly. "Does the name Jacky Morgan *mean* something to you?"

She glanced at him briefly. "Well, sure. I'm surprised you don't recognize it."

"I do. That is, it's familiar, but I can't place it."

"Well, you were only in knee pants at the time it actually happened, but it's one of those horror stories your father used to trot out every Halloween to scare you into behaving yourself. It was like—you know, traditional."

"I don't know what you mean," Matt said in a puzzled voice.

Tilly spoke slowly, emphasizing each word for full effect. *"Jacky Morgan was the boy that went over Eagle Head in a barrel."*

"What?" George asked, sitting upright with a jerk that nearly sent coffee over his lap.

"Or was it a parachute?" Tilly mused, her hands momentarily still.

"Now why didn't I just ask you in the first place," Matt said in chagrin. "Of course. And he died."

"Jesus, I'm not surprised," George said. "Eagle Head must be about a hundred and seventy feet high if it's a day."

"Lower at night, of course," Matt murmured.

"Well, you know what I mean," George said.

"Dad just used to say 'Remember the boy who went over Eagle Head'—I don't think he mentioned the *name* very often," Matt said, thinking back. "Or a barrel. But it was definitely one of his Awful Warnings. He had a million of them—no wonder it got buried in the back of my brain."

"What *happened?*" George demanded impatiently.

"It was a stupid game," Tilly said. "And like all stupid games, it went wrong." Having straightened the files to her satisfaction, she went over to get herself another cup of coffee and a second doughnut.

"What *kind* of game?" George persisted.

"Well," she said around a mouthful of cinnamon-flavored calories, "I was only about thirteen at the time, and they were older kids than me, so I never really got it straight. You know what high school gossip is like. I seem to recall it had something to do with a snipe hunt, or a tag game of some kind. Being chased, anyway. A bunch of kids were fooling around in the woods up there, having some kind of Halloween picnic, telling spooky stories, drinking beer, probably, and they eventually started up this game. A barrel came into it, somewhere. Maybe it was a beer barrel. Anyway, he took a wrong turn in the dark or something and went over. They heard him scream and couldn't find him, so they went for help. Your dad and some others finally found him smashed up on the rocks below the Head. Awful. Just awful." She took another bite of doughnut. "Not that *he* was missed, exactly—he was an obnoxious little squirt—it was more the shock of the thing, if you see what I mean. The Howl is supposed to be fun, after all. People aren't supposed to get hurt."

"Or killed," Matt said wryly. "Shame on Jacky Morgan for spoiling everyone's good time."

Tilly looked at him. "I didn't mean that, and you know it. They were only kids fooling around. They didn't *mean* any harm."

"They sound really dim," George said.

"Well, they weren't," Tilly said mildly. "They were good kids, George. Nice boys from nice families, and they were real upset."

"What happened to them?"

"Nothing official. It was an accident, after all. They probably got spanked or grounded or told off—whatever their folks thought best under the circumstances. They went back to school, grew up, got married, and had kids of their own," Tilly said, brushing crumbs from her lap and taking a final swallow of coffee before returning to her keyboard and the reports from the previous night. "Unfortunately for us."

George looked confused. "What do you mean?"

"*You* wouldn't be *here* if they hadn't."

George looked even more confused. "What?"

"I think she means one of them was your father, George," Matt said slowly. "Is that what you mean, Tilly?"

"That's what I mean," Tilly agreed.

"Well, so what?" George said defensively.

"Nothing, George, nothing. Every kid does something dumb sooner or later."

"Yeah, well then," George muttered.

Matt sank onto his chair and began to consider. If Tom Finnegan was upset enough to want to talk to Matt about something that happened thirty years ago, then it *was* possible that his mind had been affected by his illness or the drugs he was being given. Otherwise why would it suddenly have had so much significance for him? On the other hand, he had recognized Matt, and referred to his "father," not mixing up the two, so his sense of time had been intact. And during the day he died, he had talked to someone and mentioned "murder." The logical conclusion was that he had known something about Jacky Morgan's death that meant it hadn't been an accident at all, and that his own approaching death had compelled him to confess and "clear the decks," as it were. Was it worth pursuing after all this time? Tom's knowledge had died with him.

But somebody *else* had the same knowledge. Someone on the other end of that phone call. Perhaps that same someone had been driving the car that forced Tom off the road. *If* his car was forced off the road. That made Tom's death *another* murder. Could he let *that* go?

"Mind you, most of those 'boys' still live right here in town, if I recall correctly," Tilly continued. "Some of them are now men with real influence."

"Like my dad?" George asked.

"Like your dad," Tilly agreed. She didn't like the look on Matt's face. He got stubborn sometimes, about what seemed to her to be small things, and when that happened he wore the same look he was wearing now. "You don't want to get people's backs up about something that's been gone and forgotten now, Matt," she continued in a warning voice. "Not with an election coming up."

That was the second time in as many days the election had been mentioned. Matt scowled. As a matter of fact, he wasn't at all sure he *wanted* to be reelected. More than once in the previous weeks he had opened a particular desk drawer and gazed speculatively at the old offer from a small midwestern college to take up an associate professorship in their Philosophy Department. He was pretty certain he could still get them to take him on—even though it had been a good six years since he'd taught philosophy. Or even (thinking of the Wittgenstein biography) included it in his daily reflections. His father had been sheriff of Blackwater for almost forty years. When he died, taking up his shield had been merely a stopgap for Matt, who had been drifting from job to job ever since he'd taken his doctorate. Philosophers, he'd found, were about as employable as marimba players, and colleges were closing Departments of Philosophy even faster than they were building athletic stadiums.

However, Matt's law-keeping "stopgap" had grown into a six-year stop, period. And he was beginning to have his regrets. Mind you, it wasn't that he didn't enjoy the job—he did.

Or had.

It was just that now, with all this updating and modernizing, it didn't feel the same. *He* didn't feel the same. He glanced over at Tilly's computer and scowled. That was it, really. That damn computer symbolized the feeling that he was locked into a greater whole, part of a "network" instead of being free to enjoy the old, autonomous isolation.

Playing sheriff just wasn't fun anymore.

Matt looked at George, who was apparently trying to decide what attitude to take toward the revelation of his father's teenage sins. One minute he looked amused, then truculent, then embarrassed, then righteous. It was obviously a strain.

Matt's scowl returned. If he chose not to run for sheriff again, George would leap with abandon into the gap. He would run a flashy, busy campaign, and he would probably win because people would quite reasonably reckon he knew the job better than anyone coming new into the thing. This was not the case. Maybe in twenty years George would be ready to look after Blackwater County, but not now.

For a start, if elected, George would bring in some bouncy barking *dog* who would worship him and bite everyone else. George Putnam as sheriff would run around in circles, arresting people right, left, and center for imagined crimes that would prove to be strangely reminiscent of those he'd just read about in *Lawman's Monthly*. He would shoot and ask questions afterward. He would strut. He would shout. He would alienate the old, confront the young, and wonder why nobody liked him. Which would be a pity, because George was quite likable—as a deputy.

Matt sighed. Well, until and unless he gave up, he was still the sheriff. He owed a duty to the citizens of Blackwater County to protect them from all manner of trouble and despair—and that *included* George Putnam turned loose into a position of power. There was no way around it. Either he *had* to run for reelection or shoot George.

It was a straight choice.

"I think Tom Finnegan was killed because he knew something about the death of Jacky Morgan," he said in a flat voice. "I intend to find out what it was, and why he had to be murdered to keep it quiet."

Both Tilly and George groaned.

Although Matt should have known better, he almost missed the street. Signs directing people farther along the highway to Butter Beach obscured a smaller sign, nailed to a fence-post behind a mailbox. "Eagle Cove 3 miles," it said.

He drove slowly through the streets, trying to imagine how it had been all that time ago. The town of Blackwater was like any other—it seemed stable overall, but it had areas that went "up" or "down" for no apparent reason, properties bought and sold, businesses starting and failing, small areas built up or left to decay. The approach to Eagle Head lay through an area that had come down in the world for little apparent reason. Although, as the car thumped and clunked over the many potholes in the road, he wondered whether the town council had had something to do with it. Which had deteriorated first, the area or the road? And who was going to benefit in the long run?

The houses were far apart—but the space around them was filled with junk and old cars rather than grass or flowers. What thirty years ago had been pleasant middle-class residences were now shared houses badly in need of repairs—several of them were actually boarded up against squatters. Certainly he and his deputies were down here more and more often now, dealing with domestic or juvenile problems. It occurred to him, idly, that when it got bad enough, somebody would move in, buy up, and make a killing through redevelopment. Like most things, it was only a matter of time, opportunity, and a man willing to take a chance with his money.

Finally he pulled up where the road petered out in a half-circle of cracked concrete. At some time in the past the upper

part of the slope beyond had been cleared and carved into a
series of plateaus to accommodate trailers carefully angled so
that vacationers could gaze out every morning at the blue
and beckoning bay. But apparently not enough vacationers
had wanted so to gaze, for now there were only standpipes
and corroded electrical boxes to mark the places where the
trailers had once stood. Only two remained, tilted on broken axles, apparently too decrepit to tow away. The wind
was desultorily plucking at their rotted siding, clanking bits
of rusty metal together as if these structures were the vesti-
gial percussion section of some dismal and long departed
orchestra.

A sign had fallen across the entrance. Tilting his head to
accommodate the angle, Matt read that the all-new Eagle
Cove Luxury Trailer Park would be opening in May, year
unspecified. Its painted message was faded, and rust had
begun to form on its edges. He had to pry it back to get past.

From the far side of the lowermost concrete apron it was a
five-minute walk down a steep path to the cove. Grass had
begun to penetrate the sand and gravel, but the way was still
discernible. As he left the last crumbling skeleton of vacations past and started down, he began to hear the waves.

What had been scrub pine over thirty years ago was now
young forest, closing around and over him with whispers and
creaks. As he crushed needles beneath his boots, a sweet,
resinous smell rose to seduce him into relaxation, so that
when at last he emerged from the shadows of the trees onto
the rocky beach, the brightness hit him like a blow. His eyes
watered, and he took a deep breath, drawing the icy wind
deep into his lungs until his chest ached.

The steely surface of the water stretched in a wrinkled, un-
broken plateau to the horizon, glinting like beaten metal, reflecting the paler gray of the sky. A few gulls scimitared the
air above him. He turned to his left. The long, shallow curve
of the beach led the eye irresistibly around to an odd high
cliff shaped by ancient waves and retreating glaciers into a
profile resembling the hooked beak and lowering forehead of
a bird of prey. The prominence was capped by tall pines that
waved like some feathery crest above the granite silhouette.
Below the headland a jumble of huge, broken rocks sloped

down to the shoreline, where small waves crushed and frothed themselves on a graveled beach.

Here it was, even more lonely and bleak than he remembered.

The place where Jacky Morgan had died.

7

Dominic crunched his way over the stony beach, his tie blowing out to the side like a flag, aware that his dark suit contrasted oddly with the wild setting. He saw Matt Gabriel standing with his hands shoved deep in the pockets of his leather jacket, staring out at the lake. This was more his world than Dominic's—wind and wave and big sky. Dominic shouted to him, but the wind snatched the words away. He repeated them when he got closer. "Why do we have to meet like this?"

"The atmosphere in the office was a bit thick," Matt said.

Dominic's hair blew into his eyes, and he turned slightly to adjust to the wind direction. "You mean because of George?"

Over the past few weeks, Dominic had become aware that Chief Deputy George Putnam resented him. Carl Putnam seemed to think his new junior associate was the very image of the man his son should have become. Apparently Carl had always planned on George going into the law—but *not* through putting on a police uniform. Their relationship had begun to cool when in high school it became clear that George was a doer, not a thinker, and that his strengths were not academic. Putnam's interest in his eldest son had faded away, and George had been left to pursue his star without parental approval.

What made George's attitude even worse was that his

younger brother, Sam, had just been accepted at Columbia Law School, fulfilling their father's dynastic ambitions. Sam would be "ripe" to take over the practice when it came time for the elder Putnam to retire.

Dominic could understand George's feelings in the matter—it probably had been bad enough to have Sam constantly held up to him as the success of the family—but when his father began quoting Dominic Pritchard on every subject as well, it grew even rougher. George was civil to Dominic, but it was a veneer of civility only. It was patently clear to Dominic that George would love to find an excuse to land a knuckle sandwich in the teeth of his father's new associate. The sad thing was, Dominic deserved neither a knuckle sandwich nor George's resentment. He quite liked George Putnam, he found his boss Carl Putnam rather hidebound, and he thought Sam Putnam was a snotty little shit.

"It isn't important," Dominic finally said. "Listen, I'm sorry it's taken me so long to get around to this, but—"

Matt shrugged. "I haven't had time to go into it much myself. The only thing I have done is to ask the phone company for a record of Tom Finnegan's calls on the day he died—but whoever he was talking to when his wife overheard him could have made the call—in which case Finnegan's call record won't be much help. I can't do anything more until I get the forensic report from the state police. It's just—"

"A loose end," Dominic said. "I know what you mean—it's been niggling at me, too."

"Mmm. Anyway, since you've looked it up in the papers now, I thought you might be as interested as I was in seeing where the Morgan accident actually happened." He pointed toward Eagle Head. "He fell from up there."

Dominic followed the gesture and stared at the steep granite outline that hung over the jagged tumble of shoreline rocks and boulders. "Jesus, no wonder he was smashed up."

"Absolutely. The boundary is fenced now, but it wasn't then. At the time it belonged to an old miser who had it well posted against trespass and was quite happy to prosecute— which I suppose is why it seemed like such a big deal to those kids to have a sneaky midnight picnic up there." He gave Dominic the scanty outline of events he'd managed to pry out of Tilly concerning the Halloween fun and games of thirty years ago. "As you can see, the trees go right up to the edge, and then that bare, steep slope just drops away."

Dominic's eyes followed the presumed course of the falling boy and came to rest on the huge rocks at the base of the cliff. Suddenly he shivered, and scowled. "How can it be reasonably warm everywhere else today and so damned cold here?" He folded his arms and hunched against the wind. "I didn't even need a coat in town."

"It's probably why that trailer camp up there went broke," Matt said. "What did you get over at the *Chronicle*?"

"An earful from Emily Gibbons."

It was Matt's turn to smile. "Par for the course. I assume her presence there explains your eagerness to help out in my investigation?"

"Was I that obvious?"

"Of *course* not."

"Damn."

"Gave you a tough time, did she?"

"Let's just say it's hard to look good with your foot in your mouth," Dominic said mournfully. "The harder I tried, the worse it got. I ended up sounding like a game-show host."

Matt laughed—he couldn't help it. The young attorney looked so miserable recollecting his failure to achieve a winning verdict. "Listen, *I'd* take that as encouragement. From what I hear, she usually freezes out guys who try to come on to her. It means she looked at you, anyway."

"You think so?" Dominic felt pathetically in need of reassurance.

"Don't worry about it. What did you find in the files?" Matt walked over to a large twisted log of driftwood and sank down in a curve of its bleached trunk.

Dominic followed him and balanced himself gingerly on the opposite end, bracing his highly polished oxfords in the stones of the beach. "Well, there wasn't all that much, to be honest." He hesitated.

"Before you go on, I already know that your boss was one of the boys involved," Matt said.

"Ah," Dominic said, clearly relieved.

"And so does George."

"Ah," Dominic said again, in quite a different tone.

"Do you think that's where you came across the name Jacky Morgan? In Carl Putnam's office?"

"Ummm—it could be," Dominic said, reaching into an inside pocket for the sheaf of notes he'd scribbled at the newspaper office. Guilt assailed him.

He knew very well it was where he'd first seen the name, because once he'd started reading the newspaper reports it had come back to him. In one of the "inactive" cabinets in the storeroom there had been a confidential file labeled "Jacky Morgan," detailing payments made over a period of thirty years or so to a Mrs. Coral Morgan, whose address had changed many times over. The last payment had been made two years before, to an address in Florida. The amounts had been substantial, thousands per year, increasing regularly, presumably in line with inflation.

Dominic wanted to tell Matt this but felt that would be a serious breach of confidence. His boss hadn't told him not to go into the inactive files, but on the other hand he hadn't authorized him to do it, either, and certainly it was not a junior associate's place to discuss anything he found in practice files outside the office. Dominic had felt looking through the records was a quick way to get the feel of the practice. Now his initiative and industry had placed him in a difficult ethical position.

Matt didn't press the point. "What did the *Chronicle* have to say about it?" he asked impatiently.

"Well, it was pretty strange, if you ask me," Dominic said, relieved to move onto firmer ground. "I mean, it was a really dramatic story, right? And yet they kept it off the front page and only gave the facts. It was almost like they were trying to pretend it hadn't happened at all."

"Did you get the names of the boys involved?"

"Oh, sure, there doesn't appear to have been any secret about that." He read from his notes with some difficulty as the wind flapped them around his hand. "Carl Putnam, Thomas Finnegan, Albert Budd, Merrill Atwater—isn't he the mayor now?"

"He is." Matt was writing in his own notebook. "Go on."

"Peter Dill, John Fanshawe, Tyrone Molt, and Daniel Rogers."

"Well, that explains why there wasn't much in the paper about it," Matt said. "Dan Rogers was old Henry Gibbons's nephew, which would make him Granger Gibbons's cousin—they're about the same age. I think that's right." He closed his eyes for a minute. "That's right. Old Henry Gibbons would have been running the *Chronicle* when the accident actually happened, and Granger took over for him about fifteen years ago. Granger is Emily's father," he concluded. "Which I guess makes Dan Rogers her second cousin—or something like that."

"Oh, great," Dominic said wryly. How could Emily Gibbons fail to fall madly in love with a man who might be instrumental in proving someone in her family was a killer?

"Dan is also her doctor," Matt went on.

"Oh, terrific!" Not only a second cousin, but probably the Blackwater version of Albert Schweitzer as well.

"He's my doctor, too," Matt continued inexorably. "Peter Dill is a vice president of Blackwater Savings and Trust, Jack Fanshawe is a respected local realtor, and Tyrone Molt runs the Supercar Showroom over on Ventnor Avenue. He's also a town councillor." He pondered a moment. "I don't know that other one—Albert Budd? He's a mystery. Tom Finnegan is dead, of course."

"So basically you're saying that those boys who saw Jacky Morgan die now *run* Blackwater Bay?" Dominic asked, his heart sinking rapidly into his shoes. What a wonderful way to start a career—alienating the local movers and shakers.

"I don't know about running it. They're certainly not without influence, one way or another. Two of them are town councillors."

"Oh, my God. And you suspect one of them might have killed Tom Finnegan? Do you *realize* how much trouble . . ." Dominic was becoming seriously agitated.

"Things could get a little awkward," Matt agreed.

"A little *awkward?* . . ." Dominic was verging on self-strangulation. He was new in town, and by showing his hand at the newspaper, he may inadvertently have become part of something that could antagonize not only the girl he desired, but a large number of the most influential men in town.

"We might dent a few egos," Matt acknowledged.

". . . !!" Dominic choked. Wait a minute—had Emily noticed *what* he was after? Had he made any actual reference to it? Panic swept over him, visions of hot black tar, mounds of chicken feathers, and himself being ridden out of town on a rail (whatever that was, it certainly *sounded* painful) swam in his head and then receded. He was sure he hadn't said what he was looking for. It would be all right.

He cleared his throat and spoke diffidently. "Anyway, they're probably all pretty reasonable men." He waited for a moment. "Aren't they?"

Matt raised an eyebrow and tried not to smile. "Of course they are," he said, giving Dominic a reassuring slap on the shoulder. "This is a very reasonable community. And anyway, let us not forget the mysterious Albert Budd," he added, pocketing his notebook and standing up. "I must ask Tilly if she remembers Albert Budd. Did you photocopy these stories or just take notes?"

Dominic separated the sheaf of papers he'd been referring to, retaining his personal notes and handing Matt the photocopies he'd taken of the pertinent pages in the bound back issues of the *Blackwater Bay Chronicle*. He'd offered to pay for them, but Emily Gibbons had just shaken her head and taken the big books from him, checking the pages carefully as if she expected to find them somehow defaced by his interest. When he'd offered to carry them back upstairs, she'd snapped that the janitor would do it, and was there anything else he wanted?

He'd said no, thank you, and retreated in some confusion.

"Thanks for all this," Matt said to Dominic, pocketing the photocopies. They left their bumpy and rather unsteady driftwood perch and started back up the path through the pines. "I appreciate your taking the time to help me out."

"Are you actually going to follow it up?" Dominic asked warily.

"I'm afraid so," Matt said. "I gather from your expression that you don't approve."

"It's not up to me to approve or disapprove," Dominic said.

"But leave you out of it?"

Dominic was stung. "No. That is . . . well—"

"Look, I appreciate that you're in a difficult position because of Carl Putnam being your boss, and being new and all that. But there might come a time in all this when you could be useful to me, and I'd like to know now whether or not I can ask for your help," Matt said, not unreasonably. "George isn't exactly eager for me to go after this, as you can imagine, and the only other experienced deputy I have has worked nights for so long, he only recognizes people by flashlight."

Dominic looked down at his highly polished shoes, which already showed scratches and abrasions from the stones of the beach. Did he want to be highly polished and free of sin forever, or was he going to accept a few scrapes and arrows now and then? He respected Matt Gabriel, and he trusted him. That much he knew for certain. And he was, after all, an officer of the court. If a crime or crimes had been committed, it was his duty to reveal them, although it seemed a little early in his career to be faced with the possibility that his immediate *boss* might be a killer; but who was he to pick and choose his dilemmas? He knew living and working in Blackwater would entail some problems—here, almost immediately, was a doozy. Was he prepared to be a Sancho Panza to this windmill tilter or not? It was early times. If he lost this job, he could get another. And he'd obviously blown his chances with the fair Emily. What the hell? As they reached the concrete plateau of the failed trailer camp, he squinted into the light and regarded the sheriff.

"I guess Jacky Morgan and Tom Finnegan deserve proper legal representation," he said mildly.

"Fine," said Matt.

They ducked underneath the fallen sign and approached their cars. "What about all these other men? Your 'suspects'?" Dominic asked across the torn roof of his aged sports car.

"We'll see," Matt replied as he opened the door of his

own. "What will be interesting is to have a look at each of them when they attend Tom's funeral."

"Do you think they will?"

Matt glanced at him in feigned surprise. "Well, of course they will. They were all his good friends, weren't they?"

Forty minutes later they stood above the edge of Eagle Head. Behind them the woods rustled and murmured with a thousand secrets. Ahead of them the ground sloped away, its angle deceptively gradual at first, then—abruptly and terribly—it steepened and dropped.

Dominic brushed twigs and bits of undergrowth from his suit as he tried to imagine the scene that night—the pitch blackness, the shouts and drunken laughter, the hollow grating sound of a rolling barrel. When would the boy have realized he'd gone too far, that he was headed toward destruction? Here? Farther on? Had he known at all, or had his first intimation come when the barrel dropped into space and he had been momentarily weightless, heading for the rocks below?

Matt's thoughts were much the same. There would have been light coming from the lake—or rather, a lessening of darkness at the mouth of the barrel as it approached the edge. Jacky might have seen the last line of trees, he might even have seen the first naked expanse of granite glistening in the moonlight—had there been a moon that night? He'd have to check that out. But if he'd been moving fast, *really* fast . . .

How fast is too fast to a boy? Young muscles, young reflexes—couldn't he have scrambled out or swerved the barrel somehow? Couldn't they? They must have known what lay ahead. Or had they been too far behind the rolling barrel to turn it, stop it?

Had it been a gamble, a simple miscalculation?

Or intentional?

Dominic stared at the cliff edge and out over the burnished metallic surface of the lake. Jacky Morgan had not been that much younger than he. He could remember being seventeen. It wasn't so very different from how he felt now. Both strong

and vulnerable, sometimes proud, sometimes foolish, sometimes hopeful, sometimes scared.

Both men flinched as there suddenly came the scream of a
falling boy—thin, high-pitched, piercing the heart with its
knowledge of certain death.

But it was only a gull.

8

When Matt got back to the office, he was dismayed to discover that the "gendarmes" costumes had arrived. George was gleefully parading around in his. As the only mirrors available were in Tilly's compact or hanging over the basin in the bathroom, he was trying to get some idea of his appearance by angling himself toward the window, ducking and weaving and crouching so as to get something dark behind the glass and therefore produce a reflection. He looked as if someone had dropped a wet frog into his pants.

"*Bon jour, ma* petty shoe," he said with what he thought was a Gallic smirk.

"I am not your little cabbage," Matt growled, and tried to get past him.

"Is that what it means?" George asked. "I heard Louis Jourdan say it in the late movie the other night."

"I can't imagine Louis Jourdan ever saying any such thing," Matt said irritably. "He's a man of considerable intelligence—he would have objected to it."

"Do I look French?" George wanted to know, tilting his cap over one eye and swirling his cape.

Matt ignored him. "Tilly," he said, going over to stand beside her, "tell me about Albert Budd."

To his astonishment, the blood slowly drained from her round, plain face and tears welled up in her eyes. She attempted to speak, but all that came out was a thin, strangled wail. She stood up abruptly and ran into the bathroom, slamming the door behind her.

Matt stared after her, then turned to look at George in perplexity. He was further puzzled to discover George looking back at him with deep disgust as he removed his gendarme uniform. "Nice one, Matt," he said.

"What? What?" Matt demanded. "What did I say?"

"Don't you know *anything*?" George went on repressively.

"I don't know anything about Albert Budd," Matt said, and was rewarded by another wail from behind the bathroom door.

George spoke in a forced stage whisper, with a furtive glance toward the sobs and sniffs. "Albert Budd was the guy who stood Tilly up practically at the altar," he projected breathily. "They were engaged, but he ran off with some girl from Lemonville, and now he's a millionaire or something from selling funiture polish."

Matt found himself whispering back. "When did *this* happen?"

"I don't know exactly," George whispered back. "Maybe it was while you were away at college."

"That was over fifteen years ago!" Matt whispered in some astonishment.

"I know, I know—but she still feels bad," George hissed. "She showed me his picture once—funny-looking geek, if you ask me."

"It didn't do him justice," came a sepulchral voice from behind the bathroom door. "He was a lovely man, with beautiful curly red hair."

Matt gazed at the panels of the door, then turned back to George. "How come you know about this and I don't?" he demanded, still in a low voice. He was beginning to get a sore throat.

"Tilly and I spend a lot of time sitting around here," George said. "We have to talk about something, don't we?"

"It was that day you and Charley Hart were late getting back from testifying in court over in Hatchville. He got me drunk," came the voice from the bathroom.

"The hell I did," George said, outraged. "It was *your* applejack, not mine."

"Yeah, well, I could tell him a thing or two about Mariloo Gabrillowitz," the voice went on. It occurred to Matt that Tilly, in this mood, would have been an excellent choice for the role of Eeyore. George, meanwhile, had gone bright red.

"Who the hell is Mariloo Gabrillowitz?" Matt asked unsteadily.

"He met her at a Stone Roses concert," Tilly said over the sound of running water. "She had a tattoo of a lizard on her hip, and the tail ran right down between her—"

"Knock it off!" George shouted.

"Buttocks," said Tilly, emerging pink-eyed from the bathroom.

"That is the last time I tell you anything," George muttered.

"Look, Tilly, I'm sorry . . ." Matt began as his overweight and indispensable secretary picked up a Kleenex to blow her nose. She shrugged.

"No, no—you just caught me off guard, that's all," Tilly said into the Kleenex, obviously enmbarrassed.

"It's just this Jacky Morgan thing. . . ."

She stared at him. "Good Lord above, are you *still* going on about that?"

"Well, I've managed to find out more details. Albert Budd was one of the boys at the picnic that night."

Her stare turned to amazement. She tossed the now dilapidated tissue into the wastebasket and sighed in resignation. "I must be losing my mind. Do you know, I'd actually forgotten Albert was involved in all that? I only got to know him later, you see," she said slowly, obviously dismayed at forgetting such a vital fact about a man she had loved. Or thought she had loved. If you *really* cared about someone, how could you forget something like that? Recovered now from what had seemed to her almost like an accusation from Matt ("Tell me about Albert Budd"), she was beginning to realize that opening an old wound might be useful. Even instructive. In fact, she felt a lot better already.

"Well . . ." she began.

*   *   *

Dominic returned to the office of Crabtree and Putnam considerably subdued by the results of his research and the visit to Eagle Cove.

To make matters worse, he had glimpsed Emily Gibbons through the plate-glass window of the *Chronicle* building and seen her on the telephone, laughing and talking with someone. She'd been leaning on the counter as she spoke, doodling with a pencil, which she'd then stuck through her hair at a rakish angle while she reached for something else. She had looked wonderful.

He said something pleasant to Mrs. Pickering, the matronly practice secretary, and continued on into his small office. He dropped onto his chair—a dangerous thing to do at the best of times—and leaned back—also dangerous—to stare at the ceiling. After a few minutes of that, he swiveled to stare out of the window, which looked out over the length of Main Street.

On the pavement below, the citizens of Blackwater pursued their many concerns, moving in and out of various shops, sauntering along, greeting one another, pausing to exchange pleasantries and gossip. Dominic wondered if that was the reason old Phineas Crabtree had chosen these offices when the practice had started out—it gave them a crow's nest view of the town, a high point from which to observe covertly all that went on. He didn't suppose they'd assigned a member of staff as permanent overseer, but it wouldn't have surprised him if occasional glances out of the window had not tipped the balance in various cases—divorce, for instance. Many a glimpsed hand clasp or furtive conversation could have given a clue or two about what was really going on with an offending husband or wife.

However, as he watched, something a little more dramatic than a stolen kiss took place within his view. There was a distant rumbling, as of an approaching dinosaur stampede. All the people on the pavement turned, as synchronized as any tennis tournament audience.

Dominic sat up. Sure enough, it *was* dinosaurs—of a kind.

The rumble came from the arrival of huge carnival rides, lumbering on their various transporters down the length of Main Street, heading for the fields behind the high school where the Blackwater Bay Halloween Carnival took place every year. Driving by during the past week, he had noted various activities going on in the field in preparation for the carnival—but the arrival of the big beasts was the final touch.

As the big transporters disappeared up the road, the street life below gradually returned to its previous configurations, but now the conversations were more animated. There was considerably more laughing and a greater number of elbowed ribs. Plans were being made all right. He smiled and wished he had a way of eavesdropping on some of those plans. Forewarned was forearmed.

He heard Putnam's voice in the outer office and turned his chair slightly to look through his open door. His boss was handing some papers to Mrs. Pickering, explaining what he needed her to do. Carl's practice was made up of the more lucrative activities inherent in being the most senior lawyer in town. Wills, estates, house purchases, divorces, small claims, large claims, and contracts of all kinds brought the kind of income that allowed Mr. Carl Putnam to afford a large new car every year, a huge house, generous alimony payments to George's mother, who lived down in the city, plus all the expenses that accrued in the course of indulging a young and rather glamorous second wife.

Dominic scowled. He hadn't much liked the second Mrs. Putnam, although he must have hidden it well, for he was certain Carl took anything his precious Mitzi said into account when making momentous decisions such as which tie to wear and which junior associate to hire. As a matter of fact, Dominic didn't warm to Carl Putnam himself very much. He did, however, respect him as a lawyer, and it was for that reason as much as anything else (including Emily Gibbons) that he'd finally decided to stay on in Blackwater Bay. The size and peculiar dimensions of Blackwater County made it a microcosm of general legal activity. Working here for a few years meant that he would build up a lot of varied experience, the breadth of which he could never have hoped to cover if he'd gone into some big-city firm or into the public prosecutor's office, for example.

Carl Putnam was tall, lean, and exceptionally handsome—

his hair gray where George's was blond, his face taut where George's was still youthfully rounded—but otherwise he looked like a grown-up version of his elder son. He had a deep, luxurious voice and indulged himself in its use. He liked good clothes and wore them well. He played a fair game of golf, a superb game of tennis, and ostentatiously came to work on a bicycle during the summer months. He was politically correct in every way that was useful, ruthless when he knew it wouldn't show, but surprisingly honest for a man with so many opportunities to be otherwise. Despite his personal snobberies, he was sympathetic with those clients who were their own worst enemy and tough but fair to those he had to prosecute.

Considering his position and his appearance, it was not surprising he had managed to attract a younger wife. What was surprising was that he would prefer her rather shallow charms to those of his first wife, George's mother.

Dominic had met the first Mrs. Carl Putnam at a party in the city the previous spring. It was she who had told him about Blackwater Bay and suggested he might try it as a possible first place to practice. She was an elegant and intelligent woman whose beauty came from her exquisite bone structure, her lively mind, and her ready laughter. Olive Putnam had outshone all the other women in the room, just through being herself. She didn't disguise her age, or dress to stun, or make any other overt effort to stand out. She was simply one of those rare people who are entirely happy in their own skin and therefore are more interested in other people than in themselves.

Dominic supposed he'd fallen a little in love with Olive Putnam at the time—the people giving the party had believed in the power of champagne. He'd been studying too hard and was therefore supersensitive with stress. He smiled at the memory. Talking with Olive Putnam had been like walking out of the heat of his approaching bar exams into a cool and shadowed room. She had calmed him, flattered him, rested him. They'd talked for a long time.

He didn't know the ins and outs of the Putnam divorce, but on reflection it seemed to him now that Olive Putnam had probably escaped rather than been usurped. He couldn't imagine a man like Carl would have thrown away such a prize. Maybe Mitzi Putnam, the new wife, was Carl's consolation prize for having been dumped by a woman he didn't deserve. He wondered how George felt about it.

He also wondered how George felt about the possibility that his father could be a murderer. A policeman's lot could be an unnerving one. And so could a new junior associate's. He looked at Carl, standing there, and tried to imagine him young and mean drunk and capable of killing.

Moving away from his secretary's desk, Carl caught Dominic's speculative eye and came over to stand in the doorway of his office. "Everything okay?" he asked with a smile. "You look a little rattled."

"Everything's fine," Dominic said, improvising quickly. "I was just thinking about Mr. Rumplemeyer's will."

Carl grinned. "Trust old Gustav to leave his estate in a mess. Whenever he ate he used to shower the surrounding area with crumbs and splashes. His house is overflowing with everything he ever bought in his lifetime, and his garden is a jungle of plants he collected from everywhere he went. He wore out three wives and his six children adored him, even though they were convinced he was crazy. He used to say he lived life big, never mind the small."

"You liked him," Dominic said, surprised.

"I thought he was wonderful," Carl admitted, leaning against the doorpost. "I often wished I could be like that instead of worrying over how it would look if I did this, or what people would think if I did that." He shrugged. "But it's hard to shake off those kinds of considerations when it's all your parents have ever drummed into you. I even started to make the same mistake with *my* sons. Sam's turning into a prune like me, but George escaped, bless his rebellious heart. Next time you hear me complaining about him, just say 'remember Gustav Rumplemeyer,' and I'll shut up." With a final grin, Carl turned and went back into his own office.

Well, dammit, thought Dominic. And just when I was beginning to build up a really strong dislike for him, too. You just can't trust lawyers these days.

*   *   *

Coming into the house later that afternoon, Tilly found her
mother asleep in front of the television set as usual. Mrs.
Moss was esconced on her special electric easy chair, with
all her personal requirements laid out on tables to either hand
(books, magazines, cookie jar, a cooler filled with cold cans
of Vernor's ginger ale, a thermos of hot coffee, some
wrapped sandwiches, two bags of potato chips, a box of Butterfinger bars, and the TV remote control to the right, needle-
work projects to the left). Her crutches were propped beside
her, should she need to move to the bathroom. All was as
Tilly had left it during her lunch hour. A quick assessment
told her that her mother had drunk two cans of ginger ale,
eaten a sandwich, a bag of potato chips, and a Butterfinger
bar, looked at the latest *Woman's Day* magazine, and done
approximately four inches of straight quilting. A busy afternoon, then. No wonder she was tired.

Mrs. Moss had suffered a stroke some four years before.
Up until then she had been one of the busiest bodies in
Blackwater, in terms of both frenetic activity and gossip. The
former meant that she battered her way into various clubs
and organizations, always with suggestions for improve-
ments that suited her if no one else. She had also been a great
"dropper-in," pinning many women down to gossip over the
coffee cups when they would rather have been somewhere
else. This latter aspect of her mother had been both a great
help to and a great strain on Tilly. On the one hand, it meant
that she was in a position to provide Matt with a great deal of
"inside information" on Blackwater if he required it (although they had to separate carefully the grains of truth from
the chaff of rumor). On the other hand, it also meant that no
matter how much Mrs. Moss pestered her, she had to be
careful not to pass on any information she picked up in the
office.

The stroke had ended all that.

In the curious way of strokes, this one had bequeathed its
victim an eccentric pattern of aftereffects. Mrs. Moss remained weak on the left side, worse in the leg than the arm,
so that while she could not walk easily without support, she
could still do a straight quilting stitch if the pattern was a
simple one. This meant she was able to produce quite hap-

pily many brightly colored pot holders and table mats for church sales and bazaars. The stroke had altered her personality from one that was consistently irascible and impatient to one that was unfailingly cheerful and amenable. It had diminished but not destroyed her understanding, so that she was able to read magazines and enjoy light fiction of a certain level but was unable to comment on it, because she had been left virtually speechless. In short, the stroke had changed her from a difficult, demanding, and irritating person into an ideal companion as far as Tilly was concerned.

For a start, she now always knew where her mother was, because while Mrs. Moss could move around their little bungalow well enough to attend to her own personal needs, she was too timid and unsteady to venture out alone. Before the stroke Tilly never had known exactly what she was up to—except to be certain she was causing consternation somewhere.

Next, although she retained an avid interest in the goings-on of the town, Mrs. Moss could no longer speed the rumors on their way or even embellish them as before. Therefore Tilly could tell her everything in perfect safety, providing her mother with entertainment and herself with a release valve.

If Mrs. Moss felt any frustration at these considerable changes in her life-style, she never exhibited it, apparently as content as Tilly to continue thus forever. Perhaps, Tilly sometimes thought, she had grown as tired of her old self as the rest of us. Now, as she cleared away the detritus of what to her mother had been just another in a long and unquestioned line of pleasant afternoons, Aggie Moss awoke with a smile and babbled a greeting.

Tilly smiled back, kissed her, patted her hands, and in a few moments returned with a pot of tea and two cups. She poured out a libation for each of them, opened the cookie jar, helped herself to one of Mrs. Norton's Snickerdoodles, and leaned back in her own large but nonelectric armchair. "It's been a *real* peculiar day," she began.

Mrs. Moss's eyes brightened above her teacup.

9

The weekend of the Howl dawned cold and clear, with no snow and no rain forecast until the following week. For most of the residents of Blackwater County this was good news—whatever else might happen, at least their various devilish plans would not go awry because of inclement weather.

For Matt Gabriel and his staff it was bad news. Charley Hart said he'd gone so far as to actively pray for icy rain—"I swear, Matt, I got down on my goddamn knees"—and the others nodded solemnly. Nobody took the opportunity to tease Charley about praying, which unnerved him even more. George, in particular, rarely let such an opportunity go by.

It was nine o'clock Saturday morning. Charley and the two night patrolmen had stayed on to join the day rotation in making last-minute battle plans for the twenty-four hours ahead. In the worst of all possible years, and this was one of them, October 31 fell on a Saturday. This meant that not only could the school-age children stay up late for the carnival and fireworks display, it also meant that whatever adults did tonight could be slept off in the morning. Church attendance would be down—the Devil takes his due at such times—and everyone would have hangovers: the kids from overdosing on cotton candy and carnival rides, the adults from alcohol and whatever else they had gotten up to.

Tempers would not be improved by the weird sights that would greet some of the sufferers when they looked blearily into their mirrors or out of their windows on Sunday morning. Many still shuddered at the memory of the last time the Howl had fallen on a Saturday. Particularly vivid was their recall of the language uttered by a shy and newly ordained Reverend Whipple, who, having delivered himself of a memorable sermon concerning the pagan origins of Halloween and their detrimental effect on the young, discovered that the floor of the pulpit had been covered with superglue. After struggling for several minutes to free himself, he'd been forced to abandon his shoes and finish the service in his socks.

Which did not match.

So unnerved was he by this—and the sight of five male members of the congregation removing their hats to reveal shaven heads tattooed with the name of a famous beer, sufficient of which had rendered them unconscious while the shaving and decorating was carried out—that he had asked to be reassigned and was now gratefully serving the more sedate parishioners of Holy Cross, Alaska.

"Okay, let's see," Matt said, consulting his list. "Have the carnival operators been warned?"

"Yes," George said. "I talked to them yesterday while they were setting up."

Matt ticked off an item. "Has the lock on the gate of the Cecil G. Heckman Memorial Park been fixed?"

"Sure," said Glen Hardwicke. "But that's not going to stop anybody, Matt. At least, it never has before."

The atrocities carried out on the life-size bronze statue of the late Cecil G. Heckman, a local man who had attained the status of state senator around the turn of the century by somewhat questionable means, were numerous. "Decorating Cecil" had become an annual tradition, and some of the finest minds in Blackwater County were known to have been consulted over the years. No one knew who made the final decision, but the results were always spectacular.

"Have we got somebody patrolling Jack's Nature Trail?" Matt asked George.

"Sure—I swore in Bob and Jim Matthew," George said,

naming two brothers who had played pro football for several
years and then benched themselves to Blackwater Bay.
"Their knees may be shot, but they've still got nerves of
steel."

"Better them than me," Glen Hardwicke said.

"What's so terrible about Jack's Nature Trail?" Duff
Bradley asked. He was one of the new patrolmen hired in
from upstate, and this would be his first Howl.

"Nothing—normally," Matt explained. The nature trail
was an adjunct to Jack's Four Seasons Sporting Goods Store.
Carefully trimmed and tanbarked, it stretched for two beautiful miles through the forest behind the shop. Local jogging
enthusiasts paid an annual fee for the right to run the trail
whenever they liked. "But last year some college kids collected a bunch of roadkill samples—flattened beaver, wood-
chucks, foxes, skunks, and so on—and on each one they
painted a great big footprint, as if it had been stomped on by
a gigantic jogger. They scattered these all along Jack's Nature Trail on the night of the Howl. The next morning we had
a riot over there. As luck would have it, Milly Hackabush,
the coach of the high school girls' track team, brought her
girls out for a dawn run. Four of the girls had to be taken to
the hospital in hysterics."

"Jack was sure pissed off." George tried not to grin, because everybody liked Jack, but the memory of those big
footprints leading away into the distance always made him
laugh. Jack maintained his trail to a high standard and had
not appreciated the squashed additions to it. He'd wanted to
sue but hadn't been able to find anyone to nail for the prank.

"I don't know what Jack has done, but the town council
has taken out a policy against damage to *public* property for
the next twenty-four hours," Matt continued. "So, if the
fence on Heckman Memorial Park is intact and the lock is
secure, the insurance will cover any damage."

"That must have cost a lot, after last year's claims,"
Charley Hart said.

"New company," Matt said.

"They're going to run out of hayseed insurance companies
pretty soon," Hardwicke observed. "Where's this one located—Fencepost, Nebraska?"

"Something like that." Matt grinned. "Now, how about the library and the Town Hall—who's going to cover that tonight?"

"Me." Frank Boomer raised his hand. "You gave me that end of Main Street."

"And I've got the other end as far as the church," Duff Bradley said. "What the hell am I supposed to be looking for, anyway?"

They all looked at him in astonishment, then remembered he was new. This brought a certain number of speculative expressions to their faces, which Matt caught.

"All right, all right—none of that."

"What?" Hardwicke asked with an air of innocence.

"We're going to have enough problems without you guys putting Duff through it."

"Through what?" Duff asked warily.

"Would we?" Lou Buncie put on a reproachful tone.

"You damn well would," Matt said. He turned to Duff. "Weren't you told about the Howl?"

"It's a town carnival, right?" Duff asked. "My wife is looking forward to it. She was just—"

Matt interrupted. "It's a lot more than a carnival." He glared at his chief deputy. "George, you were supposed to *explain* all this."

"Was I?" George shrugged and looked around. "Who said?"

"I said, as you damn well know." Matt was irritated. "Look, I'm stating here and now that if any Howlers are played on Duff—*or* his wife—and I find out it was done by anyone here, there will be a fifty-buck fine on *everyone* and a ten percent cut in salaries until Christmas. Is that clear?"

There was a general shuffling of feet.

"Listen, I don't want to cause any trouble—" Duff began uneasily.

"Normally I wouldn't mind," Matt continued, looking at each man in turn. "In fact, I might have handcuffed him to his steering wheel or let down his tires myself—*in any other year.* But I just can't spare him, or any of you, this time around. Last year things got out of hand, if you remember, and I don't want to see it happen again. Nor do I want to see anyone hurt. I want every one of you bright and alert and available *all night long.* Is that clear?"

"Coffee's ready," called somebody over by the percolator. "But there aren't any doughnuts here."

"Where's Tilly?" Hardwicke asked.

"She's on a special assignment for me," Matt said. "She'll be back this afternoon. You'll have to do without doughnuts this morning."

There was a general aggrieved muttering while everyone poured out and adjusted to naked coffee. "Hey, do we absolutely *have* to wear these costumes George got us?" asked somebody in the rear.

"No, you don't—not if you don't want to," Matt said.

"Ah, hell, Matt—everybody's *got* to wear them, otherwise what's the point?" George complained. "Come on, guys—join in, have a laugh. It's the *Howl,* for crying out loud."

"It's up to each of you," Matt repeated. "However, it's been announced that the police will be dressed as French gendarmes this year, just so everyone knows. They'll be expecting it."

"You bet they will—I've started getting the razz already," Glen said good-humoredly. "Hell, I don't mind. It's for charity, isn't it?"

That was the proviso that Matt had finally made—that each man who wore a costume would find sponsors—thereby removing any taint of foolishness from the dressing up. There was a general murmur of assent, and George beamed at them.

They were halfway through Matt's list when the phone rang. Matt answered it, then turned back to the men. "It's started already," he said.

"I don't know how the hell they did it," Jack Fanshawe said.

"Who?" Matt asked.

"Open the phone book at any page," Jack said wryly. "I mean, this isn't fair, right? The Howl is supposed to be tonight, not last night."

"Some people like to get in early," George said, squatting down to pat the floor. "They probably waited until after midnight, anyway—that would make it officially the thirty-first."

The offices of Fanshawe Realty were normally carpeted in a neat tweed-patterned wool. When Fanshawe had opened up this Saturday morning, however, he discovered that during the previous night someone had removed all the furniture, taken up the carpet, replaced it with live turf, and then neatly replaced all the furniture just as it had been.

"Nice, soothing effect," Matt said, trying not to laugh.

"Oh, I don't know," Jack said. "I think it's kind of dull, myself." He gazed at the green expanse waving gently in the breeze from the open door. "Now someone with *real* imagination would have added a few daisies, don't you think?"

"Daisies are nice," Matt agreed.

"I like tulips, myself," George said.

"Out of season," Jack told him.

"Oh, right."

Matt produced his notebook. "Do you want to make a complaint?"

"Yeah—no daisies. Put that down—I would have preferred some daisies."

"Jack . . ."

"Oh, hell, Matt, what's the use?" Fanshawe said resignedly. Once the hero quarterback of the local high school, he was running to plumpness around jawline and waistline, his thinning blond hair was smoked with gray, and his mustache had lost its spring, but he still retained a certain oily gloss.

Although the males of Blackwater found it inexplicable, it was a fact that Jack Fanshawe had always been eagerly pursued by women. Since adolescence he'd possessed an air of good-humored sexuality that made the prospect of a dalliance with him particularly attractive, especially to married women looking for a little excitement without repercussions. Jack never told. His interest in real estate meant he knew every back alley and quiet corner where assignations or getaways could be facilitated. There had been rumors about a certain teacher who had left the high school rather suddenly when Fanshawe was only a sophomore, and it was common knowledge that both the Baugh and the Hopwood divorces were precipitated by affairs the wives had had with him. Although it hadn't come out in court, it had come out in town.

At the age of twenty-two, Fanshawe had inherited the real
estate business from his father. Four years later he'd married
the daughter of a rival real estate agent from Lemonville.
Some said he had chosen her because she was prepared to
overlook his tomcatting, others that she was too dim-witted
to realize it was going on. Being a nice girl, she was more
pitied than scorned, and after twelve years of being the quiet,
dutiful wife, she quietly passed away of heart failure one Saturday afternoon while Jack was showing a prospective customer around the Halliday farm.

Fanshawe, to everyone's surprise, took her death badly.
He had collapsed at her funeral and had had to be hospital-
ized for a week. It was then that the gray had appeared in his
hair and his mustache had begun to droop. Months passed
before he could pick up the threads of his business again.

Once his grieving seemed to be over, however, the pursuit
by the single and divorced women in town had resumed and
continued still. There were now many contenders for the title
of the second Mrs. Jack Fanshawe, but the town had never
detected a real front-runner. When leaning against the bar of
the Dirty Duck or the Golden Perch, he was often heard to
bemoan the drudgeries and loneliness of bachelorhood, but
his listeners now took that with a large pinch of salt. He
seemed in no real hurry to end his unexpected second harvest
of wild oats, but it was assumed that eventually Jack would
succumb, if only out of exhaustion.

The lady chosen would inherit a large house full of antique furniture, an even larger garden to tend, and a man who
ran his business efficiently and profitably. Gazing now at the
bucolic transformation of his office, Fanshawe considered
the many nominees for perpetrator of this particular
Howler—disappointed purchasers of less-than-perfect
houses, disappointed sellers for less-than-hoped-for prices,
ladies seeking attention, husbands seeking retribution—and
was slightly overwhelmed. "I suppose you could find out
who *bought* the turf—"

"Stolen from Garfield Gardening last night." George stood
up. "I suppose they'll want it back."

"It will have holes in it from the desk and chair legs," Jack
pointed out.

"Maybe you ought to talk to them," Matt suggested. "You could probably come to some agreement."

"Well, it's not *my* responsibility," Jack protested. "Dammit, these things are only funny until somebody has to start paying for them."

"A few holes here and there won't make a big difference in a lawn," George said. "All they have to do is find somebody with molehills to match, right?"

Matt and Fanshawe regarded him with disfavor.

"Just trying to lighten the moment," George said.

"At least it wasn't destructive," Fanshawe said. "I mean, whoever it was left the carpet rolled up out back. It will just mean a big mess to clean up and moving a lot of furniture around, I guess. It could have been worse. I suppose I'm getting old, but the Howl isn't as much fun as it used to be. When I think of the things we used to get up to . . ." He chuckled and shook his head.

"There have been bad times before," Matt said slowly.

Fanshawe was lifting one of the pieces of turf with his foot, trying to judge what degree of mud and moisture had escaped into the floorboards underneath. "Oh, yeah?" he said absently.

"Like Jacky Morgan, you mean, Matt?" George asked brightly.

Suppressing the impulse to kick him, Matt nodded. "Yes—that's a good example," he said.

Fanshawe had flinched visibly at the mention of the name, and there was a silence while he tried to decide what expression to put on. When he looked up at Matt his face was bland—the face of a man selling you a house with rot under the floorboards.

"That rings a bell," he said.

"It should . . ." George began.

"Boy who went over Eagle Head," Matt said. "You were there, weren't you, Jack?"

"Good Lord—you're right. I'd forgotten all about that," Fanshawe said with a frown. "It was pretty terrible at the time. We were all really knocked out by it. The Howl was different, then."

"Tom Finnegan was there, too, I understand," Matt said.

Fanshawe's face contracted. "Say, wasn't that awful, him dying like that? Although, since he was dying anyway, maybe it was some kind of blessing. . . ." His voice trailed off, and he was silent for a moment. Then he shook himself, like a dog shaking water from its coat. "Funny how you repress those kinds of memories, isn't it? Not the kind of thing you look back on with pleasure. How come you knew about that? You must have still been in knee pants at the time."

"Just happened to be going over some old records at the office," Matt said easily. "What with the rebuilding and all— you know how things turn up you thought were lost and so on."

Fanshawe laughed a little too loudly. "Boy, do I know what you mean. You ought to see some of the stuff we come across in the attics and basements of houses that people swear blind they've cleared out."

"Like what?" George wanted to know. "Old Master paintings and boxes of gold bars?"

"Hardly," Fanshawe said with an eagerness that revealed his relief at the change of subject. "More like cartons of dog food they bought at a sale in 1959 and forgot, or once there was a—"

There was a shriek behind them. "I don't *believe* it! Is that *real* grass in there?"

They all turned. Mitzi Putnam stood with her hands on her hips, gazing gleefully past them into the Fanshawe Realty office. Fanshawe straightened up and pulled in his stomach.

"Sure is, Mit—Mrs. Putnam," he said.

George stared at his stepmother. "Somebody did it last night," he said in a flat voice.

She glanced at him, and a frown momentarily passed over her smooth face, like a small cloud obscuring a determinedly sunny sky. "Hello, George," she said levelly.

"Hello, Mitzi," he said with an equal lack of enthusiasm. "What brings you out before noon?"

She raised an eyebrow. "Business," she said dismissively, then turned back to Fanshawe. Immediately her face took on fresh animation. "You know, that grass looks *amazing* in there. It must have taken them hours. I guess that makes you the victim of the first Howler of the year. Why don't you call the *Chronic* and have Harry Foskett come over and take a picture of it before it starts to wilt?"

Fanshawe's eyes brightened. "Say, you're right—if I'm going to have all the bother of clearing it out, I might as well get a little publicity out of it."

"Why not?" Mitzi asked, warming to the idea. She put her hand on Fanshawe's arm and leaned into the doorway. "You know, you could even make a little more of it. Jack—you could get a lawn mower and pretend to be cutting it, or maybe set out a little picnic—" She straightened and looked up at him. "I've got a nice wicker picnic basket you could borrow, and a checkered cloth . . . What do you think?"

"Sounds good to me," Fanshawe said with growing enthusiasm.

"I gather you won't be making a complaint, then?" Matt asked with as little irony as he could manage. Mitzi Putnam's perfume was having its usual effect on him—his eyes watered with the effort of suppressing a sneeze. He shared George's surprise at seeing her up and about this early in the day—she was definitely a night-blooming creature.

In fact, she was *so* amused by the grassy carpet that, for just a moment, he wondered if she had been the instigator of the prank. Not that he could imagine her getting any dirt under her perfectly manicured nails, but she had money enough to have paid for it to be done.

He considered her as she stood there burbling. She was twenty years younger than Fanshawe—but then she was twenty years younger than her husband, too. Maybe she just liked older men.

Mitzi Putnam had been the grandniece of Carl Putnam's late partner, Phineas Crabtree. She had the frothy blond hair and exaggerated figure of a Barbie doll and behaved as if she had the mentality to match. The figure probably had been augmented by implants, the hair certainly wasn't natural—and more than once Matt had caught a look in those big blue nearsighted eyes that revealed not only brains, but cunning. Little Mitzi was not at all what she appeared, and what she appeared was unmistakably a result of careful planning. She had certainly been quick to put in an appearance once Carl's first marriage broke up and had hung on tight until she'd got that ring on her finger.

He exchanged a glance with George, raising an eyebrow. Had she arranged this joke for reasons of her own? George, reading him perfectly, shook his head. Reluctantly he agreed. She would be a fool to risk her marriage to Carl Putnam for someone like Jack—she wasn't a fool—although there *did* seem to be considerable warmth in the way she patted Fanshawe on the arm and looked up into his face. Maybe she hadn't thought up the indoor lawn—but she might be thinking up something else, such as making sure she kept her husband on his toes through jealousy.

Still without speaking, he turned and glanced up the street toward the offices of Crabtree and Putnam, then looked at George again. Could it have been *Carl* Putnam, for more obvious reasons? Could he be warning Fanshawe that the grass on his own side was green enough and he'd be wise to stay on it? It was a little subtle, but the two men had been friends for years. They might have their own private signals. George followed Matt's glance, then shrugged. Maybe. George knew his father better than Matt—if *he* thought it was possible, it could well be probable.

"Well, see you, Jack," Matt said, putting away his notebook.

Fanshawe waved a vague hand at him. "Oh, right. Thanks for coming over, Matt."

"All part of the service," Matt said, but Fanshawe had turned back to his conversation with Mitzi. Matt and George started to walk back toward the office.

George glanced at his watch. "And it's only ten o'clock."

"My God," Matt said. "It's going to be worse than we thought."

He was certainly right about that.

10

If he had lived in a different country, it might have taken Tilly Moss longer to locate Albert Budd, but probably not *much* longer. Using the official information network to which her computer now gave her access, and using the powers granted by the state to the Blackwater Bay Sheriff's Department, it had still taken her several hours of hard work to find out precisely where he was presently living. It turned out to be not that far away from Blackwater Bay—in miles, anyway.

But that was only the beginning.

The reason Matt had not heard of Albert Budd—indeed, very few people had—was that Albert had become a millionaire and a recluse. He had acquired a phalanx of secretaries and minders who formed an almost impenetrable wall around him, and they permitted no access via phone or doorbell. She might, one of them suggested haughtily, make an appointment—the first they could offer her was in March of the following year. Tilly had been stymied.

And then she remembered Sam "Snakehips" Turkle.

Tilly had not told Matt about going to Snakehips for advice. Matt would not have approved. She didn't approve, either—but the snotty tones of those secretaries had made her mad. And anyway, she wanted to be back in Blackwater in time for the Howl.

Retired now—mostly through the efforts of Matt's fa-

ther—Sam Turkle had once been one of the best burglars in
the business. Quick of hand, eye, and brain but small of ambition, Sam could penetrate the most complex of defenses,
but once inside he never stole very much. It had been the
challenge of the thing that excited him, not the profit. Many
of the Turkles were like that.

They were a family whose legend had grown with their
number. There were Turkles of all sorts in Blackwater Bay
County—rich ones, poor ones, smart ones, stupid ones, busy
ones, lazy ones—but all possessed of a streak of high-caliber
cunning that facilitated their individual, if idiosyncratic, ambitions. Thus, among all the other eccentrics, there was Sam,
who loved a locked gate almost more than he loved a good
meal or a wicked woman and for whom a sophisticated
alarm system possessed almost orgasmic fascination.

He stood beside her now—white of hair, stiff of limb, and
sorely disappointed.

"What do you think, Sam?" she asked the old man.

"I think two things," Sam said. "I think you don't need me
at all, but you do need to lose fifty pounds in the next five
minutes. Now, if I had an ax—"

"Very funny," Tilly said in an acid tone. "How far could I
get on one leg?"

"You could roll," Sam said. "A rolling Moss gathers no—"

"Look, Sam," Tilly interrupted. "I offer you an exciting
challenge and you stand there—"

"So far as I can see, wire clippers, a circuit bypass, a felt
mat, and a cloak of invisibility are all you need," Sam interrupted her. "I got the first three in the car, but frankly I don't
see how anybody could miss a woman of your proportions
slipping along the garden paths in there. If it was dark,
maybe. But in sunshine like this you're a pretty big target."
He intended no insult—he was simply making a professional
assessment. "Maybe *I* better go in."

"No, I'll do it. Maybe I'm a big target, but think how
much harder I am to throw out than you are. They might get
their arms around me, but they'll never lift me. And anyway,
Albert doesn't know you."

"Well, think how thrilled he'd be to meet a living legend,"
Sam pointed out.

"Get what you need from the car, okay?" Tilly asked impatiently.

"Women just ain't fun anymore," Sam muttered to himself as he turned away. "No snap to 'em at all."

He went back to his car, which was parked behind some bushes on the gravel road that ran behind the Budd estate. All along the road, on the inner side, ran an electric perimeter fence with an inner barrier of barbed wire. Beyond that, a ring of tightly planted trees blocked the view of whatever lay in the center of the compound, although a silvery-shingled roof of considerable extent could be glimpsed through the leafless branches. The house was either built low or sunk down in some kind of hollow.

"Be a hell of a lot easier at night," Sam grumbled, returning with his "equipment." "Somebody could come along here at any damn minute, and then what?"

"That is why we are wearing these overalls," Tilly said. "We are repair persons."

"Repairing what—bushes?"

"Will you just do what you have to do, please?"

"Don't know why you're in such an all-fired hurry," Sam said as he attached the circuit bypass and cut the wires of the electric fence.

Neither did Tilly. She just felt so frustrated by Albert's minions, and so determined to stop Matt from carrying on his "investigation" any farther, that she wanted to get this over with. She had discussed it all with George. He had his own reasons for wanting Matt to leave things alone. Reasons that, though different, ran in sympathy with her own.

Matt was just getting carried away, that was all. Tilly was worried he'd make a fool of himself. He felt bad about Tom Finnegan's death, and he was building the whole thing out of all proportion simply to give himself something to do. The trouble was, if you stick a pole in a peaceful pond and stir things up, you never know what will rise from the bottom. Life in Blackwater Bay had always gone along nicely, to Tilly's way of thinking, but the events of the previous summer had sent Matt off balance. He'd got murder on the brain.

The fact that she was determined to break into the grounds of a wealthy recluse's home in broad daylight did not seem at all as odd or dangerous to Tilly as Matt Gabriel's trying to solve a thirty-year-old mystery that wasn't even a mystery at all, in her opinion, and could only lead to people getting hurt, probably.

"Okay," Sam said. "You can go in now. Just duck through here, throw the mat over the barbed wire, and walk across it. If you spot something strung up in the trees, come back." He told her what to look for. "Personally, I think the whole layout is a disgrace," he concluded. "A kid of ten could get in here."

"Maybe kids of nine are all they're worried about," Tilly said, ducking and proceeding as instructed. She waved to Sam and pushed her way through the undergrowth between the trees, glad she had worn coveralls.

There was nothing "strung up" in the trees, no dogs, no security patrols, no electric eyes or trip wires. The house, which was a beautiful sprawling mansion in old French Provincial style, lay in and followed the contours of a natural hollow in the land. Around it were gardens that seemed to be wild natural growth, but Tilly's discerning eye detected much discreet planning and control. Nobody seemed to be about, and it suddenly occurred to her that this whole "assault" had been so easily achieved because Mr. Albert Budd was not in residence, but abroad in some exotic clime—and *that* was why she couldn't speak to him or get an appointment for the next five months. Maybe he lived here only in the summer.

Crestfallen, she abruptly abandoned her furtive crouch and walked casually through the gardens. Nothing happened. No bells rang, no whistles blew, no sirens wailed.

After wandering for a while between the flower beds, she encountered a fat man wearing brown overalls much like her own. He was bending over, pruning a rosebush. The sun glinted off his smooth, bald head, and the overalls strained across his ample bottom—much as her own were doing.

"Excuse me," she said. "Is Mr. Budd away?"

The fat man started and dropped his pruning shears. He turned slowly and regarded her. After a moment he spoke.

"Holy shit," he said. "Tilly Moss."

It was Albert himself.

*   *   *

"It's easy being a recluse if you make sure nobody *wants* to see you," Albert explained. "And if you damn and blast those who do want to see you, they eventually give up."

"You haven't blasted me," Tilly pointed out.

"Mmm. Well, you still have novelty value," Albert said. "And I happen to be in a good mood today. Although I can think of a few people I'll fire before the end of next week."

"Not because of me."

He peered at her. "Why not?"

"Because as far as I'm concerned, they did their jobs correctly. I wasn't let in, I broke in. Or did you think I always walk around looking like this?"

"You *broke* in?"

"Sure."

"But there's an electric fence, wire—"

"A ten-year-old could get in here."

"Ah—but it's the nine year olds—"

"That's what I told him."

Albert regarded her suspiciously. "Told who?"

"Snakehips Turkle."

"You're kidding."

"No."

"But . . . the man's a living legend!" Albert exclaimed.

"He can be had for fifty dollars and a quart of whiskey."

"Exactly!" said Albert. He leaned down to pick up his shears and thrust them into his coveralls pocket. "In the real world he'd demand ten times that and a signed contract with health benefits and a retirement pension. Believe me, I know." He turned on his heel and marched away down the path.

"The real world?" Tilly asked, following him. "I thought you were avoiding the real world."

He came to a French door and went through, thrusting aside the billowing curtains without a thought for whether she might be behind him or not. Tilly went in and looked around.

The room could have been a beautiful one, for its proportions were excellent and the morning light flooded it with pale yellow. But what the light fell on was not the patina of

fine antiques or the rich colors of lush upholstery, but the
dull gray of metal, for it was a virtual Kennedy Control Center of office machinery.

Albert stood studying it like a pasha surveying his harem.
"The real world comes to me," he said with gloomy satisfaction, and walked through a door on the far side of the room.
Tilly followed. Having gotten this far, she was determined to
carry on.

Albert had come to a halt at a beautiful credenza that
served as a bar in a long and sunlit room that seemed to
stretch half the length of the house. This is more like it, Tilly
thought with some satisfaction. The decor was predomi-
nantly gold but with touches of peacock blue and green. The
carpet was Chinese, and the furniture, though varied and antique, was in ebony, so the room had a Chinese flavor overall. Albert, despite his brown coveralls, also had a faintly
Oriental aspect, mostly because of the fatness of his face,
which had taken on slightly Buddha-like creases and folds.
He was pouring himself a drink but offered none to Tilly.

"I hope you haven't come to serve notice of a breach of
promise suit," he growled. "Must be a statute of limitations
on that."

Tilly drew herself up. "I wouldn't dream of it," she said.

He eyed her over his glass. "Well, that's something, anyway. What the devil *do* you want? Money?"

"No!" Tilly said angrily. If he'd still had his back to her,
she would have kicked him right in the coveralls.

"What is it, then? Dammit, there must be something to
make you break into my home. Crude curiosity doesn't cut
it, somehow. Was it some kind of dare?"

"Do people ever argue with you?" Tilly asked.

"Not much."

"They should, it might teach you some manners."

"I don't need manners." Albert shrugged. "Nor do I need
the love of a good woman—I've had enough of those. Nor
do I yearn for a sled named 'Rosebud.' I am perfectly happy
tending my gardens by day and the stars by night."

"I beg your pardon?" Tilly said, bemused by this sudden
turn into poesy.

"I am an expert on floribunda roses and, if I do say so myself, an acclaimed amateur astronomer." He seemed to swell slightly. "My life is quite complete, therefore, and I have no need of anything more."

"What about your family?"

He shuddered slightly. "I have had four wives, each more beautiful and disappointing than the last. No children, no brothers and sisters, no parents. I am alone."

"How awful."

He raised an eyebrow. "You think so? I disagree. It has not been easy to slough off all emotional attachments—I do have a weakness for pretty women—but I approach the twilight of my life with—"

"Crap."

For the first time he seemed actually to see her. "I beg your pardon?"

"I said crap," Tilly repeated. "Come on, Albert, cut the fancy talk. I knew you then and I knew you well. Either you've had a head transplant—in which case they should have included hair—or you're lying through your teeth."

He sighed and sat down. "What do you want, Tilly? I'm a busy man, and—"

"More crap. Honestly, Albert, you're a real disappointment to me. You've got more money than God, and here you are looking like a handyman and acting like a road company version of Sydney Greenstreet with a migraine. I expected at least a cigarette holder and a velvet smoking jacket."

He smiled suddenly. "You remember that?"

"Sure." Tilly smiled back. Years ago Albert used to dream that a velvet smoking jacket and a cigarette holder were the absolute peak of sophistication and insisted he would one day own and use both—when he became a millionaire. He always insisted he would be a millionaire, and in that, at least, he'd been correct.

"Actually, God has more money than me—according to the last *Forbes* survey—although I'm gaining on Him," Albert said. "But you can't wear a velvet jacket when you're pruning roses, you'd get sap all over it."

"Uh-huh."

He sighed again. "As for the rest—it's a habit. Money does things to you, Tilly. You get suspicious of everyone."

"I noticed."

"Well, you have to admit, you appearing out of the blue after all these years, dressed like that and claiming to be with Snakehips Turkle . . ."

"All right, all right," Tilly conceded. "I see how it could look a little . . . fishy, but your personal assistant is absolutely the snottiest—"

He laughed. "Isn't she wonderful? You can't imagine the peace and quiet she brings me."

"Where is she, anyway? Where is everybody, for that matter? A place like this should be crawling with servants."

"It usually is," Albert agreed vaguely. "But I give most of them the weekend off. There's usually a minor secretary and a maid or two about somewhere—they work out the schedule between themselves. Jeffries, my chauffeur, has taken Cook into town to do the week's shopping. You timed your break-in perfectly. Although *why* you did it is still a mystery."

Tilly felt a little foolish but proceeded with the pretext she had decided upon, weak though it was. "I only wanted to tell you that Tom Finnegan is dead. I didn't think it would make the national papers and—"

"Who?" Albert interrupted.

She stared at him. "Tom Finnegan. Your old school buddy."

"I don't—" he frowned.

"The Tom Finnegan who was with you the night Jacky Morgan died," Tilly said in a harsh voice, annoyed by his patronizing tone, his pretended lack of recognition, and her own silly game.

His eyes widened. "What do you know about that?"

"I know you were there," she said.

"But I didn't get to know *you* until years later. You weren't one of the girls . . ."

"What girls?"

He stared at her and then seemed to collect himself. "It doesn't matter."

"It might."

He ignored this and pretended to muse. "Oh, Tom Finnegan. Of course. Became a pharmacist, had the drug-store on the corner. I remember." He smiled very, *very* brightly, then seemed to recall she had brought news of the man's death. "How sad," he said abruptly, and removed the smile.

Tilly regarded him with some dismay. Matt had asked her to contact Albert Budd. She had thought it foolish and a waste of time, but Matt was her boss, and apparently he was intent on pursuing this Jacky Morgan business to the bitter end.

She had eventually agreed to do it because she had been curious to see what had become of Albert after all these years. Matt had asked her to introduce the subject of Jacky Morgan into the conversation casually, to see Albert's reaction. She had not intended to blurt it out as she had, but in any event she had been certain that any mention of Jacky Morgan would produce little reaction from a man she had remembered as having a head of curly red hair, a figure like Fred Astaire's and a personality to match—lighthearted, light-footed, and charming.

Instead she had found this bald, grumpy old poop—who was now avoiding her gaze. Obviously the name Jacky Morgan meant quite a lot to him, none of which he was willing to discuss.

"Yes, it is sad. He was killed in a car crash. My boss—"

"You're still working for Ted Gabriel?" Albert asked warily.

"No, he passed away some time ago. I'm working for his son, Matt. He's sheriff of Blackwater now."

"Matt?" Albert frowned. "He was just a college kid when I left. Studying philosophy or something."

"Yes. Well, like I said, he's sheriff now."

"I see." Albert stood up. "Well, I appreciate your coming to tell me about Tom Finnegan, Tilly. It's a sad thing when your old friends start to disappear."

"You disappeared first," she snapped.

He flushed slightly at that. "Yes, well—I had my reasons. Nothing to do with you, of course—I hope you understood that. I had this great ambition to make my mark in the world, and Blackwater Bay was not the place to start. It was good to see you again, of course—"

"So you remember Tom Finnegan now, do you?" Tilly asked, also standing up.

"I do, and I'm most sorry for his loss."

The hell you are, Tilly thought as he began to shepherd her toward the door.

"Mind you, I can't see that it was worth all the trouble you've gone to—"

"And you remember Jacky Morgan?" she asked in an innocent voice.

"One of the tragedies of my youth," he intoned. "Best forgotten."

"I see." Tilly allowed herself to be escorted back through the office and into the garden. She still had seen no servants of any kind—Albert had served himself at the bar, and there had been no sounds of other people in the house at all. Was he really that serious about being a recluse? She stopped abruptly, and he nearly ran into her. Turning around and facing him, she stared into his eyes. "Are you happy, Albert?"

"What?" So intent had he been on showing her out smoothly and inexorably that her balk so near the exit had caught him unprepared.

"I said, are you happy? It's a simple question."

"Who knows what happiness is—" he began in a sonorous voice.

"You know it when you feel it," Tilly snapped. "Are you?"

He dropped the attitude. "I'm reasonably content. I've found that things like money and roses and stars are easier to deal with than people, that's all."

"Because they don't talk back?"

He scowled. "Because they don't talk at all. Marketing mother's furniture polish was a big success, but in the end I had enough money and I'd certainly had enough of all the intrigue and arguing and back stabbing of the business world, so I sold out. I still have to deal with the money—it keeps on growing, you see—but tending it is rather like gardening. I can handle that, but I couldn't handle all those people and their *emotions*. They're so messy, so . . . uncontrollable. I mean, you've been here less than half an hour, and you've stirred up things in me I had happily forgotten. My digestion is already suffering, and later I'll probably have a stinking headache."

"Dear me," Tilly said dryly.

"You don't understand," he said in a disappointed voice. "My nerves were under such a strain that I *had* to leave the world behind. I'm not a well man."

She assessed his eyes and skin. "You'd be a lot healthier if you lost fifty pounds," she observed.

"So would you," he retorted angrily, abandoning the little-boy-lost routine.

They glared at one another.

After a minute he spoke in a more formal tone. "Thank you for coming to tell me about Tom."

"Sure, Albert, sure." She walked down the path and then looked back. "I'll just slip out the way I came, shall I? Save you the emotional strain of waving good-bye and all."

"It was good to see you again," he called after her.

But, clearly, it hadn't been.

11

By midafternoon on Saturday there had been fifteen reported Howlers perpetrated and probably twice as many committed that people thought weren't worth bothering the law about. They ranged from the simple (a fence painted puce, detergent in the Marion Heckman Memorial Fountain causing a small mountain of bubbles to totally obscure the central nymph from whose urn the fountain flowed) to the wicked and dangerous.

Over at the hospital, Matt discovered the emergency room was already busy. From behind the curtains of the various cubicles, sounds of retching could be heard. He recognized Fred Boyle among the white faces and waved. Boyle waved back, looking even more drawn and miserable than he had a few hours earlier when he'd come in to sign his statement about Tom Finnegan's accident.

"I should have taken you up on your offer of coffee instead of going down to the Dew Drop," he called weakly. "Somebody decided to poison half the damn town."

Matt went over. "I suppose they're blaming you?"

"You bet they are." Boyle managed a weak grin. "I know I help my friends work up a few Howlers every year, but do you really think I'd be dumb enough to do this to *myself?*" His face changed suddenly, and he turned his back to vomit into a stainless-steel bowl.

"Better out than in," Matt observed.

"Don't you believe it," Boyle muttered over his shoulder.

Moving away, Matt caught sight of Dr. Dan Rogers tapping into the computer at the emergency room desk. He was looking harassed. Matt went over and asked whether the law should take an interest in this particular prank, but Rogers shook his head.

"Nobody will get more than a bad bellyache," he said. "It was only ipecac, after all." He suddenly turned grim. "Mind you, if somebody could slip ipecac into the coffee urn at the Dew Drop Inn, they could just as easily have put in some god-awful thing we *haven't* got the antidote for. We laid in a supply of everything we thought we might need over the weekend—splints, superglue solvent, paint remover, and so on. As it is, if any one of these people had a bad gastric ulcer or a weak heart, the trouble could have been a lot more serious."

"People don't think that far ahead," Matt said.

"People don't think, period," Dr. Rogers growled. He was a small, dapper man—quick in his movements, his decisions, and his opinions. Nurses quailed when he barked their names, but he took endless trouble over his patients and was an excellent diagnostician.

If, years before, people had been told that Dan Rogers would go to college at all, much less medical school, they would probably have snorted in derision. His adolescent years had been marked by wild escapades and a constant defiance of authority. They might have thought his grades merited respect, but not his attitude. His family was poor but overproud, and the pressure of their expectations seemed to weigh on him, causing outbursts of almost criminal behavior from time to time, followed by black periods of depression and remorse.

If his contemporaries had been further informed that he not only would *excel* in his medical studies, but would become a politically savvy manipulator of the local AMA, a pillar of society, and chief of medicine at Blackwater General, they would have fallen down and rolled over with merriment.

Yet all this had come to pass.

Credit for the transformation was generally given not to

Rogers himself, or to his family, or to his teachers, but to his wife, Bonnie. Having gotten into college despite the frowning doubt of his high school principal, he met the bright, laughing girl in his freshman year. His undisguised adoration of her had wrought miracles. She had been—and still was—a beautiful woman who exuded warmth and joy with every breath.

It wasn't surprising that at first she was unimpressed by the handsome but rather sulky young man who always seemed to be hanging around the edges of the group that constantly surrounded her.

Perhaps stung by their unsubtle gibes—he was neither as wealthy as her friends nor as socially accomplished—he set about improving himself. He worked hard, tried hard, and changed his entire attitude. That she did notice. Unlike her rather shallow cronies, Bonnie Roderick had considerable depth and valued both effort and excellence wherever it manifested itself.

She began to spend time with him, defying her so-called friends and his so-called superiors to comment. As they moved through university from freshman to senior, Dan Rogers shone brighter and brighter, holding his rebellious nature down tighter and tighter, controlling his impulses, and conforming to the social "rules" of his new peers. The only place where his natural passions broke free was in Bonnie's bed, and that, too, she valued and appreciated. Bonnie Roderick was many things, and none of them was foolish. They married two days after graduation.

It had proved a solid and productive relationship. She blossomed, he rose. Their children grew up straight and strong and were a credit to them. As a couple they were both admired and envied. If, occasionally, his black depressions or the urge to rebel returned, nobody but Bonnie knew. And nobody doubted him anymore.

Normally he would not have been on duty over the weekend, having attained sufficient status to regularize his schedule at everyone else's expense, but the possibilities of the Howl had worried him.

Obviously, with reason.

"You expected this?" George asked, swallowing hard as

he heard a strangled cry and yet another gush of vomit hit the floor. A nurse ran past, muttering.

Rogers shrugged and jammed his hands into his white coat pockets. "I expected *everything,*" he said. "After last year—"

He didn't need to finish the sentence. They all remembered the aftermath of the grudge fight between Blackwater High and Lemonville High—the bloody noses, the broken fingers, the kicked shins, the bruises, grazes, and abrasions, and most worrying of all, the knife slashes. There had been quite a few of those.

Matt sighed. "I don't know, Dan. Something in me wishes we could just ban the Howl—it's getting worse all the time. It's not so funny anymore."

"Was it ever?" Rogers asked.

"I think it was—when the world was young and people had a little more time to think and a little more kindness," Matt said.

"When would that have been?" asked a voice from behind them. "Seventeen ninety-two?"

They turned to see Peter Dill swinging toward them on a pair of crutches. Normally a man who carried neatness to obsessive lengths, he was both disheveled and dirty. His hair— what there was of it—hung over his forehead, his gray suit was covered in slimy streaks, and his ultraconservative dark gray tie was askew. He looked more like a drunk than a respected vice president of the local bank.

Peter Dill had always been the Boy Most Likely to Succeed and had stayed on his predicted course throughout his life. He was in line to take over as president of the bank when the present incumbent retired in two years, and he would then be one of the most powerful men in the county. The bank held many mortgages, particularly those on small farms and businesses, and had held them through good times and bad. In administering these and other loans, Dill was not unkind, but neither was he open-handed, as many bank clients would attest. He knew many secrets, but if he used them to keep account holders in line, nobody ever said. His saving grace was his sense of humor. Often directed toward himself, it would manifest itself when least expected, disarming many an opponent into making concessions never intended before discussion was opened.

While in college he had made an unfortunate marriage that had produced an even more unfortunate son, named Wayne, who had recently been released from an open prison in Kentucky, in which state he had attempted to become a marijuana baron at the age of eighteen. The state had not approved. The word was that Wayne was now working at a garage in Hatchville. Dill had not officially disowned Wayne, but he never spoke of him in public, and it was common knowledge that he and the boy didn't get on. When Dill's first wife left him for the drummer in a rock band ("What else?" he had said wryly), he had married again, this time more sensibly.

Mrs. Evelyn Dill was exactly the wife he should have had from the beginning. They both knew it, and they both said so, frequently. The daughter of a successful Chicago plastic surgeon, Evelyn had been "finished" in Switzerland and had then had a brief but fairly satisfying career in hotel administration.

They had met when he attended a banking conference at the hotel where she worked. She had been the organizer, giving him ample opportunity to assess her worth. An attractive brunette with regular features and perfect teeth, she now ran his household with the same cool efficiency she had demonstrated at the hotel. She took an active role in the country club, where she excelled at tennis, golf, and bridge, and made a point of always being at home with the martinis mixed and dinner waiting when he returned from work.

"What the hell happened to *you?*" Rogers demanded when Dill swung to a painful stop in front of them.

"Some sweet soul decided it would be funny to squirt vegetable oil under the door of the bank. It's transparent, and it had all night to spread itself thinly over the dark green marble. It was inevitable that the first person through the door would go skating across the floor like Sonja Henie. *Very* funny."

"Were you good?" Rogers asked.

"Good? I was spectacular," Dill told them. "I did a skid, a twirl, three arabesques, and a sideways leap that would have taken gold at any Winter Olympics. Unfortunately, my last trick ended badly."

"In . . . ?"

"Multiple contusions and a broken ankle," Dill said, exhibiting his newly plastered lower limb. "I'd suggest an autograph, but the plaster's still soft. My backside is also killing me, but they refused to plaster that."

"Feather pillows," Rogers suggested.

"I bet you say that to all your patients."

"Are you always the first person through the door?" Matt asked.

Dill looked at him in surprise. "Why, yes—on a Saturday morning, anyway." He got the idea. "You think it was meant for me personally?"

"Only if the person who did it knew your habits," Matt said. "Any idea who it might have been?"

"Oh, come on," Dill said irritably. "This is the Howl, remember? It was probably some kid who didn't give a damn *who* fell over. He was probably hiding in the bushes across the street and had a good laugh at my expense." He aimed a mock glare over at Rogers. "And I *mean* expense. I just had to shell out over two hundred bucks for this. Where do you buy your plaster—in Paris?"

"Of course," Rogers said. "And when you've finished with it, we'd like it back, please."

"For your collection?"

"Absolutely. Maybe you'd care to finance a new wing to house our medical museum of Howl artifacts?"

"Are you kidding?"

"No," Rogers said a little grimly as yet another member of the great Blackwater Bay public came through the ER door. This one was cradling his bleeding arm in a towel. "It would have to be a pretty big wing, though," he muttered to himself.

Dill turned to Matt. "Frankly, I'm surprised how many Howlers work every year. There are so many people out causing trouble, it's a wonder they don't trip over one another."

"They do," Rogers said wryly. "We had a pair in last year who went around undoing everything other people were setting up. When somebody doubled back to check, they got caught. Nasty."

"What they did or what was done to them?" Matt asked.

"Both," Rogers said.

"That's what I mean," Matt said. "Things are getting out of hand. I've played it down as much as I could, but the truth is the Howl hasn't really been the same since Jacky Morgan died."

There was a silence.

"You remember that, don't you?" Matt asked the two men in a neutral voice.

"I try not to," Rogers said in a low voice.

Dill said nothing. He seemed to have lost whatever vestige of humor he'd managed to retain through his own accident. After a moment he cleared his throat.

"What the devil made you think of that?" he asked.

Matt shrugged. "Oh, some old records I came across. Sad case."

"Very," Rogers agreed hurriedly, and caught the eye of a passing nurse, who paused expectantly. "Well, I've got to get on with things. Hope your ankle mends quickly, Peter." And he was off down the corridor, holding on to the nurse's elbow and issuing instructions at a furious rate.

Matt stared after him speculatively.

Beside him, Dill spoke again. "About Jacky Morgan," he said.

Matt turned. "Yes?"

"It was just high spirits that got out of hand, you know."

"That's what it said in the record."

Dill's high forehead smoothed out. "Right," he said.

"Tom Finnegan didn't agree," Matt continued.

The creases in Dill's forehead reappeared. "Tom was a very sick man," he said. "I don't think he was in his right mind at the end. Maybe he drove into that tree deliberately."

"The state police don't agree," Matt said. "He tried to brake, hard, when he went off the road."

"Oh," Dill said. "Well, he was pretty weak—"

"Oh, yes," Matt agreed. "Everybody knew how weak he was."

Dill stared at him. "You say that as if it's supposed to mean something."

"Does it?"

"Not to me," Dill said shortly.

"Fair enough." Matt waited.

Dill seemed puzzled, then shrugged. "Well, my wife is over there waiting for me—I guess I'd better get home and put my foot up. At least there's a decent football game on this afternoon."

"Enjoy it," Matt said.

Dill looked at him sharply. "I intend to." He took a few swinging steps away, then stopped and turned back to give Matt another hard look. "It's never a good idea to open doors other people have closed, you know."

Matt raised an eyebrow. "Is that a warning?"

Dill seemed surprised. "Good Lord, no. Just an observation. I simply meant most people would rather forget their youthful sins and confusions."

"Some people can't," Matt said. "Tom Finnegan was one of them. Are you going to his funeral next week?"

"Well, of course," Dill said over his shoulder as he turned and started again toward his wife. "Tom and I were old friends."

"I've hired four nightwatchmen," Tyrone Molt told Matt later that afternoon. "Last year we had *eighty-four* flat tires to pump back up, and I'm sure as hell not going through that again."

They were surveying his used-car lot. The multicolored flags strung along the wires overhead flapped in the breeze, and the shiny spinners and streamers that hung between them glittered in the occasional shafts of sunlight that shot down between the small, fast-moving clouds that scudded through the blue October sky.

"Well, at least you can lock up your new car showroom," Matt said.

"Ha," Molt said. "That didn't give me much protection last year, did it? Cost me over a thousand, that little caper."

Matt was surprised. "Is that all?" He thought back to the scene when he'd arrived on the morning after the previous year's Howl—the pickup the drunk had driven through Molt's showroom window was teetering on the sill, pouring oil and gas onto the forecourt, there was plate glass everywhere, the frame of the window had been torn away, and two of the cars inside the showroom had been total wrecks. By the time the Blackwater Bay Volunteer Fire Department had finished pouring foam and water over everything, the carpets and furnishings in the showroom had also been ruined.

Molt laughed. It was the harsh laugh of a hard man. Molt had never matched the popular image of a car salesman. Instead of oily charm, he had an abrasive personality that was long on volume and short on style. Once a handsome man with a burly frame, he had long since run to fat, and the lines on his face bespoke the sour disposition of a man who figured the return on everything to the last penny but refused to pay the cost of gentle persuasion when selling his wares.

Oddly enough, his brusque manner struck a responsive chord in many of the car-buying citizens of Blackwater County. "Got a good deal from that son of a bitch Molt," they'd say, seeing themselves as driving a hard bargain, when in fact the bargain had invariably been on Molt's side, and hard driving was what *they* were left with.

Despite repeated indications to the contrary, they seemed to think Molt's attitude was a sign of old-fashioned honesty—which it was not. His take-it-or-leave-it style had earned him much money and some enemies, but few friends.

Now he fixed Matt with a knowing eye. "It cost the insurance company over thirty thousand to straighten me out," he said. "The thousand it cost *me* was the increase on my goddamned premium this year."

"Ah," Matt said. "Well, it will probably be worth it if anything happens."

"It's a deductible running cost," Molt observed.

His little lizard eyes, sunk in a welter of fatty wrinkles, blinked complacently. In a sudden twist of breeze his black toupee lifted minutely from its mooring, briefly revealing the scant white growth beneath. He wore this hairpiece clapped on his head like a beret, not seeming to care whether people noticed it or not. He paid equally scant attention to his wardrobe, turning out most days in mismatched jacket and trousers and a frayed shirt. His one gesture toward sartorial distinction was to top whatever random ensemble he'd apparently picked up off the floor with a selection from his extensive collection of wide and revolting hand-painted silk ties, most of which featured either boss-eyed horses, ill-proportioned dogs, or impossibly colored Hawaiian sunsets. On very special occasions, there would be a bathing beauty riding his swelling paunch, coyly looking over her outthrust bust or buttocks in blissful ignorance of her surroundings.

Molt's wife had died many years back—of despair, most people said. Others claimed it was shock brought on by a sudden realization that money was not going to be enough to compensate for waking up next to Tyrone every morning for the rest of her life. He had lived alone ever since. Tilly Moss claimed Molt had a mistress in Lemonville, but Matt found it hard to believe that Tyrone would spend all that money on gas. More likely were occasional trips to a certain establishment on Cotton Street, run by a woman named Dolly Boot and known locally as the Doll House.

The laws of Blackwater County were extremely flexible when it came to prostitution, reflecting yet again their unique origin. Apparently the men who wrote the rules for Blackwater County had felt that a certain amount of sin was inevitable and had fashioned their strictures accordingly. In a sense, the whores won the ground that the bootleggers lost. Oddly enough, this beachhead had never been consolidated. Despite the vague laws and small fines, Blackwater County was no more populated by ladies of easy virtue than any other county in the state. Matt had long since decided that this had been entirely due to his father's influence, which had been benign but precise. On his deathbed, he'd told Matt that he had given the matter considerable thought and reckoned that taking into account the population of Blackwater County, its median age, and its commercial appetites, three houses and about ten summertime freelancers were sufficient, and that was the end of it. Matt had continued this policy, although lately there had been so much free amateur talent on hand that the professionals were complaining about recession.

"I hope you're paying your hired hands enough to keep them from temptation," Matt said.

Molt spat into the row of petunias by his feet. "I'm paying them plenty," he said. "They'll keep good watch."

Matt waited a moment, then spoke casually. "Shame nobody kept watch on Eagle Head the night Jacky Morgan went over."

Molt was lighting a cigar and cursed as the flame suddenly wavered across his knuckles. "Wind caught me," he said. He took some puffs on the cigar and gazed across his lot. Then he gave a patently false start and looked at Matt. "Sorry— what was that you were saying about Eagle Head?"

"Jacky Morgan," Matt repeated.

Molt frowned. "Can't say I know him," he told his cigar. "Sounds familiar, though. Is he the dentist over in—" He gave another start as he pretended to notice some people on the far side of the lot. "Uh-oh—duty calls. You'll have to excuse me, Sheriff, but it looks like I got customers. Thanks for the advice." He waved his cigar in a vague salute and bustled away.

Matt sighed and returned to his own car, where the words "Official Cars Proudly Supplied by Molt's Supercar Showroom" seemed to glare at him from almost every possible surface. As he drove away he saw the automotive baron, his magenta-and-lime-green tie flapping this way and that over his big belly, bearing down on a meek-looking couple standing beside a five-year-old sedan.

They didn't stand a chance.

12

At Mrs. Peach's Guest House, preparations for supper were already well under way. Tonight, however, there would be no huge feast set before her guests, for it was buffet only, and a light one at that. The reason it was such a simple meal was that there would be plenty of goodies at the Halloween Festival, which was the official name of the Howl, and Mrs. Peach hated to think she would be spoiling anyone's appetite.

"Do you think that's enough?" Mrs. Peach asked, surveying the dining room table.

"My God, Mother, I think you ought to be reported to Weight Watchers as an evil influence," Nonie said. "Why, they won't eat anything like all that."

"Not to start with, no—but as the Howl goes on, they may build up an appetite and come back hungry."

"And what about Mrs. Norton's cookie stall, and Mr. Naseem's Eastern Delicacies, and Roy Antonio's Pizza Pieces—will they be ignoring those, do you think?"

"If they're sensible, yes."

"The hell they will."

"Language, Nonie," Mrs. Peach said automatically.

"Mother, the real beneficiaries of your cooking are Riley Newcombe's pigs, because we throw away more than our guests eat. It's no wonder you always run at a loss. Why can't you learn—"

"Sometimes I think Riley's pigs don't *get* all of it," Mrs. Peach said vaguely. "Bessie Newcombe is a terrible cook. I wouldn't be surprised if she went through it and took out a thing or two for the family first."

"Which is why, I suppose, you wrap everything up separately before you throw it into the bin?"

"Pigs can be choosy, too. By the way, I saw your costume hanging up in your room," Mrs. Peach went on before Nonie could continue with that line of questioning. "Whom do you plan to amuse with that—a skin specialist?"

"Everybody dresses up for the Howl," Nonie said weakly. The costume had taken her weeks to make, and she hoped it would transform her from frumpy old Nonie into Winona the Wise, magical mystic from the romantic eastern deserts. Particularly in the eyes of Jack Fanshawe, whose accounts she kept and whose eye she'd been trying to catch ever since his wife had died. (She'd only started flirting with him after a decent interval, of course. Unlike some she could mention, who thought they were getting the inside track. Desperation had invented the gauzy glitter of Winona the Wise—and tonight she would be put to the test. Jack Fanshawe, look out!)

"I wouldn't call that dressing, I'd call that *un*dressing," Mrs. Peach said. "You're not going to be much help to me lying in the hospital with pneumonia."

"I'll wear a nice, thick cardigan," Nonie promised, her fingers crossed behind her back.

After all, it was the night of the Howl.

Cardigans and inhibitions were easily shed.

"You must have enough cookies and cakes here to feed a regiment," grumbled Larry Lovich as he helped Nell Norton load up his designer RV with another consignment of baked goods.

"That's nothing," called his partner, Freddy Tollett, from the far side of the graveled parking area behind the Toby cottage on Paradise Island. "You ought to heft a few of these quilts around and then see how you feel." He glanced at Margaret Toby with a grin. "What do you fill these things with, concrete?"

"Now stop that, both of you. You're only jealous because we're so brilliant and you're simply two grasshoppers in the field of life," Mrs. Norton chided, not without affection.

The two men exchanged a glance. "Now that's where you're wrong," Larry said. "We have decided to become productive members of society."

"Do tell," Mrs. Toby said disbelievingly. She and her friend were very fond of the two gay men who lived in a cottage up the island from them and added fun to their lives. They were witty, generous, loyal, and quite muscular—useful friends in every way, especially to two "widow women," as the ladies liked to call themselves.

"We have finally signed the lease on that little shop next to Daria's gallery," Freddy said. "We are going to gut it, decorate it as only we can, and next spring we are going to open a wine and quiche bar for the summer trade. So there."

"Wine and *quiche*?"

"Yes. We were wondering if you'd be interested in being a supplier," Larry said.

"Mind you, we haven't fully made up our minds yet," Freddy said, leaning against Mrs. Toby's station wagon in a reflective frame of mind. "It could be an old English tea shoppe—cakes, scones, crumpets, that sort of thing."

"I thought we'd decided on wine and quiche," Larry said, scowling. "I've been in touch with wine merchants—"

"It could be tea in the afternoon and wine at night," Freddy pointed out. "It could be anything—that's the fun of it. We can spend the whole winter planning." They exchanged a sudden, beaming smile.

"Well, when you've made up your minds, let me know," Nell Norton said briskly. "I might be interested in the sweet side, but quiches aren't my line, really." She carefully loaded the last of the coconut cakes, then straightened up and glanced at Margaret Toby. "You might want to ask Dorothy Finnegan about quiches—they're her specialty. And she might be glad of something to do next year."

The two men's smiles vanished as quickly as they'd appeared. "That's a thought," Larry said slowly. "Poor Dorothy—so terrible for her, Tom's dying like that."

"More terrible than you think," Mrs. Toby said. "Matt Gabriel doesn't even think it was an accident."

Freddy was shocked. "You mean—he did it deliberately?"

"No—worse than that," Mrs. Toby said meaningfully.

The two men stared at her, then at one another. "Oh, my God," Freddy said. "Not—"

"I'm afraid so," Mrs. Toby said. "And it has something to do with Jacky Morgan."

"But how bizarre!" Larry said in astonishment.

"Who the hell is Jacky Morgan?" Freddy asked. He was a latecomer to the area, having lived on Paradise for only eighteen years; Larry, on the other hand, had grown up there.

"I tried not to hear," Mrs. Toby said self-righteously. "I went out of the room, but—"

"It was just plain eavesdropping, Margaret," Nell said disapprovingly.

"It *wasn't.*" Mrs. Toby was indignant. "It's a small house."

"But who—" Freddy repeated plaintively.

"I'd forgotten all about that," Larry said.

"So had everybody," Mrs. Toby said. "But now Matt Gabriel has got some sort of bee in his bonnet about it, I suppose it will all be brought up again."

"Is he investigating?" Larry asked eagerly.

"Who's Jacky Morgan?" Freddy pleaded, looking from one to another.

"No—more like cogitating, I think," Mrs. Toby said. "He hasn't *arrested* anyone yet, that's for sure. We would have heard."

"Would someone—" Freddy said.

"He'll get over it," Nell Norton predicted confidently as she climbed into the RV and took a firm hold of the stacked boxes. "Deep down, Matt is a sensible sort of person."

"Do you think so?" asked Mrs. Toby, sinking down on top of her quilts.

She seemed disappointed.

The sheriff looked all over town for Merrill Atwater and finally located him at the carnival grounds, overseeing the setting-up of the stage, allocating positions to the various rides and stands—and, in general, helping out where he could.

At the moment he was carrying a huge garland of heavy leads for the head electrician of the company that provided the mechanical rides. He treated the heavy coils as if they were so many rubber bands instead of steel cables.

"Any time you want a job, buddy, just say the word," said the electrician, who was trailing behind him. "We could use a guy like you on the road."

"Already got a job, thanks," Merrill said, smiling. And it was perfectly true: he was the mayor of Blackwater.

Mayor Atwater looked like the result of an injudicious mating between a combine harvester and a grizzly bear. He was taller than Matt and weighed half again as much. His muscles constantly endeavored to escape the constriction of clothing through the shortest route possible, resulting in high bills at the Big Man's Boutique. What neck he had was as thick as a young redwood tree.

It had not always been so.

In his youth Merrill Atwater had, according to local legend, been a gawky, skinny young man of a type apt to have sand kicked in his face at the beach. Then, one memorable day, he'd read a Charles Atlas advertisement on the back of a Plastic Man comic book. He'd sent off for the brochures on the Atlas Method of Dynamic Tension and had never looked back.

Soon the muscles of Merrill Gladstone Atwater had begun to rise from their bony beds and bulge like nobody's business. He seemed to grow up as well as out and progressed from suspending himself between two kitchen chairs to working out with actual weights and dumbbells. He pounded up and down the country lanes, sweating heavily. He ate huge amounts of foods. Dissatisfied with adding mere bulk, he began to expand his spiritual dimensions, too. He read widely and absorbed strange philosophies, details of which he sent for with coupons from the various body-building magazines to which he subscribed. He contemplated the night sky. A small Japanese man was reputed to have been seen talking to him while walking in the fields—but this was

never confirmed, although there *was* an Oriental laundry in
Lemonville during those formative years.

As he grew in both girth and depth, Merrill lost his shy
ways. He took up public speaking for confidence and tap
dancing for coordination. He joined the debating team, the
football team, and the drama club. He stopped parting his
hair in the middle. His acne cleared up. His parents, quiet, respectable people, slowly seemed to fade in both color and
presence and wore oddly furtive and puzzled expressions
whenever they attended church with their burgeoning son.

Girls began to notice him. Boys began to notice him, too,
and to smile nervously when he talked, backing away to give
him plenty of room to express himself.

No more sand was kicked in his face.

These changes eventually brought their reward. He went
away to one of the "big ten" universities on a football schol-
arship, choosing to study business administration, at which
he excelled. In his senior year he was chosen as a member of
the Olympic team and won a gold medal in judo. Merrill Atwater was a fine example of the self-made midwestern
American hero.

It was unfortunate, therefore, that at his greatest moment,
while leaning forward to allow a tiny Indonesian judge to
place the gold medal around his neck, he chanced to head-
butt that gentleman into twenty minutes of oblivion.

Merrill had carried the unconscious official to the Red
Cross tent as gently as if he had been a child, the judge's little legs dangling over the huge athlete's muscular arms.
(Sadly, the judge in question was never able to erase from
the minds of his fellow countrymen this image of his ig-
nominy—televised as it had been to the entire world—and he
subsequently left public life to become a highly successful
dental supply salesman in the more remote islands of the
archipelago.)

Later that evening in the press room, under the watchful
eye of the Olympic team captain, Merrill had tried to explain
to the assembled international journalists that his gesture had
not been an intentional insult but was the kind of thing that
happened to him all the time. Chairs broke under him, orna-
ments shattered in his grasp, structures snapped when he

leaned against them. He seemed to be constantly surrounded by shards, splinters, and bruised, lurching people. He was very sorry, but it was not his fault, he insisted.

Yet even as he spoke, he had gestured widely and quite unintentionally knocked a front tooth from a slightly deaf BBC reporter who had innocently drawn near in order to hear better.

It was a bleak moment.

In his hotel room that night, Merrill Gladstone Atwater reflected on the changes that had taken place in his life. He had started out genetically programmed to be a small man and as such had been destined to lead a small and uneventful life. In overcoming that programming and denying that destiny, he had been guilty of the sin of pride and imperfect depth perception. Despite his enlarged horizons and dimensions, he had continued to move and act as if he were still a small man. His athletic triumphs could not disguise the fact that important distinctions were beginning to blur for him. It could not continue. It *would* not continue.

Armed with this revelation, and thick spectacles, Merrill Atwater returned to Blackwater Bay filled with a burning desire to share with others his realization that to embrace the larger life was to embrace equally large responsibilities, among which were regular eye tests.

He opened a sporting goods store and a martial arts center. He joined Greenpeace, Amnesty International, the World Wildlife Organization, and the church choir. He married a small, rather plain optician who spent most of her free time sewing his shirt buttons back on. He coached the local football teams—free—and created a multitude of diet and exercise programs for the overweight, the underweight, the weak and the timid and the nearsighted strong. He saw it as his mission to bring the joys and the responsibilities of physical enlightenment to all.

In his mayoral campaign two years ago, he'd made it his business to greet every citizen of Blackwater on a personal basis, looming up at them when they least expected it, smiling widely his shark-toothed smile, leaning down and taking them by the hand, booming out their names, making promises as broad as his pectorals, impressing them with his beliefs, his sincerity, and the strength of his grip. As a result practically everybody in Blackwater voted for him.

They were afraid to do anything else.

"Afternoon, Your Honor," Matt said when Atwater had deposited his burden.

"Well, hello there, Sheriff!" Atwater boomed. "What do you think of it so far?"

Ducking as the mayor gestured widely, Matt looked around the football grounds at the complicated activities involved in setting up for the festival. "It looks like chaos, as usual."

"Don't worry. We'll be ready by seven o'clock, as long as We All Pull Together!" Merrill bellowed confidently. Several people within the sound of his voice flinched and began to move a little faster. "We've always done it before, haven't we?"

"We have," agreed Matt. "That's one thing that worries me."

"What do you mean?"

Matt leaned against a strut of the Space Spider ("Spin your way to the stars!") and looked around. "People *may* be getting a little bored with the same old things. They seem to want fresh excitement, new thrills. We've had quite a few Howlers perpetrated already today. . . . "

"What, even before nightfall?" Atwater, a traditionalist, was shocked by this evidence of poor sportsmanship. The festival officially opened at seven o'clock, and that had always been the tacitly agreed time for Howlers to begin. Sneaky head starts were discouraged. He frowned, and several people cringed.

"I'd like you to say something about it to the people tonight," Matt continued. "Ask them to tone down their tricks, use more imagination and less gunpowder, remember that water-based paint is kinder to the environment—that kind of thing. You see, what worries me is that people seem to be getting nastier. Folks are getting hurt. Expenses for repairs are rising. Cruelty is creeping in. You remember the last Howl—".

The mayor scowled, and a passing town council member whimpered slightly. "The fights, you mean," Atwater said.

"Yes—that's exactly what I mean. Everything seems to be getting a little more violent, a little more—"

Atwater sighed gustily. "A Sign of the Times, my friend. Standards on a Downward Slide. Young People without Guidance. Moral Turp—"

"Whatever," Matt said hurriedly. He looked at Atwater and took a deep breath. "I think it started way back when Jacky Morgan was killed."

There was a rumble in Atwater's chest that might have meant almost anything. It grew in intensity, and then Atwater spoke. "A Ghastly Tragedy," he intoned. "I was there, you know."

"I know," Matt said.

At this the muscles in Atwater's face contracted, giving him the appearance of a thoughtful but constipated gorilla. "It Was Awful," he said. "There Was Nothing We Could Do. The Poor Kid went over and That Was That." The well-rehearsed pronouncements rolled out, one after the other, as he recalled the events of the past. "It was a Foolish Prank That Went Wrong."

"Merrill . . . "

"We Were Only Silly Kids with No Idea of What—"

"Merrill . . . "

"—We Were Doing. And Then It Was Too Late."

"Isn't that your wife calling you?"

Atwater seemed to come to himself with a start, and he looked around furtively. "Where?"

"Over there, by the coffee tent."

Atwater's huge frame shook briefly. A hunted look came into his eyes. The tiny woman who had been unsuccessfully waving for attention started toward them determinedly. "Quick," the mayor said, grabbing Matt's arm. "Think of something for me to do."

Matt, paling at the pain incurred by Atwater's grip, managed to gasp, "Like what?"

"Anything. Come on, she's getting closer. Think, man—think!"

"Oh, right . . . " He raised his voice. "We need you over at the . . . the . . . fireworks stand. The men want some help with the larger pieces. They're getting heavy."

The little woman's steps slowed.

"Why, of course," Atwater boomed jovially. "I'd be glad to help." Still gripping Matt's arm, he started away at a pace so swift that even the sheriff's long legs had to work hard to match it. As he was dragged along, Matt glanced over his shoulder and saw Mrs. Atwater—for that was the identity of the little woman—put her hands on her hips and glare, then shrug and turn away to march back to the coffee tent.

"She gone?" asked Atwater out of the corner of his mouth.

"She's given up," Matt said rather breathlessly.

Atwater slowed. "She's been after me to be one of the judges of the Beautiful Baby Contest. Have you any idea how nasty women can turn if you don't pick their kid out and kiss its sticky little face?"

"Well, no, actually . . . "

"And they pee on you, too."

"The women?" Matt asked without thinking.

Atwater guffawed. "No, the babies." His laughter faded, and he scowled. "*She* wants another one."

Matt was beginning to see spots before his eyes. "You mean—"

"Muriel wants us to have another baby," Atwater said glumly. "It was the twins that made me mayor, you know. I ran for office just to get out of the house." He gave Matt a sideways glance and slowed down a little more—he did not entirely lack compassion for his fellow man. "I'm not saying I don't *like* kids," he said.

"Of course not," Matt wheezed.

"Just babies," Atwater went on. "I'm terrified I'm going to squash one without realizing it. But Muriel thinks they're cute. She figures if I see a bunch of them at once, I'll realize how cute they are. I won't. Believe me, I won't."

"My car is over—"

"When they get older, of course, their bones harden up." Atwater mused a bit and actually came to a stop. "I think fifteen is enough, don't you?"

"Sorry?" Matt was leaning against a cotton candy machine and rubbing his arm.

"Fifteen minutes for my speech tonight. I think that's enough."

"Oh, plenty," Matt agreed. "Plenty."

Atwater nodded, and his eyes focused on the horizon. He drew a mayoral breath. "I'll Speak to the People, Matt. Tell them that we'll no longer tolerate aberrant behavior during the Howl."

"Well, that wasn't exactly—"

"Meanwhile, it's Nice to Know We Can Count on You." He thrust out his arm and shook Matt by the hand.

"I beg your pardon?" Matt asked, wincing.

"To look after things tonight. Keep order, make sure everyone is safe, that sort of thing."

"I have all my deputies—"

"Good, good." Atwater's attention had wandered. "See you tonight, then." And he was off, lumbering across the grass toward what looked like the tent of a desert prince but undoubtedly housed the portable public toilets hired for the night.

Matt walked slowly back to his patrol car, reflecting on his encounters during the day and the result of casually dropping the name of Jacky Morgan into various conversations.

He opened the door and slid in behind the wheel, but did not immediately start the engine. Through the windshield he watched people running to and fro, setting up stands, arranging displays, tacking up bunting and streamers, trying out equipment, alternately wringing their hands and laughing, but in general enjoying their nervous anticipation of the approaching night.

Jack Fanshawe claimed to have "forgotten" the incident of Jacky's death, Dr. Dan Rogers had hurried away so as not to discuss it, Peter Dill had issued a kind of warning to keep away from the subject, and Tyrone Molt had professed ignorance of the whole thing. He awaited with interest Tilly's report on Albert Budd, who at present seemed the least likely to be involved in Finnegan's death.

If anyone was involved, except Finnegan himself.

The phone company records had been no help. In fact, they had made things worse. Finnegan had not called any of the others that afternoon—*but they had each called him.*

When he'd gotten copies of all their records, he had stared unbelievingly at the printed lines. One after the other, each

of the six—including the distant Albert Budd—had called
Tom Finnegan on the afternoon of the day he'd died.

The obvious conclusion was that he was looking at a con-
spiracy of some kind, and that each of them had tried to talk
Tom Finnegan out of "confessing" what Matt had begun to
suspect—that they had been mutually responsible for Jacky
Morgan's death all those years ago and had sworn some kind
of oath about never speaking. Tom had wanted to break the
oath and confess before he died. Instead, he'd died before he
could confess. And that, too, was too much of a "coincidence."

He was already out on a limb on this. Asking for the
records of the other six had been definitely out of line, an
abuse of privilege for which he had no excuse. Indeed, if the
six found out about it—and they included a doctor and a
lawyer whose records could be considered privileged in
themselves—they could cause him a lot of trouble.

This whole thing was causing him a lot of trouble.

Maybe Daria was right. Maybe he was trying to build a
nice new mountain out of a very old molehill, so he could
stand up there and show everyone how clever he was. The
temptation was a strong one, after his successes of the summer. They hadn't been his triumphs alone—the vacationing
Jack Stryker had had a lot to do with it—but he was pretty
much alone now.

If he was right, he could take all the credit.

If he was wrong, he would get all the blame.

He turned the key and started the engine. He'd wasted
enough time on this idle and probably pointless "investigation." The state police were probably right. Tom Finnegan
had simply lost control of his car, and his dying words were
mere babble, without any meaning or importance. The conversation that Dorothy had overheard was irrelevant, too. It
was recalled under stress, she could have misunderstood, she
could be subconsciously searching for someone to blame.

And so could he.

Maybe it was time to stop thinking like a Sherlock and to
start thinking like a sheriff. It was the Howl—and there was
a long night ahead.

13

"*I*t usually starts with elves," Nonie Peach confided to Dominic, who was using the hall mirror to make a final check of his Robin Hood costume. He had decided to take full part in the Howl—after all, if he was going to become a Blackwater Bay attorney, he needed to know all aspects of its unique personality. Besides, he might see Emily at the carnival—and the Robin Hood outfit was particularly flattering. He felt quite dashing.

"The kids under seven do the early rounds," Nonie continued, taking a peek out of the narrow window beside the door. "Their parents are still at the 'isn't she adorable' stage, so it's all pixies, ghosties, fairies, and little ETs."

"Sounds more like the DTs," Dominic observed goodnaturedly. "Heaven help any poor wino who ventures out this evening, losing track of the dates the way they do. Imagine some poor drunk running into a troop of elves without warning. It could send him straight to the loony bin."

"It gets worse later on." Nonie chuckled. "Imagine coming upon a troop of Teenage Mutant Ninja Turtles, melting monsters, Frankensteins, witches, goblins . . . "

"I get the idea." Dominic glanced down at the array of special cookies and candies she'd made during the day. "Do you go to this kind of trouble every year?" he asked in some amazement.

"Sure," Nonie said. "Why not?"

"Halloween in the city lost its innocence years ago," he said rather grimly. "Trick-or-treating has disappeared because the streets are too dangerous for ordinary muggers, much less weirdly dressed children slowed down by bags full of dentist's delights."

"Is it true some people put poison and razor blades and things like that in the kids' treats?" Nonie asked.

"I'm afraid so," he said. "A lot of hospitals offer a free X-ray service so children can bring in their booty bags and check them out. Ground glass doesn't show up on an X-ray, of course," he added sadly.

"My God," Nonie said, shaking her head. "Who needs Halloween when there are real ghouls walking the streets already?"

Dominic nodded agreement, having always had a soft spot for Halloween himself. He gave a start as the doorbell went. "Uh-oh, stand by; the Hoarders from Hell are here."

"Wow!" said Daria, regarding Matt in his gendarme outfit.

"The same to you," he said, taking in the shimmer of her shimmy. Daria was dressed as a twenties flapper. Everything about her was silver, from her curving wig to her strappy little shoes. Every time she moved even slightly, there was a tremble and glitter of stranded fringe that drew the eye to a figure that was unsuccessfully suppressed by the straight line of her costume.

"Are we a success?" asked Daria, hooking her arm through his. They started toward the bright lights of the festival grounds.

"You are," Matt said. "*I* feel like an idiot."

"Nonsense. But you should be carrying a machine gun, you know. That's what the gendarmerie carry in Paris now."

"Today Paris, tomorrow Blackwater Bay? I hope not."

"You said things were getting worse."

"Not *that* much worse." They were joined by a melting corpse, a Tin Man of Oz, a ghost in paper chains, and a two-headed calf. As they drew closer to the gate, the parade of masked and costumed citizens of Blackwater grew thicker and more varied. Many were luridly lit by the jack-o'-lanterns they carried for entry into the pumpkin-carving contest, the prize for which had been boosted to $250 by the local chapter of the Algonawana Lodge. He looked around at the gathering grotesques. "That is, I *hope* they aren't getting worse."

Tilly straightened up and emitted a small groan. "Now I know what they mean about the Victorians being strait-laced," she said. She turned and glared down at her mother, who smirked up at her with a slight air of triumph. "You didn't have to do them up so *tight,* did you?"

Mrs. Moss made a noise that could have been a giggle. Tilly grinned back at her. "I guess you did." She walked over to regard herself in the full-length mirror and sighed. "Well, it's nice to have a waist again, even if it's only temporary. I certainly won't be able to stuff myself with taffy apples and Nell Norton's cookies *this* year." Exchanging a glance with her mother in the mirror, she saw what was definitely a wink. "Oh, I get it. You want me to catch a man, is that it?"

Another wink.

"Fat chance. And I *mean,* fat chance," Tilly said. She gave a last tug to her costume and went back to her mother. Grasping it by the handles she propelled the wheelchair into the sitting room. "I think it's just you and me forever, kid," she said, and began to add the finishing touches to her mother's outfit. "We make a lovely pair."

Tilly had begun designing their costumes on the first of November the previous year. She'd made not only the dresses, but all the trimmings, which included her hat and her mother's lace mittens and cap, and she'd also knitted the long, warm shawls Victorian ladies often wore instead of coats. The thermal underwear she and her mother wore be-neath their costumes was a modern addition (although after poring over reproductions of *Godey's Lady's Book* and simi-lar sources, Tilly wasn't altogether certain the ladies of that time didn't also have their secrets when it came to keeping warm in winter).

Mrs. Moss was "done up" as Queen Victoria in her later days. The long black wool dress spread over her knees and down to her ankles, and the silver wig and white lace trim-mings made her look quite elegant. Tilly was dressed as a fashionable lady-in-waiting in a gown of iridescent taffeta of a greenish amber shade that was very flattering to her tawny coloring. She had spent two hours in the beauty parlor that afternoon, getting Nora Cray to tint her hair and do it up in a French twist with curls and tendrils that fitted around the little hat that tipped over her forehead.

The doorbell rang.

"That will be Lem Turkle and the taxi," Tilly said. She wrapped her mother in her shawl, tucked a patchwork quilt over her knees, and went to open the front door, collecting her own warm shawl on the way. She opened the door, an admonition about being late as usual on her lips, and gasped.

It was not Lem Turkle who stood there, but Albert Budd in full evening dress. She gaped at him openmouthed, from the diamond studs in his dress shirt to the tips of his patent-leather dancing pumps.

"I've come to apologize," Albert said. "I'm sorry I was so churlish this morning. I have no excuse. Will you forgive me?"

"Well . . . sure," Tilly said. She wasn't one to carry grudges—at least, not this one. Her romantic memories of Albert had been forever buried during her time under the dryer that afternoon, and she'd felt a great relief. She certainly had never expected to see him again. Recovering herself, she said, "We were just going to the Howl—I thought you were the taxi."

"I took the liberty of sending Mr. Turkle on to his next fare," Albert said. "I hope you don't mind. Jeffries will take charge of your mother's chair—there is plenty of room."

Tilly glanced beyond his shoulder and saw a uniformed chauffeur standing on the steps and beyond him, at the curb, a huge black stretch limousine.

"Well, I . . . I . . . " Behind her she heard a squeak. Turning, she discovered her mother had managed to roll her chair to the door—a feat of considerable determination on her part. Curiosity had both impelled and propelled her—and now she was glaring at Albert. She looked cross. "Mother, you remember Albert, don't you?"

Her mother's lip curled.

Albert smiled. "I know you must still be angry at me for

deserting Tilly the way I did, Mrs. Moss. I do understand. Won't you let me make up for it, now?" He stood aside to display the chauffeur and the limo. Mrs. Moss's lip uncurled as her mouth dropped open.

"I told you, Mother," Tilly said through clenched teeth. "I *told* you he was . . . different."

Mrs. Moss managed a simper, Tilly managed a smile, Albert managed a wink at Tilly, and Jeffries managed the wheelchair down the stairs. He lifted Mrs. Moss into the front passenger seat as gently and easily as if she had been a costumed doll. He was young and handsome, and as Tilly climbed onto the backseat, she reckoned he was going to break at least a dozen hearts in the next few hours. The girls of Blackwater Bay had never seen anything like *him* before, that was for sure.

While Jeffries folded the wheelchair and stowed it in the luggage compartment, Tilly and Albert settled themselves on the backseat, for all the world like a Victorian couple ensconced in a brougham. He proffered a nosegay, done in antique style. "You mentioned your choice of costume," he said. "I told the florist to make up something that would be suitable."

Tilly accepted the flowers. "Listen, Albert—"

"No, you listen first," he interrupted in a quiet voice. "After you left I went back to my roses. But something happened to me." He turned to face her. "I felt *lonely* after you left, Tilly. It was a shock. I haven't felt lonely for years and years. But seeing you again brought back memories of what my life used to be like when I lived here."

Tilly wanted to believe him, but his voice was almost *too* winsome. "You didn't like it enough to stay," she reminded him.

"No, but I see now that it would have been much better if I had taken you with me. That was my real mistake, not leaving." He sighed heavily. "However, that is what I did, and I have had to live with the consequences. Anyway, you might have changed if you'd gone with me, Tilly. Mightn't you?"

She heard the plea in his voice, the wish to have his selfish cruelty excused on the grounds that he had left her unspoiled and pristine, a far, far better thing than he actually had done.

"Oh, sure," she said with heavy irony. "I might have stayed thin and had lots of beautiful clothes to wear, I might have gotten an education, I might have traveled all over the world, I might have met lots of interesting people, I might have——"

"All right, all right," he said sharply. "Mea culpa."

She relented—blame was not her style. "All right, so you felt lonely. But what a night to pick for your return."

He brightened. "Ah, but that was what tipped the scale. What a night indeed! Everybody here, in festive mood, full of fun and happiness——"

She managed not to snort. "Full of hell, you mean. My God, you have a lousy memory. Don't you remember this is the time for practical jokes and pranks and all kinds of mischief?"

"I do," he said gravely. "Shake hands, Tilly." He reached for her hand and took it, giving her a jolt with a hand buzzer. She squealed and snatched her hand back. "We stopped at a joke shop on the way. I came prepared," he said, smirking.

"Hmmph," she said, rubbing her hand. "You only think you did."

Jeffries had apparently been given prior instructions, for they were now pulling up at the high school parking lot. Beyond the wire fence that encircled the athletic field lay the bright and beckoning lights of the festival. The high narrow circle of the Big Wheel turned against the sky, the merry-go-round was a striated whirl of colored lights, and the rising and falling arms of the Octopus carried a waving load of celebrants. Already screams and shrieks could be heard above the cacophony of music and mechanical clacks and clatters as various indecencies were committed between not necessarily consenting adults. Jeffries stopped the car.

"Ummm—I don't think you should park here," Tilly said, only too aware of the effect a Rolls-Royce limo would have on the local lads—especially after a few beers.

"No, we won't. Jeffries will drop us here and then whiz the car back to the hotel garage, where I am assured it will be watched."

"Assured by who?"

"Archy Ventnor, of course."

"Ha—you'll be lucky to still *have* a car by morning. Archy is one of the worst."

"I said I would sue him if anything happened to the car, purely as a point of law. My lawyers could outlast his lawyers any day in court, of course."

"Mmmm—well, that *might* do it," Tilly conceded. "As long as he stays sober, that is."

"Cars can be replaced," Albert said calmly. "People can be replaced, too. If he causes trouble, I'll simply buy his damned hotel and burn it down."

Tilly glanced at him. That sounded more like the Albert she'd encountered in the rose garden. The reason he'd given for coming back tonight had not convinced her—but the bitter undertone in his voice did. He had his reasons, even if they were not the ones he gave her. She was merely serving as expedient camouflage, a bridge between Albert and old friends. She gave a mental shrug. It was more interesting than most of the things that happened to her these days. Why not?

"Come along, let's join the festivities," Albert said with grim determination. Whatever he had in mind, he'd had to brace himself for it.

Jeffries produced the wheelchair and decanted Mrs. Moss into it, then drove slowly away, having arranged to meet them by the merry-go-round in fifteen minutes. As she straightened her mother's costume, Tilly looked up into Albert's face and gave him one last chance. "Are you sure you want to do this tonight?"

"Absolutely positive," Albert said briskly, and taking hold of Mrs. Moss's wheelchair handles, he proceeded to sail majestically into the heart of the Howl. "Tonight's the *only* night it would work," he said over his shoulder.

Tilly stared after him. Now what the hell did he mean by that? she wondered.

Dominic had practically given up when he finally spotted Emily Gibbons going past him on the merry-go-round. Risking life and all limbs, he leaped onto the platform and made his way toward her, much to the annoyance of the operator, who yelled something pithy about breaking his goddamn neck.

"Hi," Dominic said, his head going up and down synchronously with Emily's rise and fall.

Emily, who had been searching the crowd as she circled, gave a start and gazed down at what should have been Prince Charming but was, in fact, Robin Hood. Close enough, she thought, and gave him her most devastating smile.

As Dominic had not reappeared in the *Chronicle* office, and since she fully intended to find out why he was interested in Jacky Morgan's death (a comprehensive perusal of the pages he'd wanted photocopied had easily produced a correlation that triggered her reporter's instinct), she was very glad to see him. If there were additional and more personal reasons why she longed to gaze again upon his broken nose and firm young body, she would have admitted it to no one.

Now, here he was, looking up at her with every evidence of devotion—or, at the very least, lust. This made him putty in a reporter's hands. Further, having gazed upon, dated, and rejected most of the available male population of Blackwater and its environs, Emily saw in Dominic the possibility not only of news, but of destiny. For despite all her attempts at becoming a hard-nosed newshoundette, the truth was that at heart Emily Gibbons was a hopeless romantic. Dominic Pritchard's appearance first in town, then in the *Chronicle* office, and now here on the platform of the merry-go-round satisfied all her requirements for the way love's young dream should proceed.

But there was an imperfection.

Although he looked rather dashing taken overall, Dominic's false mustache was curling up at one end thanks to some rather elderly glue. It spoiled Emily's idea of how participants in romantic trysts should appear. Ever a creature of impulse, she leaned down and tried to smooth it back into place. Unfortunately, the rise of her flying horse at that particular juncture caused her inadvertently to grasp the mustache, ripping it off.

"Ouch!" Dominic yelled—the glue hadn't been *that* elderly.

"Oh, God, I'm sorry," Emily said.

"No, you're not," Dominic grumbled, rubbing his upper lip.

"I am too," she snapped. "I *meant* to smooth it down."

"I can twirl my own mustache, thank you," he huffed. "Well, I could when I *had* one."

She handed him the strip of gauze and false hair. As she was still rising and falling, he had to make several passes at it before it was in his grasp. "I really am sorry," she said in a very contrite tone.

He gazed up—and down—and up at her. She was dressed as Carmen Miranda, and the tower of artificial mixed fruit on her head was extremely becoming, as was the frilled and flounced dress below it. She had wonderful shoulders.

"I was wondering—before you assaulted me—whether you would—" Dominic began.

"It was an accident," she interrupted coolly, going down.

"Whatever—could we—"

"I wouldn't want you to think I am in the habit of—" Up.

"Look, couldn't we—"

"—causing pain to people I hardly know." Down.

"I've never been to a Howl—"

"I didn't *ask* you to jump onto this thing." Up.

"The other day in the—"

"There are plenty of people I'd rather talk to." Down.

Dominic was beginning to feel sick, what with going around and around and Emily going up and down and the feather in his hat tickling him on the back of his neck. Desperation, frustration, and nausea led him, as usual, astray.

"I think you should know I intend to marry you!" he shouted at the very moment the merry-go-round and its wheezy music stopped. His words seemed to echo out into the night. Several people turned. Somebody laughed. The proprietor of the merry-go-round, who had been on the verge of demanding a fare from Dominic, halted, hovered, and then retired. He, too, was a romantic—and this kind of thing was good for business.

Emily's horse, by chance, had stopped at a point when her eyes were perfectly level with Dominic's. They gazed at one another for a long time.

"I intend to have a career in journalism," she said.

"I have no objection to that."

"I refuse to iron shirts."

"We'll send them out."

"I have expensive tastes."

"You can pay for those yourself."

"I like junk food."

"We'll take out extra medical insurance."

"My favorite color is puce."

"The hell it is."

"This is totally ridiculous."

"I am aware of that."

"*You* are totally ridiculous."

"I'm not the one with fruit on my head."

Emily hopped down off the horse and took his arm.

"I thought you'd never ask," she said mildly, and led him off the platform and out into the Howl.

Harry Foskett, in his guise as official Howl photographer, was doing his best to light up the night. Cameras and electronic flash at the ready, he was circulating through the crowd, dutifully immortalizing the efforts of the citizens of Blackwater Bay to be the worst-/best-costumed person in town.

He caught all kinds of people in all kinds of situations, some of which were printable in the *Chronicle* and many of which were not. Harry was discreet. He knew his neighbors and what was fit to print. On the other hand, Harry the newly emergent photographic artiste ("hanging in a goddamned art gallery, for crying out loud!" he had bragged to his cronies) would *never* throw anything away again. Creative dreams of photomontages, meaningful distortions, impressionistic blurs, and insights into personality by the use of uncompromising closeups danced in his head. And so he went his way, snapping and snapping.

He caught Nell Norton just as she sprayed Harriet Crabbe with the purple dye that Fred Boyle had concocted for her, and he caught Fred Boyle completely shrouded in special-effects sticky cobwebbing that Archy Ventnor had gone all the way to Cleveland to buy. Fred did not look happy—but then, Fred never did.

He caught Emily Gibbons in the warm embrace of one Robin Hood behind the hot-dog stand, then caught several *more* Robin Hoods engaged in various other activities. There were an awful lot of Robin Hoods at the Howl—all inspired, no doubt, by the film that had been held over in town for six weeks that summer.

In contrast to many of the others, however, Peter Dill's Robin Hood costume was extremely detailed, and Fred took several snaps of him. Dill or his wife had obviously done a lot of research, and he looked amazingly authentic, even down to the shortbow slung over his shoulder and the quiver of real arrows beside it. But all the effort was somewhat in vain, as he was probably the first Robin Hood in history to be walking on crutches—had he tripped over a root in Sherwood Forest? Harry wondered. Mrs. Dill looked very uncomfortable posing beside her husband as Maid Marian, especially as she kept checking her wristwatch every few moments, rather undermining the antique illusion of her costume, which was otherwise impeccable. As always.

Harry thanked them for posing and hurried on to the rifle-shoot booth, where he furtively snapped Nonie Peach gazing at Jack Fanshawe with considerable longing. Jack (dressed as the sheik of Araby) was trying to win a teddy bear for Mitzi Putnam (costumed as a fluffy baby chick), and the flash of Harry's camera spoiled his aim. Mitzi pouted and Jack told Harry to shoot somewhere else, please. Also caught in the flash was Clarence Toogood, standing behind Nonie in a hurriedly assembled Roman costume (Mrs. Peach's second-best tablecloth plus a circle of fake laurel that was raising a rash on his forehead) and looking with intense interest at the retreating Dills.

As Harry moved on through the crowd, he caught sight of Blackwater Bay's ultimate summer visitors—the Adcocks. They had been returning annually for as long as he could remember: mother, father (both teachers), and two daughters. They were so familiar to everyone that they would almost have been considered locals, if it weren't for one outstanding familial characteristic. Each season, without fail, they arrived

displaying total devotion to some new craze—eating only
raw vegetables one year, speaking only Urdu the next. Last
summer it had been cycling, and they had been ubiquitous in
parrot-bright cycling gear, gravely pedaling everywhere on a
pair of tandems.

Now here they were again—on an off-season visit. Harry
stared. Instead of wearing a bizarre and colorful costume like
all the other local celebrants, the Adcocks were dressed in
dark three-piece suits, white shirts, and silk four-in-hand ties.
The father's piercing eyes looked out from under an impeccable homburg, and the mother wore a Borsalino tilted at exactly the right angle. The two daughters looked equally
formal in tidy school blazers. Each wore a red carnation in
their buttonholes.

It was a perfect disguise.

Harry took eight separate shots, because otherwise nobody
would have believed him, and then moved on.

From behind the ticket booth he photographed George
Putnam twirling his French police baton and knocking Councilman Berringer in the ear with it, and he caught Matt
Gabriel with his mouth unbecomingly full of Nell Norton's
best oatmeal-and-raisin cookies. He thought both shots were
definite "musts" for the *Chronicle*'s center spread.

After failing to ring the bell on the Test Your Strength machine, Harry snapped Margaret Toby dressed as the Patchwork Girl of Oz selling a drunkard's path quilt to Fran
Robinson, who was, in turn, dressed as Baby Snooks—short
skirt, pinafore, knee socks, outsized hairbow, and all. Nice
ankles, he noted.

Larry Lovich and Freddy Tollett cut a wide swath as
Tweedledum and Tweedledee, with blue satin shorts, red-
and-white-striped shirts, and little school caps—just as in the
Tenniel illustrations. The fact that they were padded out as
round as balls and walked everywhere arm in arm, in perfect
unison, meant they needed plenty of room for maneuver. It
also meant he couldn't get both of them in the frame at once.

From a high seat on a momentarily halted Big Wheel, he
photographed an odd trio with his telephoto lens—Dr. Dan
Rogers dressed as an accident victim (*very* realistic), arguing
with Tyrone Molt (who was, as always, dressed as Tyrone

Molt) and Mayor Atwater, who was dressed as Tarzan (who else?).

While standing behind the cotton candy machine, he snapped Mrs. Atwater, who was supposedly overseeing the homemade preserves stand, calmly knitting something very small while two teenage hoodlums dressed as teenage hoodlums shoplifted five jars of strawberry jam from under her unaware nose.

After changing films behind the first-aid tent, he caught Dolly Boot, Blackwater's finest madam (costumed as a Puritan maid—a novel variation on cross-dressing, he thought), having a deeply absorbing conversation with a gorilla who turned out to be Carl Putnam, perspiring so heavily that he had to lift his mask now and then in order to breathe.

He caught Don Robinson disguised as the king of Bohemia, followed by his pretty daughter, Debbie, dressed as a princess in pink satin and lace, her long red hair topped with a glittering tiara. In case any of the local boys got the idea she could be whisked away by some Prince Charming, however, she was flanked on either side by her two large brothers, Donnie and Richard, who wore suitably intimidating gear—one Rambo, one Terminator.

Harry wondered briefly if Debbie really wanted all that protection, for she had a merry eye and looked ready for mischief. He made a bet with himself about how long it would take her to escape her myrmidons—after all, it was the Howl. He heard a growl behind him—Mona Pickering giving a good imitation of a prowling tiger. Through the open flap of the dance tent he saw Daria Shanks glittering through an impromptu Charleston, partnered by a surprisingly agile Isaiah Naseem, just recognizable under his Frankenstein costume.

He was, as they say, overwhelmed by choice, and had only a few hours to photograph the normally respectable citizens of Blackwater, Lemonville, Hatchville, Peskett, Larchmont, Oscogee, and points between, all let loose under a witch's moon.

And then he caught sight of Albert Budd.

14

"*I* don't believe it!" Harry Foskett exclaimed.

Albert turned and scowled.

"I *do* believe it," Harry said, and raised his camera, fully expecting Albert to dash it from his hands, as was the millionaire's reputed wont with unwanted intruders into his privacy.

But Albert smiled.

Harry, having snapped several frames, lowered the camera and stared at his quarry. Albert Budd cut a striking figure beside Tilly Moss and the handsome but somberly uniformed chauffeur who was propelling Mrs. Moss's wheelchair. Albert's bald head and expanded waist seemed to suit him better than the red curls and athletic form of his youth. In fact, Harry decided, he bore a startling resemblance to Daddy Warbucks as portrayed by Albert Finney. Perhaps there was something about being called Albert that lent them a similar distinction.

Then doubt began to creep into Harry's mind. Albert Budd was *supposed* to be a bad-tempered recluse, walled in by money and inaccessible to all. This guy was smiling. Was it some kind of Howler that Tilly was playing on everybody? He wouldn't put it past her—Tilly, for all her good humor, was a bit of a dark horse.

"It is Albert Budd, isn't it?" he asked cautiously. "Blackwater Bay's only famous son after Cecil G. Heckman?"

"No," said Albert. "It's Al Budd, who used to sit behind you in grade school, you dumb ox. Have you graduated yet?"

"Oh, hell, yes," said Harry, relieved. "Last June."

They slapped each other on the back and shoulders for a while, as Tilly looked on. She was growing a little weary of this ritual, which had been repeated time after time as they'd walked through the Howl, looking at the various stands, games, and contests. Albert would recognize or be recognized by some old crony, and there would have to be the game of back slapping and shoulder pounding and exclaiming, a brief exchange of information followed by promises to meet and talk soon, and then they would continue on. Standing close to him, Tilly could see the perspiration on his upper lip and sense the tension in his body. Albert was not enjoying himself. Why was he doing it?

Matt, seeing the moving knot of people, walked over to see what the fuss was about. This time Albert had been stopped by Dan Rogers, who was giving him a quizzical once-over

"Too many late nights and fatty foods, not enough roughage," was his considered medical opinion, delivered with a wave of his "bloodied" and bandaged arms. "What happened to all that red hair you used to have?"

"The same thing that happened to most of the brown hair *you* used to have," Albert countered. "And you're not looking very healthy yourself, at the moment. You crash your car on the way over or what?" There was a gasp from someone nearby.

Dr. Rogers was unperturbed. "Actually, this costume is supposed to be an accurate depiction of a man who has been attacked by werewolves. What do you think?"

"I know just how he felt," Albert said. "Only most of the wolves I've met up with were on Wall Street."

Tilly gazed around at the crowd, caught Matt's eye, and made her way to his side.

"Sorry I couldn't catch up with you this afternoon," Tilly said. "I was late for my hair appointment."

"I got your note," Matt said. "I never realized you brought him back with you."

"I didn't. After the talk we had, I never thought he'd show

up in Blackwater again. It's a real turnaround." She described her interview with Albert. "We didn't exactly part on the best of terms," she concluded, then lowered her voice as much as she could over the noise of the rides and games. "But he did say one thing that might be important."

"Oh?"

"Yes—he said there were girls there that night."

Matt was startled. "Girls?" he demanded. "What girls?"

"Shhh—I don't know. When I asked for names he got all vague and changed the subject. Is it important?"

"I'm sure it is," Matt said.

Albert had begun to move through the crowd again; Jeffries was following alongside, pushing Mrs. Moss, who was looking a bit overexcited.

"I think I'd better get back to Mother," Tilly said in a worried voice. "I'll try to get him to be a bit more specific, but it's kind of difficult to work it into the conversation. If I find out any more, I'll call you tomorrow, okay?"

"Fine," Matt agreed—there was little else he could do under the circumstances. He looked at Albert Budd and wondered. If he had fought coming back all this time, why come back at all? And why now? Why tonight?

"Matt?"

He turned around, startled, and found himself confronted by Robin Hood on crutches. "Looking for Little John?" he asked Peter Dill.

"No—for you," Dill said. He seemed edgy, eyeing Albert Budd and the crowd of cronies around him uneasily. "I wanted to tell you something. I don't know if you'll want to take any action about it—I don't really have any proof—"

"Let me worry about proving it, you just—"

"Maybe we could talk later," Dill said hurriedly as Albert and the others started toward them. "Or tomorrow? We could talk tomorrow, after all this is over."

"Fine with me," Matt said, not wanting to push Dill too far. He hoped whatever the bank manager had to say would be the breakthrough he was waiting for concerning the death of Jacky Morgan. Dill certainly looked worried. He watched the man stump off on his crutches, bending down to hear what his wife was saying. She was pointing to her watch. They made an odd pair.

Daria came back to Matt. She had been trying her luck at pumpkin carving. "Well," she said, "I might have been artistically trained, but it's of absolutely no help at all when it comes to a knife and a squash. It's a wonder I still have a thumb left."

"Did you hurt yourself?" Matt asked, worry about her distracting him from further conjecture about Peter Dill.

She held up a bandaged hand. "Just a scratch. I had it looked at in the first-aid tent. For them it was pretty mild—they actually had a kid in there with a lobster clamped to his nose. Apparently somebody put the thing into one of the apple-dunking buckets."

"I believe it," Matt said. "Tonight I believe anything."

"It's a madhouse all right." Daria laughed. "I haven't seen such a wild variety of costumes and things to eat since my last Greenwich Village party. It's great."

"Yeah," Matt said dourly. "Almost like old times."

"Oh, pooh. You should have come as Grumpy, one of the seven dwarfs, instead of a gendarme."

"Come on," Matt said, looking down from his six feet four inches. "Can you honestly see me as a dwarf?"

She tilted her head to one side. "I have to admit, it would be a feat of engineering," she conceded. "But I don't mind trying to cut you down to size."

"Now wait a minute—" he said as she began to advance on him with a certain mischief in her eye.

"You'd better win me something wonderful in the next five minutes," Daria warned, "or you're in trouble, Grumpy."

They moved off into the crowd.

"I can get you a great deal on a Rolls-Royce," Tyrone Molt was saying to Albert as Tilly returned to his side.

"Thanks," Albert said. "But I already have two here, and another at my place in Florida."

"Still buying things three at a time, hey, Albert?" It was Fred Boyle, trailing cobwebs.

"Fred?" Albert seemed genuinely astonished. "What the blue hell are *you* still doing in Blackwater?"

"Teaching chemistry at the high school," Boyle said. "What else?"

"What else? Why, anything else. I thought you'd have set up your own laboratory by now," Albert said.

Boyle shrugged. "Well, you know how it is—"

"No, I don't," Albert said, looking blank. "After all, you didn't *have* to stay here. Why, with what you made on that last deal alone you could have—"

Fred was peeling cobwebs from his face. "My wife died last year," he said in a flat tone.

Albert's face fell. "Oh, I see. I'm sorry, Fred, I didn't know."

"No reason why you should," Boyle said shortly, and turned away, trailing gray swathes.

"We should talk," Albert called after him. Fred waved a webby arm and disappeared around the fortune-teller's tent.

Albert was looking at Tilly. "I don't understand—"

"He's still grieving," Tilly said. "Everybody makes allowances for him—he'll get over it soon."

"Jesus—Albert?" It was Granger Gibbons's turn to be astonished. As his reporter daughter was nowhere to be seen, it had fallen to him as editor of the *Chronicle* to cover the big news story of the week, which was patently no longer the Howl, but instead the return of the prodigal millionaire. "What the devil are *you* doing here?"

And so it continued, wherever they went. Jeffries's handsome face never changed expression as he pushed Mrs. Moss along over the beaten-down grass of the field. Mrs. Moss clearly loved being the off center of attention, but Tilly soon tired of the fuss and the inescapable feeling that Albert was enjoying his "royal progress" through the festival grounds a little too much. While on the one hand it was pleasant to be part of a parade, she found herself overhearing whispered questions as people speculated on Albert's sudden return, why she was at Albert's side, and what it all meant. She didn't know what it meant, and that made her uneasy.

Finally she made an excuse about nose powdering and escaped toward the toilet tent. There she encountered Nonie Peach, who was trying to repair her makeup in a tiny mirror. Nonie's costume was very revealing—but what it mostly revealed was a considerable vista of goosepimples. And Nonie was not happy.

"Did you *see* that Mitzi Putnam, hanging around Jack Fanshawe like a coat on a rack?" she demanded of Tilly. "Isn't she satisfied with catching *one* rich man?"

Tilly was sympathetic. After all, she too had once fancied her chances with Jack Fanshawe—before reality set in. Nonie, however, still lived partly in this world and partly in the fantasy world her mother wove so gently and inescapably around her. Not that Mrs. Peach did it intentionally—far from it. was just that the scent of magnolias and gracious living seemed to emanate from her, engulfing her large and rather ungainly daughter in one or two dreams too many. It had always seemed strange to Tilly that in Nonie Peach there seemed to exist two people—Nonie the accountant, clear-sighted and practical, and Nonie the fey, who took every opportunity to wallow in her own fertile imagination.

"At least Jack Fanshawe is single," Tilly said mildly. "Carl Putnam was still married when she set her sights on him."

"Oh, she doesn't want to marry Jack," Nonie snapped. "Just drain his crankcase a little. The bleached bitch."

"Dear me," Tilly said, amused. Nonie glared at her, then managed a weak grin.

"Oh, all right, I'm being stupid and I know it."

"Well, that's better than believing it," Tilly acknowledged. "Can I borrow your mirror for a minute, please?"

"Sure." Nonie handed it over, taking in the unusual sparkle in Tilly's eyes. "Is that really Albert Budd who keeps grabbing your hand?"

Tilly felt herself blushing. She looked at Nonie and suddenly had an image of the two of them standing there while other women swished past them to and from the cubicles. Most of the women attending the Howl were either young and giddy or older and wiser—yet there they stood together, the two of them, plump middle-aged spinsters, speculating on possibilities that were really impossibilities dressed up for Halloween.

"Yes," Tilly admitted. "And who is the bouncy little guy who keeps following you around?"

Nonie was dismissive. "Oh, that's only Clarence Too-good."

"And who is Clarence Toogood?" Tilly persisted.

Nonie started to answer, then paused. "You know, aside from the fact that he's rooming with us and writing a book, I haven't the vaguest idea *who* he is."

"Or what he might be?"

"Or what he might be. I never thought about it before."

"Well, maybe you should," Tilly said, glad to divert any further questions about Albert Budd.

Nonie stared at her. "You mean—he might be danger-ous?"

Tilly handed back her mirror. "Well, you never know," she said mysteriously, and escaped back into the night. At least Nonie Peach would now stop thinking about Jack Fan-shawe and start worrying about somebody else, she thought. Do her good.

Tyrone Molt stood beside the popcorn stand, watching Al-bert Budd moving around the grounds. He belched and turned to find Fred Boyle beside him. "What the hell *is* that stuff all over you?" Molt demanded. "You look like some kind of walking fungus."

Boyle peeled off a few more strands. Underneath the man-tle of gray-white webs there was just visible his original Robin Hood costume. "I don't know, but I plan to analyze it tomorrow," he said, holding up a piece against the lights of the popcorn machine. He continued peeling for a moment, then stopped. "Oh, the hell with it—I'll pretend to be Robin Hood come back from the dead."

"A novel approach," Molt said.

"Too many Robin Hoods as it is," Boyle continued. "Haven't you noticed?"

"There does seem to be a lot of green men," Molt agreed. "There also seems to be a lot of Albert Budd."

Boyle said nothing.

"He's a smart one, though," Molt went on, envy tightening his voice. "Parlayed that furniture polish recipe of his old lady's into millions. Lucky bastard."

"He didn't do it alone," Boyle grumbled.

Molt looked at him. "What do you mean?"

"I helped him adapt that formula," Boyle said.

"No kidding?" Molt said without conviction. Boyle had been prone to exaggerate his accomplishments ever since he was a kid, but he was harmless. "He pay you for it?"

"Oh, yeah, he paid me," Boyle said. "And he made me sign papers, too. Papers I was too young and dumb to realize cut my share down to a token few bucks now and again. I thought he was just blowing smoke, talking big. He wasn't any better than me, just a Blackwater bum like me, how was *I* to know he'd make a million, for crying out loud? If I'd been smarter and gotten some decent advice, I'd have been rich like him. Then maybe Maryam wouldn't have—"

"We all miss chances," Molt interrupted before Boyle could start in yet again on his wife's death. "We all make wrong moves."

"Yeah, sure," Boyle said bitterly.

"Look at Tom Finnegan, for instance," Molt went on. "One wrong move and he went straight into a tree!" He laughed loudly, then cut it short, becoming suddenly serious. "You got to go careful in this town, Boyle," he observed heavily. "Maybe that's why Albert Budd got out and stayed out. Now he's back, wrapped in money like he thinks it would protect him. Well, if you ask me, he's acting very dumb. *Very* stupid. You aren't the only one's got reason to hate him." He extracted a cigar from his jacket pocket and stripped the cellophane, then bit off and spat out the end. "Smoke?" he asked, reaching for another.

"No thanks." Boyle glanced at him as the big man replaced the proffered cigar and blew fat blue smoke rings toward the full moon that had just risen. The smoke carried with it a strong odor of cheap whiskey—the only kind Molt ever drank. "Ever heard of spontaneous combustion?" Boyle asked with a sneer.

"Yeah," Molt said, unperturbed. "Aren't they that rock group started up over in Hatchville last year?"

The Howl—or, to put it officially, the Blackwater Bay Harvest and Halloween Festival—had been opened at seven o'clock by the mayor, who had made a lusty speech about

Having Fun Safely and Being Kind to One Another that ful-
filled all of Sheriff Matt Gabriel's requirements without convincing anyone. Even as the mayor spoke, there were many
in his restless audience turning over plans they fully intended
to put into effect at the first opportunity—plans that required
darkness and stealth and imagination.

Some of these eager souls had already slipped away during the evening to set up their Howlers. As most of the
townspeople were at the festival, leaving the town populated
mainly by sleeping children and baby-sitters, and since the
shadows between the houses were somehow deepened by
their contrast with the brightness of the festival lights, it was
the perfect time.

In one sense, it was with each victim's tacit permission
that all these pranks were perpetrated. Those who did not
want to risk it could perfectly well stay at home—but they
didn't. In another sense it was seen as a kind of compliment
if somebody went to a lot of trouble to, say, plant three hundred plastic daffodils on your lawn or to invisibly lard the
kindling in your fireplace with firecrackers.

Many upon whom these unkindnesses were visited would
call it only justice, having perpetrated their own pranks
meanwhile. Some would grumble, some would swear, some
would vow revenge, and some would just laugh themselves
silly.

But none of them would be really surprised.

It was the Howl. It was tradition. It was just one of the
things that set Blackwater apart from ordinary places.

There were others.

The annual fireworks display was scheduled to begin at
eight-thirty. Long before that, people began to settle down
into the bleachers that lined the long sides of the athletic
field. Many of them had brought picnic meals from home;
others had collected various edible items from the booths
that encircled the central area of the festival. Nell Norton's
cookies and cakes had been sold out by eight, as had Roy
Antonio's pizza slices, May Berringer's sandwiches, and
Harriet Crabbe's homemade ginger ale. Other foods on offer
ranged from Tex-Mex burritos to Chinese noodles, and the

exotic aromas from the various stands plus the heartier smells of coffee and hamburgers from the main food tent combined to make the Howl a treat for the nose as well as the eyes and ears.

The powerful lights that normally lit the field for football in winter and baseball in summer shone down on the whirling, coruscating colored lights of the rides and the glowing yellow lights of the hurricane lamps and jack-o'-lanterns that illuminated individual stands. On the northern end of the field dark shadows could be seen, moving around large, peculiarly shaped structures as the professionals hired for the occasion prepared to set off the fireworks display.

George Putnam was watching the fireworks men, fending off people—particularly children—whose curiosity drew them too close. He had been in his element as the Howl progressed. Many young women had complimented him on his "new uniform," and Molly Turkle had made a suggestion for mutual activities they might indulge in later on. She did this in broken French that owed nothing to Mrs. Dutton's high school lessons. George had been wanting to slip away to find a French/English dictionary ever since, but there hadn't been an opportunity. Her tone had pretty well conveyed the message, however, and he was looking forward to their assignation, scheduled for midnight.

He hoped Matt wouldn't notice his absence.

He hoped even more that it wasn't a Howler.

But then, Molly had owed him revenge for the past three years and hadn't taken it yet. The tension of wondering whether she was setting him up for a fall was both terrible and wonderful, but mostly terrible. Molly might have hair as shiny as midnight and eyes as blue as a kingfisher's wing, but she was a Turkle, after all. She might even have invited an audience.

"How's it going, George?" asked a gorilla, looming up out of the darkness.

George, after a moment's unease, recognized his father's voice. "Okay—so far."

"You're right to be cautious—it's a weird night."

"Cautious isn't halfway good enough. It's going to be a real bitch tonight." He told Carl some of the things they'd already had to investigate, including the greening of Jack Fanshawe's office. "I kind of wondered whether that one was you."

Carl took off his gorilla mask and wiped his forehead with a hairy forearm. "Not guilty," he said. "Although I wish I'd thought of it. No, it's his turn this year. Last year I broke into his office and replaced his desk calendar with one from the year before. It was one of those that you flip over a page each day? I copied all his notes for appointments, very carefully—you know how good I am at forging things."

"It's always worried me," George said wryly.

"Yeah, well—I didn't start it on November first—he would have noticed that right away. No, I replaced the pages starting a week later. It's easy to do because Saturday and Sunday are on the same page, and most people flip them over without really looking. After that the *days* made sense, but the dates were wrong. Took him a week to discover it." Carl started to laugh. "He got into one hell of an argument with some mortgage broker over in Hatchville and nearly lost a sale." He sighed. "So I will be very careful tonight when I go home, and when I go into the office on Monday. I don't know what he's got planned, but it will be good."

"Guess you and I don't have the same definition of 'good,'" George said.

Carl raised an eyebrow. "You sound glum, chum. Problems?"

George shrugged his shoulders, gazing at the crowd, then glanced sideways at his father. "The name Jacky Morgan mean anything to you?"

Carl seemed startled. "That's the second time this evening somebody's asked me that."

"Well?"

"Old news. Bad news. Jacky was a kid I knew who died when I was younger than you are, must be thirty years ago, now."

"Thirty-one," George said.

Carl frowned. "Why are you asking me if you already know about it?"

George shrugged again. "Something Tom Finnegan said before he died has spooked Matt. He hasn't talked much about it to me, but he's *thinking* about it."

Carl, too, gazed out at the crowd. "Matt's a thinker all right. Works things out."

"Yeah." George shifted his baton from one hand to the other. "Does that worry you?"

Carl didn't speak for a long time. "No," he finally said. He looked into his son's face. "Does it worry *you?*"

"I don't know," George admitted. "Some things worry me a lot. Like why you married her." He nodded toward Mitzi, who was waving at them from beside the bleachers.

"Don't I have a right to be happy?" Carl asked. "She makes me feel young again."

"But for how long?" George burst out suddenly. "Eventually she's going to make you feel a hell of a lot *older.* Then what?"

Carl looked at Mitzi, then looked away. "I'll tell you something, George. Everything has a price. You look at what you want, and you decide if you're willing to pay."

"But you have to pay *sometime,*" George said.

"Yes."

"And Jacky Morgan? What about that? What was the price on that?"

Carl's eyes met his son's. "I don't know the final cost, George. All I know is, I'm still paying it."

"You want to tell me about it?" George asked, not really wanting to know, not ever wanting to know.

Carl shook his head. "You can't afford it, son." And Carl loped away, his neat gray-blond head looking small and odd above the hairy bulk of the gorilla costume. From under his arm the scowling gorilla mask glared back at George.

The fireworks were spectacular and very, very noisy.

In a pretended ecstasy of fear, Emily clung to Dominic's arm every time one of the big bangers went off and oohed and ahhed with the best of them when the spangles and colored stars curved up and flowered out against the night sky, making even the moon look a little dull by comparison. They had spent the past hours walking and talking, and although nothing was ever mentioned about Dominic's outburst concerning marriage, the knowledge that it had been said was within them.

They would see.

Meanwhile, there were all the discoveries of one another to be made. And all the arguments to enjoy. Because whatever the physical attraction between them, it was already clear that conversational sparks could fly when least expected. It wouldn't be an easy relationship, but—like the fireworks—it would add a certain spectacle to their lives for as long as the romance lasted—which could be for a week or forever.

When the display was over, the crowd surged down off the bleachers toward the parking lot. Families with children usually went home now, leaving the "grown-ups" to continue the revels. The rides were still operating, there were craft stalls and game booths to explore, and the main food tent was still serving beer and hot dogs and other indigestibles.

And, of course, it was now that the canoodling would start.

Emily wasn't certain that Dominic quite understood about "canoodling." She had tried to explain about how kissing (at the very least) during the Howl didn't count, but she hadn't put too strong an emphasis on it. After all, she had noticed some of her friends giving Dominic the eye when they went past, and she knew they would all be out for what time they could make with him—especially since she hadn't publicly declared her proprietary interest yet. So when they became separated in the crowd, she grew a little alarmed. Not a lot—just enough to be excited.

She thought back to what they had said earlier. Was it to be the Big Wheel next? She thought that was what he had said, but it could have been that he absolutely hated the Big Wheel. There was so much noise, half the time they hadn't been able to hear one another properly. Maybe it was a ride through the Bonechiller. Yes, that was it!

She headed toward the ghoulish tunnel that had been constructed around the southern perimeter of the festival. A trip through the Bonechiller was definitely what they had planned to do next.

Emily felt a shiver of delight and anticipation go through her. She just *loved* being scared to death.

15

The proprietor of the Bonechiller was a lanky, slightly wall-eyed man named Milt Bickerstaff. He was justly proud of his variation of the classic Ghost Train. The Bonechiller was more than that old snake-and-spider ride. It had taken him years to design and perfect, and it was the star attraction of the carnival—as usual. Everywhere he took it the lines were long, as giggling and pale-faced people waited to be scared half to death and back. He had done many years apprenticeship in various carnivals and fairs around the country. He had learned early that people—especially courting couples and teenagers—loved to be scared. Hence the success of horror films like *Friday the 13th*.

He had learned a lot from those, too—how to create life-like monsters and mutations displaying the grotesque wounds and deformities that would chill the blood, freeze the marrow, and probably stunt the growth. He spent his nights studying manuals and drawing up plans for his baby, his own beautiful creation. It had taken all his savings to build and required a day and a half to set up at each venue. Everything was computerized and so complex that it needed its own generator to power all the mechanical horrors that fell, leapt out, dangled, tickled, and generally terrified the passengers on the little train that passed through it.

The Bonechiller was indeed a masterpiece.

Yet even Milt hadn't realized how scary the thing could be, given the proper circumstances. During the early part of this particular evening, he'd been busy. Even during the fireworks display he'd had plenty of customers and was very satisfied with himself. This was good business—more than he'd expected from such a small town.

But for the past half hour or so it had gotten *better*. He finally decided it must be the conjunction of Halloween and booze that was doing it. His latest customers had been coming out really white-faced and shaky. It was wonderful. Most of them had avoided his eye when they got out of the little carriages and sort of helped one another away. He was beginning to think he must be a genius! Maybe he should take the thing to Disney or Industrial Light and Magic after all. It had been a dream of his to do this a few years down the road, but if he could produce this kind of reaction in a little nowhere town in the Midwest, then he *must* be good!

Milt beamed at the girl in the Carmen Miranda costume. She was a dish all right. She'd been pacing back and forth by the gate for about ten minutes now, obviously waiting for her boyfriend. He gave her the eye—well, you never knew—but she wasn't having any. He turned to his next customer and handed over the ticket. The line grew longer, but the girl still didn't join it.

He checked his watch—another thirty seconds and the first car of the little train would emerge from the exit, bearing its load of frightened people. He had to admit, some of them were wearing Halloween costumes that matched his efforts and then some. Maybe this wasn't such a nothing little town after all. They sure went to some trouble to scare the wits out of each other.

The exit doors of the tunnel burst open, and the train came out. In the first car the couple were pale, and the rest looked pretty stunned, too. When the train came to a stop, Lena Turkle, who had been riding in the first car and was known for her sensitive nature, threw up over the side.

Her escort, Wilber (Weasel) Rumplemeyer, looked a little green himself. He left Lena to clean herself up and came over to Milt. "Listen, buddy—don't you think some of that stuff in there is a little . . . well . . . *strong* . . . for a family fair?"

Milt went on the defensive. "No worse than stuff you see in the movies. I got a limit, you notice, nobody allowed in under fourteen." He pointed to the sign. "I'm a socially responsible guy."

"Maybe. But that last corpse but one is pretty god-awful, if you ask me."

"What, the guy with the acid burns? Why, he's my best . . ."

But Weasel was shaking his head. "No, not that one—that one's okay. I mean the Robin Hood body—the one with the smashed-in skull and the arrow sticking out of his chest. I think it's the way his mushed-up brain sort of . . . oozes and steams . . . and the way the blood runs down his neck into that puddle. . . ."

"What the hell are you talking about?" Milt asked.

"The blood on the—"

"I haven't *got* no dead Robin Hood with blood dripping—" Milt began hotly.

"The hell you don't. Why—"

"The hell I do!"

Weasel stared at him. "I *seen* the goddamn thing!" he shouted in outrage. "Whaddya mean there's no—"

"I mean, if there's a dead body in there dressed in a Robin Hood outfit, it's got nothin' to do with me, that's what I mean!" Milt shouted back belligerently.

Behind him, the girl in the Carmen Miranda costume began to scream, and scream, and scream.

There had been plenty of shrieks during the festival—it wasn't nicknamed the Howl for nothing. People on the rides, winners at the rifle shoot, and old friends greeting old friends and laughing at their costumes all contributed their excited yips, yells, and bellows to the overall cacophony.

But, as mothers wake in the night or whirl around and start running in supermarkets and playgrounds at the sound of a child in pain, so Matt Gabriel responded to Emily Gibbons's scream.

He just *knew.*

*   *   *

Emily's terror proved to be communicable, and by the time Matt skidded to a stop at the entrance gate to the Bonechiller, even Milt Bickerstaff was shouting. His Tennessee twang rose above Lena Turkle's wails, instructing her to shut the hell up. Lena was the lead soprano in the local Baptist choir. She had a piercing and powerful high C, but it had considerable competition from the other women in the crowd that had immediately gathered, sensing drama.

"What's wrong—what is it?" Matt shouted as he came up.

"Accident!"

"Murder!"

"Dominic . . . Dominic . . . " Emily sobbed.

"What?" asked Dominic, coming up behind her. "What's wrong? Are you hurt? Who did it? Where is he? I'll knock his block off!"

Emily whirled, stared at him openmouthed as she wavered between relief and hysteria, then threw herself into his arms. Dominic, gratified but overbalanced, stepped sideways and trod on the toes of Councilman Berringer, who yelped and backed straight into Mrs. Atwater's knitting needles.

Mr. Berringer had not been having a good evening. His head still ached from where George Putnam had accidentally clipped him with his nightstick, some obnoxious child had snapped off the tail of his lizard costume, and now the peace of the festival was threatened by this ridiculous uproar. After glaring at Mrs. Atwater with watering eyes, he crossed his arms and glared at Matt.

"Young Rumplemeyer's claiming there's a real body in that thing," he said, nodding toward the Bonechiller. "Personally, I don't believe a word of it. It's just his idea of a Howler."

George Putnam came running up. "Did he say what I thought he said?" George demanded.

Milt Bickerstaff pushed through the crowd and waved his arms at Matt. "Listen, you got to do something about this! I got a decent attraction here. It's a class attraction, cost me twenty thousand to build, maybe more! I resent people leaving their dead bodies in it."

"It's just a dummy," someone in the train shouted uneasily.

"Now, look—" said Weasel Rumplemeyer. "I know what we saw. It was definitely a dead man in a Robin Hood outfit with his head smashed to pieces, blood everywhere, and with—"

"With an arrow sticking out of his chest, yeah, yeah," shouted one of his buddies in the little train. "Come on, Weasel, get real. We all saw it. It was just a dummy."

"No it wasn't," Weasel said stubbornly.

"Sure it was," said someone else.

"No it *wasn't*," repeated Weasel.

"They aren't *dummies,* dammit, they're animatronic struc—" Milt began.

"Why don't we just take a look?" Matt suggested. "Can you turn off the juice or whatever, please?"

Milt drew himself up, his anger somewhat diluted by pride. "No problem. I'll have the computer put the tunnel into access mode—that way you'll have plenty of light."

"Fine."

"And I'm coming with you to make sure you don't step on anything. My insurance don't cover—"

"All right, all right," Matt growled. "Just do what you have to do and let's get going. Folks are getting upset here."

Milt, muttering under his breath, turned to his computer console and tapped in his instructions.

"Looks like Cape Kennedy," George murmured.

"I use a lot of similar hardware," Milt said stiffly. "This is a high-quality operation. State of the art."

"Of the what?" Councilman Berringer asked, looking at the lurid posters and illustrations that surrounded the installation.

"Listen, I'm a member of the BEE, and—" Milt began.

"What the hell is that?" George asked as they climbed over the gate and followed Matt back along the narrow track and through the wooden doors into the alley.

"The Brotherhood of Electronic Exhibitors," Bickerstaff said sullenly. His voice became strangely muffled as they pushed through the door flaps and entered the Bonechiller tunnel. It might have been computerized, but its outer structure was made of canvas, plastic, and cheap wood. "We got standards," Milt continued.

"And we've got trouble," Matt said. He was about ten feet in front of them and stood staring down. His face was white.

Wedged between the track and the outer canvas wall, his Lincoln green costume harshly bright under the glare of the working lights, lay Peter Dill, his head bloodied and mis-shapen.

He was real, he was dead, and he had obviously been mur-dered.

Suddenly things weren't so funny anymore.

16

"Two down, six to go," muttered Matt.

"What?" asked Milt Bickerstaff, who was clearly shocked by the sight of real death as opposed to the plastic facsimiles he was so proud of creating. For one thing, real death *smelled* bad. "You know this guy?"

Matt took a deep breath and glanced at George. "He's the vice president of our local bank."

"Ho," Milt began. "The rate of interest those guys charge, it's no surprise somebody . . . " His voice trailed off as he realized the impropriety of humor at this particular moment.

Matt ignored him and spoke to George. "Make the necessary calls. And see if you can spot Dr. Willis out there. Or any doctor." As George started back down the track, he called after him. "Any doctor but Dan Rogers, that is."

George stopped, turned, and stared. "You don't mean you think *this* has to do with Jacky Morgan, do you?"

"Don't you?" countered Matt.

"No!" George said, then swallowed. "Well, maybe . . . " he added miserably. "I don't know." He looked at Matt a moment longer, then left to carry out his assignment.

"Who's Jacky Morgan?" Bickerstaff asked without really wanting to know. "Hey, listen, how soon can you get this thing out of here so I can—" He paused as Matt turned to look at him. He cleared his throat and sniffed. "So I guess you're saying I'm finished for the night?"

"I am," Matt said stolidly. *"You're* finished for the night. *We're* just starting."

"An hour at the most," Dr. Willis said, straightening up with some difficulty. His sciatica had returned with the frosts of autumn, and the tightness of Rhett Butler's trousers was not conducive to comfort. "From the look of things, he was killed close by and then just shoved under the canvas out of sight."

"Except that the light from that thing"—Matt indicated the looming figure of a two-headed Monster from Mars—"shone straight onto him every time the train passed by." He grimaced. "Unless the killer was familiar with the inside of this thing and the way the lights come on and off, he couldn't have known that."

"He or she," Doc Willis said.

"Do you mean all *that* could have been done by a woman?" George asked in some astonishment. His surprise was understandable, for the wounds on the corpse were severe. Dill's skull was shattered and the brains were horribly crushed. Gray matter oozed from several fissures in the scalp.

"Oh, yes," Willis said, unperturbed. "The first blow probably would have knocked him out. After that it would just have been a matter of continuing the blows until the frenzy wore itself out. It was a frenzy, by the way. Even at this point I can identify no less than six separate blows with the traditional blunt object. An ordinary rock, at a guess. About the size of a grapefruit. With sharp, irregular edges."

"Like that one," Matt said, pointing at a stained rock that lay half-out and half-under the lower edge of the canvas about three feet from the dead man. It, along with four or five others, was weighting the base of one of the rough uprights supporting the canvas shrouding of the Bonechiller.

Doc Willis lowered his head and peered over the top of his glasses. "Definitely like that one," he agreed.

"George," Matt said, pointing to the rock.

"Right," George nodded and produced a clean handkerchief from the back pocket of his gendarme's uniform. He wrapped the handkerchief around the rock, picked it up rather gingerly, and straightened, holding it at arm's length. "No plastic bags," he said in a worried voice. "Didn't think we'd need them tonight."

"Do the best you can," Matt said.

George looked puzzled for a moment, and then his brow cleared. From his back pocket he produced a packet of condoms, removed one, unwrapped it, and—with some difficulty—proceeded to engulf the suspected murder weapon within its flexible confines.

"Jesus, George," Matt said plaintively.

"What the hell," George said. "It's sterile, isn't it?" He marched off in some triumph, the outline of the condom packet showing clearly in the back pocket of his tight-fitting costume trousers. He seemed to be cooperating, but with a degree of attitude, and the reason was obvious.

George Putnam now knew that Matt was actively considering the possibility that one of the six surviving participants in what he thought of as "the Jacky Morgan case" could well have killed Peter Dill—and among those six was his own father. He might not get on all that well with Carl Putnam, but that didn't mean he liked having him suspected of murder.

"This is all very unfortunate," Dr. Willis said in a low voice. "Peter was well respected in Blackwater. Has his wife been told?"

"Charley is looking for her now," Matt said. "I told him to just tell her there'd been an accident and to take her to the first-aid tent."

"Do you want me to tell her?" Willis asked.

"I'd be really grateful to you," Matt said. "You'll be better at it than me."

"Ought to be," Willis agreed. "Forty years in practice must add up to about a million cases, and I haven't won them all by a long shot. You get used to telling folks the bad news."

"Do you really?" Matt asked.

Willis sighed. "No," he said ponderously. "That was a lie. But I guess you get used to telling those, too."

When Matt emerged from the Bonechiller, Tilly and Albert Budd were in the crowd, still standing around watching Milt

Bickerstaff putting up an "Out of Order Due to Mechanical Difficulties" sign.

"That's not true, is it? About mechanical difficulties?" Tilly asked in a low voice, barely audible above the noise of the carnival. News of Dill's death had not yet spread much farther than the first row of booths beyond the Bonechiller—but it would.

Matt sighed. "No, it's not," he agreed. He told her what had happened. Albert Budd looked shocked and somehow irritated.

"Damn, that's inconvenient," he muttered. "I'd arranged to talk to Peter about some business matters tomorrow. Apparently there's been some confusion about paym—"

"That doesn't matter now, Albert," Tilly interrupted firmly.

He looked down at her. "No . . . no, I suppose not," he said slowly. "Sorry, Til. Force of habit. I keep forgetting it's people and only think about the . . . " He raised his hands and waved them vaguely. "You have to understand that I gave up being a decent human being deliberately," he said solemnly. "When you're building up a big business, social considerations take up too much time and energy. You just have to get on with things."

"Well, what else are you going to do with your precious damn time and energy now you've *sold* the business?" Tilly demanded impatiently. "Discover a new planet or grow a black rose?"

He managed a grin. "That would be nice, wouldn't it?"

Glen Hardwicke came running up, his red-lined gendarme's cape fluttering in the breeze. The longer this went on, the more ludicrous they all looked, it seemed to Matt. He wished, heartily, for his usual khaki trousers and leather jacket. For one thing, he had all the pockets sorted out, pencils here, notebooks there, and so on. He kept slapping his chest and sides, expecting to find things in their usual place. Trying to be "official" while feeling like a fool was difficult.

"I just heard from George about the—" Glen paused delicately, glancing at the crowd. "What do you want me to do, Matt?"

"Damned if I know," Matt said. "There's absolutely no

way we can contain everybody that's here—and the killer
has probably left the grounds anyway."

"We can lock the gates and take names," Glen began.

"Half of them will just walk off around the back," Matt
said, glancing at Albert. "Just a waste of time and energy."

"Exactly," Albert said, smacking a fist into his palm.
"First you've got to decide what's important and then deal
with each item in proper order. Prioritize."

"And leave out human beings," Tilly added with some asperity.

"Well, it may not be nice, but it works," Albert snapped.

"Doc Willis says Peter has been dead over an hour but less
than two," Matt muttered as he stared out over the milling
throngs that were still enjoying themselves. The air was
filled with the rumble of the rides and the various tunes that
accompanied each of them, the peep and beep of space in-
vader machines, the shouts and laughter, the heavy metal
thump from the disco pavilion—the party continued while he
stood here, pondering how to "prioritize" the murder of a respected citizen of the community.

It wouldn't last.

The people who had been near or in the Bonechiller when
the grisly discovery had been made were even now filtering
out through the crowds, carrying the news—or various versions of it. By the time it reached the far end of the carnival,
the story would be that there were nineteen dead and forty-
three maimed in the Bonechiller owing to (1) the train being
derailed (2) a madman running amok with an ax (3) electro-
cution via a short circuit, or (4) Martians. There was nothing
he could do about it. There would be enough opinions, suspicions, and alibis to fill six notebooks, and all of them useless.

The case he'd dealt with over the summer was about as
complex as a canary kidnapping compared to the mess he
faced now. To start with, this was not a contained physical
situation. Although there was a cyclone fence around the
playing fields, it was breached in many places where kids
had made shortcuts into the school grounds. People had been
coming and going all evening. It was a night where everyone
expected people to be sneaking around and looking furtive.
If anybody had witnessed anything suspicious, they would

have dismissed it as part of a Howler. And any witnesses could long since have gone home, forgotten the whole thing.

On the other hand, there were still plenty of people here. Too many, looking at it in terms of keeping order. Certainly there were enough to cause trouble, especially since many of them ranged in condition from pleasantly high to practically falling-down drunk. Soon the crowds would stop their celebrations and gather around the Bonechiller in strength, the women with their shrill, demanding voices, the men filled with grim but as yet undefined purpose. They would press in and—

"Oh, shit," he said suddenly, snapping out of his useless reverie. "Glen—see if you can find Bill Crowley or any of the others we use as temporary deputies and get them over here. I want the whole of this area blocked off and taped. We'll need floodlights and . . . " He went on listing his requirements for protecting the crime scene. As he spoke, Matt glanced at Albert and noted his apparent approval. Does he think I'm "prioritizing" and behaving like a professional? How little Albert knows of how little Matt knows, he thought.

"Tilly," he said, "you go back to the office and call the coroner over in Hatchville. Tell them what we've got and get someone over here to do the official song and dance. We want—" He broke off as a woman burst out of the costumed crowd and ran toward him. It was Mrs. Dill in her Maid Marian outfit.

"Now, Evelyn—" Matt began, spreading his arms and moving to fend her off. As he did so, he both heard and felt the shoulder seams in his rented costume split. Now he not only felt like an idiot, he looked like one. No doubt the pants would go next.

"He's not dead, he's *not*—" Evelyn Dill was sobbing. "I want to see, let me see—"

Tilly stepped forward. "No, Evelyn," she said, and wrapped her arms around the hysterical woman, forcing her to a halt. "You don't want to see him now. Come on . . . come on . . . "

"I've sent for the car," Albert said, looking surprisingly distressed for a man who'd deliberately given up being human. "We can take her home." He looked around. "Is there anyone—"

Nonie Peach emerged from between a six-foot grasshopper and an equally large Mickey Mouse. "I'll go with her," she said.

Evelyn looked up, wild-eyed, at the vision of a rather voluptuous belly dancer coming toward her with arms outstretched. She stepped back. "Who are you?" she demanded, hiccuping and choking.

"I'm Nonie, Mrs. Peach's daughter," Nonie said in a practical voice. "I live across the street from you."

"Oh," said Evelyn, slightly mollified. "Yes. I'm sorry—you look so—different."

Nonie looked down at her costume. "Yes, well—it is a change from my usual jeans and sweater, I must admit."

Doc Willis came up, puffing gently. He hadn't been able to keep pace with his erstwhile patient. "I'll send around some pills for her to take," he said to Nonie in a low wheeze. "She'd be best off sleeping until tomorrow."

"I'll see she takes them and settle her down," Nonie promised. "Come on, Mrs. Dill."

"I really don't know you very well," Evelyn Dill protested in a dull voice, but she went along obediently, her face pale, her steps wavering. Nonie put a strong arm around her, and the crowd parted for them and then re-formed, like quicksand around a fallen stone. They were quiet now. Just staring. Just watching the show.

For the first time Matt became actively conscious of the bizarre scene they all presented. American policemen dressed as French policemen surrounded by costumed figures representing practically every known animal, insect, comic-book hero, and historical personage, plus a few unnameable products of definitely lunatic imaginations. The lurid lights of the Bonechiller and the carnival beyond lent the scene a demonic glow. The front rank of the crowd was visible in garish color, but those behind it were only weirdly shaped shadows, with extra arms, antennae, and other inhuman appendages. Overhead the huge, multi-faceted field lights were misted with shrouds of whirling insects drawn irresistibly to the white-hot glow. Swifts shrieked as they cut and crisscrossed the evening air, feasting on this unexpected and unseasonal harvest. Bats, too, slid silently through the darkness, graceful and voracious, adding their sinister shadows to the scene. Matt felt as if he had stumbled into a painting by Bosch, and he did not, he definitely did not, want to be a part of it.

Unfortunately, he had a job to do.

Two hours later the party was over.

The rides were motionless, the music was stilled, the shouts and laughter had been finally silenced. What had seemed an evening of fun and excitement had proved to be a little too exciting and—in its conclusion—no fun at all. People had arrived full of joy and anticipation, wearing their costumes with pride. They departed drooping miserably and feeling more than a little silly.

The Howlers that had been perpetrated before the news of Peter Dill's death had been discovered were no longer funny or welcome. Those who went home to find their living room furniture nailed to the ceiling or all the labels removed from their canned goods or the apples on their prize apple tree replaced with sweet potatoes merely sighed wearily and went to bed.

The young medic from the coroner's office in Hatchville had come and gone, taking the battered body of Peter Dill with him in a black bag. Before it was removed, Harry Foskett had the dubious honour of photographing it in situ, along with shots of the whole of the Bonechiller, inside and out. The pictures would not be appearing in the *Chronicle,* but their subjects would be appearing in his dreams for some time to come. He thought that one day, maybe, he could make something of the negatives, a photographic statement that would be meaningful and important—but not now.

Emily Gibbons had mustered enough of her newly acquired professional energy to make a few impressionistic notes in order to write a report for the next edition of the *Chronicle,* but her father—a newspaperman trained in a harder school—had already gleaned sufficient factual details to prepare a story for the wire services and had returned to the office to efficiently relay it in time for the morning editions of the main Grantham City papers.

Once again, Blackwater Bay would be in the news. The unexpected presence of eccentric millionaire Albert Budd was additional reason for the big papers to take an interest. His actual presence was proving to be less than a boon, however. He seemed to think that his advice was required at every turn. If it wasn't "I wonder if you should do that . . . " it was "It seems to me that if you . . . " or "Shouldn't you just try . . . " until they were all ready to turn him into a second victim. Finally Matt had to tell him that if he *really* wanted to help, he should go over to the first-aid tent and tell Frank Boomer to take the group he'd gathered down to the office. He told Albert to go with them.

After Albert had bustled off, filled with purpose, they continued their close search of the area along the outer canvas side of the Bonechiller. Matt was certain he'd found the precise location of the murder and had marked it out with stakes within the taped and screened-off perimeter. His temporary deputies—they'd managed to locate six of them—were on their hands and knees in the grass, crawling and looking. So far, all that had been found were two used condoms, twenty-nine wrappers from candy bars, six rocket sticks from the fireworks display, the leg of a doll, quite a bit of dog dung, and a dead grass snake.

With the area lit by floodlights, it was more difficult to imagine the scene as it had been when the murder took place. The outer side of the tunnel would have been in pitch darkness, curving around the lower end of the field as it did. The lights from the carnival on the opposite side would have made this area seem even blacker—an excellent choice of venue for a private rendezvous between people who had no wish to be seen together in public. It seemed likely that it *had* been a planned meeting—Matt couldn't imagine anyone wandering around there for no reason at all—always discounting the used condoms. In which case, it seemed likely that Peter Dill had known and trusted his killer.

Or killers.

"That make sense to you?" Matt asked George.

"I guess so," George said. He was looking a little pale, and it was not because he'd had to look at a victim of extreme violence, either. He'd seen worse. He took a breath.

"I don't see why you're so hipped on this Jacky Morgan business," he finally burst out, causing some of the other deputies to turn and stare. "Why the hell couldn't this just have been a mugging? Or a jealous husband? Or some drunk from Lemonville looking for . . . "

"For what?" Matt asked.

"Money."

"There was still about fifty bucks in his costume pocket," Matt pointed out.

"Well, probably he heard someone coming and didn't have a chance to search the body," George countered. "That's why he shoved it under the canvas," he finished triumphantly.

"He could have done that to give himself time to get away," Matt said.

"All he would have needed was two minutes to get back into the crowd," George said.

"Or she," Glen Hardwicke said. "Didn't Doc Willis say it could have been a woman?"

"Yeah," George said, looking a little more cheerful. "Yeah, he did."

"I haven't accused anyone yet," Matt pointed out.

"Oh, sure—but you *are* thinking about the Jacky Morgan business, aren't you?"

"It does seem quite a coincidence," Matt said.

"Well, hell, you're always saying coincidences are more common than people realize," George retorted. "If Tom Finnegan had died of cancer and *then* this had happened, you wouldn't think two thoughts about it, would you?"

"No," Matt admitted. "I wouldn't. But Tom didn't die of cancer, he crashed his car in suspicious circumstances, and—"

"The state police are satisfied it was an accident," George said, his voice rising a little.

Matt stood up. "Take it easy, George," he said. "You're protesting too much."

"What the hell does that mean?" George wanted to know.

Matt sighed. "It means you sound a bit *too* worried about your father. As if you think he might have done it after all."

"I never said that!" George shouted.

Matt raised an eyebrow. "And neither did I, George," he said quietly. "Neither did I."

"But you're thinking about it," George said again.

"Oh, sure," Matt agreed. "I'm thinking about a lot of things. That's just one of them."

Max's usual night routine had been badly upset. First Tilly had burst into the sheriff's office, bustled about making phone calls and muttering to herself, and then shot out, banging the door behind her. He was just resettling himself in one of the boxes of old files when the door burst open again, and Frank Boomer came in, followed by six angry men, all shouting. Resignedly, the big ginger cat stood up, stretched, then folded his paws under and settled down to observe.

Half an hour later Matt left his car and approached the office. He paused briefly to look in through the window. Waiting for him were eight men: his deputies Charley Hart and Frank Boomer, plus Tyrone Molt, Jack Fanshawe, Dan Rogers, Albert Budd, Carl Putnam, and Merrill Atwater. Tilly had obviously performed her duties and gone gratefully home.

The six "suspects" were keeping well apart, he noticed, and were not looking at one another, either. Thinking back, he realized that over the years he'd never really noticed any of them together in the sense of being friends or cronies. Whatever had happened in the past had not brought them closer.

Frank and Charley were the only ones in the room who didn't look annoyed. Taking a deep breath, Matt opened the

door and went in. Nine heads swiveled toward him—Max's,
and the eight men.

It was the mayor who spoke first, in an attempt at joviality
that fell rather flat. "Well, Matt? We're wondering why
you've called us all together."

Matt smiled wearily and turned to his deputies. "Thanks,
boys." He pulled off his costume jacket, regarded the torn
seams ruefully, and exchanged it for his old blue cardigan
hanging on the hat stand.

"You want us both to stay?" Frank asked. He was not usually on night duty.

"Please." Matt turned to the others. "You've all heard
about Peter Dill?"

"Of course." This was from Dan Rogers, whose costume
of an accident victim looked, if anything, more vivid and
ghastly than it had earlier in the evening. "Albert here claims
he was murdered. I presume this is some kind of morbid
Howler you've dreamed up?"

"I'm afraid not," Matt said. "Peter Dill *is* dead. His head
was beaten in with a rock, and one of the arrows from his
costume was shoved through his chest. The killer was apparently the kind of person who liked to make sure. Mr. Dill's
body was then shoved under the edge of the canvas shrouding that encloses the ride named the Bonechiller. The killer
presumably hoped it would be well hidden there, giving
him—or her—time to escape. Unfortunately the place chosen was directly under a light that came on whenever the
train passed by. The light was meant to illuminate the figure
of a two-headed monster. It also lit up the body of Peter Dill.
His face was turned away from the track, and his plastered
ankle was twisted up in the canvas, so no one made any connection with a real person. There were a number of men
dressed as Robin Hood at the carnival tonight. Because of
the rather sensational nature of the Bonechiller ride, it was
some time before customers began to actually complain to
the owner, a Mr. Bickerstaff, that his display of a dead Robin
Hood was too realistic. He, of course, had no such display."

"Dear God," Rogers murmured, and sank back onto
George's chair, clinging to his crutches as if they were a prop
and mainstay.

"Okay, okay. Come on, Matt," Jack Fanshawe said, rising from his place on the wide windowsill, his Arab robes swirling around him dramatically. The outfit, with its romantic headdress and encrustations of braid, suited him admirably. Valentino would have been jealous. "Albert here was very impressive, talking about the body and so on, although how you roped him into it I'll never know. Anyway, if it makes you happy, I feel *real* intimidated. But I am also damn tired, and I'd like to go home, now."

"Not joking," Matt said flatly.

"You said 'or her,'" Carl Putnam said. "Are you saying the killer could be a woman?"

Fanshawe turned on him. "What killer, for crying out loud? Can't you see this is Matt's idea of a joke? There's no killer, no body. I bet Peter is back home already, sound asleep. Or in on it." He turned back to Matt. "Am I right? Is he in on it as well as our nonresident millionaire here? Is he going to come walking in here in a few minutes, laughing like hell? Come on, Matt—it's late, and this really isn't funny."

Matt ignored him and answered Putnam's question. "*I'm* not saying it could have been a woman—Doc Willis is," he said, sinking a hip onto the corner of his desk and running his fingers through his hair. "I don't happen to agree with him, but he probably knows more about it than I do. I think Peter Dill was killed by a man. Or men."

"Just a moment. Am I to understand you suspect one of us?" Albert Budd asked. His tone was more one of curiosity than resentment. Obviously, despite being asked to wait here with the others, this possibility had not occurred to him before. He was sitting on Matt's chair as if it were his right to do so.

"Oh, come *on,*" Dan Rogers said. "This has gone far enough."

"I'll have to agree, Matt," Mayor Atwater said. "Your men herded us over here without letting us talk to anyone, acting all very serious and official. Then they said we couldn't leave, even laid hands on their guns to make it all look good—"

"But it isn't funny," Fanshawe finished for him.

"It isn't meant to be funny, and it isn't my idea of a joke," Matt said with growing irritation. "If you had talked to other people, you'd know what I'm telling you is the truth. If you hadn't been isolated in here on my orders, you would have seen the coroner's wagon arrive and then take Peter Dill's body away, you would have seen me marking the area off around the ride in question, and you would have seen my men going over the ground inch by inch under floodlights. They're still doing it. Albert Budd is not acting as a straight man, and this is not a joke. Peter Dill has been murdered." He turned to Rogers. "Dan, I'd like you to take off those bandages and leave them here. Hope you've got a jacket or something with you."

Rogers stood up angrily. "Why?"

"Because I can think of no better way to disguise real bloodstains than to combine them with fake ones," Matt said evenly. "I could be wrong, but you seem to be a bit more gory now than you were earlier this evening. What's more, you've acquired some crutches—and Dill's crutches are missing."

Rogers reddened. "Dammit, I resent this. You're right, I am bloodier than I was, because Mary Wendell's middle boy had a nosebleed on the Ferris wheel—purely psychological, of course, altitude has nothing . . . Anyway, I took care of him." He waved a bandaged arm. "This is the kid's blood, not Dill's, and the rest isn't real."

"But it could be, couldn't it?" Matt asked.

"No, it could not, because I didn't *kill* Peter Dill," Rogers said with some asperity. "I am a doctor, not a murderer. However, to indulge your little fantasy, I am only too happy to offer you my poor wrappings if it pleases you. As for the crutches, I found them earlier, lying on the ground. They're stamped with the hospital marking. I held on to them in case they were called for or needed."

"Where did you find them?"

"By the . . . " Rogers suddenly looked horrified. "By the gate near the end of that Bonechiller ride." He dropped the crutches. "My God—they must be his."

"And now we have a perfect reason for finding your fingerprints on them," Matt pointed out.

Rogers glared at him. "Well, I guess you have it all figured out."

"Not at all. I just want you to realize that this is very, very serious. Give your 'costume' to Frank, please."

Rogers looked ready to explode, but after a minute he began pulling off the bandages. "I assume you'll be requiring the clothing of my friends here as well?" he asked in a snide voice.

"I will," Matt said.

"But . . . but . . . that's preposterous!" Tyrone Molt exploded. "Goddammit to hell, Gabriel, what do you think you're doing? Why the hell should *we* give you our clothes? I can see fake bloodstains might make you suspect Dan, but what about all the hundreds of other people who were at the carnival? I don't see you dragging *them* over here and asking them to strip off. Why the hell were *we* dragged in here? Why do you think one of *us* might have killed Peter?"

"Because of Jacky Morgan," Matt said.

For a moment, there was dead silence.

Then everyone spoke at once.

It was the first time Nonie Peach had crossed the threshold of the Dill residence, which was one of the recently restored homes on Sycamore Avenue. She was not at all surprised, however, to find it exactly as she had imagined—perfect in every respect. From the large silk Chinese rugs that seemed to float on the background of richly polished floorboards, to the swagged gold velvet drapes, to the furniture that gleamed with French brocade upholstery, it spoke of money and immaculate taste.

That it was also faintly reminiscent of the lobby of a good hotel she dismissed as envy.

Evelyn Dill was a wreck. She had collapsed weeping in Nonie's lap in the dark recesses of Albert Budd's limousine, and her face was swollen and red. Her normally beautiful grooming was a thing forgotten in her grief. The depth of her reaction rather startled Nonie, who had always thought of Evelyn as tight-assed and totally cold. Apparently Peter Dill had been more than just a "good catch"—she must have really loved him.

As they staggered in from the hall, the baby-sitter looked up in surprise. It was Molly Turkle's mother, Belinda, a placid plump woman of good heart but limited education. The magazine she had been thumbing through slid to the floor as she rose and came across the room, responding spontaneously to the sight of unhappiness.

"Land alive, what's happened?" she asked, taking Evelyn's weight from Nonie and escorting her to the sofa. Evelyn dropped like a stone and broke into a fresh round of sobbing, burying her face in a pillow.

"I'm afraid Mr. Dill has been killed," Nonie said.

"You don't tell me!" expostulated Mrs. Turkle. "An accident on one of the rides? I always said to Lem that them things was a temptation to the devil, flinging folks around—"

"No," Nonie said quietly, drawing Mrs. Turkle slightly aside. "I'm afraid it's worse than that. Somebody killed him."

"Who?" demanded Belinda, not questioning the deed, but avid for the name of the doer.

"They don't know."

"One of them no-goods from Lemonville or Hatchville, I'll bet. Or . . . " Her eyes widened as the thought passed between them. There was a slight pause, and then Belinda continued as if they had spoken Wayne Dill's name aloud. "They never did get on, you know," she said in a half whisper. "And he did go to jail, didn't he?"

"Not for violence," Nonie whispered back. "Just for selling dope."

Wayne Dill, the bad seed, the evil son. Could it be?

"No," Nonie said after a minute. "I can't believe that."

Belinda shrugged. Then her glance fell on a silver-framed photograph on one of the side tables. "Oh, them poor little girls," she said. "Poor babies to lose their father so young." The twins were around ten, Nonie recalled, and while pretty enough and bright enough and polite enough, they seemed also to have their mother's normal air of intense reserve and control. She looked at Evelyn, limp now and silent save for an occasional shudder, her face still buried in the pillow. Would the twins, too, fall prey to this storm of grief? Or would they fold their hands and look primly out at a world that had failed them, disapproval in every line of their small, identical faces?

That's unfair, Nonie told herself. You may not warm to them, but they are still just little girls, and deserve better than that. What were their names again?

"Caryl and Sheryl," Belinda said, following Nonie's train of thought perfectly. That she seemed to read Nonie's mind surprised neither of them—all the Turkles were intuitive.

"Oh, no—how can I tell them?" Evelyn asked, sitting up suddenly, fresh tears appearing in her reddened eyes. "What can I say? It's horrible . . . it's so horrible."

Nonie knew that Peter Dill's father and mother were both dead. "What about your parents?" she asked Evelyn, sitting down beside her. Belinda sat on her other side, the two of them bulwarking the new widow, lending fleshly support if nothing else. "Would you like me to telephone them? Could they come?"

Evelyn seemed to be seeking counsel from a tall chinoiserie lamp on the far side of the room. After a moment she spoke in a small, childish voice. "Mummy would come," she said. "Daddy's always *busy.*" She managed to add a sulky tone of resentment to this piece of information.

"Where will I find the number?" Nonie asked, standing up.

"In the book by the phone in the hall," Evelyn said, still in that little-girl voice that was extremely unnerving. Nonie thought it was the first sign of a complete breakdown, which did not bode well for the twins. They would need *their* mother, too." It's under M for Mummy," Evelyn said.

And giggled.

Dear God, thought Nonie as she went into the hall, where are those pills Doctor Willis was supposed to send over? But even as she found and dialed the Chicago number, the doorbell rang, and Belinda went to answer it.

In the sitting room, Evelyn was still giggling.

"Good evening," Nonie said to the voice that answered sleepily. "I am sorry to disturb you so late, but I'm afraid it's an emergency."

"My husband is already at the hospital," said the woman on the other end of the line.

"No, you misunderstand. I'm phoning from Blackwater Bay. I'm a neighbor of your daughter's."

"Oh, my God—is Evelyn all right? The girls—is it one of the girls?" All too wide awake, now.

"No, they're all right. But I'm afraid there's bad news. Your son-in-law has been killed."

"An accident? Are you *sure* Evelyn is—"

"Your daughter and granddaughters are fine." Nonie paused. "I'm afraid it wasn't an accident, Mrs. . . . Mrs. . . . I'm afraid I don't—"

"Mrs. Parks," snapped the woman. "Do you mean he's killed *himself,* is that what you're saying?"

Nonie was startled. Why should she think that?

"No, not at all. I'm afraid it was . . . "

"Murder? Is that what you're saying? He was murdered?"

Nonie let her breath out suddenly, relieved of having to speak the actual word. "Yes."

"A robbery? A bank robbery? Don't tell me he died protecting all that wonderful money of his. . . . " There was a surprising tinge of distaste in the voice.

"No, not that, either. Your son-in-law was killed by a person or persons unknown." The phrase, so familiar from television, felt peculiar in her mouth. "Evelyn is very broken up, Mrs. Parks, and there are your granddaughters to consider. I think it would be a great help if you could come—"

"I'm getting dressed now," said Mrs. Parks, and from the sounds coming over the phone that was exactly what she was doing. "I'll catch the first available plane to Grantham and rent a car. Is there someone who could stay with her until—"

"I'll stay with her," Nonie heard herself saying. "The doctor has sent some pills to ease her through the first few hours. There's a baby-sitter here, but if she can't spend the night, I will. I live just across the street."

"You're very kind." Mrs. Parks grunted—obviously bending over to put on shoes or pull a suitcase out of a closet. Nonie could picture her somehow, like listening to a radio program about a woman getting dressed and packed. It was an odd sensation.

"Good night, then, Mrs. Parks," Nonie said. "And . . . I'm sorry about your loss."

"No loss of mine," retorted Mrs. Parks. "Good night."

Nonie put down the phone and turned to Belinda Turkle still standing by the front door, holding a small package— obviously the pills sent over by the doctor. But she wasn't looking at the pills or at Nonie. She was looking at something over Nonie's head. Nonie looked up.

Two faces looked down at her. Two small, identical faces peering over the balustrade on the floor above. Same nightgowns, white with pink sprigs. Same long dark hair. Same pointed chins.

Same slow, tidy tears.

"It's so hard to believe," Emily said to Dominic.

They were sitting in the front room of Mrs. Peach's Guest House. Dominic had discarded his Robin Hood costume in favor of jeans and a sweatshirt, and one of his thicker cardigans was wrapped around Emily's shoulders, making up for the deficiency of the Carmen Miranda costume.

Before them lay empty plates that not long before had held generous helpings of the various riches available from Mrs. Peach's buffet. When Emily had started to shiver at the carnival grounds, Dominic had remembered the food, the fireplace, and the emptiness of the house, in that order. Soon after the coroner's wagon had departed with the departed, they'd come back here.

"And when he said it was Robin Hood who was dead," Emily was continuing, "well . . . "

"I heard you scream halfway across the grounds." Dominic grinned. "I thought you'd caught someone eating the fruit off your hat."

The hat in question lay on the floor. Dominic gathered up a strand or two of the tawny hair that now tumbled loosely over Emily's shoulders and gave the curl a small, gentle tug. "You shouldn't dwell on it," he said softly.

"Oh, I know." Emily sighed. "But awful as it was, it's the most exciting thing that's ever happened to me, so you'll have to forgive the tendency to croon over the sensations."

"There's excitement and excitement," Dominic pointed out. "Some kinds we can do without."

"There speaks a man whose blood has too often raced

through his veins," Emily retorted. "I, on the other hand, hold the record for slow-flowing life force, the lowest BP ever recorded, and—"

He kissed her.

"—as for the highlights of my career, you could count them on the fingers of one hand," she concluded when the kiss was over. Emily did not approve of loose ends, conversational or otherwise. She glanced at him sideways. "Stop kissing me," she added. "It interrupts my train of thought."

He burst out laughing. "Never have I heard such a lack of conviction," he finally managed to say. He reached for her again but was interrupted by the sound of the front door opening.

It was Clarence Toogood. He stood in the archway to the hall, his toga hanging loose and lopsided over his sportcoat and trousers, his laurel wreath awry.

"I can't find Nonie anywhere," he said morosely.

"Oh, she's upstairs," Emily said. "She's going to stay with Mrs. Dill and the girls until their grandmother can get here from Chicago. She dashed over a while ago so she could get changed and pack a few things while the baby-sitter was still there. She'll be back sometime in the morning, I expect, depending on the grandmother."

"Ah," said Clarence, and sank onto his favorite easy chair on the opposite side of the fireplace. "I wonder if I should go over with her. There might be something I can do to help. Checking windows and the furnace—that kind of thing."

"You'd be better off getting yourself something to eat," Dominic said, thinking his wistful expression was caused by cold and hunger. "The buffet is still laid out. Mrs. Peach came through and turned off the warming trays on her way to bed a little while ago, but the food is still warm, I imagine. I recommend the chili."

"And I recommend everything else," Emily said, speaking from enthusiastic experience. The evening's dramatic events seemed to have stimulated her appetite, much to her dismay. A quiet life was obviously preferable for maintaining her figure. On the other hand, as she watched Mr. Toogood heading for the dining room, she recalled that she had been through a lot this evening. Encountering love and murder within hours of one another would be a strain on anybody's nervous system, especially a sensitive, intelligent person such as she had recently decided to be.

She stood up and collected her empty plate. A second helping of macaroni and cheese and perhaps a tiny triangle of apple pie would finally calm her nerves. Mrs. Peach, expecting a jolly party of friends to return after the carnival as usual, had provided plenty of everything, and it seemed a shame to waste it.

Mr. and Mrs. Stevens had been no help at all. They had avoided the carnival by going to the movies in Lemonville, returned home full of righteous buttered popcorn, and had long since gone to bed. They had been so scathing about the Howl that neither Dominic nor Emily had felt like telling them about Dill's murder—they would only have said "Told you so" and sniffed patronizingly. They could read about it in the city papers when they arrived in the morning.

As the three of them stood around the dining room table helping themselves, Nonie appeared in the doorway. "Ah— what a good idea. Maybe I'll put together a picnic to take back. If they eat, it might make them sleepy enough to settle down."

She didn't have to identify the "they" in question—she'd told them about the twins overhearing her phone call to their grandmother and of Evelyn Dill's hysteria.

"You look exhausted," said Clarence Toogood. "I hope this won't be too much for you."

Nonie glanced at him in gratified surprise. "I'm fine, thanks. Glad I can help. She's always been a bit snobby, but ... well, she's really upset. You can't help feeling sorry for someone when they're like that, can you?" They all murmured that you couldn't help it, no, you really couldn't.

Nonie went into the kitchen and appeared with various plastic bowls. "Now, then—let's see," she said, and proceeded to claim most of the food still available. Indeed, it was only by sleight of hand and quickness of wrist that Emily managed to snare that piece of apple pie she'd planned on for her second dessert.

"I'll help you carry it all across the street," Clarence said eagerly, putting down his plate. "We don't want you to slip on the ice or anything, do we?"

As they went out the door, laden with barely balanced trays of food, Emily turned to Dominic. "Do we?"

"Do we what?" Dominic asked slowly, looking after the departed couple.

"Want her to slip or anything?"

"Heavens, no!" Dominic said.

"Am I wrong in thinking that Mr. Toogood is sweet on Miss Peach?" Emily continued.

"I think you are," replied Dominic. "It seems more like nosiness than concern to me. Not that he isn't sympathetic and all that, but . . ."

"But what?"

"Well, he seems a bit eager to get over there."

"You have a very suspicious mind," Emily said.

"I know," Dominic agreed. "It's all part of the training."

"Is this something your girlfriends have to learn to tolerate?" Emily asked as they returned with their own trays to the living room.

"I haven't had any complaints," he said.

"Obviously you have only gone for the submissive type, then," Emily said. "I am different."

"I had noticed," Dominic acknowledged. "But I'm prepared to overlook your many flaws."

"How kind. I hope you're equally prepared to overlook a piece of apple pie in your ear," Emily said demurely.

They had just settled down when Clarence returned, blown down the hall by a gust of cold air. "Starting to freeze out there," he announced. "Ice forming on the puddle in the drive."

Emily glanced at the mantel clock. It was nearly one A.M. "First of November," she said. "The season's over."

"It is for Peter Dill," Clarence said, retrieving his food from the dining room. He settled onto the chair opposite. "That's one hell of a house they've got over there. Have you been in it?"

"No," they murmured, avoiding one another's eyes.

"The furnishings alone must have cost a fortune, to say nothing of all the restoration work on the fabric of the place.

Craftsmanship like that doesn't come cheap." He seemed to be adding it all up in his mind. After a moment or two of gazing into space, he readdressed himself to his meal. "And to think I almost had him, too."

Emily and Dominic stared at him. "I beg your pardon?" Dominic finally managed.

Toogood glanced up at them and smiled. "Writing books about debauched storm-door salesmen isn't my *only* job," he said.

18

When his suspects had settled down, Matt looked at each of them in turn. "First, Tom Finnegan died in what I consider to be suspicious circumstances, with the name of Jacky Morgan and a wish to confess something on his lips. I subsequently discovered that Tom and Peter Dill and the six of you were somehow involved in the death of a boy named Jacky Morgan—an incident that seemed to haunt Tom Finnegan."

"We were not 'involved,'" Carl Putnam put in. "We were simply there at the time."

"Thank you. I was curious about the apparent coincidence, but had no reason to continue my investigation."

"What investigation?" Tyrone Molt demanded.

Matt ignored him. "Tonight Dill—*another* of the original group—is blatantly murdered. And lo and behold! you're all on the scene *again*—just as you were thirty years ago. Including Albert, who hasn't been seen back here in Blackwater Bay for years. Now, I'm a reasonable man—I accept that there are coincidences happening around us all the time. Nevertheless, this is beginning to look slightly excessive in that department. So I want to know what happened that night."

"Which night?" Albert Budd demanded. "The night Tom crashed his car? I wasn't in Blackwater then, and I can prove it."

"No—the night Jacky Morgan died."

They all stared at him. Tyrone Molt was the first to recover. "Jesus, that was over thirty years ago! I can't even remember what the hell I was doing last week!" He looked around at the others, but they managed to avoid his eye. "Well, can *you* remember what you were doing on a specific night last week?" he finally challenged Merrill Atwater.

"Hell, no," Merrill mumbled.

"You?" Molt asked Jack Fanshawe.

"If it was after nine, I could make a guess," Fanshawe said, leering.

"*I* was tracking a comet," Albert Budd said. "I've been tracking it all month. I should be doing it now, in fact. There's a—" He began to wax enthusiastic about his hobby of astronomy.

"And the night Jacky Morgan died? Would you have been tracking it then?" Matt interrupted.

"Of course not. We were a poor family. I didn't have a telescope of sufficient power to do that then."

"Did you kill Jacky Morgan?" Matt asked abruptly.

The bald man blinked and went pale. "Good Lord," he said. "What a question!"

"Now listen, Gabriel," Carl Putnam said, standing up. "This is ridiculous. You should be investigating *Peter's* death, not shilly-shallying around with an accident that happened years ago and has absolutely nothing to do with it, or trying to turn another accident into murder. You're not doing your proper job on this. You were elected to protect the people who voted for you, not to play around with history. You have no more reason to hold us than to hold anyone else, and unless you actually intend to *arrest* us on suspicion of murder, I suggest that we end this right now. Do you intend to arrest us? All of us? Any of us?"

Matt met Putnam's eye. "I don't know," he admitted.

"Well, when you do know, we'll be available as usual. Until then, we're leaving. Good night." He started out the door.

"Frank?" Matt said quietly.

Boomer stepped to the door his hand on his holster, his eyes flinty. He was loving this and could hardly wait to tell his wife all about it. He settled himself, feet apart, ready for action, the way he'd seen T.J. Hooker do it on television. Come on, smart-ass, just try getting past me, he said to himself.

"Get out of my way, Frank," Putnam said, and Boomer blinked.

"Sheriff Gabriel isn't through talking to you," Frank said with a dry mouth. After assessing Putnam's expression, and the confident way he was coming through the door, he was having second thoughts about imitating art at the cost of his job. Being ready was one thing; actually doing something was another. This was, after all, Carl Putnam. If it had been Molt, now—that would be different. He wouldn't have minded arresting Molt—if only for that clunker of an '89 sedan he'd sold the wife. But Carl Putnam? He threw a quick look at Matt. Did he really want him to manhandle Carl Putnam, for crying out loud?

Charley spoke up. "You'll have to make a choice, Matt," he said. "We haven't got room to keep all of them. Not yet, anyway."

"Ha," said Tyrone Molt. "Ha, ha." There was little mirth in the sound, but considerable triumph. The others looked at one another and then at Matt. Smiles began to flicker.

"Well?" Putnam asked, turning to Matt. "Are you going to charge me or not?"

Matt looked at him and then at the others.

He looked at Frank, at Charley, and finally at Max.

They've got me, Max, he thought. I've got no grounds other than my own uneasy feelings, and not enough room at the inn.

He conceded temporary defeat but issued cautions about not leaving town. At least that would mean he knew where *somebody* was in the morning.

Frank Boomer took Carl Putnam and Dan Rogers home, waiting for and taking each of their costumes as they removed them. Charley Hart took Mayor Atwater and Jack Fanshawe home and did the same. Matt took Tyrone Molt home and Albert Budd to the Ventnor Hotel, also collecting their clothing for forensic examination.

Each of the six men complained about being "harassed,"

each of them complained about being suspected on the basis of an "ancient" crime, and each of them protested his complete innocence in connection with Dill's or any other death.

They were right about the harassment, of course, Matt thought to himself as he headed back to the fairgrounds to see that everything at the scene of the crime had been taken care of and was being protected to his satisfaction. But what were his alternatives?

Hold and interview the several thousand people who had been at the Howl? Hardly feasible with his staff.

Arrest Dill's wife? A possibility—but unless she was the world's greatest actress, he believed her shock and grief were genuine.

Arrest Dill's son? He had already sent out a request to the Hatchville police to locate Wayne Dill, but that interview would take place tomorrow. It was routine, because in addition to being related to the victim, Wayne had a record—although not of violence. Apparently he and Peter didn't get along, or at least they seemed to have little or no contact with one another. So it could have been Wayne, although what could have set him off and/or what he would have gained by killing his father remained to be discovered.

Arrest Milt Bickerstaff?

Arrest any of the other ride operators? They were unknown and transient but could all be contacted at their next venue, which was a two-week booking at Kisco Beach. As far as he knew at present, none of them had any connection with Dill or Blackwater Bay. Of course, if one of *them* was missing . . .

But all of that was general. Only his six were specific.

You have to know someone to hate them.

And whoever had killed Dill had killed with hate.

It was one or all of the six men who had been involved in the death of Jacky Morgan—he was sure of it. He felt it in his bones.

He also felt exhaustion, confusion, and a great need for the comfort of Daria. Instead he settled for cold chili in a dark and silent guest house and an otherwise empty bed.

Back in the sheriff's office, darkness and quiet also reigned. Max sighed, stretched, and resettled himself in his

currently preferred box. Beneath him the papers crunched
and rustled and crumpled—including, among them, the pale
blue accident report on one Jacky Morgan, aged seventeen,
filled in so carefully by Sheriff Ted Gabriel over thirty years
before.

19

"**W**here are they?"

When Matt arrived at the office late the next morning, the two Mrs. Matthews, in search of missing husbands, had George cornered. Phyllis—small, peppery, determined—and Joan—gentle, soft-spoken, but equally determined—were standing with hands on hips, glaring down at the hapless chief deputy.

"Look, I told you—I deputized them yesterday. They were supposed to be patrolling Jack's Nature Trail until eight this morning," George said uneasily, not knowing whether the Matthew brothers had used this as an excuse for a night out or whether something had really happened to them.

"Well, they haven't come back," Phyllis added. "*Do* something."

"Like what?"

"Like get up off your lazy backside and find them," Phyllis suggested.

"They might be hurt," Joan said.

"Or they might be drunk," Phyllis snapped. "Either way, they'll need to be looked after, and we're the girls who can do it. Find them, George. Get moving."

"Okay, okay. . . . " George stood up and winced slightly.

"And we don't want to hear about *your* hangover, either," Joan added. "We've heard it all before."

"Who said I had a hangover?" George protested.

"Your little red eyes give you away," Phyllis said. "I don't see you moving, George. Git!"

"But—"

"Git!" echoed Joan.

Directing a look of despair toward Matt, George put on his jacket and got.

Phyllis stopped at the door. "We'll be in the Golden Perch having breakfast," she informed Matt.

"Sounds good," said Matt, who had had to content himself with a quick coffee. It had been a low-calorie start to what promised to be a very high-tension day.

The Ventnor Hotel's dining room was high-ceilinged and airy. Fresh white muslin curtains stirred gently at the long windows as waitresses passed to and fro with their trays. Sundays were special, and this particular Sunday was more special than most, for the hotel allowed for the fact that its patrons might have been kept up late by the Carnival and always extended its serving hours on November 1.

Late-season tourists who had not attended the carnival were catching up on what they had missed by means of the city papers, both of which had given the murder of Peter Dill considerable coverage. Locals who had attended the carnival, and for whom Sunday breakfast at the Ventnor Inn was a tradition, had their heads together discussing the murder. As a result, many glances were directed toward the large bald man in the corner.

Albert Budd sat alone, surrounded by the detritus of a large, high-cholesterol breakfast. He nodded his appreciation as a passing waitress filled his coffee cup for the fourth time. Ignoring the glares of nearby patrons, he lit a large cigar. Then he added a generous dollop of cream to his coffee cup, stirred it reflectively, and sipped between draws on the cigar. As most of the other breakfast guests at the Ventnor were wearing casual clothing, his extreme formality of dress— three-piece dark gray suit, white silk shirt, and dark red tie— set him apart even more than his expression, his girth, or his reputation. He sat like a king and surveyed the lesser members of society. He might have maintained this lofty position for some time had he not been visited by an agitated Tilly

Moss, wearing her church best: a pleated beige skirt with a drooping hemline and a cream jacket covered with big red dots. The ensemble was completed by a large-brimmed hat that unfortunately made her look like a perambulating mushroom as she came across the room, dodging between the tables, her eyes fixed on her goal.

She stopped beside the table and looked down at Albert. "We have to talk," she said in a whisper that reached the far corners of the room.

"Sit down, sit down," Albert said hurriedly, beckoning a waitress over. "Have some breakfast."

"Oh, I ate hours ago," Tilly said. "Just some coffee, thanks. Oh, and maybe one of those Danish pastries."

"Well?" Albert asked when the waitress had served Tilly and rushed away to inform her colleagues in the kitchen about the arrival of the sheriff's secretary in a "state."

Albert leaned forward. "Before you speak, however, I suggest you keep your voice down. This room has unfortunate acoustics. In fact . . . " His voice faded as he watched her rapidly consuming the pastry. He cleared his throat. "In fact, perhaps we ought to adjourn to my suite."

Tilly looked up at him, startled. She had been worried about coming here. Going to Albert's room would make things even worse. Worries about disloyalty to Matt had caused her to drive back and forth in front of the hotel for half an hour before parking and coming in. She had a duty to Matt, but she also had one to herself. Something she had said or done had caused Albert to come here and get involved in a murder investigation. She didn't want to think he blamed her for that. "But what will people think?" she heard herself say.

Albert smiled the smile of a crocodile watching a small animal teetering along the edge of his pool. "With any luck they will think we are retiring to indulge in bizarre sexual antics," he replied calmly. "However, common sense will soon reassert itself, and they will think nothing at all about it." He stood up. "At any rate, it is a suite, not a room, and Jeffries is in attendance, so it will be quite proper. I thought you might have moved with the times, Tilly, but I see Blackwater Bay still has a hold on your imagination. Come along."

"But—"

He was already halfway across the room. Tilly took a last sip of the Ventnor's delicious coffee and followed him, still chewing a corner of pastry but keeping her head high. She might as well go through with it, now.

She hadn't known the Ventnor ran to suites and was surprised at the luxurious standard of the top-floor accommodation to which Albert led her. Sitting room, two bedrooms, two baths, all newly decorated just like a magazine.

"Drink?" Albert asked, hesitating by a tray of bottles near a bay window that looked out over the intervening buildings and permitted a glimpse of the glittering bay.

"No, thank you," Tilly said primly.

"I believe I will," said Albert, helping himself to what looked like brandy. He came across and sat down on the opposite end of the sofa to Tilly, toasting her across the expanse of beige velvet. "Now—if we are going to talk, I leave it to you to introduce the subject."

"Well, for heaven's sake, the murder, of course," Tilly said in some exasperation. "What else?"

"Almost anything else would be preferable," Albert said coolly, having sniffed and sipped his brandy. "I had nightmares all night—that poor man." He sipped again and eyed Tilly over the rim of the glass.

"Oh, knock it off," Tilly said impatiently. "Matt had you all hauled in for a grilling, didn't he? He suspects you. I'm sorry I brought you here—"

"You didn't bring me here," Albert said.

"Well, if I hadn't come to see you, would you have come?"

"I might have," Albert said. "But the sheriff's conduct is hardly your responsibility."

"Well, sometimes I feel like it is," Tilly said restlessly. "I've been there longer than he has, so I *should* know better about some things. I've tried to talk him out of it, but it's no good. He's even more stubborn than his father was. He's had some kind of bee in his bonnet ever since Ton Finnegan's accident. I don't understand it, and neither does George. Matt's not usually so . . . so . . . balky. Mind you, he *was* like that as

a kid, wouldn't let go of an idea until he'd worked it right
through."

"But it's a perfectly logical assumption," Albert said.
"Why should you talk him out of it?"

Tilly gaped at him. Was this a confession?

Albert went on, obviously enjoying himself. "For all you
know, I *did* kill Peter Dill. I had the opportunity—I was here.
What is more, it wasn't until I *was* here, after an absence of
thirty years, that Dill was killed. Apparently, one could reason, he was perfectly safe as long as I wasn't around. The
weapon was at hand—the rock. As for motive—"

Tilly's mouth remained open as Albert went on.

"Presumably he attributes to me the same motive he attributes to the others—a wish to silence Peter Dill concerning
the death of Jacky Morgan."

Tilly's mouth snapped shut.

"What he does not have," Albert continued inexorably, "is
any indication that there was anything suspicious about
young Morgan's death—because there wasn't."

"Perhaps Mr. Dill *threatened* to speak," Tilly managed.

"Have you proof of that?"

"No."

"Does he?"

"Not as far as I know."

"Well then?"

"Well, maybe he thinks you were *afraid* he'd speak."

"Has he any proof or indication of *that?*"

"No, but—"

"Exactly. And so you see, my dear Tilly, I have nothing to
fear from your sheriff, nor do any of my friends." He smiled
at her, a blank, bland smile that did not reach his eyes. "What
shall we talk about now?"

Jack Fanshawe opened one eye and looked around the room
cautiously. He recognized nothing. Opening the other eye, he
took in the lilac-sprigged wallpaper, the matching curtains,
the purple frills on the dressing table, and the profusion of
perfume and lotion bottles that cluttered its top. He tried to
slide his eyes sideways to see if he could recognize the fea-

tures of the warm female body that lay beside him, but she had her face turned away on the pillow.

Blond, no dark roots.

He moved his head slightly and took in the back of her neck, the shoulders, the curve of the spine. Over forty.

She stirred, flung out a hand.

Uh-oh. Wedding ring.

He raised an arm slowly and examined his watch. Christ! Almost noon! Stifling a moan at the jab of pain that shot through both eyeballs and struck at the center of his brain, he eased himself out of the soft bed and began to look for his clothes.

He heard a rustling of the sheets and a sleepy, muffled question from the bed behind him. He looked back. She had turned on her side to face him, blue eyes buffered by puffy lids, a long thin nose, lips pale and full, the beginnings of a double chin.

He hadn't the vaguest idea who she was.

Dr. Dan Rogers bent over the bed of the old man who had been brought in during the night with a suspected heart attack brought on by an ill-timed giant firecracker going off not four feet from him.

"Now, Mr. Parish, I don't want you to worry. This has been a warning, not a sentence. We'll be doing more tests during the morning, but I am reasonably certain that you'll be back on your feet in no time. What you do after that will determine whether we see you again in one year or in twenty—all right?"

The man nodded, reassured by Rogers's touch on his hand and the warmth of his smile. "Thank you, Doctor."

"I'm going out to see your wife now, to talk about things like diet and exercise."

"Boring," Mr. Parish said wheezily.

"Not half as boring as a quadruple bypass," Rogers said firmly. "You get some rest, and I'll see you later. All right?"

"All right." As Rogers went out the door, Parish called after him. "Does this mean no more French fries?"

Rogers turned. "I'm afraid it does."

"Good," Parish said, pulling up the covers and closing his eyes. "Can't stand the damn things."

Mayor Merrill Atwater was in his gym, working out. Sweat poured down his face and chest. As the weights clattered for the last time into their sockets, he rose and reached for a towel to wipe himself down. Turning away, he glanced at his reflection in the mirrored wall opposite. Not bad for a man his age.

But not so good, either.

He went closer and examined his face. Bags under the eyes. A thickening at the jawline. A coarsening of the pores of the nose and scattered thread veins appearing in the cheeks.

"You're Getting Old, Atwater," he said aloud, his voice filling the huge space and making the nearest apparatus jingle slightly. He took a deep breath and let it out. "But you're also Getting Better." He smiled at his reflection.

Above his head, the wall-mounted intercom speaker crackled, and the voice of Mrs. Atwater filled the gym with a shrill, tooth-rattling sound.

"Merrill, there's somebody on the phone for you from the governor's office about the murder, and you have to get dressed for church or we'll be late, so don't take too long."

Atwater's shoulders slumped, and his belly muscles sagged. "I'll be right there," he said.

"And your breakfast is getting cold. You *know* what it does to your stomach if you eat cold bacon, Merrill. I called you ten minutes ago."

"Sorry, my dear, the weights were—"

The speaker clicked off, and Atwater headed toward the door of the gym. Just as he reached for it, the speaker crackled again. "By the way, Mrs. James is coming around after church with her new baby. I want you to be extra nice to her, because she had a hard time. But it's a *sweet* baby, with curly red hair, just like our Denny. You'll love it." The speaker clicked off.

Atwater closed his eyes. After a moment the speaker crackled again. "Merrill? What's that noise?"

The mayor didn't answer but continued to gently bang his head against the varnished surface of the gym door.

Bump, bump, bump, bump, bump.

Tyrone Molt was paying off his temporary nightwatchmen.

"You done real good," he said grudgingly. "No trouble, no damage. Must be a record."

"Glad to be of help," the three men said, accepting their pay and getting into the blue pickup in which they had arrived from the city the previous night.

It wasn't until an hour later, while drinking his coffee and sucking the raisins from his third Danish out of a hollow tooth, that Molt noticed the row of used cars at the very rear of the lot was three short. They had been carefully respaced and reparked to cover the discrepancy.

And he hadn't even taken down the number of the pickup.

Carl Putnam stood on the eighth tee, waiting his turn. Archy Ventnor, his partner for the morning round, swung, hit, and shaded his eyes to follow the ball down the fairway. "That will make two funerals this week," he said. "Good for business—relatives from out of town usually put up at the hotel."

"That's a callous attitude," Carl protested as he plunged his tee into the hard ground. "They were good men."

"Yeah, sure. But Finnegan was going to go soon, anyway."

"And Peter Dill?"

Ventnor shrugged. He was a handsome man, much younger than Putnam, dressed in a tartan golfing outfit with a Coors baseball cap on the back of his head. "People die," he said.

"Dill was murdered."

"People die or get murdered—either way it means a funeral. So? As long as it isn't me or mine, I have to look on the practical side and make certain we have enough rooms ready. I'm not going to walk around with a long face saying nice things about a guy I hardly knew and didn't much like. Was Dill a big buddy of yours?"

"I went to school with him." Putnam swung, and his ball sailed high and straight down the fairway.

"Oh. Okay. Sorry." Ventnor wasn't embarrassed. "Nice shot."

"Thanks," Putnam said, going back to the cart and shoving his driver into his bag. He sat behind the wheel and waited for Ventnor to store his club and sit beside him. "Nothing wrong with a practical attitude, Archy, but you have to remember that people have feelings."

"All right, all right—I'm sorry if Dill was a friend of yours," Ventnor said defensively.

Putnam started the cart moving. "I didn't say *that*," he commented, and steered carefully down the slope.

Dominic Pritchard and Emily Gibbons were walking in the Cecil G. Heckman Memorial Park, admiring the sharp reds and yellows of the autumn trees and one another. After driving her home, Dominic had spent the remaining hours of the previous night tossing and turning, his imagination bright with images of what might have been if he'd been living in a place of his own instead of at Mrs. Peach's Guest House.

Today it was becoming clear to him that—in this, at least—he had been mistaken. To a healthy and love-struck young man, Emily Gibbons was that most terrible of things—a good girl.

This was not to say she was either frigid or a prude. Just careful. She was not the type to leap into bed at the first rise of hormones, and it was therefore going to take time for his fervid imaginings to become reality—which was just as well, as he had more pressing concerns at the moment than the well-being of his glandular infrastructure.

"You *do* understand, don't you?"

"I understand that you're trusting me not to give in to my baser instincts and publish a huge editorial on it," Emily said, hooking her arm through his. He did look very attractive, despite the circles under his eyes, and they'd passed by several of her acquaintances already. She was content—except for all this fuss he was making about the murder. What he'd had to say so far would have been interesting—very interesting—if there had been a story in it. But before going on, he had demanded that she not publish a word.

"You promise?"

"I promise—on my mother's life."

So he told her about the file.

"I'm in a bit of a quandary about it," he said morosely.

"I've always thought that sounded kind of like a big—"

"*Listen,* will you!"

"Sorry." He was even cuter when he was agitated. She was enjoying herself immensely.

"A lawyer's files are confidential, but lawyers are also officers of the court, and so if they *know* about a crime—"

"Paying money to some poor old woman isn't a crime."

"It is if the payments are for blackmail."

"Oh. But she's dead, isn't she?"

"The payments stopped—that doesn't mean she's dead. The last payment was a big one—maybe it was a settlement of some kind."

Emily kicked through the leaves along the edge of the path. "Did you try to contact her at that last address?"

"No. I haven't done anything yet. I told you, I'm in a —"

"Quandary, yes, I know."

"Well? What do you think I should do?"

"I suppose you ought to ask Mr. Putnam about it."

It was Dominic's turn to kick leaves. "Oh, swell—and admit I was burrowing through his files without permission?"

She shrugged. "Did he tell you not to go through them?"

"Well, no, but—"

"Then you can say you thought you were supposed to do it."

"Yes, but—"

"Alternatively, you and I can go there now and look

through this file, and then I might be in a better position to advise you," Emily concluded with a bright smile.

"I don't need advice, I just need to—"

Emily withdrew her arm. "Then why have you told me about all this?" she demanded. "It's not *my* problem."

He stopped and looked at her in sudden dismay. "I thought you wanted to know what was worrying me," he said in a plaintive voice. "I thought you *cared* about—"

"Oh, I do, I do," she agreed absently, staring over his shoulder. "I really do."

Hurt at her sudden change of attitude and apparent disinterest, he turned to see what she was looking at. They were not the only ones to stare.

Magnificent on his marble pediment, the life-size bronze of Cecil G. Heckman stared out over the park that bore his name. Noble head outlined against the brilliant blue of the sky, he made an impressive and memorable focus for the four broad paths that led to the cobbled circle that surrounded the statue. Below the beautifully sculpted lines of his face, the delineation of his clothing was perfect in every detail, right down to the last button on his coat.

Which was painted bright purple.

And his trousers.

Which were painted bubblegum pink.

And his waistcoat.

Which was painted neon orange.

And his shoes.

Which were painted banana yellow.

With green spots.

But it was the head that held the eyes. Cascading over the old senator's cast-bronze curls was red paint—paint that spoke eloquently and horribly of blood. Whether the jokesters who had decorated Cecil G. Heckman had known about the murder of Peter Dill or not was a moot point. It was even possible that the red paint had been added by someone else after the initial "artwork" had been completed.

Whoever had been responsible, the fact was that they had
provided everyone in Blackwater Bay with a ghastly reminder of what had been done to one of its leading citizens
the night before. Even when the paint had been removed, the
memory would linger.

Emily and Dominic were silent for a while. Then Dominic
stirred and took hold of Emily's arm. "Let's go look at that
damned file," he said.

20

At the best of times, Wayne Dill was not a prepossessing young man—and this was hardly his best of times. Roused early from a bed he'd inhabited for only three hours, he was unshaven, bleary-eyed, and pale. Coming over from Hatchville in the patrol car, they'd had to stop twice to let him throw up some of the beer he'd consumed the previous night.

When he arrived at Matt's office he looked terrible, smelled worse, and was, furthermore, still drunk.

And angry.

"You got no right—!!" he shouted, swaying from side to side until Duff Bradley pushed him onto a chair.

"Wayne, I have bad news for you," Matt began.

"And I got news for *you*, asshole," shouted Wayne. "You got no goddamn right bringing me here. I ain't done nothin', and you ain't got a warrant, and what's more, anyway, just because—"

"Wayne, listen to me!" Matt shouted back. Into the stunned moment of silence that ensued while Wayne took a breath to continue his tirade, he dropped the simple words: "Wayne, your father is dead."

Mouth still open but no sound emerging, Wayne stared at him.

"Do you understand?" Matt asked after a moment.

Wayne closed his mouth and blinked. "No," he said.

"Your father is dead," Matt repeated. "He was killed last night. Did you do it?" With drunks, he'd found, a frontal attack was often best.

"Do what?" Wayne asked, a sly glint appearing in his eyes.

"Did you kill your father?"

"My father? Kill my father?"

"Yes."

"Show him to me, I'll give him a medal."

"Who?"

"Who killed my father, that's who." There was a pause. "Thisizza joke, right?" The shaggy head moved from side to side as he looked at each of them in turn—Matt, Duff Bradley, and Frank Boomer. He scowled. "Not very funny."

Then he leaned over and threw up into the wastebasket. "Bull's-eye!" he said triumphantly, wiping the nauseous slime from his loose mouth onto his sleeve. "Never spilled a drop, right? No sense keeping it when the good is all got out of it, right?"

And he laughed.

It took quite a while to make him understand, and when he did understand he began to cry, and that took quite a while, too.

"Well, hell," he blubbered with a drunkard's childish naiveté, "he didn't deserve that, did he? Maybe we didn't get along these last few years, but he was my old man. I hated his guts, but he was my old man, and before it all started we were okay, we spent time together, and like that."

"Before all what started, Wayne?" Matt asked softly.

"All that stuff with Vic Moss," Wayne snuffled. "It wasn't my fault, but he blamed me for it, he wouldn't pay, and I got beat up—" He stopped abruptly, some instinct warning him to protect even the dead from the long nose of the law.

Matt leaned back, trying not to show his surprise. Victor Moss was Hatchville's major villain, running high-ticket women and gambling out of a mansion that would have made an automotive giant envious. But he was a villain of the old school, a Hollywood gent, his appearance a cross between the MGM lion and *Tyrannosaurus rex*, informed equally by *GQ* and the streets of Grantham, where he'd grown up from gutter to criminal grandee. Whatever went on in his name, even perhaps under his own eyes, never seemed to actually touch him. Set in the lush surroundings of a large private estate, Moss's empire was allowed to flourish because he was discreet, well behaved, and serviced the vices of many of the leading politicians in the county.

So, young Wayne had developed a gambling habit that Dill refused to finance, leaving his son to the untender mercies of Moss's collection men? Matt surveyed Wayne Dill and almost felt sympathy for him. Almost. Whatever the boy had started out to be, whatever Dill's plans for him had been, there was no denying that he was now pretty much a drifting disaster waiting to slop onto somebody's shore. Even so, to be rejected by your father was tough and obviously enough to make a grown man cry into his beer. Repeatedly.

"How much do you owe?" Matt asked.

Wayne looked up in surprise. "Me? *Me?* I don't owe nothin', man. *I'm* no gambler—anyway, Vic Moss don't allow bums like me into his fancy-ass place, does he?"

Matt leaned forward, trying not to show his dismay. "Are you telling me your *father* owed money to Moss?"

"I never said that!" Wayne shouted, too quickly, too loudly.

"No," Matt agreed sadly. "You never said that."

"Well, then . . ." Wayne subsided.

Further questioning elicited the information that Wayne had been with friends in a bar in Hatchville for the whole of the evening of October 31 and could not have been his father's killer. Pending interviews with these "friends," Matt had nothing on which to hold him. Even so, he held him, hoping that the coming of sobriety would herald the coming of sense.

It was not to be.

Sobriety merely brought out the natural cunning of a privately educated ex-convict, well schooled in the remarkably similar traditions of both societies.

Sober, Wayne maintained that his inadvertent mention of being beaten up had absolutely nothing to do with his father. Last year he, Wayne, had asked his father for money, but his father had been unable to help him, having at the time a lot

of personal expenses—the twins had needed orthodontal
work, apparently—so Wayne had borrowed money from one
of Victor Moss's "agents" and had run up a debt he was unable to repay, hence the beating. Nothing to do with his father. Nothing to do with Matt, either. Here he sat, a son
who'd lost his father in violent circumstances—didn't that
mean he was due a little respect instead of bullying and harassment?

Matt had tried to break through the boy's barriers, but a
sober Wayne—shaggy and sullen though he might be—was
a match for him. From within the flaccid facial muscles of
overindulgence there shone eyes of considerable intelligence
and guile. Wayne had nothing to say.

As Matt had, equally, nothing with which to charge him,
Wayne Dill was reluctantly returned to Hatchville.

"Have we any way of getting information out of Victor
Moss's bunch?" Matt asked Frank Boomer. Boomer was a
reliable man most of the time, but he did have a preference
for mixing with the lower element of the county. A good ol'
boy, and useful because of it.

Boomer considered. "We might. What do you want to
know?"

"Whether Peter Dill was a regular at Moss's place,
whether he was a gambler or a womanizer—dope seems unlikely—and if so, what he owed."

"Mr. Dill the banker, you mean, or his son?" Boomer
asked.

"I mean Mr. Dill the banker and recent corpse," Matt said.

"Shit—you don't think he was killed on *Moss's* orders, do
you?" Boomer's amazement said it all.

"I hope not," Matt said. "I truly do hope not."

"Because we haven't a hope in—"

"I know, I know." Matt sighed. "Just find out what you
can, will you?"

"Sure," Boomer agreed. "I'll make some calls."

"Quietly, Frank. Very quietly."

Boomer looked at him reproachfully.

Matt grinned. "Sorry," he said.

*   *   *

George Putnam returned twenty minutes later. "Found Bob and Jim Matthew," he said.

"Where were they?" Matt asked, expecting anything.

"On Jack's Nature Trail," George said wearily, hanging up his jacket and hat. "Both of them roped facedown on the path, madder than hell, and each one with a great big footprint painted on his back."

The giant jogger had struck again.

When Tilly came in after lunch, she seemed very subdued. Matt asked her if there was anything wrong, was her mother ill, was *she* ill, did she want to skip work for the day—all questions she answered with a shake of the head.

"I'm just tired, Matt. Last night was very upsetting, and it took me a long time to get Mother to sleep. But I know you need me here, so . . ." she shrugged and managed a smile. "Here I am. What would you like me to do?"

"I want you to do the impossible, Tilly."

"Well, sure," she said, managing a grin. "I do that all the time."

"I know you do." He grinned, too, but his eyes were serious. "I want you to draw me up a timetable—one that will cover all six men—"

"Which—"

"You know which six men. And—"

"You're still hipped on that Jacky Morgan business? Matt, I really don't think—"

"Well, if you don't agree with me—and I know you don't, and George doesn't, and probably nobody else does, either—here's one way to settle it once and for all. I want a timetable running from the start of the carnival to the time of the murder, and I want it for all six men, and I want it broken down in twenty-minute increments. Then we'll assign one deputy to each name, and all they have to do is find someone to vouch for seeing the men at each of the times. It shouldn't be all that difficult—they're all well known, and most of them were with their families anyway, so there should be very few gaps. Can you do that?"

"Yes, I can. And I can fill in Albert Budd's timetable my-

self, so that will be one less deputy out annoying people,"
she snapped.

"Fine."

It took her about an hour, and when she was finished
charting out what was required, she brought the master sheet
and several smaller sheets of paper to Matt. She seemed, if
anything, a little more subdued than before. "I couldn't quite
complete Albert's timetable after all. When I thought back,
there were two times when we were apart: once when he was
talking to Mr. Berringer—but Jeffries and Mother were still
with him—"

"Then Berringer could verify that," Matt said, making a
note to call him.

"And during the fireworks. I stayed with Mother at the
foot of the bleachers because of her being in her wheelchair
and all, but Albert said he wanted to go higher up because he
hates the smell of gunpowder and the air would be fresher up
there. I didn't see him again until the fireworks were finished. He came right down, though, and we were together
until you found Peter Dill's body."

"Well, he must have sat next to somebody," Matt said easily. "We can check that out." He looked over the other charts
and found he could make a few entries himself, as he realized he'd unconsciously been keeping an eye out for the six
men through the evening. It hadn't been suspicion—after all,
he had hardly expected Dill to be murdered—but they had
been on his mind because of both Jacky Morgan and Tom
Finnegan, so he'd been more aware of them. Even so, the
times he filled in were but few and approximate—as everyone else's would be. He sighed.

"It's just a shot in the dark, Tilly, and maybe it is a waste
of everyone's time, but I think it's worth doing."

"Whatever you say, Matt." Tilly went back to her desk
and stared unseeing at her computer screen. "What should I
do now?"

"What we do with any case, Tilly," Matt said gently.
"Open a file on the investigation, make some coffee, fill in
the appropriate forms, make some coffee, enter the details on
the computer, make some coffee . . . you know." He went

over to her and put his hand on her shoulder. "And stop worrying. I'm sure Albert had nothing to do with it."

She smiled up at him gratefully, aware—as he was—that he was bullshitting just to make her feel better.

Emily and Dominic stared at one another. The last payment listed in Mrs. Coral Morgan's file hadn't been for ten thousand dollars, as he'd vaguely remembered. He'd missed out a few zeros. The payment had been for over *one hundred thousand* dollars, and it had been invoiced by a company called Sunshine Forever, Incorporated, with an address near St. Petersburg, Florida.

They were sitting side by side on the rather elderly chaise longue in Dominic's office, going through the papers in the dusty manila folder. The afternoon sunlight slanted in through the window, its touch surprisingly warm considering how cold it was outside, and from the street below came the sounds of people talking in tones that ranged from amazement to shock. The occasional rumble of the huge carnival rides being transported away to their next venue caused the conversations to pause—and then they continued, making a rise and fall of noise like surf.

"It sounds like one of those retirement villages," Emily finally said. "There are a lot of them in Florida, and out west, too. Do you suppose she's still alive?"

"Well, she probably isn't that old, you know," Dominic said. "When Jacky died he was seventeen—his mother *could* even have been in her early thirties then, which would only put her in her sixties now. She might have been older—we could check the county birth records in Hatchville or search church records for the date of her marriage or the hospital for—"

"Wouldn't it be easier just to call this place and ask?" Emily interrupted.

"Er—yes, I guess it would," he said, chagrined.

Emily stood up and went over to the phone. As she dialed the number shown on the headed invoice, she smiled at him. "You're going to be a very successful lawyer, and we are going to be very rich," Emily said. "How nice."

"What makes you say that?" He was puzzled.

"You obviously have a knack for turning simple tasks into

complex efforts, thus building up your charges. What a pity I
don't believe in wearing fur—we could probably afford
sable, or—" She lifted her head suddenly. "Sunshine Forever? Good afternoon. I'm calling in reference to one of
your . . . clients. A Mrs. Coral Morgan. I'm her niece, and I've
been living abroad for some years. Is she . . . still with you?"

Dominic stared openmouthed as she continued with her
rapidly manufactured tale of "getting in touch with Aunt
Coral after all these years." She was right: he would have
made long, hard work of it, whereas she did the simple,
straightforward thing.

She lied.

"I understand completely," Emily was saying. "And really, I'm very grateful. I should be able to get down there tomorrow just before lunch—do you think she will be feeling
strong enough to see me then?" A pause, and Emily nodded
into the air, her eyes on Dominic and one thumb raised in
success mode. "Wonderful. Thank you so much. Oh—and
don't tell her I'm coming, I'd like it to be a surprise. Would
that be all right? Her heart isn't . . . Oh, wonderful. And your
name? Mrs. Perkins. Well, thank you, Mrs. Perkins. I'm
Emily Morgan, by the way, and I look forward to meeting
you in person. Thanks again. Good-bye."

"Now, look—" Dominic was saying as she put the phone
down.

"Well, isn't it the quickest way to find out what we want
to know?" Emily asked innocently, coming back to sit beside
him. "Aren't you proud of me?"

"Yes, but—"

"I can fly down and talk to her and find out all about it,"
she said happily. "Then we'll know whether we should tell
the sheriff or not."

"Why should *you* go?" he finally managed. "It's got nothing to do with you. *I* should go."

"And how would you explain your sudden journey to Mr.
Putnam?" Emily asked, wide-eyed. "Besides, I'm a woman."

"I noticed," Dominic said.

"And I could probably get a lot more information out of
Mrs. Coral Morgan than you could," she continued, snapping
the file shut. "Kiss me."

"What?" He had been about to protest that he was perfectly capable of interviewing old ladies, and her sudden command confused him.

"Kiss me, I said. Someone's coming up the stairs."

He turned toward the door, but she turned him back around and enclosed him in a sudden and passionate embrace, so that when Mr. Carl Putnam came into the outer office, he had a good view of a courting couple caught in the act.

"Oops," he said with a grin of pretended embarrassment. "I see you have acquired a new client, Dominic."

Dominic stood up, shedding Emily's arms, horrified at being caught with—with—he looked down. The file had vanished.

"Sorry, sir. You see . . ."

"I see very clearly." Putnam smiled sympathetically. "Hello, Emily. How are your parents?"

"Oh, just fine, thanks, Mr. Putnam. I'll tell them you said hello."

"Good. Do that. Don't mind me, I just came in to get some money out of the safe." He started toward his office, then turned and came toward Dominic, who stepped back involuntarily. Putnam reached in and took hold of Dominic's office door and drew it toward him. "You must never forget the most important requirement of successful legal practice."

"Sir?"

Putnam winked as he closed Dominic's office door. "Discretion, Dom. Always proceed with discretion."

His footsteps went away, and his office door closed.

"Jesus wept," Dominic said, wilting back onto the chaise longue. He looked around. "I thought he'd see the file. Where is it?"

Emily lifted the edge of her wide skirt, revealing a corner of the manila folder. "Discretion, Dom," she said, with a grin. "Always proceed with discretion."

By the evening, when the last deputy had returned the last individual timetable, one thing was very clear. It hadn't been a wasted effort.

Matt stared down at the large master chart, so carefully divided into squares, with the names of the "suspects" down one side and the time in twenty-minute increments across the top. Running through the entire chart were two glaring blank lines.

During the entire duration of the fireworks display—some forty minutes in all—nobody had seen any of the men.

For forty whole minutes, during the noisiest period of the evening, Merrill Atwater, Carl Putnam, Jack Fanshawe, Tyrone Molt, Daniel Rogers, and Albert Budd had been missing from view.

And so had Peter Dill.

21

"*D*ammit, Max, move—now I've *got* to find out what actually happened that night!"

The big ginger cat protested as he was pushed off onto the fourth box from the left, and from there to the fifth, as Matt began hauling out papers and sorting through them.

Max sighed heavily, and Matt looked up.

"All right, all right—I know that sound. I'm sorry, but it has to be done. There are just too many coincidences."

Max yawned.

"It may not interest you, but it fascinates me. Here we have eight young men who shared a common experience, presumably a harrowing experience. They were seventeen, eighteen years old at the time—it was dramatic, exciting, scary—just the stuff to draw the girls. And yet none of them has ever spoken about it. Years later, when Tom Finnegan finally *wanted* to talk about it, the others apparently tried to convince him to keep his mouth shut. Why? What really happened? What were they so determined to hide? When Tom seemed *determined* to talk to me about it despite their best efforts to dissuade him, he got killed in an 'accident.'"

Max began washing a paw.

"His wife says she overheard him talking to someone—and we know he talked to all of them—on the afternoon he died. She says he spoke of 'murder.' Despite that, the state

police are not prepared to spend any more time on it. Okay—
I accept their decision, they have their priorities and I have
mine. So now we have seven of them left, seven men *still* not
prepared to talk about what happened the night Jacky Morgan died.

"Suddenly, for no apparent reason, one of them who left
town years ago and has never seen fit to return comes back.
The seven are together again—and what happens almost immediately? *Another* one of them dies. But this time, *this*
time, Max, it isn't a fall from a high cliff or a car crashing off
the road—it's clearly murder.

"The seven have now become six. You'd think, wouldn't
you, that they would be worried about it, that they might *notice* they were dying off one by one. But they *aren't* worried,
Max. They're all as calm as can be. What does that tell you?"

Max looked out of the window.

"It tells *me* that they're in it *together*. The doctor says that
as far as he can see from a preliminary examination, there
were at least six blows to Dill's head. *Six*, mind you. If he's
right—that's one blow each. And now I find they were all
unaccounted for at the same time—so they had a chance to
gang up on Dill and finish him off. Maybe that was the same
way they finished Jacky Morgan off!"

Matt continued to talk as he rummaged through the next
box. "Now, I'm *trying* to be sensible about this. I admit that
if George came up with this *Murder on the Orient Express*
idea I'd laugh him out of the office. I admit that it's kind of
farfetched and unbelievable. I admit that. But if I can just
find out—*hah!*"

Max gave a start at his shout, then made for the cat flap.
No self-respecting feline would stay in an office where a pre-
viously sensible human was jumping up and down and waving a piece of blue paper in the air.

Matt did not notice the clunk of the cat flap—he was
too busy sorting out the rest of the Jacky Morgan file.
When he had collected all the relevant documents he
could find, he took them back to his desk and began to
read.

Accident Report

Date: November 1, 1962
Place: Blackwater Bay
Recording Officer: Theodore J. Gabriel, Sheriff

During the evening of 31 October, 1962, the following
people trespassed on the land of Mr. G. G. Osborne for
the purpose of "having a picnic" to celebrate Halloween:
Carl Putnam (17), Daniel Rogers (18), Peter Dill (18), Tyrone (Mouldy) Molt (19) Merrill (Merry) Atwater (17),
John (Jack) Fanshawe (17), Albert (Red) Budd
(18), Thomas (Tom) Finnegan (17), John (Jacky) Morgan
(17), Maureen (Micky) Ventnor (16), Jane Heckman (16),
Mildred (Milly) Hackabush (17), and Martha Turkle (17).

The land in question is the wooded area known locally
as Ghost Glen, located on top of Eagle Head. The picnic
was in the nature of a dare, as the area has the reputation
of being haunted and is also posted clearly against trespass by Mr. Osborne, who has been known to prosecute
past offenders. I believe this trespass was not done with
malicious intent, but was simply an example of Halloween high spirits, typical of the activities indulged in by
young people at this time of year.

According to those present (see attached personal statements), they had driven to the woods in three cars, belonging to Rogers, Molt, and Budd. They parked some
distance away and went into the woods "deep enough so
nobody could see." They gathered branches for a fire. In
the course of their exploration, they came across the remains of a "still" (see Report 2128, March '62) once operated by Osborne. After building the fire in a clearing
near this site, they roasted wieners and marshmallows,
told ghost stories, and indulged in various forms of horse-
play. About an hour after they had arrived, John (Jacky)
Morgan joined them, having gotten there on foot. The
girls left shortly afterward, saying the boys were "getting
too rowdy." It is clear from evidence found near the
campfire that some beer and whiskey was consumed, and

the boys say that this was provided by Morgan. According to Peter Dill (see attached), they soon got bored with "sitting around" and decided to investigate the old still, in case some whiskey had been "overlooked." They found none, but began a game of dares—climbing trees, etc. The subsequently fatal dare involved the one whole barrel found at the site. They devised a "game" which involved taking turns being "rolled in the barrel" to see how far each would go toward the cliff before losing his nerve. They tied a rope to the barrel for safety, but the rope was old and partially rotted. Morgan drew the short straw and went first. The rope parted, and he went over the cliff, falling to his death.

Rogers and the others climbed down the cliff to see if they could help Morgan, while Atwater drove to town for help. I accompanied Atwater back to Eagle Cove, arriving on the scene at 11:53 P.M., along with my deputy, Harry Jorganson. We located Morgan's body on the rocks. The others were nearby. Rogers was weeping openly. Apparently he had some first-aid training and had hoped to help Morgan but had been unable to do anything for him as he was obviously dead when they got to him. Rogers was extremely distressed and was subsequently treated for shock at the hospital, as were the others. The parents of the boys were called to the hospital, where they were informed of what had occurred and their sons' part in it. All of the boys showed genuine regret and guilt over what had happened.

This morning I returned to the scene with the boys, who were very cooperative. With their help, I reconstructed the events of the previous evening and found physical evidence to confirm their version of their own activities, i.e. empty beer bottles, an empty whiskey bottle, the fire, remains of food and food packaging, etc.

In my opinion, Morgan's death was the result of a stupid but innocent dare rising out of alcoholic bravado and could have been avoided had any of the boys shown simple common sense. Instead they behaved stupidly and without any evidence of responsibility or care. Although there was a full moon, it was dark enough in the woods to prevent their seeing the true condition of the rope on which they were depending for safety. But their judgment was impaired by alcohol, and they took no secondary precautions whatsoever. It might be said the result was inevitable.

Signed
Theodore Gabriel, Sheriff

Attached were the individual statements of the boys and the coroner's report, which stated that John (Jacky) Morgan died of "multiple injuries among which were a fractured skull, several broken ribs, one of which had penetrated the right lung and lacerated the heart, a broken arm, broken legs, and a broken back, all consistent with a fall from a height of some one hundred and seventy feet onto the rocks."

There was a rough sketch of the cliff in profile, showing the probable course of the fall, and several photographs of the body in situ among the rocks, surrounded by the broken hoops and shattered staves of the barrel. The glare of the flash reflected from the water that lapped the rocks, but the white face of the boy was clear and curiously blank above the cruelly distorted limbs.

The old man had been thorough all right.

He'd also been angry and disgusted.

But had he been suspicious?

According to Ted Gabriel, all the boys had shown "sincere regret" and "distress" about Jacky Morgan's death. They had been "very cooperative." Although distressed, they had gone back to the woods with the sheriff and his deputy to show him exactly what had happened. And, to be fair, his father had no reason to doubt those boys. They did not have "bad" reputations, they all came of respectable families, some quite well-to-do, and they all had good school records. They had never even been cautioned for speeding, still the most common offense among the local young.

True, they had been trespassing—but the sheriff concluded that it was due to "Halloween and youthful high spirits"—and that there had been no "malicious intent."

In short, a stupid, avoidable, but nonetheless tragic accident.

He was about to put the report into a folder when he noticed, in the curled-over bottom right-hand corner, a small
mark. Looking more closely, he saw it was not a mark as
such, but some letters and numbers written in very small
script—CDB6/12.

In his father's code—"See day book six, page twelve."

Ted Gabriel had been a complex man. On the surface bluff
and good-humored, he'd also had a tendency to secret depression coupled with a frustrated creativity that had never
found an outlet. In the long months of his dying, he'd confided to his son that he'd kept day books, or what he called
his "dark books," in which he wrote out all the anger and
confusion that he felt unable to express in public or within
his family. When he'd told Matt about it, he said his first impulse had been to ask him simply to burn the books unread.
But on later consideration, when he'd learned that Matt intended to run for sheriff himself, he had advised him to leave
them where they were. Now, staring at the small letters in the
corner of the report, Matt tried to remember where his father
had kept the collection of stiff-covered notebooks.

His father had closed his eyes against a wave of pain,
sinking back onto the pillows until it had passed. When he'd
spoken again, his voice had been weaker, and Matt had had
to lean forward to catch his words. "Don't read them just to
read them—I'll be embarrassed enough knowing they're still
around—but if sometime you get in a corner, they might be
of some help. Just knowing somebody else went through bad
times too can make it easier. You sure you want to do this,
son?" He'd meant was Matt sure about being sheriff.

"I'm sure, Dad." Although he hadn't been, and still
wasn't.

"Then just remember where they are."

Finally it came to him, and he retrieved the box from a
dusty gap behind the office safe. Number six was there—and
he quickly thumbed through to page twelve. He scanned it
quickly, then read it again more slowly, remembering that
Belling had been the coroner until 1972. Ted Gabriel's con-
tempt for him was clear.

Belling says "maybe" the kid could have been dead when he went over. There was so little blood, but that could have been washed away by the shallow water where he landed. What can I do? I can't accuse these boys of murder, their parents would raise holy hell, nobody would believe me, it would split the town wide open. I have no proof, no reason, nothing. Just my feeling that they're lying, and Belling's chicken-shit "maybe" which he won't say out loud in any court because he's afraid of losing his goddamn extra pension money. I hate his gutless sniveling and can't wait until he retires. The kid wasn't liked, I know that. His mother is a slut and a drunk, nobody cares about the boy's death except her. The town wouldn't appreciate my spending money trying to make her happy by taking on some long investigation that goes nowhere. And as long as these boys stick together, it *will* go nowhere. So I give up. Another one that slides by, when you know you should do something and you haven't got the time or the guts yourself to stand up to everyone and push it to the limit. Maybe I'm like Belling. Maybe I'm worse than Belling. I'm tired. I'm going home. Fuck it.

Matt stared at the book. Old deaths, old suspicions, old books, and old stories. How much of the past slides its tentacles into the present, curling and tightening in secret around this soul and that heart, strangling, sickening, crushing? The "boys" were still sticking together, the "boys" were still telling the same story, the same lies.

He started to swear, quietly at first and then with increasing intensity and volume.

Max, returning via the cat flap, paused and backed out again. He'd heard that kind of noise before.

Perhaps another patrol of his territory was in order.

22

"*I* suppose you think this is funny," Tilly said when Matt walked in the next morning. She was bent over the boxes he'd been rummaging through the previous evening, trying to put them in some kind of order. "I mean, this is the *second* time, Matt. Didn't you say you'd ask me for what you needed in future?"

"Sorry, Tilly. It won't happen again—I found what I wanted."

"Well, congratulations." She didn't sound as if she were pleased at his success. In fact, she had been acting less than pleased about everything since the night of the Howl. He was sorry about that.

"Where's George?" he asked.

"Gone over to Hatchville for the coroner's report on Dill."

"Oh." He helped himself to coffee and a doughnut. At least Tilly's resentment had not extended to taking strike action over the office refreshments.

He'd gone home the night before absolutely exhausted and more than a little confused himself. He understood Tilly's feelings better than she knew, and he didn't like what he was having to do. But Tom Finnegan deserved his best efforts, and so did Peter Dill. So he ignored Tilly's resentful thumps as she sorted through the boxes, just as he'd had to ignore Dominic Pritchard's strange behavior last night.

The Sunday evening meal at Mrs. Peach's Guest House

was another buffet affair, the main meal of the day being served at midday. He had missed it, suffering indigestion from a hurriedly snatched hamburger instead of enjoying one of Mrs. Peach's sumptuous Sunday lunches.

While he'd been filling his plate, Dominic had come in with Emily Gibbons. They'd both looked at Matt with almost furtive expressions and had returned his tired greetings with equally offhand smiles. This was so counter to Dominic's usual enthusiasm that Matt's curiosity had been aroused. He'd tried to open a conversation with them, but they had given only monosyllabic responses, and in the end he'd given up, taking his dessert up to his room with the excuse that he was going to eat it later. As he'd gone up the stairs he'd seen Dominic watching him, an almost guilty look suffusing his features, but when he'd paused the boy had looked away to concentrate on his food. Matt had continued up the stairs feeling something of a pariah, and eaten his cookies while trying to read a book. Eventually he had fallen into a deep but oddly unrefreshing sleep.

When he'd come down to breakfast this morning, it was to find that Dominic had already eaten and left—another unusual action for a man who usually lingered over his coffee in order to walk to town with Matt every morning.

There was no doubt about it: Dominic Pritchard was avoiding him. Was it because of Carl Putnam? By now most of the town had heard about Matt's immediate questioning of six of the town's most important men following the murder of Peter Dill. He had no doubt there were many who were feeling confused by his actions as well as his inactions concerning the murder investigation.

Was Dominic afraid of losing his job? Eager to help Matt before, he now seemed more eager to distance himself from the entire affair. It was disappointing, but no more than Matt had come to expect. One by one he was alienating everyone—Tilly, George, and now Dominic.

He sat down at his desk, feeling hard done by and not a little lonely. He looked through his father's old accident report on Jacky Morgan again and noted the names of the girls who had been there in the woods during the first part of the evening.

Jane Heckman. She was unavailable, dead of cancer
shortly after he'd been elected sheriff. As far as he knew,
Martha Turkle was alive, but she had married and moved
away from Blackwater years before. He thought he might be
able to track her down if he really needed to, as Turkles good
and bad always kept in touch.

Maureen (Micky) Ventnor? It took him a moment to rec-
oncile the tomboyish nickname with the dignified woman,
now Mrs. Arthur Hudson, who was a leading light in the
Blackwater Bay Operatic and Musical Society. Now that was
not an encounter he looked forward to by any means.

Milly Hackabush. He grinned. She was still around, teaching physical education at the local high school. He decided to
talk to Milly first and to Mrs. Hudson afterward, if necessary. If he couldn't get the truth out of his suspects, perhaps
the "girls" could give him some insight into the events of
thirty years ago.

"Do we have a number for Arthur Hudson?" he asked
Tilly.

She turned and looked at him in some surprise. "What on
earth do you want with Arthur Hudson?" she asked.

"Nothing, actually—I want to talk to his wife."

She straightened up at that. "His *wife*?"

Did he have to explain everything? "She was Maureen
Ventnor before she married Hudson, wasn't she?"

"Yes."

"Fine."

"We don't have their present number, though." She'd
turned back to the boxes but seemed to sense when he
reached for the phone book. "No point looking in there."

"Why not?"

"Because they're in Venice at the moment. I don't know
which hotel."

"Oh, terrific." He couldn't decide whether he was disappointed or relieved.

"Why did you want to talk to her, anyway?"

He was speaking to her backside, which was broad and
covered in jeans that were doing more than their normal
duty. "She was up on Eagle Head the night Jacky Morgan—"

"Damn it!" Tilly straightened up. "Damn it, Matt!"

"I have to find out, Tilly."

"It was a tramp who killed Mr. Dill. Or some drunk from Hatchville. Nothing to do with—"

"And a tramp or a drunk who killed Tom Finnegan?"

She frowned. "That was an *accident*!"

"I don't think so."

"You don't think so," she mimicked derisively. "And that makes it true, does it?"

"It makes me want to find out *if* it's true, yes. You'd be happier if I just left it alone, wouldn't you?" He'd unconsciously raised his voice in response to her scorn. "You'd all be happier if I just let things alone, didn't bother the important men, didn't stir up trouble, overlooked things like lies and murder and—"

"I don't want you to ignore anything, I just think you should investigate what's real instead of silly suspicions that don't have any foundation—" Her voice was shrill.

"There's plenty of foundation, those bastards are lying—"

"They're respectable men—"

George, walking in, was startled.

"Hey—cool it, you two."

"Stay out of this, George," Matt snapped. "It's got nothing to do with you."

"Oh, yes it does—it's his father you're accusing of murder—" Tilly said, tears of anger in her eyes.

"You're accusing my father of murder?" George gasped.

"No, of course not," Matt began.

"He might as well be," Tilly said. "He's still going on about Jacky Morgan—"

"Oh, come *on*, Matt," George said.

"And now he wants to talk to Arthur Hudson's wife—"

George looked confused. "What's she got to do with—"

"She was there, on Eagle Head—" Tilly said.

Matt stood up. "It's simply a matter of clarifying—"

"I didn't know *she* was there," George said. "How do you—"

"It's all here," Matt said, throwing the accident report at George. "Read it yourself. Both of you. Read it right through, and then tell me I should start interviewing every tramp and every drunk and every goddamn person who was

at the Howl on Saturday night. And while you're at it, look
at that time chart Tilly made. I spent an hour last night corre-
lating all the reports. Note the gap. And *then* tell me I'm the
idiot you both seem to think I am. I don't care. Think what
you damn well like. I can only do what I think is right, that's
what they elected me for and that's my goddamn *job!* If you
don't like the way I run things, you can both go and work at
McDonald's!" He grabbed his jacket and slammed out of the
office, leaving them openmouthed.

It was not like him to lose his temper, and having done so
left him unsettled and slightly wobbly. He went to the Dew
Drop Inn and risked being poisoned. There was no trace of
ipecac in his coffee—they'd obviously scrubbed out the coffee urn well—but he noted that there were not as many customers as usual on a Monday morning. That suited him fine.
He was not in the mood for light conversation.

One way or another, he was being thwarted. Perhaps, like
his father, he ought to accept the inevitable and simply conduct a routine investigation on Peter Dill's murder. He was
leaving all that to George, who was doing a reasonable job
so far. Most of the deputies were out asking questions, and
he'd called in the state police forensic unit to cover the scene
of the crime. George had to learn sometime—especially if he
was going to be sheriff one day. Maybe that would come
sooner rather than later. Meanwhile, Matt was determined to
carry his own investigation as far as he could. Stubbornness
was his most abiding fault, Daria had told him. She was
right. He also insisted it was one of his virtues, but she had
laughed at him. Well, maybe he deserved being laughed at,
affectionately or otherwise. He paid for his coffee and drove
out to the high school. Death, upward mobility, and vacations had left him only Milly Hackabush.

She, however, more than made up for the absence of her old
friends. "Not friends, exactly—not any more," Milly informed him.

"Any special reason?"

"Oh, just the usual drifting apart, different life-styles, different goals, you know the sort of thing. Well, maybe you don't. . . ."

Milly Hackabush was a tall, skinny woman with a good deal of gray hair barely contained by an elastic band into a ponytail that seemed to have an electric life of its own. Her flat-chested and sinewy form was presently encased in a rather worn gray leotard and skirt. He could see the outline of her breastbone as it descended into the neckline of the leotard. A fine sheen of moisture overlaid her pale skin. She had been teaching her "modern dance" class, which seemed to consist mainly of girls running around in circles trailing long pieces of filmy cloth. They were running around still, leaping and spinning with a seriousness of intent that totally belied the jollity of the music that filled the gymnasium beyond the glass of Milly's office.

"I understand that people grow up and apart," Matt agreed. "But from what I recall of Mrs. Hudson, she hardly seems . . . well . . ."

Milly grinned, showing big white teeth. "It's often difficult to detect the girl in the woman," she said cheerfully. She reached for an open can of Gatorade and drank deeply, wiping her face with the towel she had draped around her neck. "Micky Ventnor was *fun* when she was young—before Arthur Hudson got hold of her, that is. He's an absolute dud, if you ask me. Not a laugh in him."

"He's very wealthy," Matt said.

She snorted. "Yes, well—maybe that gives Micky something to chortle about in the long nights, but I doubt it. Still—it's what she wanted."

"And you?"

Again, the big-toothed grin. "I've got a life," Milly said. "It may not suit everyone, but it suits me. I do some good, occasionally—rescue a girl from being bamboozled by boys, booze, or drugs, build up confidence, beat the blues, that kind of thing. My various teams have lost a few and won a few more. I am beholden to no one. I earn my keep. I have a nice house, I have three cats who think I'm wonderful—which I am, when it comes to opening the catfood—I take terrific vacations every summer, I know a lot of interesting people, and I'm never sick. I'm not beautiful or rich, but by God I'm healthy!" And she laughed.

"And thirty years ago?"

She stared at him, perplexed. "Thirty? Why thirty?"

"I'm interested in the events of a particular night thirty years ago," Matt explained. "A Howl night, when you, and Micky Ventnor, and Jane Heckman, and Martha Turkle went with some boys out to Ghost Woods on Eagle Head."

"Wait a minute." She went to the door of her office and shouted over the music. "Yvonne, that's enough. Switch that thing off and everybody hit the showers. You've got ten minutes before the bell goes." The music stopped abruptly in midphrase. There was a chorus of breathless birdsong as the girls began to gossip, heading toward the changing rooms with a leaden thudding of bare feet. He wondered how they could have been so light on their toes moments before and yet sound like a herd of elephants now. Another of those damn female mysteries, he supposed.

Milly closed the office door, turned back to Matt, and sank one bony haunch onto the corner of her desk. "Run that by me again?"

He did.

"That's what I thought you said." She gazed at him. "I heard it, but I don't believe it. How the hell could *you* know about what I was up to on one particular night thirty years ago?"

"Because of what happened that night *after* you left."

She continued to stare at him, and then her face suddenly cleared. "Oh, Lord—you mean Jacky Morgan."

"That's it."

She was still confused. "But we *left*—as you said. We left before it happened."

"Yes, I know. But I'm hoping you could give me a little sense of what the atmosphere was like, what the people were like."

"Ask them yourself. They're all still arou—" She stopped. "No, they're not, are they?" She was not a stupid woman, and it did not take her more than a moment to see the way his mind was working. "Two funerals this week," she said. "Tom and Peter."

"Yes."

"And you think . . . Peter's murder and Jacky's death . . ."

"I'm looking into every possible angle."

"You're looking a hell of a long way back, then."

"I said every possible."

She considered him for a moment, then reached for a large brown handbag hanging off the back of a chair. She fished out a pack of cigarettes and a lighter, craning her neck to see if any of the girls were still in the gym. "You smoke," she said, lighting up.

"No, I don't."

"Yes, you do. If anybody comes in, this is yours."

He smiled. "All right."

She picked a bit of tobacco off the end of her tongue and resettled herself on the desk. "Let's see." She closed her eyes, then opened them again a minute later. "Jesus, you'd think I could remember . . ." She smiled ruefully. "Maybe I'm not old enough. They say the older you get, the better you remember the early part of your life." She sighed. "I was what? Sixteen?"

"Seventeen."

She nodded. "But just. I'm a Leo—August nineteenth. Sweet seventeen, hey?" She laughed and took another drag on the cigarette. She did it awkwardly, keeping an eye on the gymnasium, thrusting the cigarette into pursed lips as if unaccustomed to it, as if it contained sustenance of some kind.

"Well, we went in Danny Rogers's car—that is, Jane and Micky and I did. Martha went with Peter Dill—she had a thing for him. Not that he was interested, but—" She sighed again. "I had a 'thing' for Danny—and he *was* interested, for a while anyway. Until he went away to college. Just as well—we would have been a disaster if it had lasted. Anyway, we went out to the woods sort of on a dare. Well, you know the Howl. It hasn't changed much."

"Hasn't it?"

She raised an eyebrow. "You sound disapproving."

"Only of the trouble we've had the last few years. *People* have changed."

"I suppose you'd know," she said quietly.

"Go on about that night," he urged.

She shrugged. "It was damn cold, I remember that. I remember Micky saying there wouldn't be much trouble with the boys—you know—because nobody would want to take their pants off in that weather." She smiled. "I told you she'd changed."

"So you did. Too bad Arthur didn't know her then."

"Mmm. Anyway, we parked a few blocks away, climbed old man Osborne's fence, and went into the trees. It was real spooky—which I guess was the point. We kind of hung on to each other, lots of giggling, you can imagine the scene."

"Yes."

"Well, we eventually came to this clearing, and there was all this stuff lying around. Copper tubing and a big boiler thing—Moldy said it was a still. Or had been a still—and I guess he'd know. Moldy Molt was not exactly a golden boy, even then."

Matt nodded. "My father broke up that still a couple of years before you got there. Osborne had been so damned fussy about trespassers that Dad got suspicious and went in one day. He wasn't much on turning people in for that kind of thing. Some Prohibition traditions still hold, after all. Anyway, according to my dad this was a small still, and Osborne was only running it for himself. So Dad just broke it up. He figured Osborne moved operations to his basement after that, but he didn't pursue the matter. It wasn't that Osborne *needed* to make hooch, he had plenty of money, but he'd *been* making it since Prohibition and had gotten the taste. Good whiskey just didn't do it for him."

Milly started to laugh. "My God, the things you learn when it's too late. We knew he was a mean old bastard, but we never knew *that*. We thought it had been *from* Prohibition times—although, come to think of it, the copper tubing wasn't all *that* green."

"Anyway—"

"Oh, right. Anyway, we gathered up some wood and made a fire, and those that wanted to eat ate and those that wanted to . . ." She paused with unusual delicacy.

"That wanted to neck . . ."

"Necked, right. And it was spooky and funny and . . ." She frowned.,

"And?"

"And then Jacky came."

"Bad news?"

"He was a pain, frankly. First of all he brought some whiskey with him and made a big show of it. Then it turned out that some of the guys had brought booze, too, although they hadn't told us. Or offered it around, either, come to think of it." A line appeared between her eyebrows. "Stinkers. Anyway, that wasn't really the problem."

"Oh?"

She shook her head. "The problem—as always—was Jacky himself. You didn't know him."

"I was only a little kid when he died."

"I forget all the policemen are getting younger." She smiled. "Well, Jacky was a pain in the ass. He was always hanging around, trying to be part of the group, and he had this kind of habit of teasing people in a weasely, whiny way. Sort of, I don't know, sort of implying that he knew more than he was saying, if you see what I mean. Real kid stuff. He was always insinuating that he was 'best buddies' with everybody, knew all their secrets and dreams kind of thing, when in fact nobody liked him much at all. I don't know why they put up with him, in fact."

"But they did?"

"Well, *some* of them did. Moldy and Merry did, I remember. And Danny was nicer to him than he deserved. And Fanny—oh, he was Fanny's best friend—according to Jacky. He kept referring to himself as one of 'the Two Jacks'—as if he and Jack Fanshawe were some kind of team. Which they weren't."

"Are you sure?"

Suddenly two things happened in quick succession. Milly Hackabush blushed, and she slipped her nearly finished cigarette between Matt's fingers. Five seconds later the office door opened and a rather lovely young girl stuck in her head, wrinkling her nose at the smoky atmosphere. She looked saucily at Matt.

"Hasn't she read you the riot act about that cigarette yet?" she asked with what might have been a wink.

"That's enough, Yvonne," Milly snapped. "What's the problem?"

"No problem. I just wanted to tell you that I put the tapes and the player under the bleachers—is that okay? I'd have put them away, but we've got rehearsal later and—"

"That's fine. Thanks. Haven't you got a class?"

Yvonne's eyes went to the clock on the wall. She scowled. "Yes—God, I don't know why they make us teach personal hygiene to them—the girls already know more about sex than *I* ever will." She looked again at Matt. "Unless I get very, very lucky, that is." With another very obvious wink, she was gone.

Milly cleared her throat and reclaimed her cigarette. She took a last drag and then ground it out on the side of the wastebasket. "My teaching assistant," she said dryly, straightening up. "Now, where were we?"

"You were saying that Jacky Morgan and Jack Fanshawe were not close. That you were sure they weren't. Why?"

The blush returned. "Wow," she said with a wary laugh. "All the secrets have to come out, don't they?"

"Not if you don't want them to."

"Oh, I don't mind, really. I know they weren't best friends because that summer *I* had been Jack's best friend—in every way, you might say. He wouldn't have had time for Jacky Morgan, believe me. And, of course, Jacky made sure everybody knew it, which made me angry, because by that time I was going off Jack Fanshawe and—as I said—had a 'thing' for Danny Rogers." Laughter suddenly burbled up in her throat. "*Listen* to me, my God, it sounds like Peyton Place for real, doesn't it? But that's the way it was then. You had a summer romance—and *everybody* had a romance with Fanshawe at *some* time—that summer it was just my turn. But Jacky started right in on it practically the minute he arrived. 'Your buttons are all wrong,' he said to me—and they weren't, but I reached for them, which is what he wanted, of course. 'You two just come back out of the bushes?' he said in that snide voice of his. Everybody laughed. Including Danny Rogers. So much for my chances with *him*, I remember thinking. Then Jacky started in on Peter about Mary Turkle—"

"*Mary* Turkle?" This was a new name to him—he couldn't remember any Turkle girl named Mary.

"I guess you wouldn't know about her. Mary was Martha's older sister, and she and Peter Dill had been dating for about a year when she killed herself. It was awful. She didn't tell anyone she had taken the pills, they all thought she had the flu, Peter was even there earlier in the evening, visiting her, and she never even told *him*, can you imagine? She was depressed about not getting into the college that Peter was going to, because they'd be separated. Martha said Mary was certain he would find somebody else when he was away and couldn't face losing him. My God—it's hard to remember how *important* all that was to us then. How deeply everything hurt, and how wonderful love was, and all of that. I see it every day, and it still throws me to see how much these girls can suffer over things a grown-up would dismiss." She scowled. "That grown-ups *do* dismiss, unfortunately, which contributes to the problems. Anyway, Jacky started saying unpleasant things about Mary, and Martha started to cry, which seemed to satisfy him. So he turned on Moldy and started in about his father being arrested over in Hatchville, I think it was, and then Albert for going bald, and on Merry about being a wimp—" She grinned suddenly. "And isn't *that* hard to believe? Merrill Atwater a ninety-pound weakling? Have you been to his gym?"

"Once or twice."

"I work out there three times a week, but you can see what good it does me."

"You're slim."

"Hah! I'm skinny, a skinny old maid!" She laughed. "No matter what I do to build myself up, I still stay stringy, bony, and flat. Whatever I had at seventeen—and it wasn't much—has long gone. Still—I have my moments." She reached again for the Gatorade.

"So what happened then?" Matt prodded gently.

She shrugged. "When he'd had a good old dig at everyone he sort of settled down. It was as if he had to cut everyone down a little to his size—metaphorically speaking—and then he was happy. *He* didn't exactly come from a fine home, after all. His mother—" She stopped and made a face.

"What?" Matt asked.

She had become reflective. "I suppose that if I had Jacky Morgan as a student now, I'd feel sorry for him. From an adult point of view, he had it rough. His father was dead, his mother was not only a drinker, she was also the town . . ." She cleared her throat. "Well, what the hell. The point is, Jacky was left out, put out, *sent* out of the house on many an evening, hence his tendency to hang around whomever he could find. We all knew it, and he knew we knew it. So he stuck his knife in first. The funny thing is, none of us would have referred to it for the world. It was too serious, too hurt-ful, you don't tease a person for that—not in your teen years, anyway. Children do—children are cruel. But teenagers are too vulnerable themselves to . . ." She paused. "Anyway, that's how it was for him. Nowadays he'd have his own so-cial worker and be seeing a therapist and the whole schle-mozzle—but then, he just . . ." She looked away. "Stupid. How stupid to care after all this time."

"About Jacky Morgan?"

"About *all* of us." When she turned back he saw there was anger in her eyes. "All the kids who suffered, and who will suffer, the torments of adolescence. When we become adults we lose that vulnerability, we turn hard and say 'Well, they all have to go through it.' We shut it out. Now you make me remember my own pain, the pains of my friends. I'm not grateful." She passed the back of her hand across her eyes.

"I'm sorry." He was surprised.

She managed a smile. "Oh, don't mind me. I'm being silly—and I don't usually allow myself to be silly. Waste of time. But that was the last year we had, all of us. The last year of—God, how trite—the last year of innocence, of *be-lieving* things, the last year of really letting anyone *in*. After that, we were different."

"You mean after Jacky Morgan died?"

"Do I? Was that it? I don't know. Something happened. Jacky died. Mary died. The boys went away to college or Vietnam. Our parents turned gray. The usual."

"You girls left the woods shortly after Jacky arrived."

"You just don't give up, do you?"

"I need to know, Milly."

"Why?"

"My job. Peter Dill was murdered, and I have to find out who did it. Simple as that. At the moment I think it might be because of what happened that night."

"Really? After all this time?"

"I think so."

Somewhere beyond the doors of the gymnasium, a bell rang. There was a sound of slamming doors and pounding feet in the halls beyond the gym. Boys started to pour in through the double doors and head toward the changing rooms. Milly was silent for a moment, considering.

"Well, I don't know what more I can tell you. The boys began drinking and roughhousing after that. It got sort of competitive, the way boys are. I can drink more than you, I can tell dirtier stories than you, and so on. It was obvious to all of us that it was only going to get worse, and Martha was feeling down anyway, so we decided to leave them to do whatever they wanted to do. When we left, Merry had already thrown up once—they forced him to drink a whole bottle of beer straight down. That was how it was going. No place for nice girls." Her expression was wry. "So, if it started *that* night, I think you're in trouble. The only person there who might have wanted to kill Peter was Jacky Morgan himself—because he wanted to kill all of us, in a way. We all had nice families, we were all going to college, we were all okay—and he wasn't. In a way I suppose . . . God, this sounds terrible."

"What?"

"You want me to say it?"

"Please."

"Well, in a way, if anybody had to die that night, it was probably better that it was Jacky Morgan, because he had the least to lose and the least to look forward to. His life was crap, frankly, and it was probably never going to get better. If he finished high school, and that was open to question—he wasn't all that bright—then what could he expect out of life? A low-paid job, no more. And he wasn't exactly prepossessing, so he might never have found a wife. At the time I despised him—we all did. But, looking back, seeing him with adult eyes—he seems pretty pathetic. If he tried to make other people's life crap, it was only to make his own bearable. We didn't cry for him then, but I could right now. If I let myself, that is." She glared at him. "I don't let myself. Ever. Not anymore. Nothing more useless than a crying woman, my mother used to say. And she was right."

"Was she?" Matt asked gently.

Milly Hackabush sniffed and tossed her head back to rid herself of whatever vestige of nostalgic, romantic, useless tears might remain in her eyes. "Most of the time," she said.

He stood up. "Guess that's the best we can hope for," he said. "To be right most of the time." He started for the door, then turned. "Although I'd settle for being right just once in a while, frankly. Thanks, Milly."

"Sure," she said. "Sure."

And watched him as he pushed his way through the noisy boys and out into the crowded halls.

Sunshine Forever was practically a city in itself. There were winding streets of small red-roofed bungalows surrounded by well-tended gardens, some with displays of extraordinary flowers. These streets—none too long for a nice afternoon walk—all curved toward a central plaza that contained a surprising variety of shops, a supermarket, and a large administration building cum medical facility.

Emily was very impressed.

Most of the people strolling in the central plaza were over sixty-five, but she expected that. This was one of the many retirement villages that had sprung up in Florida and other sunny climes to cater to semiaffluent retirees. The younger people she encountered—male and female nurses, security men, and so on—were wearing uniforms. Even the administrative staff in the central building wore bright golden yellow, although there were individual variations in style and accessories.

Coral Morgan was registered as living in one of the small bungalows, but she was presently in the medical facility, having suffered a perforated ulcer. She was mending, but still weak. On the flight down Emily had conjectured what Mrs. Morgan might be like. She had finally settled on the image of a fragile, timid, white-haired old lady—and was therefore rather stunned to find a long, bony woman with spiky bright red hair and snapping black eyes sitting up in the bed of the room to which she had been directed.

"Who the hell are you?" this vision demanded as Emily knocked gently and stuck her head around the door.

"I, the hell, am Emily Gibbons," she answered briskly.

And Coral Morgan grinned.

"Come on in, Emily Gibbons," she said. "Thank God you're wearing blue," she continued as Emily complied. "I am so goddamned sick and tired of white and 'sunshine yellow' that I could puke purple. In fact, I did—which is why I'm here. They said it was an ulcer, but it was really the sight of all those goddamn fatuous smiles that finally did it. Take the medicine, they say, and they smile. Lie back and rest, pay the bill, turn over for the enema, sign your life away, but they smile. What*ever* they do, they smile. Dental paradise, this place. Who needs sun, with all those *teeth* shining at you? What do you want? And don't smile."

Emily laughed. "Sorry," she said, and attempted a scowl.

"Christ, that's worse," Coral said wearily. "I don't suppose you have any cigarettes on you, do you?"

"I'm sorry, I—"

"Don't smoke. I knew it."

"I had to give it up," Emily continued. "It gave me sinus problems."

"Shame," Coral said unsympathetically. "Booze? Any booze in your bag?"

"No, I—"

"Then get the hell out of here," Coral said. "You've got nothing I need." And she meant it.

When Emily returned twenty minutes later, it was with a heavy handbag and an even heavier heart. It was wrong, she knew, to give whiskey or cigarettes to a sick woman, but—

"You got the message, I see," Coral said when she knocked again. "I thought you might. Gimme."

Without speaking, Emily extracted the pack of cigarettes she'd purchased at the supermarket and handed it to Coral Morgan, who snorted derisively. "Well, well—one twenties, with filter and low tar. Looking after my health, are you? How kind. Light?"

Still without saying anything, Emily produced a match-book and handed it to the old woman. Now that she was by the bed she could see, in the cruel clear sunlight that streamed in from outside, that Coral Morgan was well into her seventies and not bearing up. Her tanned face was as lined as a monkey's, and her teeth were gappy and decayed. As she lit the cigarette the black eyes flicked up and caught Emily's expression.

"I can see I shoulda kept my back to the light," Coral said. "How about the booze? Got *that* with a filter, too?" She stared, then started a cackling laugh as Emily produced a miniature bottle of Johnnie Walker Red Label. "Jeeze, last of the big spenders." She reached out a red-tipped hand and snatched, wrenching the little top off and upending the bottle into her mouth. This sudden intake of smoke and liquor was received with a savage bout of coughing that the old woman seemed, somehow, to relish.

"Wonderful," she said, her eyes streaming tears. "Like old times." But she put the little bottle aside and stubbed out the cigarette after one more drag. She squinted up at Emily through the last exhalation of smoke. "It's okay, you haven't killed me. I just wanted to know if I was still alive. What do you want in exchange for these precious gifts?"

"I want to talk to you about your son," Emily said, dragging over a chair.

"I ain't got a son," Mrs. Morgan said. "And I didn't invite you to sit down, neither."

Nevertheless, Emily sat down and, after scrabbling in her handbag yet again, produced a notebook and ballpoint pen. "About your son, Jacky," she said steadily.

"Oh, shit," Coral said. "What's the little bastard done now?"

23

*C*oral began to laugh. "Your face," she said. "You should see your face."

"Very funny," Emily said. "You were expecting me, weren't you?"

"I was expecting someone I didn't know," Coral agreed. She took pity on Emily, who was feeling very foolish. "Honey, look—I'm an old broad, and I ain't stupid. I can count my friends on one hand and my relatives on one finger—a no-good spinster sister who lives in Poughkeepsie. I've got no brothers. So when they tell me a 'niece' is coming to see me—"

"I asked them not to say anything," Emily grumbled.

"They like to torment me," Coral said. "Anyway, they're afraid if I pop off because of shock they won't be able to run up more bills, so they told me about your call. I keep asking you what you want, but I know it must be something about Jacky because there's nothing else about me anybody would want to know. Besides, I got a call warning me to keep my mouth shut."

Emily sat up. "Who from?" she demanded. "From whom, I mean."

"From never you mind," Coral said. "I don't intend to pay any attention to it." She leaned forward. "Look, sweetheart, I said I wasn't stupid. They say this in here—" she indicated her flat middle—"is a perforated ulcer, but I know better.

That's what they say to all of us with stomach kick-ups, but we got a library here, and I can read as good as anybody. If it was operable, they'd have operated—they get a good price from the insurance for that. But they didn't, so it's gone beyond that."

"I . . . I'm—" Emily didn't know what to say.

"Please, hold the onions. I've had a good run, and I'm tired as hell. If they can make it painless—and I know they can because my friend Bernice had the same thing and she went off smiling in a high old state—then I'm ready for the ride. The point I'm making is that I don't like being told what to do. Or what not to do, right? So I'm going to talk. There—how's that?"

"That . . . that's fine," Emily said. "What about?"

Coral looked confused and a little disappointed. "Why, Jacky, of course. What they done to him. What they done to me, or for me, to keep me quiet. All that stuff. Isn't that what you want to know?"

"Yes, but . . ."

"But what, for pig's sake?"

"He fell."

"Uh-uh. He was pushed."

"What?"

"Oh, hey, listen, kid. Why the hell would they pay me to move away and shut up about it? When I got thrown out of my last boarding house, why did that Albert Budd come down here and get me a place here at Sunshine Forever? Why did they buy me off with a house of my own, and why does he pay the bills? Because he murdered my son, that's why, and you can believe it."

"But, surely, if your son was *deliberately* killed—"

"I didn't say it was deliberate, did I? But they all did it, they all got together and said let's scare the shit out of him by pushing him over the edge. They wasn't to know he had thin bones—family trait, thin bones, but they wasn't to know. They probably thought maybe a broken leg or arm, and he'd leave them alone. More likely they didn't think at all, but they were right, he probably would have stopped bothering them, the little weasel."

Emily was growing more and more astonished by Coral

Morgan. She was obviously a woman who had lived hard and who was facing death with equanimity, even courage. Yet she seemed to think little of a son who had been lost to her at an early age.

Coral's plucked eyebrow went up. "You shocked that I should call him a little weasel?" Emily wondered if imminent death sharpened instincts—Coral certainly had no trouble reading her mind, or her face.

"Well, I—"

"Don't your parents ever call you names?"

Emily started to smile. "Sure. Especially when they get mad."

"Yeah, well—I been mad at Jacky for thirty years, and his being dead doesn't change that. I loved him, of course I did, although he made it a pretty uphill road. Around about the age of six, when his old man turned against us, he went wormy on me. Turned into a sly little liar and a sneak. I can't abide a sneak, and I did my best to strap it out of him, but it didn't do any good. That boy just loved more than anything to go slipping around and looking in folks' windows, listening at their doors, teasing and tormenting them. It was a surprise to me he lived as long as he did—I was always waiting for Sheriff Ted to come by one night and tell me somebody strung Jacky up from a tree or beat the living hell out of him. Finally he did come, only it was over a cliff instead of strung from a tree."

"You mean—"

Coral picked up the miniature bottle and finished it off, tossing it across the room into a wastebasket with surprising accuracy. Then she had another good cough and wiped her eyes on the sheet. "I mean he was a weasel, and he got killed because of it. And that was the worst thing and the best thing that ever happened to me, because those boys were guilty and their families knew it. They paid me to go away, and I've lived good since. Thirty years I've been comfortable, thanks to Jacky getting pushed off a cliff." Despite her hard words, Emily noticed the glint of tears in her eyes. "He was ugly and he was stupid, really. But he didn't need to be as stupid as he was, and that's why I'm mad at him. Maybe he never would have been president and all that, but he would have been *here*, and we could have managed something. Between us, we would have made out okay."

There was a long silence. Emily reached for the cigarettes. "Would you like another?"

"Hell, yes—hand them over." When the cigarette was lit and the rest of the pack hidden in the bedside table drawer, Coral regarded Emily thoughtfully. "You think I'm a terrible old woman, don't you?"

"No, not really. I don't know anything about Jacky except that he died in that awful way—"

"At least it was quick," Coral observed, glancing out of the window. "I envy him that, poor little snipe."

"Why do you say he was stupid, Mrs. Morgan?"

Coral twisted herself in the bed and punched the pillows into a more comfortable shape. "Well, like I said—he teased and tormented people. He was stupid because he risked making them mad enough to do something to him, and he was even more stupid because he never *made* anything out of it. He knew a lot of things about a lot of people—we used to laugh like crazy over some of the things he'd found out. Not just about his friends—hell, that was small stuff. But things about adults, things that could have made us some money, if you see what I mean. Shocked?"

Emily was, but she knew a good reporter never showed emotion, so she simply shook her head.

"Look—you have to understand, girlie. We had nothing and we *was* nothing. You got to make your wad where you can or you go under. I told him I could get money for what he knew, but that didn't interest him. Even when I told him we *needed* it, the little bastard didn't care. All he liked was the knowing, the power it gave him, even if he never used it. Stupid, like I said. Narrow-sighted, like his old man. So, when he was dead, *I* used it instead. Those eight boys thought they was the only ones paying, but they weren't. I've had plenty over the years, thanks to Jacky. One way or another, he's kept me—although he never knew it, never would have done it if he'd lived. You want to hear some of it?"

"Yes," Emily said simply. "But I think you should know I'm a reporter."

"I know the name Gibbons, honey. I knew your grand-

dad—in more ways than how-de-do, if you see what I mean.
I know what I'm doing, talking to you."

"What *are* you doing, talking to me?"

Coral Morgan's face suddenly contorted. Emily never
knew whether it was pain from the cancer or pain from the
past, but pain it surely was. "I'm getting back at them,
honey. For my boy. I'm getting back at all the smug, smart,
snotty know-alls who ever turned away from him and me.
Can you understand that?"

"Oh, yes," Emily said softly. "I can understand that very
well. But before you start, there's one point I'd like to clear
up."

"Go on, then." Coral was relaxed, enjoying her moment.

"I know you were Jacky's mother—"

"For my sins," Coral agreed genially.

"Well, then—who was Jacky's father?" Emily asked.

"So, you see, I was sent ahead to do a preliminary overview
of Dill, to check out the life-style, the habits, and so on. It's
routine. The same with the other bank employees. We knew
there was something wrong, but the regular audit hadn't
shown anything up." Clarence Toogood leaned forward on
his chair. "I have a nose for this kind of thing, you see. I may
be slow—but I'm cheap." He cackled at his own joke.

"I sure am getting a different picture of Peter Dill than I
had a few days ago," Matt said.

"Some men don't wear their sins on their sleeve,"
Clarence said. "I would have to agree with your conclusion
from the interview with the son—Dill was a gambler, and he
was playing with the wrong people. The official auditors will
be going in anyway—death of a major bank official gives
them the excuse—and now they'll be paying close attention
to anything Dill had his hands on. Something tells me it will
be mortgages on nonexistent property, always an old favorite. But you never know—that's what makes the work so
exciting."

"Does it?" Matt was having trouble reconciling this new
Clarence Toogood with the old. Somehow the persona of the
eccentric overhearty author seemed to suit him more than
that of the professional snoop. And yet snoop wasn't quite it.

What had his self-description been? "Indian scout," that was it. The one who went ahead and spied out the lie of the land. Or, rather, the lies of the subject—in this case, Peter Dill.

"According to my landlady's daughter, Mrs. Dill is talking about selling up and moving back to Chicago after the funeral," Matt said.

"Ah, well—it might be better if she held back on that," Clarence said. "The proceeds from the sale might not be hers, you see. If the auditors find discrepancies, well—"

"She could end up with nothing?"

Clarence shrugged. "It's happened before. Very sad, of course—but bigger crooks than Peter Dill have left broken-hearted women behind them."

"Broken-hearted *poor* women," Matt said.

"Indeed. Of course, the man wasn't stupid."

"No, he wasn't."

"He may have put the house and other assets in his wife's name. Do you think that's possible?"

"I think it wouldn't be too difficult to find out."

Clarence stood up. "Then that's what I'll be doing next. I suppose he would have bought his house through Fanshawe?"

"Most people in Blackwater do."

"Then I'll pay him a visit." Clarence chuckled. "Assuming, of course, that the grass is no longer growing under his feet."

"I think that's all cleared up," Matt allowed.

"Fine." Clarence turned back at the door. "I'm sorry not to have let you in on all this from the beginning, but I like to work quietly. You understand."

"Oh, I understand all right. No other way to proceed, in a town this size."

Clarence nodded. "But you don't smile, Sheriff. You don't like it."

"No reason for me to like it or not like it. You're a private investigator, not a public official. You have no legal requirement to inform me of your activities."

"But we broke beautiful bread together, isn't that it?"

Matt acquiesced with a shrug, and Clarence sighed. "I'll let you know what I find out from here on in—especially

anything I think might have a bearing on Dill's murder. I mean, if he was cheating people—"

"I'd appreciate any help you can give me," Matt said.

"Fine. Fine." Clarence seemed reluctant to leave on this note but eventually went out with a wave.

"Well there, see?" Tilly crowed. "Old Dill was probably bashed by some poor person he cheated, nothing to do with Jacky Morgan at all."

"It could be," Matt said noncommittally.

"But you don't buy it," said George, who had been surprisingly silent during Toogood's goodwill visit. "You still want to work on that old accident theory."

"I want to work on *all* theories, however strange," Matt said. "I'm glad to open any doors that might lead somewhere, but I'm not closing any."

"Sure getting drafty around here, with all these doors open," Tilly muttered at her keyboard.

Matt stood up. "Well, I'm going home," he said, ignoring Tilly.

George looked surprised. "For lunch?"

"No—to change for Tom Finnegan's funeral. I leave everything in your capable hands."

"Yeah, but what am I supposed to do next?" George wanted to know, a little panic showing in his eyes.

"Talk to the forensic people," Matt suggested. "See what they've come up with at the murder scene. Follow up on some of the interviews. The usual."

"Yes, but—"

"Tell him, Tilly," Matt said. "You taught me—you can teach him."

And he walked out.

He drove home because before changing into his dark suit and tie, he wanted to talk to Evelyn Dill.

Matt didn't recognize the woman who came to the door of the Dill residence. He introduced himself, and she told him she was Mrs. Parks, Evelyn's mother. She was an upright woman with a short mane of white hair brushed straight back from her face in a sculptured halo that only a master cutter could have achieved. From her simple hairstyle to her simple dress and shoes, it was apparent that Mrs. Parks spent money quietly and well. Quite a lot of money, in fact.

"I would like to speak to Evelyn for a few minutes, if that's possible," Matt told Mrs. Parks.

"Is it absolutely necessary?"

"Yes," Matt said, and added nothing.

After a moment of steady eye contact, she stepped back and permitted him to enter. "Evelyn is not at her best at the moment," Mrs. Parks said, leading him down the hall and through the archway to the sitting room, where two young girls, startlingly alike, assessed him with dark, unreadable eyes.

"Girls, run up and tell your mother the sheriff would like to speak with her," Mrs. Parks directed her twin granddaughters.

"She's sleeping," the one in the blue skirt said.

"She took a pill," the one in the red skirt said.

"No, she didn't, because I have the pills and she didn't ask for one," Mrs. Parks said firmly. "Run along, and take your things with you. We'll require some privacy." She pronounced the word in the British way, and Matt's eyes slid sideways to take her in once more. She sensed his curiosity.

"I was a war bride," she informed him briskly. "My husband was stationed in one of the hospitals in London, and I was a surgical nurse. Occasionally my English vowels show."

"Yes, ma'am," he said.

She chuckled. "And the more English I become, the more John Wayne you become. We'll have to watch it."

So she was not as correct as he'd first thought. In fact, in a dignified and amused way, she was flirting with him. He found himself feeling awkward, which was probably her intention. She was a far from ordinary woman.

"Yes, Mother?" came a voice behind him.

Mrs. Parks's eyes went over his shoulder and narrowed with concern, but along with her English pronunciation she had also retained English control. Or perhaps it was the medical training. "The sheriff wants to speak with you, Evelyn. Come in and sit down so we can get it over with. Would you like some coffee or tea, Sheriff Gabriel?"

"No, thank you," he said.

Evelyn swished past him, cat-quiet in gold slippers. She wore a long velvet robe in a pale cream, but even this gentle color contrasted cruelly with the white of her face. Fair-skinned despite her dark hair, she had lost what little coloring she'd once had, and her complexion seemed almost transparent. Her hair, still sleek but dulled, fell forward over each cheek, partially obscuring her face. She sat down abruptly and remained very still, holding her shoulders slightly angled, as if expecting a blow.

"This won't take long," he said, aware of her fatigue.

"Indeed, it had better not," Mrs. Parks said, sitting down beside her daughter and taking her hand. "Fire away, then."

"I'd rather talk to—"

"I will remain," Mrs. Parks said firmly. "Evelyn is not up to being on her own yet. She is . . ." She hesitated. "She is upset."

Matt's glance went to Evelyn Dill, and he suddenly saw what he hadn't seen before—a certain blankness in the blue eyes, a childlike laxity around the well-shaped mouth. Evelyn Dill had fallen apart, and only her mother's presence in the house and in this room was holding her together. She had come down from her room only as an obedient child would come. He revised the questions he had been rehearsing on the way over.

"I'm sorry to disturb you at this time," he began formally.

"That's all right," Evelyn said automatically, matching his formal tone. She looked and spoke like a doll, perfectly groomed and perfectly empty. He glanced at Mrs. Parks, whose eyes apologized but who said nothing.

"I'd like to ask you what may seem like an odd question," he said. "But I wonder if you can remember where your husband was between seven and eight o'clock last Thursday evening."

"My husband is dead," Evelyn said.

"Yes, I know, Mrs. Dill, and I'm sorry. But if you could remember—"

"He was at the bank. He was late that night, and the roast had dried out. I was angry. He apologized. He said he had been working at the bank and had lost track of the time." She spoke very carefully, as if taking part in an oral exam. "He often does that. He works very hard." She closed her mouth with a snap. After a moment she added, "He worked very hard."

"Yes, I know he did. Was anyone working there with him?"

"No. He said he was alone and that was why he hadn't noticed the time. Someone else would have complained, he said."

"Did you know your husband was a gambler, Mrs. Dill?"

"My husband is dead," she said again.

"Yes, I'm sorry. I see the car in the drive is white. Is that your husband's car?"

"No."

"Where is your husband's car?"

"In the garage."

"And what color is it?"

"Red."

Damn, he thought. Red on red. Any paint transferred from Tom Finnegan's car would take an inch-by-inch inspection to find.

"What has his car to do with his murder?" asked Mrs. Parks.

"I'm trying to ascertain some background," he said.

"And the gambling?"

"Well, I—"

"He *was* a gambler," Mrs. Parks said. "A secret gambler. He borrowed money from my husband several times to pay off debts. I only learned this the other day, when I told my husband that Peter was dead."

"Peter is dead," echoed Evelyn, to no one in particular.

"Do you know how long he had been a gambler?" Matt asked.

"I think for many years," Mrs. Parks said. Her tone, her facial expression, told him she had not esteemed her late son-in-law. Far from it. "I don't think Evelyn had any idea. I hope not."

"You haven't asked her?"

Mrs. Parks glanced at her daughter, who was now staring

fixedly at Matt. "There didn't seem much point, frankly. Not now."

"He was a good provider," Evelyn said. "You can see, all around you, what a good husband he was. We had all— everything—we wanted. He loved us."

"I'm sure he did, Mrs. Dill." Matt wished he had never started this; the woman was obviously on the verge of flying apart—nobody wound that tight could hope to remain so for long. When she let go it would be spectacular. He could see Mrs. Parks's knuckles were white, holding on fiercely to her daughter's sanity for her.

"He loved his daughters."

"Of course."

"He even loved that awful son of his, Wayne. He was a man full of love."

Mrs. Parks's eyes said "He was a man full of shit."

"And he loved animals, too." Evelyn was beginning to croon.

Mrs. Parks's eyes said "He loved nobody but himself."

"Everybody at the bank thought he was wonderful." Evelyn continued her litany.

Mrs. Parks's eyes said "They hated him and I hated him."

"He must have fallen and hit his head," Evelyn concluded.

Mrs. Parks's eyes said "I wish I'd done it myself."

Matt thought briefly of asking for Mrs. Parks's alibi, then remembered that Nonie had told him she'd rung her in Chicago and she'd been in bed at the time Peter Dill was murdered.

"Were you aware of any irregularities at the bank, Mrs. Dill?" Matt asked doggedly. "Did your husband ever mention any problems at the bank?"

"No."

"Of course," Mrs. Parks's eyes said. "Of course." And aloud she said, "My husband refused to lend him more money when he never offered to repay the first loan." She smiled sadly. "My husband is a forgiving man, but not to thieves."

"He put up the house as collateral," Evelyn said.

"Then you *did* know your husband was a gambler?" Matt asked.

"It's my house," Evelyn said. "My father, too."

"She means he would never have—"

"I realize what she means," Matt interrupted. "You say it's *your* house, Mrs. Dill? In your name, you mean?"

Evelyn nodded, and went on nodding. "My house, my furs, my jewelry, my daughters, my life." Suddenly there was intelligence in her eyes. "*I'm* not a gambler, Mr. Gabriel."

Both Mrs. Parks and Matt stared at her in dismay, suddenly sensing that within the childlike woman who was apparently devastated by her husband's death, there was still someone quite cold and efficient, someone who may have loved her man but who had never quite surrendered control to him. The blankness returned, and she stood up. "I want to go to sleep now. Give me a pill, Mother. One pill."

Mrs. Parks looked at Matt, who shrugged in resignation. It was clear that beneath her apparent helplessness was a spine of steel——Evelyn Dill instinctively sensed that hiding was safer than facing reality. It was equally clear that anything she said in this state could not be considered reliable evidence, and she knew that, too. She was deliberately permitting herself this fugue, this suspension of normalcy. The control she would never have surrendered to her husband she was willingly surrendering to her mother.

She may have loved Peter Dill, but she hadn't trusted him.

Matt may not have had all his questions answered, but that one had been. Once the pill had been produced from a bottle in Mrs. Parks's pocket, and Evelyn Dill had departed, moving in her tranced and mannered way, Mrs. Parks walked him to the door.

"She . . ." She paused.

"I understand, Mrs. Parks," Matt said. "She's not really herself at the moment."

Mrs. Parks's eyes met his, bleakly. "Isn't she?" she asked.

24

*I*t was definitely the Monday afternoon after.

On Sunday everyone except the sheriff's department had rested. But as Matt drove from Mrs. Peach's Guest House to collect Daria, he noted the usual post-Howl activities taking place throughout the town. A strong aroma of paint remover floated on the November air. Cars passed him on the way to the town dump with a multiplicity of odd objects stacked on their backseats. Through his partly opened window he could hear the sounds of hammering and sawing as victims repaired or rebuilt or removed the evidence of successful Howlers perpetrated on their homes. Workmen on ladders were removing "things" from trees, and others could be seen clearing rubbish from the athletic grounds of the high school. And in the various windows on Main Street shopkeepers could be seen taking down orange-and-black decorations and replacing them with Thanksgiving turkey displays.

As if Monday weren't bad enough, he thought glumly.

Daria was ready and waiting just inside the door of the art gallery. Her black suit and small tilted hat were very much souvenirs of her recently rejected life in New York. She would be the most fashionable attendee of Tom Finnegan's funeral service, and probably the most beautiful. He wished, as he kissed her briefly, that he felt more like appreciating her fragile loveliness instead of wanting to simply go hide in a cave somewhere. She gave him a sharp look.

"*You* certainly look ready for a funeral," she observed. "Are you all right?"

"Physically fine, mentally and emotionally with one foot in a metaphorical grave," he said glumly.

She grinned. "Dear me. How deep is a metaphorical grave?"

He held his hand up to just under his chin. "About up to here," he said. "Tilly is hardly speaking to me, George is about as calm as a cat in a roomful of rocking chairs, and speaking of cats, even Max is giving me the cold shoulder these days. Young Dominic acts as if I've developed some contagious disease, and I seem to be alienating half the movers and shakers in Blackwater."

"Hardly half," Daria said. "Just six."

"But who's counting?" Matt asked as they turned into the church parking lot. He angled into a space and turned off the engine. "Daria, am I being pigheaded about this Jacky Morgan connection?"

"Maybe—a little. Have you any other angle to explore?"

"Not really—just the possibility that Dill was killed by one of about five thousand people with any of five thousand different motives, or maybe a mugger with no motive at all. But *both* Tom Finnegan and Peter Dill seemed about to tell me something before they died, and since they have so little in common *except* Jacky Morgan, I can't simply ignore that."

"They might have been about quite separate things," Daria said kindly. "Two and two don't *always* have to be put together."

"I am a compulsive put-together-er," Matt said. "I think it comes from studying philosophy—I'm always looking for a logical construct or a consistency in ideas or events which—when they are human—isn't always possible. Or even likely."

"People *is* peculiar," Daria agreed.

He smiled at her. "You're not," he said. "You're wonderful."

"Of course I am," she said with mock complacency.

"Don't I have the heart of the most gorgeous and least boring man in town?"

"Who is he—I'll punch his lights out!"

She laughed and leaned over to kiss him. "Come on, let's face the awful music of that old harmonium. I am sorry, really sorry, about Tom Finnegan—but I don't know if I can keep a straight face if Mrs. Crabbe is still hitting all those clinkers in 'Nearer My God to Thee.' "

They joined what turned out to be a considerable congregation. Tom Finnegan had been much loved in Blackwater, and not only because of the banana splits. There were faces both old and young in the pews. Mrs. Crabbe did her best, but Daria had to grip her hymn book very tightly to keep herself in order during a spirited if somewhat random rendition of "Jerusalem."

Dorothy Finnegan remained upright and clear-eyed throughout the service, but when they gathered again at the graveside, Matt could see that in these last moments before the earth closed over her husband, she was in difficulty. Knowing Tom was dying, that there was a finite time to share, had been bad enough. No doubt she had subconsciously planned each stage in her grieving to run a certain length of time, to prepare herself for the day when the cancer finally claimed him.

But that time had been cut short.

And now she was neither certain nor ready.

The weather cooperated in mourning. It was now not only dark, but raining steadily. Umbrellas were produced by the funeral director's staff, so Tom's final moments seemed to be attended by an outbreak of black mushrooms. Bayview Cemetery—true to its name—extended across the top of the hills behind Butter Beach and would have commanded an excellent vista of Blackwater Bay had rain not been falling. As it was, he could see the yellow sands of the beach below and a small stretch of gray-green water, but the far side of the bay might not have existed at all.

He could, however, see Eagle Head.

Its sharp outline was veiled and softened by the rain, but it loomed darkly in the middle distance, a stark attendant at this

occasion and a reminder of both his duty and his present ob-
session.

In the crowd across from him he saw the six men who carried their secret to this grave. He regarded each in turn, seeking some flicker of remorse, some indefinable indication of
guilt; but there was none.

Tyrone Molt wore a gray suit that had seen much service
and, for him, quite a discreet tie—four wild geese in flight
against a blue sky. Jack Fanshawe was bareheaded, the rain
dripping freely from his hair and chin. Dr. Rogers looked
grim—whether through accident or disease, he apparently
still took death as a personal defeat. Merrill Atwater said a
few words, as befitted his position as both friend and mayor,
but his voice was uncharacteristically inaudible beneath the
drumming of the rain on the umbrellas. Carl Putnam looked
pale and ill, his knuckles white where he gripped his hands
in front of him. Arthur Budd's suit had the casually draped
cut that bespoke expensive Italian tailoring, oddly fitting his
ponderous figure. Tilly did not meet Matt's eye during the
whole of the mercifully brief interment.

Matt felt himself growing angry all over again. Those six
men needed to be knocked apart from one another, somehow. They had to be shocked or scared into revealing the
truth. Only then would he know whether he was right or
wrong. Of course, in the process of doing this, he could lose
more than he gained, but it was a risk worth taking. He
hoped.

When it was over they all made their way across the slip-
pery wet grass to their various cars. Dorothy—supported by
her two eldest children—was weeping openly now and near
collapse. Matt and Daria went to her and said a few gentle
words, but he didn't think she heard them. Tim, her oldest
son, nodded gratefully and apologetically as he saw his
mother into the limousine at the head of the line.

By the time they reached the Finnegan house, managed to
find a place to park on the rutted, winding road, and then
trudged around all the muddy puddles to mount the steps and
enter the house, Dorothy was nowhere to be seen. Sent to
bed, no doubt. The temporarily returned young of the house
were accepting condolences on her behalf.

The Finnegans had many friends and acquaintances, as they had been active in several town organizations. There was a splendid buffet, catered by Mrs. Peach. Mrs. Toby and Mrs. Norton were overseeing the distribution of food, and Larry Lovich and Freddy Tollett were practicing the art of bonhomie by seeing that everyone had just a little more than enough to drink. All of the Blackwater Bay Magpies were there. Many men wore the gull-feather emblem of the Algo-nawana Lodge, of which Tom had been a past chief. Isaiah Naseem, the present chief, wore his full formal regalia—sans headdress, of course—and made a colorful contrast to the generally dark-clothed crowd. Some people had come from as far away as Hatchville, Oscogee, and Peskett to give their sympathy to Dorothy.

After helping themselves to food, Daria waded straight into the crowd, but Matt stood back, not yet ready to make his move. Gradually the self-conscious silence melted away as people greeted one another, shared memories of Tom, and then moved on to more recent events—foremost of which was Peter Dill's murder. Even in the window seat where he was sheltering, he could hear the low-voiced comments and questions.

The Dill funeral would be on Friday, bracketing the week with ritual farewell. Many glances slid Matt's way, and he knew people were wondering what he was doing about find-ing Dill's killer, whether he would be successful before the funeral, and whether it would turn out to be someone they knew. Someone here, perhaps?

He knew how fervently they did not want that to happen. They wanted it to be some stranger, some passing person un-connected with their lives, their emotions, their consciences. Someone they could dislike without hesitation or confusion.

Matt did not think they would have their wish.

Molt, Rogers, Fanshawe, Atwater, Putnam, and Budd were all here now, smiling, talking to people but not to one another, circulating through the crowded rooms with paper plates and drinks in hand, performing an elaborate dance of avoidance that, if seen from above, would be amazing in its complexity.

And could not be anything but deliberate.

It was as if they trailed banners, invisible to all but Matt, saying, "We Are Not Connected."

He intercepted Molt near the buffet table and noted that there was now a generous supply of spots on his clothing, for Tyrone was the kind of man who gestured as he spoke as he ate. The geese were no longer the only thing on that tie. "Good spread," said Tyrone, chewing strongly.

"Yes. They must have spent a lot of time on it," Matt agreed solemnly.

"Tried that orange thing over there?" Molt asked. "Or these lobster sandwiches?"

"No, I—"

"Damn good. Damn fine."

"About Peter Dill."

Molt's eyes rolled, like a startled horse, and he actually reared back slightly. Matt wanted to shout, "Whoa, boy!" but refrained. "Listen, one dead guy a day is my limit," Molt said.

"There were at least six blows to his head," Matt went on.

"I don't want to hear about it," Molt said, moving away. "Unless you want me to puke up on this nice carpet here."

He tried Dan Rogers next. "I've had the forensic report on your clothing," he began.

"Oh?" Rogers asked, turning his back on Carl Putnam as he went past.

"The blood on your bandages was mostly animal—but there were several splashes of A-negative."

"Oh?" Rogers said, sipping his drink.

"That's a relatively rare type, I'm told," Matt said. "Did the boy with the nosebleed have that type?"

Rogers's expression had been vague as he stared out over the crowd, but his eyes came quickly to focus on Matt's face. "I don't know," he said. "Did Peter Dill—or did you forget to check?" He smiled blandly at Matt and walked away.

Carl Putnam was standing by the front windows, gazing out at the dripping garden and the line of cars at the foot of the lawn.

"I understand your father used to be pretty friendly with Jacky Morgan's mother," Matt said to Putnam. "Were they business partners or just good friends?"

"Where the hell did you hear that?" Putnam demanded.

"I have my sources," Matt said evasively. In fact, it had been one of the peripheral observations in his father's old day books. He'd been reading them steadily since retrieving them from behind the safe. Aside from their salty humor, which he relished, and their common sense, which he tried to absorb, they were providing him with the support he needed to stick to his guns. His father had been a stubborn, opinionated bastard, too.

Putnam almost snarled. "I'm warning you, Matt, don't push me too far."

"You mean the way someone pushed Jacky Morgan?" Matt asked. Putnam whitened and abruptly turned and moved through the crowd like a man in urgent need of seclusion and a place to vomit.

His next quarry swam into view almost literally, because it was obvious that Jack Fanshawe had had far more than usual to drink, even though he had been here less than half an hour. Perhaps he'd taken a load on before the funeral, Matt thought, but it hadn't showed until now.

"Hey, take it easy," he said as Fanshawe lurched into him, spilling part of his drink down himself. "You're wasting some."

"So what?" Fanshawe asked belligerently. "Finnegan was a good man. Miss him already, the dumb old son of a bitch."

"He wasn't so dumb, Jack," Matt said. "He talked a lot to me before he died."

Fanshawe's eyes widened. "What do you mean, talked a lot?"

"He felt bad about Jacky Morgan."

"So what, so what? We all felt bad about Jacky. Who wouldn't?"

"Somebody didn't," Matt suggested. "Someone was glad."

Fanshawe went a little pale. "Who told you?" he demanded, more loudly than he'd intended. Worse, his question fell into one of those lulls that often occur at random in large gatherings. Several people turned, including Merrill Atwater and Albert Budd, who both scowled and quickly turned away.

"I'd rather not say just yet," Matt told Fanshawe in a

deeply confidential tone, and walked out into the hall. He
hadn't expected Fanshawe or Putnam to bite so easily; it had
caught him unprepared. Whether it was the booze or the funeral, Putnam was sickened and Fanshawe was on the edge
of fighting drunk, and the last thing he wanted to do was start
a scene at Tom Finnegan's wake.

But he'd gotten a response! There *was* something to be
told. And judging from both Putnam's and Fanshawe's reac-
tions, each was afraid one of the others would tell it. No
wonder they were avoiding one another. No wonder they always had. He felt triumph for an instant, then the inevitable
letdown.

All right, he'd found a chink in the closed box of what had
happened thirty years ago—but he still had to insert a crow-
bar.

And then find a way to press it down.

Because of her efforts on behalf of the grieving Dorothy
Finnegan, Mrs. Peach had warned her guests that there
would be no evening meal on Monday. Dominic had accepted this without question, but Rita and Arthur Stevens
had demanded an appropriate reduction in their weekly bill,
which was duly given. Now, driving through the rain to the
airport on the other side of Grantham, Dominic wished he
had stopped to eat something before setting out on the long
trip. His stomach was actually growling. He hoped there
would be time to grab something at the airport before
Emily's plane landed.

She had sounded so upset on the telephone. He felt worse
than ever that she, instead of he, had gone down to talk to
Coral Morgan. If he had gone, giving some excuse or other
for his absence, maybe he would have been able to avoid the
confrontation he'd had with Carl Putnam just before leaving
the office.

Putnam had come in just before five, white-faced and furious, and had gone straight into the closet where the old filing
cabinets were lined up, emerging a few minutes later to demand of Mona Pickering the location of "the Morgan file."
She, of course, professed total ignorance of the file or its
whereabouts. The argument had escalated, ending in her

leaving the office in tears while Putnam raged about in his own room, slamming drawers and kicking his wastebasket. There had been a moment, quite early on in all this, when Dominic could have emerged from his office and handed over the file. But the moment had passed, and the file had remained, burning like a brand in his own imagination, within his own filing cabinet, its contents reallocated to a folder marked "Gibbons."

When Putnam had crashed into his office, asking whether he had seen the file, Dominic—having learned something of the art from Emily—had simply lied. Simplicity, she had told him, was the essence of it. No elaboration, no complication, just a straight-out lie and a smile. And don't stare the person straight in the eye; liars always do that. Just look at him, then away, then *do* something with your hands. Keep busy.

So he'd said to Putnam, "No, sir—I don't believe I have a file labeled 'Morgan.' Is it a new client or—" And he had gone on sharpening his pencils.

Putnam had shaken his head like a stunned ox and gone out, slamming the outer door.

Oh, that Emily.

She had told him about lying so as to ensure their relationship was a strong one. "I want to tell you all my faults and tricks," she'd said on Sunday evening when they'd left his office after reading the file. "That way I can't fool you."

But he knew she would try a trick or two from time to time, just to see if she could fool him. And he might try to catch her out, and he might not, because he knew it would only ever be over small things, never anything important. It would be a game, and he approved of games. They kept everyone on their toes.

The thought of her, and her challenges, and her complexities, and her big dark eyes, and her silliness, and her slender, sexy figure enchanted him momentarily, and he found himself doing ninety before he realized it. He snatched his foot from the accelerator and glanced in the mirror to see if any patrol cars were around. Safe for the moment. He gave a sigh of relief. "Just thinking of my girl, Officer" somehow didn't cut it as a legal defense for speeding.

He saw the sign for the turn-off to the airport and moved

into the exit lane. Glancing at his watch in the light from the sign, he saw that if he was quick to park, he might just have time for a hamburger before she landed.

He reminded himself to say "No onions."

In his office, Merrill Atwater put down the phone and stared at the wall. Something had to be done. He didn't know if he could take much more of this pressure. He got up and went into his gym, where the two Matthew brothers were working out.

"One of you feel like a judo lesson?" he asked.

He felt like throwing someone around.

In his suite at the Ventnor Hotel, Albert Budd was also on the phone. He had sat down at the desk while the room service waiter removed the remains of his dinner and then begun dialing the first number on a list he'd made out while eating.

The sheriff had made it clear he wanted Albert Budd to remain in town for another day or two. Albert knew he could not be forced to stay without legal action being taken, but it did seem expedient to cooperate at this juncture. Still, it raised difficulties. He had to rearrange several conference calls that had been scheduled, as well as have a talk with his broker, his long-suffering secretary, and his lawyer.

His first evening back had been amusing—and useful—despite the murder. Sunday had been restful—despite the sheriff's suspicion. But the strain of today's funeral and the ghastly gathering afterward had been almost too much for the reclusive millionaire.

Albert Budd was extremely peeved.

Tyrone Molt pressed down on the accelerator. It had been a long time since he'd bothered to take this little trip to Lemonville. In the past few years it had never seemed worth the time, or the gas, or the sweat. Clara understood. Their phone conversations had come to be more exciting for him than actual sex had ever been, and the price was the same. But now he needed real flesh and bone. The effort seemed more than worth it. In fact, it seemed desperately, hungrily,

angrily necessary. It was either that or smash something.
And the trouble with smashing something is that you have to
pay for it.

Eventually.

In the prep room at the hospital, Dan Rogers stared down at
his hands. Scrubbed and powdered, they were ready to be
gloved for the emergency appendectomy that had just been
brought in. But the hands were shaking. He wiped his forehead with his arm and closed his eyes. He held his breath for
a long time, then inhaled slowly and regularly for a full
minute. He looked down at his hands again.

They were still shaking.

In the bathroom of his beautifully furnished and otherwise
empty house, Jack Fanshawe sat on the floor of his mint-
green en suite bathroom and leaned his forehead against the
cool porcelain of the toilet.

Booze, he'd very recently decided, did not help.

In the back of the Blackwater Bay Savings and Loan, the two
auditors raised their heads from the records and gazed at one
another in wild surmise.

"I'll be damned," said one.

"Probably," said the other.

25

When Matt finally climbed the stairs at Mrs. Peach's Guest House, it was after one o'clock. He had taken Daria home and spent several hours with her, celebrating life and the fact that her aunt had left that very morning to visit relatives in Florida. But after the lovemaking and the soft talk, she had been ready for sleep, while his mind was still racing with conjecture and possibility. In the end he had left her there, curled up like a child, and had come back to toss and turn alone.

As his head rose above the level of the top floor, he saw that there was a thin line of light under the door of his room. He stopped, then proceeded slowly. Of course—when he'd come home to change for the funeral, it had been darkening before the rain, and he'd carelessly left the light on.

He opened the door, expecting only that, and was astonished to find two people sitting on his bed. One of them had been crying.

"Hi," said Dominic. "We've got some stuff to tell you."

First of all, Dominic explained about the confidential file. "I knew about it practically from the beginning," he said, avoiding Matt's gaze. "Until Dill was killed, I didn't think it would make much difference—Tom Finnegan was dead, and the state police were satisfied . . ."

"I wasn't," Matt said shortly. "You knew I wasn't."

"Yes," Dominic agreed. "But the file wouldn't have told you anything about Finnegan's death. Knowing about it wouldn't have gotten you any farther."

"It might have given me some leverage," Matt pointed out.

"And it might have lost him his job," Emily put in.

Matt looked at her. He had seen her grow up, knew her to be ambitious, sharp-tongued, with little time for the local boys. Yet she clung to Dominic's hand with the fierce clutch of a reclaimed child. This white-faced, pink-eyed girl was not the budding media personality he'd had cause to avoid during the past summer's madness.

"I don't understand how you got involved in this," he said, shortly.

"We're engaged," Dominic said firmly. Matt raised an eyebrow but said nothing. The young lawyer went on. "I know it was quick, but—well, that's just how it is."

"It's a trial engagement," Emily said with a slightly faltering grin. "He's engaged, but I'm on trial."

Dominic ignored that. "Anyway, after Dill was murdered I knew the file could be helpful, but I was still worried about breaking confidentiality. I talked it over with Emily—"

"A newspaper reporter," Matt reminded him.

"She promised not to use anything I told her."

"They promise lots of things," Matt said sourly.

"I meant it," Emily said. "Besides, it wasn't really a story then, was it?"

"You see?" Matt said. "An easy promise—until she knew more."

"No," Dominic said steadfastly. "She knows more now— she has a story now—but she's not going to use it. Any of it."

"I don't understand."

So they told him about Emily's trip to Florida.

At that, Matt really got angry. "You had no right—" he began, then stopped. She had the right to talk to anyone she wanted, including Coral Morgan, if they would talk to her. And, apparently, they did.

"I could hardly tell Carl Putnam I was off to talk to somebody in one of his confidential files," Dominic explained.

"But Emily is a free agent—she thought the old woman might talk to her more easily than she'd talk to me."

"And I was right. She wouldn't have talked to Dominic," Emily said. "Not once she knew he worked for Carl Putnam."

And then she told him how the interview had begun—and how it had ended.

At first the old woman had seemed an amusing, feisty person, but as she recalled old hurts and horrors, she had changed. Her voice had become shrill, her lips had drawn back in a feral display, and her clawed hands had clutched the blanket as if it were a woven substitute for human flesh.

The hate Coral Morgan felt for Blackwater Bay and its denizens seemed to grow and fill the room. Although she had started to make notes, Emily's pen had soon stopped moving and she had sat there, bathed in the brilliant Florida sunshine but surrounded by darkness. She had been surprised to discover how upset she'd become during Coral Morgan's gush of vengeful gossip.

"If that . . . was the kind of thing he heard at home, it was no wonder that Jacky Morgan grew up to be . . . unlovable," she said to Matt in an unsteady voice. Even now, hours away from the experience, it shook her. "It was like seeing a wound burst and being sprayed with pus," she said. "She went on and on, telling me the most terrible, disgusting things about people I have known all my life, grown-ups I respected—the things they did when they were younger, the sins, the corruption, the petty cruelties and the big ones . . . things I didn't want to hear. Things I wish I didn't know. I mean, did you know that—" She stopped and shook her head. "You wouldn't want to know, either," she said. "Truly, you wouldn't."

"I would if it would help me catch a killer," Matt said. "And, by the way, I probably know a lot of what she told you already. It's my job to know."

"Well, it isn't mine," Emily said with a deep, shuddering sigh. "I'm going to marry Dominic and make quilts and write children's books instead."

"Don't be silly," Dominic said. "You're going to be a brilliant newspaperwoman and support me in the manner to which I wish to become accustomed."

"I thought *you* were going to make the money," Emily said.

"I might make *some*," Dominic conceded. "But I plan to be a big spender. Go on about Coral Morgan."

Matt saw that he was trying to tease her through what had obviously been a traumatic experience. The truth did not always set you free.

Reluctantly, Emily concluded her recitation. As Coral Morgan's voice had weakened, so had the Florida sunlight, changing from glaring white to deep gold with a touch of scarlet as the sun set behind the hospital. When, at last, the croaking monologue had ceased and Coral Morgan had lapsed into a twitching, uneasy sleep, Emily realized she was weeping. A voice spoke behind her in the gloom.

"That may have been hard on you, but it was good for her," said a nurse coming into the room.

"How long have you been there?" Emily had asked.

"About ten minutes," the nurse said, handing Emily a tissue. "They were just names to me, but I guess you know them?"

"Yes," Emily said. "She was a—"

"I know what she was," the nurse said. "And I've heard some of it before—she ran a fever a few days ago and was delirious off and on. The point is, she must have been carrying that crap around in her for years. She wasn't all that well liked around the village, she had a vicious tongue and no friends, but it never went any farther than that. She didn't actually *do* anything, or attempt to take up her former profession. I suppose some of the old guys might have been glad if she had, as long as she kept her mouth shut, but . . ." The nurse shrugged. "Some old people can turn nasty. Maybe it was the drinking that made her worse than most. She never showed it, you know. Until she was brought in here and we did blood tests, nobody but the garbage men knew how much she must have been putting away in a day, and they work for the city, not Sunshine, so it never got back to us. No trouble, no staggers, no visible signs. She must have gone into the city to buy it—or had it delivered by taxi. They get pretty cunning—and as long as they have the money, well . . . they get what they want."

"You say a lot of them turn nasty?" Emily asked.

"Some. Bitter, I guess would be more accurate," the nurse said with a sigh. "Like wasps at the end of summer. They sense their time is short, and they don't want to let go of life. They see young people and hate them for their beauty and their energy and the years they've still got ahead of them—it takes them hard, sometimes. Not all, but a few." She crossed over to the bed and drew the covers over Coral Morgan, tucking them in gently around the old woman. Then she turned, and Emily saw she was not a young woman herself.

"All that poison is gone, now. Whatever you said broke the dam. . . ."

"I wish I hadn't asked."

"It wasn't nice for you, I know," the nurse said kindly. "The point is, she's laid down her burden, honey. I suggest you just try and do the same."

Now, in the stillness of the sleeping house, Emily looked over at Matt and managed a smile. "And I've been trying to do that," she said. "All the way home, I've been trying. I just don't know how I'll feel when I meet the people she talked about. It wasn't just her customers, you see. She knew or was told things about other people. Friends of my parents, teachers, even church people . . ."

"Try viewing them with a little charity," Matt suggested. "If you grew up respecting them, there must have been a reason. Stick to that, forgive the rest."

"Yes . . . well . . . I'll try," she sniffed, and wiped her eyes. Telling him had brought it back again.

Matt thought how young she suddenly looked, how vulnerable—a side of her personality she had never before shown. She was only just out of college, after all, she probably had ideals—he had been judging her by her chosen career, not herself. Her own wry sense of humor would save her from the excesses of that career—and he'd be willing to bet those books about bunnies would never be written, unless they were very unusual bunnies.

"The point is, some of the things she learned *are* going to be useful to you," Dominic said in a low voice. "At least, it looks that way. And she can't really start to forget until she tells you. . . ."

"Go on, then," Matt said, leaning back on the rocking chair and feeling a faint draft on his neck from the loose-fitting window. He shivered.

Emily began. "You know she used to be a prostitute? She worked at the Doll House—only it wasn't called that then, when she was young—but when she got pregnant with Jacky, she was set up in a cottage of her own by the father. She knew who it was because . . . well, the circumstances made it pretty clear, apparently. Something about dates and 'regulars' and so on. Anyway, he paid her something for the upkeep of the child at first, but they fought and that stopped. So she went back to what she knew." Emily managed this part of it in a straightforward manner—it was the history of strangers, after all.

"She was discreet about it, but—well . . . Jacky apparently was a sharp little kid, and he knew more or less what went on when he was at school. It's no wonder he . . ." She paused. "Do you know what she said? She said she hated him—hated her own child—because he didn't have the guts to use what he knew. She knew about the grown-ups, he knew about the kids—she got paid for keeping quiet, but he just used it to get 'friends,' she said. She thought that was weak, and she despised him for it. My God . . . how do people *get* like that? What makes them . . ." she faltered.

"You can go back generations looking for someone to blame and still not know," Dominic said. "Just tell him what he has to know, and then we can leave the rest. Go on."

"I asked her who Jacky's father was. She told me it was Theodore Putnam, Carl's father," Emily blurted out.

"It was his signature on the first checks in the file," Dominic said.

"Good Lord," Matt said. "Then Jacky Morgan was Carl Putnam's bastard half brother."

"Yes," Dominic said. "But I don't know if he knew it, or even if he knows it now. The checks in the file only date from a month or so after Jacky's death. How the old man paid Coral Morgan before that I guess we'll never know. Carl started signing the checks only after his father died.

From what I can gather from those records, all the parents gave money to Theodore and later on to Carl, who then passed the total on to Mrs. Morgan on the basis of her leaving Blackwater Bay and never returning. However, the last payment—the big one—"

"Was made by Albert Budd," Emily said. "She got thrown out of where she was living—I think she must have been either drinking too much or trying prostitution again—and she threatened to come back to Blackwater Bay."

"Budd was the only one with enough money to finance her retirement," Dominic said flatly. "Even together the others couldn't have given that kind of money. He could—and did. He bought her apartment at the retirement village, and he set up a trust fund to augment her Social Security on the understanding that it was a once-and-for-all settlement. She stuck to the agreement, and that was why the file was put away under 'inactive.'"

"She hasn't much longer to live," Emily said. "She's dying, and she knows it. When she's gone, that will be the end of it."

"That *would* have been the end of it," Dominic corrected her. "Now, of course, Dill has been murdered."

"Which doesn't make sense," Emily said.

And she told Matt why.

26

Two very busy days later, Matt looked around the conference room of Crabtree and Putnam. Intermittent rain lashed the glass behind him, and the wind whined around the edges of the window frame. The first real winter storm was sweeping toward Blackwater Bay, and although it was early afternoon, the lights were on and needed to be.

"I think you *know* why I've called you all together," Matt said to the six men who were gathered there.

Silence, except for the storm outside.

"I want to talk about Jacky Morgan. More particularly, how he died and why he died," Matt continued, ignoring the stolid expressions of the six men and their refusal to meet one another's eyes—or his.

"Jacky Morgan was, in his way, something of a monster," Matt said, leaning against the windowsill. "He was a sneak, an eavesdropper, a Peeping Tom, a creep, and a talebearer. He liked knowing things, and he liked even better the power that knowing things gave him." His glance traveled over the men one by one. "He knew things about each of you. Things that would have gotten you into trouble with your parents, maybe even with the authorities. He knew, for example, that he was Carl's illegitimate half brother."

The other five looked at Carl in surprise.

271

"He knew that Tyrone had paid teachers for the answers to exam questions in advance."

They looked at Tyrone.

"He knew that Jack was having an affair with a certain lady teacher twice his age."

"Everybody knew that," Jack said.

"Your parents didn't, did they?" asked Matt, and Jack was silent.

"Jacky knew that Merrill was experimenting with certain drugs to bolster his performance in sports because Merrill wasn't yet the man he later became."

They all looked at Merrill, who blushed deeply.

"He knew that Albert's mother stole from her employers, and that her 'magic polish' was just two commercial polishes mixed together and repackaged."

"I deny that," Albert snarled. "I hold patents on the formula."

Matt ignored the interruption. "He knew that Tom Finnegan both took and sold LSD, which he manufactured in the chemistry lab after school. He knew that Mary Turkle killed herself not because she was afraid of losing Peter Dill, but because she was pregnant by him. And he knew that Dan Rogers had performed several amateur but successful abortions, because Peter had suggested that she go to Dan for 'help.' "

"My God, do you have to take all this up now?" Dan asked in horror.

"Yes," Matt said. "I do. I want you to know that *I* know you *all* had good reason for killing Jacky Morgan. And that ever since Tom Finnegan died trying to tell me about it, I have been convinced that your *threw* Jacky Morgan to his death over that cliff."

They all looked at him then, startled and plainly horrified.

"I have now revised that theory," Matt continued.

"I should damn well hope so," muttered Dan Rogers.

"I suggest to you that he was dead *before* you threw him over," Matt said. "I suggest that you got drunk, ganged up on him, beat and kicked him, and then discovered that you had, in fact, killed him. Jacky Morgan had thin, brittle bones. One hard kick to the head would have killed him easily. He knew your secrets, taunted you, blackmailed you emotionally, and—on that particular evening—drove you too far."

"Now wait a minute—" Tyrone Molt said.

"When you realized what had happened, you panicked. Your first thought was to leave him there in the woods and run for it. But somebody thought quicker than the rest, somebody said 'Wait a minute.' Who was it? You, Dan? Peter? Carl?"

Silence. The window rattled in its frame, and a horn blared outside in the street. Matt continued.

"Whoever it was made out the following case. There were girls who knew you had been up there with Jacky. They knew you were drinking. They would be questioned, you would be questioned and, inevitably, accused. You would be shamed, tried, and possibly convicted. Instead of going to college, you'd go to jail. Or, if acquitted, you would be denied college and probably be sent to Vietnam. Neither alternative was attractive. But, if you could make it look like an *accident* instead of the cowardly, shameful gang killing it had really been, if you could all pretend to be deeply sorry that it happened, then—maybe—it would be all right. People would be angry, they would think you careless and foolish, but they would not think that you were the craven murderers you really were."

"Now listen—" Merrill Atwater said.

"So you looked around, you found the barrel and the rotten rope, and you thought of the 'game' of push-the-barrel. A dumb, drunken game—but one that was *just* believable given the situation and the circumstances. You put Jacky's already broken body into the barrel, tied the rotten rope around it, and then sent it rolling toward the edge of Eagle Head. The rope broke, and poor Jacky's dead body went over onto the rocks below. Those rocks did the business—they disguised the kicks and blows, they took the blame for what you had done to that young boy yourselves. And you got away with it, didn't you? You all got away with it—until now. Because Tom Finnegan couldn't live with what he had done. He told you he planned to confess the truth. And—"

"No!" shouted Carl Putnam. "You've got it all wrong."

"You don't understand," cried Albert. "It's true we were

afraid, and it's true we didn't want to have any of those things happen to us, but we didn't kill Jacky Morgan."

"Oh, no?" Matt asked disbelievingly.

"No," Jack Fanshawe said in a weary voice. "He was already dead when we found him."

The wind shrieked suddenly, and in the outer office the phone rang and then was silenced. From the rear of the building came the unmistakable sound of a tree branch cracking away from the trunk, but in the room nobody spoke. Finally Carl Putnam shrugged and cleared his throat.

"It's true—at least what you said about me was true," he said. "I don't know about the rest of the things, and I don't *want* to know. None of it matters now, anyway." His tone was belligerent as he looked around at the others. His eyes came back to Matt. "It's true about the drinking, too, and the anger we felt toward Jacky, who was truly awful that night. He never brayed his knowledge out in public, though, the way you just did. His habit was to sidle up to you and whisper in your ear whatever it was he knew, along with assurances that he'd *never* tell anyone because you were his friend, weren't you? He was the complete little bastard, officially and otherwise. I didn't believe what he told me then—about his being my father's by-blow—but my father admitted later that it was so. I was pretty devastated about it when I realized it was true—but that night I was just drunk. Drunk and furious. We all were."

"Yeah," Tyrone Molt agreed. "But we never threw him over the cliff to kill him the way you said. And we never kicked him to death, either. We just chased the little son of a bitch through the woods, trying to scare the shit out of him once and for all."

"Separately, or as a pack?"

"As a pack, first—but then we got separated," admitted Merrill Atwater. "It was so dark in those woods, with the trees overhead, and the moon popping out now and again, causing shadows that made you jump—we could hear one another running . . . and panting . . . and crashing through the undergrowth . . ."

"Eventually we called it off. But when we got back to that

clearing he was just lying there." Jack Fanshawe took up the tale. "We could see right away he was dead—and then we did panic, like you said."

"Who stopped you?"

They looked at one another. Finally Carl spoke. "I think it was Peter, actually."

Matt looked satisfied. "Yes," he said. "I thought it might have been."

"He said that one of us must have killed Jacky because there was nobody else in the woods."

"Are you certain of that?" Matt asked. "You could have said you saw someone or heard someone, a tramp, a stranger . . ."

"We didn't think of that until later," Dan admitted. "At the time we were spooked, we just accepted that it was one of us and that we would be considered accessories, at the very least, because we'd been chasing him and so on—"

"Couldn't he have just fallen and hit his head on a rock?" Matt asked curiously.

They all shook their heads—the first sign of the old cama- raderie they'd demonstrated. "There was a piece of wood with blood on it lying beside him," Albert said. "We thought right away about fingerprints, but Carl said the surface was too rough to take them, and that anyway, we—"

There was another silence as they all remembered, vividly remembered, their horror, their fear, their craven desperation to get out of being accused either individually or collec- tively.

"What happened to the piece of wood?" Matt asked.

Albert heaved a deep sigh. "We threw it on the fire. After- ward." He leaned forward. "You have to understand, we were *friends*, we had to stick together—"

"No, you didn't," Matt said, leaving the windowsill and coming to sit at the head of the table. It was more than the storm that was making him feel cold. "One of you was a murderer. You didn't have to stick with *him* at all. Didn't you wonder who it was? Weren't you even curious?"

"Well, of course we were," Carl said in disgust. "Don't you think we thought about it—have kept on thinking about it, ever since? Our friendship ended right there, right then. How could we trust one another, when one of us—" He stopped, then continued. "We went away to different colleges, which helped, but we all came home again. Albert got away eventually, but the rest of us had to do business with one another, we met at parties and attended one another's weddings and said 'hello' when we passed in the street, because to do otherwise would have been noticed. But we were never *friends* again. Ever. Not like before. We were afraid to trust one another because the one we trusted could be a killer."

Albert managed a wry smile. "Does anyone think we'll be friends now?"

Carl looked at Matt. "You had this figured out, didn't you?"

"Oh, yes," Matt agreed. "I did. But I wanted to hear your version of events, or your various versions, perhaps. That's why I brought you all together after talking to you individually. You're a closemouthed bunch, I'll give you that. Nobody broke down. Maybe somebody would have, eventually—but it could have taken a long, long time. I finally figured that only by forcing you together would I get a response. I knew you were all getting very nervous. I *wanted* you to be nervous. I let each of you think I knew more than I was saying. Which, by the way, I do, thanks to information received."

"Oh, yes?" Tyrone Molt asked sarcastically. "I suppose *you* know which of us killed Jacky, then?"

"Sure," said Matt. "Peter Dill killed him."

Again he received the collective stare, which he returned to them one by one. Beyond the conference room door someone walked across the outer office, opened a file drawer, closed it, walked back. There was another phone call. The wind blew.

"How do you know that?" Jack finally asked.

"Because I am reasonably certain that Peter Dill had killed

once before—so he had more to lose than anyone if Jacky talked."

"What?" Their voices made a regular chorale. Now he'd *really* astonished them.

"You see, after I looked up the coroner's report on Mary Turkle, and confirmed the pregnancy, I talked to old Mrs. Turkle. I discovered that Peter had dropped in to see Mary on the night she killed herself. He arrived at eight and he sat with her until after ten o'clock. But the coroner's report said that she took her overdose around eight o'clock—so she took the pills either in his presence or just before he arrived. I can't believe he didn't know. Her taking them *then* only makes sense if she did it in order to pressure him into marrying him. I think he told her he *would* marry her. I think he said he would call the doctor for her, and perhaps even left the room briefly, pretending to do so. She probably fell asleep trusting him—as she'd trusted him once too often before. Then I think he just sat there until she slipped into her coma. Old Mrs. Turkle says that he came out of the bedroom around ten and announced that Mary was sleeping and he didn't think anybody should disturb her until morning. He actually *said* that sleep was the best thing for flu. Them being Turkles and him being a Dill, they accepted his opinion. They let her sleep—and she never woke up. Apparently at her funeral he told them he'd had no idea she'd taken the pills, and they believed that, too."

"That's not murder," Carl pointed out reluctantly.

"Not legal murder, no," Matt agreed. "Murder by omission, perhaps? Manslaughter? You're the lawyer. Moral murder, certainly. Jacky would have called it murder. And Jacky might well have threatened to tell. Peter couldn't have that—so he killed him."

"You don't *know* that," Merrill said reflectively.

"No," Matt agreed. "It's a guess all right, but I think it's a pretty good guess, because Peter Dill killed Tom Finnegan, too. And I *do* have proof of that." It had taken a long time, but the state police forensic lab, finally chided into action by

Matt, had discovered a thin scab of the red paint of Tom
Finnegan's car overlying the red paint of Peter Dill's car. No
obvious marks, no dents—just the long, thin scrape of paint.
He'd run the weaker man off the road and into that tree with
very little effort.

"But—if Peter Dill killed Tom Finnegan—who killed
Peter Dill?" Dan Rogers asked finally.

"Well, there are six of you left," Matt said. "You were all
unaccounted for during the fireworks display—the time
when Peter was killed. Do I get a confession now—or would
you care to draw straws?"

27

Emily Gibbons had announced to her astonished parents that she was engaged. Her parents had met the nice young lawyer and pronounced themselves satisfied but concerned about his ability to support a dingbat like their daughter, as due to his helping Matt Gabriel to his employer's possible detriment there seemed to be a chance that he would be setting up on his own in the near future, resulting in a certain amount of penury. Emily said that in that case she would take in washing.

Dominic, his head a little on the spin, was now in the newspaper office scanning the city papers under Job Opportunities, Legal. After all, there was a chance that he not only might be fired, but would have to leave town as well. Maybe in a hurry.

For the past two days he had been studiously avoiding his employer, Carl Putnam. Although Putnam had not been told, Dominic was certain that he suspected the identity of Matt Gabriel's private source of information. This, even though Dominic had cunningly replaced the implicative file in the wrong drawer where Putnam had eventually discovered it. It had subsequently disappeared, but Matt had taken careful photocopies of everything in it, so there were no worries there. Dominic particularly wanted to avoid being in the vicinity of the meeting he knew was as that very moment taking place in Putnam's conference room, hence his presence in the offices of the *Chronicle*.

Emily was working on the special Halloween edition with Harry Foskett. They were going over the photographs he'd taken on the night of the Howl—excluding those destined for the coroner's files—and Emily had become quite excited. A good night's sleep had reignited her journalistic flame. She was also in the process of adding detection to her list of accomplishments.

"If only your camera printed the *time* as well as the date on the film," she enthused. "It might give us a clue as to the killer!"

"I think there *is* a camera that does that," Harry said. "But I sure as hell can't afford it. Look, I can pretty well work out a time sequence myself. I started taking pictures about seven-fifteen and broke off about nine-thirty, when I had to start taking pictures of Dill's body for the sheriff. All we have to do is line the contact prints up in order—and then I could try and remember when exactly I'd taken some of them."

"Well," Emily said reluctantly, "it's better than nothing, I suppose."

"It's the best you're going to get," Harry said, completing the display on the large table. "Okay. I started with these two kids dressed as bumblebees." He checked his notebook. "They're the Dill twins, Sheryl and Caryl." He suddenly realized what he'd said. "Oh. I guess we can't use *that* one."

"It might cheer them up to be in the paper," Emily said.

"They're probably fed up with being in the papers," Harry said. "The city guys played up the 'two fatherless little girls' angle really big in their murder coverage."

Emily sighed. "So they did. Okay, that's the first roll—what's the next one?"

"There's an opening in Lemonville," Dominic called.

"Lemonville stinks," Emily informed him.

"There's no need to get ratty about it," Dominic protested.

"No, I mean literally," Emily said. "It stinks to high heaven—there's a cellophane plant there. Some days it's not so bad, but when the wind is in the right direction—yechhh."

"I see," said Dominic. "Scratch Lemonville, then."

"Exactly how most people react," Emily agreed. She bent over the next sheet of contact prints with her magnifying glass. "Who the heck is *that*?"

Harry Foskett leaned over, too, his head next to hers as he tried to look through the glass. "Darned if I know—wait a minute, I'll look at my list." He examined the notepad whereon he'd noted the correct spelling of the names of each person he'd snapped during the Howl. "Good Lord—that's Mrs. Mayhew, the minister's wife."

"You're kidding," said Emily, dumbfounded. They gazed together at the photograph of a large marshmallow with long, lissome legs. "Where's her head, for crying out loud?"

"Inside the marshmallow with the rest of her," Harry said. "I had to talk through a little hole in the side so she could hear me. Those sexy tights weren't keeping her very warm, but inside that marshmallow she had on about ninety-five sweaters and a knitted hat that would have won a prize by itself. Looked like a big strawberry."

"I've seen it." Emily grinned. "She knitted it for Mr. Mayhew, but he refused to wear it." She lifted her head and gazed across the table. "You sure have a lot of pictures of Albert Budd," she observed as Harry laid out the next contact sheet. "Practically that whole roll—Albert with Tilly Moss, Albert with Dr. Rogers, Albert with a grasshopper, Albert with a white fuzzy blob, Albert with the sheriff, Albert with Robin Hood—which Robin Hood is that?"

"I *think* it's Dill," Harry said, reaching for the magnifying glass. They bent closer. "It's got a big white foot."

"Bingo," murmured Emily. "Dom—come here a minute."

"It looks to me like they're not too happy with one another," Harry was saying.

"Who?"

"Dill and Albert. Here, take a look." He handed her the magnifying glass, and she bent over the table.

"You're right," she said.

"About what?" Dominic wanted to know as he came up behind them.

"The late Mr. Dill and Albert Budd having an argument, from the look of it," Emily said, moving aside and handing him the glass. "See?"

"Oh, I wouldn't say that was an argument, exactly—the fat man is scowling, but Robin Hood looks like he's just sort of—"

"Sort of what?"

"I don't know. Worried, maybe? Concerned? Uneasy? Wary?"

"He'd be plenty wary if Albert Budd was threatening to *kill* him," Emily said.

"No way," Dominic said. "I don't know what he's actually saying, but he definitely isn't threatening him—the body language is all wrong."

"Suddenly you're an expert in body language?" Emily asked coldly.

He grinned at her. "Got an A in the course at law school," he said.

"Oh." She was taken aback. "Then you *do* know."

"I know something," he said carefully. "Not everything."

"Here's another one of Dill—talking to another white blob," Harry put in.

They all bent down to look. "That blob isn't fuzzy like the other one—it's blotchy. That's Dr. Rogers," Emily said.

"*They* don't look angry," Harry observed.

"More furtive than angry," Emily decided. "Here's another one of Albert Budd with Mrs. Moss and that gorgeous chauffeur of Mr. Budd's who was pushing her wheelchair. There's another Robin Hood in the background. Listen, who don't we separate out *all* the pictures of Dill? With anybody."

"That's not going to be easy—there were about ten Robin Hoods at the Howl," Harry said. "If I caught them from the back, there's no way of telling them apart."

"Yes, there is," Dominic said. "He's wearing a quiver full of arrows—see?"

Emily shuddered. "One of those was stuck through his chest later on," she recalled. "Remember?"

"Only after he was dead," Dominic said. He had learned this from Matt, who had gotten it from the coroner.

"Why would anyone do that?" Harry wondered.

"Good question," Dominic said approvingly. "*Good* question."

"Well," Harry said modestly, "I mean, it does seem sort of like gilding the lily, doesn't it?"

"More like hate or vengeance," Emily said. "And there were plenty of people—" She stopped abruptly and pressed her lips together.

Harry looked at her with interest. "Plenty of people who what?" he asked.

"Nothing." She shook her shoulders as if ridding herself of something. "Let's have a look at the rest of the shots. What on earth is *this*?" She indicated what looked like an anthill.

"Oh, I took some shots from the top of the Ferris wheel when it was stopped during the fireworks," Harry said. "That's the refreshment tent, I think." He pointed a long, chemical-stained finger. "This is that Bonechiller thing, this is the dance tent, this is . . ." He bent closer. "I don't know what the hell that is."

"An explosion?" Dominic suggested.

"A passing cloud of gnats?" Emily offered.

"Oh, *I* know." Harry laughed. "It's cotton candy. The kid in the seat below me was—"

"What's this?" Dominic interrupted, pointing. They all bent down again.

"It's that fuzzy white blob again," Harry said in exasperation. "Maybe I better have that camera looked at."

Dominic was using the glass now, his nose practically on the shiny surface of the contact sheet. "Could you blow this shot up?" he asked.

"Big as you want," Harry bragged. "Only thing is, the bigger it goes, the grainier it gets—nothing I can do about that. It won't tell you much, I promise you. Anyway, why?"

"Curiosity," Dominic said.

"You know what that did to the cat," Emily reminded him.

"Curiosity killed the cat, but satisfaction brought him back," Dominic quoted. "Not many people remember the second part."

"I hope this isn't a wild-goose chase," Harry grumbled, picking up the contact sheet and heading toward the darkroom.

"More like goose feathers," Emily said, eyeing Dominic. "What do you expect to find, anyway?"

He grinned. "Oh, what else? The vital clue that will solve the entire thing, of course. I will be famous. Hundreds of beautiful women will throw themselves at my feet. . . ."

"Then you'd better start changing your socks more often," Emily said, and turned back to the photographs.

In the Crabtree and Putnam conference room, Matt was still waiting for one of his six suspects to break down—but it looked like a lifetime occupation.

"Look, I *know* you each disappeared during the fireworks," he said wearily.

"What do you mean, 'disappeared'?" demanded Tyrone Molt.

"Well, let's say you were 'unaccounted for,' " Matt said.

They looked at one another and in some unspoken way seemed to agree. Carl Putnam cleared his throat.

"All right—we were *together* during the fireworks. And what's more, we were together with Peter. We met him outside that Bonechiller thing because we thought he was going to tell you about Jacky. He said he never had any intention of telling you a damn thing about Jacky, and so that was fine. We agreed that we would all continue to remain silent, as we have done, and we separated. He was alive when *I* left him, I assure you."

They *all* stated that Dill was alive when they left him.

"And can you prove it?" Matt asked. "I now have you all at the scene, at the relevant time, with the weapon to hand, and consensus between you about remaining silent. I only have your word that Dill agreed to that. If he didn't—"

"He did, dammit!"

"Then what did he want to talk to me about?" countered Matt.

Dan Rogers actually laughed. "Don't you know? He'd found out who put that damned oil on the floor of the bank. It was—"

The door opened and Mona Pickering stuck her head in.

"I'm sorry to interrupt, but there's a call for the sheriff. It's urgent, apparently."

"Can you put it through here?" Matt asked. He didn't want to leave them to talk together. Not yet.

"Sure." She disappeared, and after a moment a button lit up on the telephone that sat on a small table against the wall.

"There you are," Carl Putnam said. "Just press the button and pick it up."

Matt stood up and did so. He was surprised to hear Clarence Toogood's voice. "Ah—finally found you. Listen, I think we might have discovered where a lot of Dill's outside money was coming from. Not a light skimming from a lot of small accounts, like *I* thought, but an out-and-out plunder of just one. Absolutely obvious, once we knew where to look. Do you want to see the evidence? I'm at the bank."

"I suppose—" Matt began.

"And you'd better bring Mr. Albert Budd along, too, if you can find him," Toogood continued. "Do you know where he is?"

Matt turned and regarded the six men who were sitting around the long polished table, watching him. "Oh, yes," he said. "I know *exactly* where he is."

"I think the sheriff ought to see this," Dominic said.

"But it doesn't really *show* anything," Emily objected.

"And I still say it's a flaw in the negative," Harry Foskett muttered.

"It shows somebody or something with what could be Peter Dill standing behind the Bonechiller," Dominic insisted stubbornly. "At about the right time, too, if Harry's timing is right."

" 'If,' 'might be,' 'could be'—it's *nothing*," Emily objected.

"I disagree," Dominic said. "Anyway, it can't do any harm—the worst he can do is laugh at me."

"And you don't mind that?"

"I'm getting more used to it every day," Dominic said grimly. "I have a feeling it's good preparation for my future."

"Well, I'll come with you, then," Emily said, convinced he was insane but ready to stand beside him through snigger and snort. But when they had put on their coats and gone out of the newspaper office, he turned left instead of right. She halted, leaning against the wind.

"The sheriff's office is over there," she protested.

"Yes, but *he's* over here," Dominic told her.

"Are you sure?" She trotted after him.

"Yep," Dominic said. "I know *exactly* where he is."

"I was going to discuss it with Peter on Sunday," Albert Budd said, staring down at the columns of figures. "I realized something had gone wrong the minute I saw him there at the Howl."

"But you never got the chance."

"I never got the chance," Albert agreed. "And then, when Peter was *killed*, it went right out of my head." He glanced at Matt in some exasperation. "Well, I mean to say. What with you *suspecting* all of us, and—"

"I get the idea," Matt said. "And you didn't mention this when you saw Dill at the Howl?"

"I was with the others. It wasn't something to bring up at that time—our concern then was with our mutual protection. I simply informed him we would talk privately on Sunday."

"And he was alive when you left him?"

"*Yes*," Albert snapped. "As I told you earlier."

"And you didn't go back—have it out with him then and there?"

"Certainly not."

Matt looked at the overweight object of Tilly's maiden dreams and felt rising irritation. It was obvious Budd still thought himself immune through wealth. Something in his expression seemed to remind everyone that he could buy the best lawyers in the country and that to even *suspect* him was in the worst possible taste.

"I'll want corroboration of this," Matt said. "I'll have to talk to him myself."

"Go right ahead. He'll only confirm what I've told you."

"Do you know where he lives?" Clarence Toogood asked.

Matt sighed. "Yes. I'll go over there and—"

"I don't think he'll *be* at home," Albert said.

Matt's eyes narrowed. "Why not?"

"Because he is seeking escape—"

"Escape?" Matt demanded. "You mean—"

"Escape from care," Albert finished with a glare of annoyance at being interrupted.

Clarence Toogood had been watching the overweight millionaire. Unlike Matt, he had no case to solve now, no ax to grind, and no memories to overcome. Beneath the defensive veneer of pomp and circumstance that Albert Budd wrapped around himself, he sensed something else. "Do you have any idea where he might be?" he asked in a gentle voice.

"Oh, yes," Albert said sadly. "I know *exactly* where he is."

28

The gusting wind buffeted the car as Matt drove down the street and pulled into the circular apron at the end. The storm was picking up, but the clouds were still broken. It would be a while yet before the full force of it hit them. He jammed his hat down and lowered his head against the thrust of the wind as he and George left the car, walked through the flattened grass, and climbed across the fallen wire fence.

When they reached the expanse of broken concrete that had once been the bedrock of the defunct trailer park, George finally snapped. "*Here?* You can't be serious!" he said.

"I'm assuming Albert knew what he was talking about," Matt shouted over his shoulder. "It's too crazy to be anything but the truth."

"Not if you consider the source," George shouted back, holding his own hat on as it fought to fly free. The glowering scarlet vestiges of the sunset that lit the clouds from behind were merging into night, but over the trees a thin line of steel gray still showed where the angry lake met the sky. Even at this distance the whitecaps were visible, the bay churned to fury by the force of the approaching storm. And it was cold, bitterly cold. Matt could already feel his ears and the tip of his nose growing numb.

The two remaining structures of the once lively trailer park were still musically banging and rattling their bits of broken siding, but now there was a faint glow behind the corroded plastic windows of the one that was nearly intact. "Somebody's there all right," Matt said.

They lurched across the broken concrete, fighting the wind, and Matt hammered on the flimsy door. "Hey! Open up!"

Nothing.

"It's Matt Gabriel. I'm coming in."

He turned the handle and swung open the door. A cascade of fuggy warmth and the mixed odor of whiskey and kerosene poured over them before the wind caught the door and snatched it from his hand. It banged into George and then swung back against Matt, giving him a reproachful blow on the shoulder before he could catch hold of it again. The step was long gone, and they had to lift their boots high to gain access.

Inside the trailer there was little to see, and that was visible only by the light of two kerosene lanterns that swung from makeshift hooks in the partly exposed ceiling ribs of the disintegrating structure. The built-in sofa that curved around the forward end of the trailer was broken, and one side had dropped, giving it the appearance of a kneeling camel. Its upholstery, once a soft beige tweed, was now stiff and blackened from meals spilled and bottoms dragged over its surface. On the far wall there was a plywood cupboard hanging by a few twisted screws, and what had once been a shower room and toilet was now only a cubicle containing broken ends of plumbing. There were bald patches on the pale green walls, attesting to a previous presence of units that had provided cooking and storage amenities. To their left was the narrow passage that led to the bedroom—now only a space containing a stained mattress. Rags of curtains were hanging over the gappy windows where cardboard and odd bits of plywood had replaced most of the glazing. What few panels of plastic that remained had long since clouded over and in the daytime could have admitted little light through their purply-gray discoloration.

A fairly new kerosene heater stood in the middle of this desolation, filling the space with eye-watering warmth—most of which had escaped through the door as Matt and

George had entered. The entire trailer rocked gently as the wind caught it first from one side, then the other. It was not a comforting motion, and Matt was irresistibly reminded of a nursery song line that had always worried him—"When the wind blows, the cradle will fall. . . ."

There was a mound on the mattress, a fetally curved figure covered with an old feather quilt. Beside it, on the cracked linoleum, lay one empty whiskey bottle and another about a quarter full, the latter not far from the outflung hand of Fred Boyle.

"Jesus, what a stink," George complained.

They balanced themselves carefully, aware that their presence had made the trailer even more unstable than before. Many of the props that had once supported it were now missing, and only someone very familiar with it could have walked its length with any confidence.

Matt knelt beside the mattress and prodded the mound under the quilt. "Come on, Fred. Wake up. I want to talk to you."

Nothing.

He poked harder, finally grabbing what looked like a shoulder and shaking the man awake.

"Wha' want?" Boyle's voice was as cracked and broken as the trailer itself. "Whooosit?"

"My God," George muttered. This was the same Mr. Boyle who had attempted to teach him chemistry in the not so long ago, and he had remembered him with respect and some affection. His classroom demonstrations had always had an element of fun or surprise in them. Mr. Boyle had approached both chemistry and recalcitrant teenagers with a light heart then. However, what the death of his wife had begun, the whiskey was apparently finishing.

If George found it difficult to believe this was the same man, he found it even more difficult to believe what had brought them here. Albert Budd had told them what his old friend had revealed to him—that when his grief became too much to bear, Boyle came to this desolate and disgusting place to drink himself into oblivion and out the other side. At those times he didn't want to risk being seen by neighbors, colleagues, or students at his home. Blackwater was a small town. There weren't many places to hide there.

"Come on, Fred. We have to talk."

Boyle, his eyes bleary and several days' beard growth disguising his chin, groaned. "Fuck . . . off," he said, and slumped back onto the mattress.

But Matt didn't give up, and eventually he had the high school teacher sitting up and grasping his whiskey bottle like a baby roused from sleep and seeking nourishment. "Lemme straighten out," Boyle muttered, and took a long swig from the bottle.

"I never understood why that makes you feel better," George commented from the doorway. He hadn't ventured farther, repelled by both sight and smell.

"Doesn't," Boyle mumbled. "Makes you feel . . . less worse."

"Time to get up, Fred," Matt insisted.

Boyle turned his head to look at him and instantly seemed to regret the gesture. "Godda pee," he announced, and lurching over onto all fours, he crawled past George and into what had been the toilet cubicle. The trailer tilted alarmingly to one side, and there was the sound a man might make climbing erect with the help of a wall, followed by the hiss of liquid against a floor. A moment later Boyle appeared, zipping up the fly of his filthy corduroys.

He grinned amiably. "Hole in the floor in the corner," he announced. "Runs down and out, rain washes it away. Gravity plumbing. Not *nice* . . . but 'fective. Other stuff you have to go outside, not foul own nest, you know," he concluded owlishly.

Matt stood up and started forward, pushing past George, who seemed almost old-maid shocked by this final nonclassroom demonstration of moral degeneration. "Let's sit down and talk, Fred." Matt's voice was gentle, persuasive.

"Bottle . . . bottle," Fred said, waving toward the mattress.

"Bring him his bottle, George," Matt said over his shoulder as he guided Boyle around the kerosene heater, ducked him under the lanterns, and lowered him onto one of the more solid-appearing sections of the sofa. Muttering, George complied, then leaned against the wall gingerly, as if half expecting to fall through it, as well he might.

Matt watched Boyle take another long swig of the whiskey, waiting patiently until the reddened eyes focused in his direction. "Whadda want?"

"I want to talk to you about Peter Dill," Matt said. "According to Albert Budd, you were regularly remitted large sums of money as part of your percentage of the profits from the furniture polish you helped him perfect. These were paid into an account managed by Peter Dill."

"Bastard," Boyle muttered.

"This was done according to an agreement you made and signed a long time ago. Because you were not good at handling money, and preferred to have a regular income you could count on rather than money in irregular amounts, is that right?"

Boyle nodded ponderously. "Never good with money," he said slowly. "Have it, spend it. Don't have it, spend it anyway. Dill insisted because I was always writing bad checks by mistake."

"This was done at a time when you didn't really expect anything to come of Albert's project, is that right?"

"Dumb. I know. How expected to figure he'd make all that money, anyway? Joke. Laughed, all laughed. Never figured. Never."

"But you only ever received a small proportion of the money, is *that* right?"

"Needed more. Asked for more," Boyle said, opening his eyes very wide and peering earnestly into Matt's face. "*Begged*. For Maryam. Dying, you know."

"I know," Matt said gently. "I remember."

"Went to Dill, said ask Albert, ask old Albert for more. Albert rich now, see in all the papers. Would have asked myself, but Dill said Albert was recluse. Never saw anybody. Said he would *write*. Later gave me four hundred dollars. Only *four hundred*. Said it was all old Albert sent." He blinked. "Never asked him, you know. Found out other night. Albert said Rotten Pete never asked him, he never knew Maryam ill. Said sent lots over the years. Didn't *get* lots. Got lillel." He shook his head. "Li*tt*le."

"I see," Matt said.

"Shudda had lots!" Boyle suddenly shouted. *"Shudda died gentle in dark night, but died hard, died screaming in end!"*

"Yes, I know, I know," Matt said, patting the other man's hand. "Dr. Rogers told me."

Boyle was crying, now. "Was terrible to see. To hear. Someone you love—screaming—pleading—"

"Yes," Matt agreed.

"Oh, Jesus wept," George muttered miserably. His face was pale. George had joined the police to hunt villains, and he kept finding victims instead.

"Doctor did best," Boyle said, more quietly. "Tried *hard*."

"Yes."

"Albert sorry. *Said* sorry. Said he would make it right, but it's too late. Maryam gone now. Nothing left."

"When was this?" Matt asked. "When did you tell Albert?"

"At Howl. Albert *very* angry at bastard Dill. Said he should be shot, boiled, drawn, and quartered. Always talked like that. But I could tell Albert was *furious* his money gone."

"Was this before the fireworks or after?"

Boyle seemed to be thinking—it was hard to tell. "After," he finally said. "*After* the fireworks."

And after Budd and the others claimed to have left Dill alive, Matt thought with growing satisfaction. "Albert was very angry at Dill *after* the fireworks?" he asked, wanting this to be very clear before he went back to face the fat man.

Boyle began to shake his head slowly from side to side. He kept on shaking it, as if once started he found it impossible to stop. "Not old Albert's fault. Poor bald old Albert. Bald like Maryam. Hair gone. Teeth gone. She was very beautiful, you know."

"Yes, I remember." Matt nodded. He was holding Boyle's hands so tightly, his own were white-knuckled, but neither seemed to notice. Maryam Boyle had *not* been beautiful, but she had been kind and sweet-natured, and she had adored her husband.

"Where did Albert go then?" Matt asked.

"When?"

"After you told him about not getting the money? Did he go after Dill?"

"Don't remember," Boyle said, still shaking his head with metronomic regularity. "Don't remember, don't remember, don't remember—"

Matt interrupted the litany impatiently. "Peter Dill is dead."

"Yes," Boyle agreed. "Dill is dead."

"Do you think it's possible that Albert Budd killed him?"

"Of course not." Boyle stopped shaking his head from side to side and began nodding it, up and down. "*I* killed him. Wouldn't you?" He stopped nodding and grinned suddenly, horribly, his face still streaked with tears. "Prop him up and I'll do it again," he suggested in a confiding tone.

This abrupt revelation threw Matt momentarily. He had been expecting corroboration, not confession. There was a silence, during which Boyle gazed at him expectantly.

"Well?" Boyle finally said. "What?"

Feeling entirely foolish, Matt heard himself say, "That was wrong, Fred."

Boyle's face grew dark, and his voice roughened and once again started to rise. "So is robbing. So is stealing. So is taking money a man could have used to help his wife to live comfortably, happily. *She might never have got cancer if her life had been easier. It should have been easier. It should have been wonderful!* The bastard deserved more than dying, he deserved torturing, agony, the same kind of pain she had . . . but I let him off. Dumb bastard that I am, I let him off too easy. I should have *waited*, I should have done something *slow. I should have killed his kids, I should have killed* his *wife, I should have—*"

A particularly strong gust of wind rocked the trailer hard, causing George to brace himself against the wall and nearly knocking Matt and Boyle from the sofa. Matt sighed and stood up. "We can't stay here. Come on, let's go back to town. I need to get this down. . . ."

"I'm not *finished* !!" Boyle protested wildly.

"Yes, you are," Matt said.

29

*B*etween them, he and George got the windmilling, reangered Boyle out of the trailer and into the equally wild night. In the darkness the wind seemed like a guerrilla force, sneaking up and attacking hard from one side, then the other. The pine trees that surrounded the path down to the bay cracked and snapped together, their black spiky profile whiplashing against the slightly paler sky.

Boyle had no coat and began to shiver. "Jesis Chri," he said, wrapping his arms around himself, abruptly shocked from his frenzy into something like acquiescence. "Freezing."

"See if there's some kind of coat in there, George," Matt said over his shoulder. "He must have had something on when he came down here."

Grumbling, George let go of the shocked and shaken Boyle and climbed back in the trailer. "Put out the lanterns and heater while you're at it," Matt called. "If this rattletrap goes over and catches fire, the wind could carry the embers right over the trees and onto people's roofs."

"All right, all right," George shouted back. There were thumps and bumps from within, and finally George appeared, holding out a threadbare red-and-black mackinaw he'd discovered in the corner of the "bedroom." "Here." He turned back to take care of the lanterns and heater.

Matt forced the arms of the shivering and apparently be-

wildered Boyle into the sleeves of the mackinaw and but-
toned him up like a child. "It will be warmer in the car, Fred.
Come on," he said, and taking Boyle's arm, he started toward the broken gate. Boyle came along easily enough,
stumbling now and again over the broken concrete, once
catching the leg of his trousers in a rolling ball of weed and
nearly falling.

"What happens now?" he suddenly shouted over the wind
in what seemed sober and rational curiosity.

"We go back to the office and take a formal statement,"
Matt shouted back, grasping Boyle with one hand and holding his hat on with the other. "After that it's due process."
He was eager to return to the car now. The scene in the disintegrating trailer had had a surreal quality he did not want to
maintain. He wanted control again, not this mad maelstrom
of storm and reluctant duty. As the wind blew through the
half-strung wire fence, it made a low, mourning sound,
backed in bass by a louder roar as it swept up the length of
the street all the way to Eagle Head and down over the farther slope.

Although it was now virtually night, the darker mass of
the forest and the top of Eagle Head were visible against the
paler background of the low, racing cloud. He could no
longer see the Bay, but he could hear the steady thunder of
the surf against the pebbles and rocks of the beach below the
deserted trailer park.

They reached the car. Forced to momentarily release either
Boyle or his hat, Matt let the now quiet teacher go and
reached into his pocket for his car keys. Boyle collapsed
against the car and threw up. George, coming up the path
from the deserted trailer park, shouted in dismay. "Hey!"

"Oh, for crying out loud," Matt said in disgust. They
waited until Boyle had finished, then bundled him onto the
backseat and covered him with a blanket.

They got on the front seat. Matt started the engine, re-
versed, and got the car on to the coast road, intending to go
along it to the highway.

Over the hum of the heater the action of the wind was now
like a silent movie projected onto the windows of the car, the
trees bowing and thrashing, the bushes in the gardens of the

few houses whipping about as if trying to escape the clutch of their own roots. The windows of the houses glowed yellow with lamplight or flickered with the blue gray of television programs watched by people who were no doubt saying "My land, listen to that wind out there." Nobody looked out.

As they reached the peak of the hill, the engine coughed and died. "Damn wind," Matt said, reaching for the ignition.

Suddenly the wind was with them, filling the car, and the back door snapped open against its hinges.

"Oh, shit," George exclaimed suddenly. "He's making a break for it. Damn it, Matt, we should have handcuffed him to the floor."

Boyle, in a surprising burst of energy, had suddenly kicked open the back door with both feet and was running toward the dark mass of the forest. He leapt the first break in the fence and disappeared between the trees.

"He can't get far," Matt said, jamming on the brakes and putting the car into park as he reached for the door handle.

"He can get far enough," George said. "He could get *away*."

Matt picked up the radio mike and thrust it into George's hand. "Call the others. I'll get him."

He got out, pushing the door against the wind, which allowed him to emerge, then snatched the door and slammed it shut behind him. It then took his hat and sent it skimming along the roadway. Matt left it to spin in the sudden glare of approaching headlights as he ran around the car and into the woods after Fred Boyle. There was a screech of brakes behind him, but he didn't turn.

George was there.

Dominic bent down and rapped on the steamy window of the patrol car. The far door opened and George Putnam got out, looking angry and impatient.

"Is Matt with you?" Dominic shouted across the roof of the car, the wind whipping his hair around his face, stinging his cheeks with the ends.

"He's gone after Boyle," George shouted back.

"Who?"

"Fred Boyle. He killed Dill. We got a confession out of him and then—"

Dominic's hand went to the pocket where he had put the blowup of the photograph that he had been convinced would prove that Dr. Dan Rogers had been the murderer of Peter Dill. Surely that white blur had been Rogers's bandages? Who the hell was Fred Boyle, anyway? "But I thought—" he began.

"Look, I'm going to help Matt," George shouted. "You wait here and send the others in when they arrive, okay?"

Dominic watched George run into the woods before he could answer. "Couldn't we just leave a note?" he shouted after him.

The woods were dark and deep.

As Matt tripped and thrashed through the underbrush, he cursed Boyle but cursed himself even more. "Look where philosophy got you this time, Prof," he grunted to himself as he cannoned into yet another tree. "You've managed to suspect everyone in town except the real killer, and now your foolish compassion has let *him* slip through your fingers."

As he ran he managed to fish his flashlight out of the holding strap on his belt. Even if it didn't help him to locate Boyle, it would keep him from bloodying his nose on some damn tree. The huge trunks sprang into ghostly life in the beam of the flashlight, startling him with their size and nearness. High above him he could hear the somehow triumphant howl of the wind through the top branches. Well, Boyle was an idiot to run in here, he thought as he stumbled along. There was no escape this way. Not for anyone, but especially not for a man in his condition. He'd simply run in circles until he collapsed. It was a wonder he was still on his feet.

Even as this thought passed through his mind, he went down himself, caught at the ankle by an arching root. Winded, he took a moment to recover, then scrambled to his feet once more. If only he could figure out which direction Boyle was taking! This far in, there seemed no guidelines, no paths or trails of any kind. Even though it was now public land, this was not a frequented area. There were easier places to picnic, and being so near to the water yet far above it bore little attraction.

He stopped.

He had reached a clearing in which lay a clutter of rusting metal and wood. Not fallen branches, but wood that had been shaped and cut many years before and was now silvery gray and rotting in his flashlight beam.

Old G. G. Osborne's still.

He had missed it the other day when he'd come up here. Now he felt a brief frisson as he gazed on the muddle. His own father had reduced it to rubble. Here and there were marks and cuts on the wood that might have been made by his ax. Somewhere around here had been the fire those trespassing kids had built thirty years ago. No sign of it now, of course. Somewhere around here there had been giggling and the sweet charred smell of burning marshmallows and the snide, insinuating voice of Jacky Morgan. He seemed to hear, in the roar of the wind, a girl sobbing, boys arguing, a sudden shout—

"Have you found him?" said a voice behind him.

Matt jumped and whirled around, his flashlight beam crossing the remains of the still, the trunks of the surrounding trees, and finally coming to rest on the face of Dominic Pritchard.

"What the hell are *you* doing here?" Matt demanded, suddenly aware of the thudding of his heart in his chest. Dominic's voice had been so young, so penetrating, for a moment he'd thought—

"I've been looking all over for you," Dominic said. "I thought I had—" He stopped. "It doesn't matter now. Have you found this man you're looking for?"

"Does it look like I have?" Matt snapped.

"Well, I—"

"Sorry, no. But he can't be far. He's not a young man, and he's drunk as hell. . . ."

"I'll go with you," Dominic said.

Matt started to argue, then shrugged. He might need help—God knew when George and the others would get there. "Come on, then."

They crossed the clearing and plunged again into the trees,

picking their way carefully, Matt looking for signs that
Boyle had passed this way, wishing he'd had instruction at
the knee of some kindly old Indian scout who knew about
this kind of thing. He stopped and held up his hand. "Let's
listen a minute," he suggested. "We might hear him."

They stood still, side by side, and listened. Dominic's top-
coat flapped around his knees, and he pulled the lapels shut
over his chest. He was warm from the running and the work
of forcing a way through the underbrush, but the air was
cold, as every intake of breath reminded him. Pneumonia
was not his idea of an engagement present for Emily.

He stiffened suddenly. "There," he said. "Up ahead."

"Yeah, I heard it, too," Matt agreed. "Come on."

The roar of the wind overhead was almost faint now, compared with a more savage noise—the waves of Blackwater
Bay, pounding and clawing at the base of Eagle Head. They
moved forward, and the darkness grew slightly less as the
trees thinned. Matt lowered his flashlight beam to illuminate
only the forest floor, not wanting to alarm or warn Boyle of
their approach.

He needn't have bothered.

They could see Boyle now, standing with his hands in his
mackinaw pockets, gazing out over the invisible tumult of
the surf. The clouds, racing in tatters before the wind, shone
now and again with a faint glimmer of moonlight from
above, giving an eerie, magical light to the scene. Boyle's
thinning hair was flying in an aureole about his head, and he
looked like some modern Prospero commanding the far dark
waters, which glinted now and again in the momentary shafts
of light that struck from between the clouds.

Although the waves were very far below, their noise was
almost deafening. What they had heard, even above the crash
of the waves, was Boyle talking to his wife. He was standing
on the far side of the fence, his feet planted wide on the bare
granite slope of Eagle Head, shouting up to the sky. His intention seemed clear.

"I should have hurt him, Maryam," he said in a loud wail.
"I should have done something awful to him, something terrible, instead of just—"

"Boyle!" Matt shouted. "Come away from the edge."

Boyle turned and shook his head. "What for?"

"We have to go back into town now," Matt called.

Again defiance. "Why?"

"I hope you've got a good answer to that," Dominic said.

"Listen," Matt cried. "It won't be too bad. You had some justification. I don't think a jury would—"

"Oh, we're up to juries now, are we?" Boyle called. "I haven't even made a statement and we're up to juries already." He seemed to have lost all vestige of drunkenness and stood quite steadily, legs apart, as he leaned into the wind. It seemed to hold him up, like a friend.

"I'd be happy to represent you, Mr. Boyle," Dominic shouted.

"Who the hell are you?" Boyle wanted to know.

"My name is Dominic Pritchard," the young lawyer said, feeling rather like an ambulance chaser.

"Hello, Dominic," Boyle shouted, removing one hand from his mackinaw to wave.

"Hello," Dominic shouted back. "Really, it will be much easier in the long run if you just come back now."

"I'm sure it would be," Boyle agreed. "But I don't think I will, thanks very much."

"I don't want to have to come out there and get you," Matt shouted.

Boyle smiled—they could see the white of his teeth. "Then don't," he agreed. And turned his back on them.

"Oh, hell," Matt said. "Oh, damn it to hell. He wasn't running away—he was running *to*."

There was a crashing behind them and George appeared, panting, his hat jammed down over his ears. He came up to them and then spotted Boyle. "What's he doing out there?"

"What do you think?" Matt said.

"Not practicing his tap dancing, that's for sure," George said. "I *told* you we should have—"

"Yeah," Matt agreed. "I should have."

"Are you going to try to get him back off there?" George wanted to know.

"Of course."

"By reasoning with him?" George persisted.

"Of course not."

George seemed gratified. "Just checking," he said. "Unfortunately, I left my lariat back at the office."

"Stay here," Matt directed.

"Like hell," George and Dominic both said.

They advanced to the fence. Boyle, hearing their heels on the exposed stone even above the wind and surf, glanced over his shoulder and turned to face them. "Please don't," he shouted. Out here, away from the extra darkness of the forest cover, his face looked pale but very calm. "There is no one for me to live for now. I am quite alone. I will serve no purpose by staying around."

"You won't serve any purpose by dying, either," Matt said.

"Oh, I don't know," Boyle said. "I might meet Dill in hell and help the devils to push him back into a boiling cauldron or two. It's worth a try."

"I never thought you were a stupid man," Matt said, taking a step closer.

"Certainly not sufficiently stupid to miss your pathetic attempt at a stealthy advance," Boyle said. "Just stupid enough to kill out of anger and not out of cold vengeance. Talk about missed opportunities."

"We could certainly get the charge reduced to manslaughter," Dominic pointed out. "And as Matt said, no jury—"

"I am the jury and I am the judge—of me," Boyle said, stepping back as Matt stepped forward to the fence. "I am passing sentence, not you, and not a bunch of strangers, either."

"Look, Fred—" Matt began.

It all happened at once—Boyle's leather heels slipping on the smooth rounded slope of the naked stone, Matt throwing himself forward over the fence and grabbing the falling man's arms, Dominic and George grabbing Matt's legs, and a moment later the four of them were suddenly, irrevocably, stretched out in a long line from trees to open space.

Boyle's legs hung over the darkness.

Matt was sprawled across the fence, its wire biting into his chest.

Dominic hung on to one leg, George the other.

And nobody could move.

It would have been funny—if it weren't for the drop beneath Boyle, and the snarling hunger of the waves as they crashed onto and withdrew from the cruel teeth of the rocks, their swirling, sucking presence all the worse because of their invisibility. It was like holding Boyle suspended over a den of lions.

"Let go," Boyle shouted. "Let go or you'll go with me."

"I'm not letting go," Matt gasped, feeling as if his arms were slowly being pulled out of their sockets, feeling the wire cutting into his flesh even through his clothing, feeling the sudden sting of sleet beginning to fall, feeling the desperate grasp of the two men on his legs. The sleet would form ice, the ice would make holding on more and more difficult for them all. If someone didn't come soon—

He felt himself growing angry at Boyle. "You stupid bastard, you're *not* going over like Jacky Morgan."

Boyle looked up at him, his face only inches away, and then he jerked one arm free from Matt's grasp. Involuntarily Matt tightened his hold on the other arm and reached out to catch the free one, but Boyle just kept staring at him as slowly, carefully, he began to unbutton his mackinaw.

With a lunge that nearly pulled him from the saving grasp of Dominic and George, Matt once again tried to regrasp Boyle's moving arm, but he failed.

"Who the hell is Jacky Morgan?" Boyle shouted—and then, without a further sound, he slid away into the blackness, leaving Matt holding on to an empty, flapping, red-and-black mackinaw.

30

*T*here are few sights as bleak as the face of a county sheriff staring at himself in the shaving mirror after a case is over. Especially one he'd managed to mess up completely.

It was solved, of course. Everything was answered.

But to whose satisfaction?

Certainly not his own.

He toweled himself dry and went back to his room to put on a fresh uniform, wondering if it would be neater and easier to put in his resignation now and force the election to be moved back. Or, if he simply walked out, they'd have to put George in charge for the interim. The result would no doubt be the same.

He went downstairs to breakfast.

Dominic was there, finishing his coffee. "I'll wait for you," he said, and poured himself another cup. "The scrambled eggs are perfect, as usual. And the sausage patties are . . ." He paused. "Do you suppose Emily can cook?"

Matt smiled as he filled his plate. "I don't think she's had much chance to learn. Gibbons is always saying his wife is the worst cook in town because she's too busy doing yoga or putting on some damn pageant to even fry him an egg, much less cook anything that involved something as complicated as a recipe."

304

"Oh, God," said Dominic in a mournful voice, looking at the array of hot plates and warmers that Mrs. Peach and Nonie used to present an American version of an English country-house breakfast. "Maybe Mrs. Peach could teach her—"

"I'm not in the teaching business," Mrs. Peach said, coming in from the kitchen with a fresh plate of toast for Matt. "She can read, can't she?"

"Well, of course—"

"Then she can use a cookbook. Anyone with an ounce of common sense can cook."

"Ah," said Dominic. "Really."

Mrs. Peach paused and stood looking at him with her hands on her hips. "Emily Gibbons, isn't it? That you're thinking of marrying?"

"Yes."

"Mmm. Well, you can always keep your room here and come back for meals," she said with a twinkle in her eye, and went into the kitchen.

"Don't worry," Matt said. "It will be all right."

"I suppose so," Dominic said, surrendering. He stirred his coffee and watched Matt consuming a huge breakfast. "Planning on setting out for the South Pole this afternoon?" he asked.

"Might as well," Matt said, buttering some toast. "Don't much feel like staying around here at the moment."

"Oh, it will all blow over," Dominic said. "Like the storm."

"That was only the *first* storm," Matt said glumly. "There will be more."

"I hope so," Dominic said with the exhausting optimism of youth. Matt just glowered at him.

"I take it you still have a job with Crabtree and Putnam?"

"Well, he hasn't actually told me to leave," Dominic said. "I wouldn't say our relationship has been improved by all this, but since he can't *prove* I took that file, and you'll never have to produce those photocopies in any trial . . ." He paused. "Does he ever have to know?"

Matt shook his head. "Nobody has to know anything," he

said. "Everybody's dead." He took a big swallow of coffee.
"Including the sheriff."

"Oh, come on," Dominic said.

Matt shrugged. "Look—Peter Dill and Fred Boyle would
both be alive if I hadn't gotten nuts about Jacky Morgan—all
because of a few words from a dying man. Tilly wouldn't
have gone to see Albert, Albert wouldn't have come back to
Blackwater, Fred would probably never have found out
about the money . . ."

"Oh, yes, he would. Clarence's investigation would have
eventually brought it out," Dominic said. "Dill would be in
jail for fraud as well as for killing Tom Finnegan," he added.
"His wife and children would have been put through the hell
of a trial, public exposure, all that. I admit Boyle still *might
be* alive, but I don't think he would have been alive much
longer. Even if his liver had lasted, his nerve wouldn't have.
He was a man bent on suicide, slow or fast."

"Is that supposed to help?"

"You haven't done anything *wrong*," Dominic insisted.

"Maybe not," Matt agreed, folding his napkin. "But have I
done anything right?" He finished up, and they got into their
coats and boots.

About three inches of snow had fallen in the night, and the
entire town was wrapped in a soft bandage of white, conceal-
ing all its imperfections and turning it into an early Christmas card.

The rain had frozen to the trees before it turned to snow,
and every branch glittered with a coating of ice. Where sun
had struck the trees this morning the ice coating had melted
sufficiently to slip off each twig. Little glassy tubes littered
the surface of the snow below the branches, the light winking
off their angularities. The air was clear and very cold, and
they were surrounded by sounds that seemed to come from
great distances—the scrape of snow shovels on concrete,
children laughing as they threw the first snowballs of the
season, dogs barking and doors slamming, odd booms and
clatters that could never be placed and could have come from

anywhere. The first morning of winter, when the soft sweetness of summer became a memory, and clarity reigned.

Some clarities, however, were not welcome.

As they crunched along, Dominic tried to convince Matt that whatever harm had been done was going to be covered over, too—not by snow, but by time.

"You can't change any of it now," Dominic said.

"No, I can't," Matt agreed. "But I can change myself."

They argued about it all the way into town.

When he entered the office, Matt was surprised to see Daria sitting at Tilly's desk. Max was on her lap, purring and gazing up adoringly into her face.

Matt took off his coat and struggled out of his boots, then threw himself onto his chair without speaking.

Daria regarded him for a while, taking in his glum misery. "I've been thinking," she finally began in a determined voice. "The gallery won't take up much of my time off season. Mrs. Toby has said she'll be as happy to sit there and sew and greet the odd customer as sit at home. But I can't really settle to my painting until the builders finish converting the big house."

"So?"

"So, that frees me to oversee the conversion of the rooms *over* the gallery into a nice little apartment," Daria continued, blithely ignoring his scowl. "I don't know why I didn't think of it before. It's just the right size, and it should be ready by the time Aunt Clary comes back from Florida. You and Max can live there until the office conversion is completed and you have a place of your own again. After that I can rent the flat out."

He stared at her. Live *without* Mrs. Peach's cooking? At the moment it seemed his only consolation.

"And of course, it means *I* can drop in anytime," Daria added pointedly.

"Ah," he said. His scowl cleared slightly.

The door burst open with a swirl of snow. George and Charley Hart came in, stomping their snow-caked boots and looking very grim and official. "We found Boyle," George said. "Washed up near Peskett, like I expected."

They went over to get some coffee and complained about the lack of doughnuts. Tilly had not arrived yet.

"George, how would you like to be sheriff?" Matt suddenly asked.

There was a long and terrible silence in the room.

"What on earth?" Daria asked in a horrified voice. Even Max looked startled as her lap stiffened beneath him.

Charley Hart and George stared at Matt with virtually equal dismay. "Are you kidding?" George demanded.

"I'm thinking about stepping down, that's all," Matt said. "I never intended to spend my whole life being sheriff of Blackwater Bay anyway. I've had an offer from a little college out west—" He leaned down and began to look through his bottom desk drawer.

"I threw that out," Tilly said from the doorway. "You said the other day to throw out anything over five years old, so I did." They all turned as Tilly came in, stomping snow from her boots. The pattern of the new linoleum was rapidly disappearing under a pool of melting slush. "And if you think you're going to leave this town in the hands of George Putnam, you've got another think coming."

"Look, Tilly, I'm *tired*—" Matt began.

"It would be like having the Howl all year around," Tilly continued implacably.

"I resent that," George said. Then, in a burst of rare good sense, he said, "I'm not ready to be sheriff yet, Matt. And though maybe you feel down because you messed up on this whole thing—"

"Thanks a lot, George," Matt said.

"I think you did as good a job as anybody could have. Almost anybody, anyway."

"Uh-huh."

"And maybe the mayor *is* mad at you, and the DA won't cooperate for a while, and Dr. Rogers will give you laxatives every time you cut your finger, and Mr. Budd won't leave you a million bucks in his will, and Tyrone Molt won't do our lube jobs for free anymore, and Jack Fanshawe—"

"There's not much Jack Fanshawe can do to you," Charley said encouragingly.

"Unless I want to buy a house," Matt said.

"Do you want to buy a house?" Daria asked in a dangerous voice.

"Not when I have the offer of a fine apartment," Matt said quickly. "Think of the money I'll be saving the town."

"Well, there you are," Charley said triumphantly. "That will soothe down the mayor right off!"

"So we don't want to hear any more about you going out to some fleabag college to teach philosophy to hicks," George said. He turned to glare at Tilly. "Or about me turning the town into a Howl."

Tilly was unabashed and proceeded to arrange the day's supply of doughnuts in the earthenware crock beside the coffee maker. "Speaking of the Howl, I just passed Harvey Matlock, and he says he wants to press charges against Weasel Rumplemeyer because he just found out that Weasel and his buddies were the ones who filled his boat with tapioca pudding. He only noticed it this morning when he went out to check the engine wasn't froze. He says he didn't mind his entire pile of winter firewood being cemented together last year, or the horse manure in his bathtub the year before, but if there's anything he hates, it's tapioca pudding. He says he'll be in later."

"I can't stand it," Matt said weakly. The phone rang, and he reached for it in a resigned manner.

Max jumped down from Daria's lap and up onto the windowsill, settling his rump into a patch of weak sunlight. He seemed to enjoy watching people slipping and sliding past on the icy pavement—they presented such a variety of movement. Some flailed their arms as if they were trying to take off, some went skidding for quite a distance before crashing into something, some scattered whatever they were carrying as they grabbed their companions or the nearest stable object, and some just went straight down and sat there, swearing blue murder. It was a totally different scene from summer—less colorful, of course, but filled with all those human activities that are both fascinating and incomprehensible to a cat.

Despite the altered seasonal view outside, nothing in the office seemed to have changed. Everybody was talking at once, and as usual the sheriff's voice rose in weary exasperation above the rest.

"It *can't* be a body, Mrs. Berringer," Matt said. "No, you must be mistaken. . . . In a *tree?* Come on. Probably a black plastic trash bag blown up there by the storm. . . . Well, I can't spare a man just now. . . . Yes, I *know* your husband is the town clerk. . . . Yes. . . . No, it couldn't be an animal escaped from some circus, there are no circuses in the area just now. . . . Mrs. Berringer. . . . Mrs. Berringer . . . Mrs. Berringer, just calm down a minute, would you, please? . . ."